TEMPORAL DREAMS

Also by Lesley L. Smith

Temporal Dreams
Neutrino Warning
Kat Cubed
Reality Alternatives
Conservation of Luck

The Quantum Cop Series:
Book 1: *The Quantum Cop*
Book 2: *Quantum Murder*
Book 3: *Quantum Mayhem*

The Space Operetta Series
Book 1: *A Jack By Any Other Name*
Book 2: *A Jack In The Dark*
Book 3: *A Jack For All Seasons*

Temporal Dreams

By Lesley L. Smith

Quarky Media
Boulder Colorado

Temporal Dreams
Published by Quarky Media, PO Box 3332, Boulder, CO 80307
www.quarkymedia.com

Copyright © 2016 Lesley L. Smith

ISBN: 978-0-9861350-1-9 (ebook)
ISBN: 978-0-9861350-0-2 (print)

TEMPORAL DREAMS

Chapter One
Kairi: Boulder, Colorado, 2019

The small velvet box thumped onto the blacktop like a tiny eight-hundred-pound gorilla. Kairi was packing the car for her spring break road trip when it fell out of her boyfriend Josh's duffel bag.

After checking to see if anyone else in the dorm parking lot had seen (they hadn't), she stared at it for at least a minute. She was surprised. They'd been dating for less than a year. Did people get engaged after less than a year? But marrying him would be awesome. She'd wanted a family forever. Her heart was thumping so loudly people must have been able to hear it all over Colorado.

Maybe she was overreacting. Maybe it wasn't an engagement ring.

Kairi did pick up the box and look inside. The lid opened with a snap, exposing a smallish diamond on a silver-colored band. She didn't know anything about diamonds, or silver-colored bands for that matter, but it was really pretty.

She did not try the ring on. That was her story, and she was sticking to it.

Suffice it to say, when her roommate, Dakota, came up behind her, she jumped sky-high.

"Have you still been having those weird dreams, Kairi? Ooh! What's that?" Dakota asked. As she leaned over, Kairi got a whiff of pot from her hair. "Oh, my God! Are you engaged?" She squealed.

Quickly, Kairi shoved the ring back into the duffel. "No, I'm not engaged. He hasn't asked me yet."

"But you're going to say yes when he asks, right?" Dakota asked.

Visions of a perfect family life were running through Kairi's head: sharing her experiences of the day at dinnertime, waking up with that special someone, knowing for sure she had someone in her corner. And the holidays—they would be great, filled with fun and love instead of boredom, loneliness and worse. Her life so far had been pretty horrible. Josh was by far the best thing that had happened to her.

"Kairi?" Dakota frowned. "Are you considering saying no?" Dakota was also one of the best things that had happened to her. She was like a sister, even though they looked so different: Dakota so light and Kairi so dark.

"No, I'm not going to say no." But he hadn't actually asked her. She was so confused. Why would he ask her to marry him? He came from a good family, and she didn't even know where she came from. Of course, she'd been fantasizing that he'd ask her someday. "You don't think the ring might be for someone else, do you?"

"What? His secret girlfriend? No way, girl. You're getting married!" Dakota squealed again. "Pam is so going to kill you!" Pam was her foster mom.

"Pam would not kill me if I got engaged," Kairi said.

"Yeah, huh, she would," Dakota said. "She totally would. You swore you'd get your degree."

"Maybe we'll just have a long engagement," she said.

"Yeah, right," Dakota said. "That's realistic."

"Hey, Dakota." Josh's voice rang out across the parking lot.

"Shh," Kairi whispered and held up her bare finger. "Not a word. You don't know a thing."

"Hey, Josh," Dakota said in a singsong voice as he approached them. "So... any special plans for spring break?"

Josh grinned. "You mean besides driving across the country to drink beer on the beach?"

"Oh, you know?" Dakota started to say, but Kairi poked her with her elbow.

"We should get going," Kairi said. "We're burning daylight." Dakota giggled. "Burning."

Josh leaned around Kairi and put Electromagnetic Theory and Special Relativity books on top of the suitcases.

Kairi smiled. "A little light reading?"

He put his arms around her waist and kissed the back of her neck. "Yep," he said in his low, husky, sexy voice. She loved that voice. The brush of his lips and his warm breath on her neck made her warm all over.

The edges of his eyes crinkled as he smiled when she twisted around and looked at him. He let go of her and said, "Ready to roll?"

"Yep." She turned to Dakota. "Bye, D."

"Bye." Dakota giggled and started walking back to the dorm. Then she stopped and turned around. "Call me! Let me know what happens."

"Am I mistaken, or is she high again?" Josh asked.

Kairi watched her try to unlock the dorm door. "Oh, be nice. Dakota's been through a lot."

"So have you, and I don't see you toking up all the time," Josh said. "I know you think of her as a sister, but you're too easy on her."

At least one person on earth should be easy on her. Kairi slammed the trunk closed. "She was my foster sister, and I'm not too easy on her." But she didn't want to have this argument again. "Let's talk about it later." Or not at all.

Kairi walked toward the passenger seat. Now that she knew about the ring, the suspense was killing her. Was he going to ask her? How would he do it? In the car? On the beach? Maybe on the beach at sunset.

He was unlocking the driver's door. "It's around twenty hours till we get to Padre." He smiled at her over the roof of the car. "I think we'll have a chance to talk."

She said, "Can't argue with that."

As they drove through Boulder, she kept staring at him. If they got married, what kind of husband would he be? What kind of wife would she be? What would their kids be like? What would they look like? They had nothing in common in the looks department except dark-brown wavy hair. And eyebrows. They both had thick dark-brown eyebrows. But he had gray-blue eyes, and hers were brown. He had white skin, and hers was the color of chai tea.

He shot her a glance. "What?"

"What do you mean what?"

"What's up? Why've you been staring at me? Wait."
He flashed his teeth at her. "Don't tell me, I look particularly handsome today."

He did look handsome, but she couldn't say that. He'd get even cockier than he already was. "Uh, just wondering what you were thinking." When he bought that ring. Could he really want to marry her?

He grinned. "Thinking, when?"

"Uh, well, I was packing your duffel in the back, and something fell out." Enter gorilla; welcome to spring break. Shoot. So much for a romantic setting.

"Oh?" His face stilled, and he shot her another glance.

"You know I really care about you, right?" Kairi mustered up what she hoped was a warm smile. Ask me. Ask me. Ask me.

"Care about me?" he choked out. "Gee, thanks. I thought it was more than that."

Crap. "It is. It is more than that. You're important to me. Really important." She needed to say it: the I-word. But she'd never said the I-word to anyone.

His face was turning red.

Shit. Say it. "You're the most important person in the world to me." Say it, Kair! She couldn't say it. He needed to hear it, and she needed to say it. And she felt horrible and mad at herself about it. What was wrong with her? Her mind skittered away from the back seat of that car years ago...

"Kairi, what's wrong?" Josh was staring at her instead of the road, clutching the wheel with an iron grip.

"Watch the road," she managed to say.

He pulled the car off onto the shoulder. "What's wrong?" His face was turning red, and he clenched and unclenched his fists. But she knew he'd never hurt her--unlike other people--that was one of the things that was so wonderful about him.

She just looked at him.

"Excuse me," he said, "if the thought of marrying me makes you upset. It's not like I even asked you yet!"

She'd never seen him so hurt. She had to do some damage control, or this relationship was over. Now. That was the last thing she wanted. "I, uh, apologize if I hurt you. I didn't mean to. The idea of marrying you doesn't make me upset." She took a deep breath. It was now or never. "I do love you. I love you--and that's the first time I've ever said that to anyone."

His face smoothed. "So, what's going on? Why are you so upset?"

"I'm not sure." She swallowed. Figure it out, girl. "I guess I'm just scared."

"Just a sec." He bounded out of the car, opened the trunk and rooted around in his duffel bag. When he came back, he handed her a ...tissue.

She took the tissue, laughing, and blew her nose. She'd been sure he was going to expose the gorilla. She wiped her eyes and heard The Snap.

When she looked back at Josh, sure enough, he had the ring out and looked deadly serious. "This isn't how I planned to ask you, and it's not romantic, I know. But I just love you so much. I want to spend the rest of my life with you." He held his breath, holding the ring out.

It seemed as if time stopped. She looked at his wonderful face, eyes filled with hope, and it felt as if her chest was being crushed. She was so afraid that she couldn't breathe. Did he really want her? Did that mean he didn't really know her? She wished, no prayed, he did want her.

Finally, she said, "Josh..."

As she hesitated, the naïve look of hope on his face was morphing into something else. Something sad.

"Uh," she said. "Yes."

"Really?" His voice got all high and squeaky.

"Sure," she said.

"I love you so much," Josh said and reached for her.

"I love you, too," she said. It was getting easier to say. They kissed for quite a while.

"I love you no matter what," he said when they finally separated. He held out the box. "So, put it on."

"I, uh," she said. There were those hopeful eyes again. "Okay." She took the ring and slipped it on her finger. "So, maybe we should get going?"

"Yes, ma'am. Yes, fiancée!" He gave a grin and saluted her. "Your wish is my command."

As they pulled back into traffic, she concentrated on calming down. What was wrong with her? Josh was great. She'd never find a better guy, and he loved her. She did love him. And it was her dream to have a family. If they got married, he'd be her family. So, why did she feel terrified?

"Is there anything you want to ask me?" he asked.

Like, why would a guy like him love a girl like her? When would he stop being in love with her? What's it like to have everything easy? What's it like having a mom and dad? But she knew asking any of those questions would be a mistake. "Uh. Boxers or briefs today?" She forced a laugh.

Josh snickered. "In honor of spring break, I'm free-dogging it today."

Now it was her turn to snicker.

Southeast Colorado was downright boring. The view out the windows was of unending worn-out grass, and the hum of tires on the pavement was practically a lullaby.

Northeast Oklahoma wasn't any better, and she was dozing when that annoying emergency alert blared on the radio. "The National Weather Service has issued a tornado warning for Union County in northeast New Mexico. National Weather Service Doppler Radar indicated a funnel cloud near the ground ten miles southwest of Clayton. Residents in the area should seek shelter immediately." The radio was overcome with static, and Josh switched it off.

She realized while she'd been sleeping, it had clouded over. "Maybe we should seek shelter?"

Josh snorted. "It's all the way over in New Mexico. We're in Oklahoma, babe."

She had no idea where Union County was, but she could see the clouds overhead were very dark. "It can't be a good sign that we heard the emergency alert on the radio."

"We're fine," Josh said.

She just looked at him.

"I'm sure, Kair," he said, reaching over to squeeze her hand.

"Okay, if you're sure," she said and settled back in her seat.

She dreamt of a freight train coming to run her over, roaring louder and louder as it got closer and closer.

And then she woke up, lying on the side of the highway. In the sun. It took a couple of seconds for it to register.

Where was she?

She stood up.

Where was Josh?

Where was the car?

What the hell was going on?

"Josh!" she yelled. But it was no use. She could see a long way, and all she saw was sad old grass and an unbroken ribbon of empty highway.

Chapter Two
Kyle: Sydney, Australia, 2019

Just as Kyle stepped off the Eastern Suburbs Line into Kings Cross Station, his mobile rang. Caller ID said it was St. Vincent Hospital. He screwed up his courage before answering, praying it wasn't some nurse calling to tell him his dad died when he was only a block away.

He jogged through the station and started up along Victoria Street.

"Yeah. This is Kyle Barada."

"Kyle?" A tired old man's voice was on the other end, Dad's voice.

Kyle let out a breath and slowed his pace to a fast walk. "Yeah, Dad. Are you okay?" His image on the little screen looked horrible, like death warmed over. "What's happening?"

"Have you been Dreaming, Traveling?" Dad asked.

Kyle knew he didn't mean the train. "No."

"Did you feel it?" he asked. "A disturbance?"

"No." Kyle shook his head. "I didn't feel anything. But I just got off the train. I'm down the block from the hospital. I'll be right there."

In person, if anything, Dad looked worse with a grayish cast to his brown skin, but Kyle couldn't say that. "Dad," he said. "Good to see you. You look good." He definitely didn't go up to the bed and touch him even though he really wanted to.

"Bastard," Dad said in a weak voice, but Kyle caught a hint of a smile. "I know you're lying. I look like crap, but I had a good run. I'm dying. I know it, and you know it."

One of the nurses, a gray-haired old-timer, bustled in. "Let's have a Captain Cook." She looked the older man over, nodded, and adjusted the pillows behind his back. "There we go. That's better." She checked the younger man out. "Who's this cobber, then? Another Aborigine by the looks of 'im."

"This," Dad said, "is my oldest, Kyle. My pride and joy. He's taking over an important part of the family business for me."

Kyle was taking over because Dad wasn't strong enough to handle it anymore. Suddenly, his eyes felt heavy with moisture, damn them. He blinked it away.

The nurse crossed her arms in front of her. "It's about time someone came to visit." She pointed her chin at him. "What took you so long?"

What took so long was Kyle knew he'd want to hug his dad to say goodbye, and that would make both their lives shorter. Instead of saying that, he said stiffly, "Couldn't be helped. I was busy." He was lucky he'd been allowed to come at all. His younger brother Oliver wasn't supposedly for his own protection. And Mom had been estranged since the divorce.

"Well, don't just stand there. Give him a hug or something," the nurse said.

Would that he could.

Dad cleared his throat. "It's not our way."

She raised her eyebrows high and turned for the door. Kyle thought he heard her mutter something about a "No-hoper son if I ever saw one."

Once she left, Kyle closed the door firmly behind her.

He dragged the chair up near the bed but not too close. "So what's this about a disturbance?" he asked quietly.

Dad slowly shook his head. "I was hoping it was you making a little jaunt, maybe testing things out..."

Kyle shook his head. He wanted to try The Dreaming with all his heart and soul, but it was against the rules. There could be only one Dreamer at a time. Period.

"I know it's against the rules, but..." Dad said. He was one to break rules. That's what got him in this mess--at least that's what Dad said. He'd been very vague about the particulars, however.

Kyle would have to be a fool not to learn from his dad's mistakes. He shook his head again. "Wasn't me."

Dad collapsed back against the bed. "I don't understand,

15

then. I felt something. It felt like someone Dreamed."

Kyle leaned forward. This stuff was fascinating. He couldn't wait to try it--with the obvious drawback that his dad would have to be dead for him to do so. "Did they change anything?"

"Change anything!" Dad had to stop and catch his breath after his outburst. "What kind of crappy training are you getting?"

Kyle leaned back. "I know we're not supposed to change things, but if there was an unauthorized Dreaming, who knows what's going on?"

"*Hhmpf.*" Dad frowned. "Good point." He was silent for a few moments, thinking. "I need you to check with all your aunts, uncles, and cousins and make sure none of them have been Dreaming."

"But none of them can Dream, can they?" Kyle asked. "I mean, you're the Dreamer of your generation, and I'm the Dreamer of my generation. Oliver can't even Dream."

"Yeah." Dad steepled his fingers. "Maybe you better see if any of your cousins have had any babies we don't know about."

Yeah. Like Kyle wanted to have those conversations. But he didn't have a choice. "Yes, sir."

As he turned to go, Dad said, "I love you, Kyle. And I'm proud of you, son, no matter what."

Kyle shifted back in his direction. He knew his dad was saying those things in case he died tonight, and he did look done for in that damn hospital bed.

Kyle had a hard time talking around the lump in his throat. "Don't be such a pessimist, Dad. You're going to be fine. I'll be by tomorrow, first thing."

He pivoted and strode for the door. But at the door, he couldn't seem to step through without saying more. He turned to face him again. "I love you, too, Dad. And I'm proud of you."

Now, both their eyes were heavy.

Dad managed to give him a nod.

Kyle returned it and hurried out.

In Sydney, Kyle had planned on staying with Liam, his mate from university. He got to the flat, retrieved the key from Liam's hiding place, and let himself in. Of course, Liam's flat was decorated in rich bachelor, including the requisite huge flat-screen TV, cutting-edge gaming system, and ginormous sound system. Kyle didn't let it distract him and started making his calls.

At tea time, after Kyle'd offended all his cousins by asking them about unplanned pregnancies, Liam finally got home from work. "Kyle! There you are!" He smiled widely and came right over and gave him a big bear hug. Kyle didn't know if it was true that all the white folks in Australia were descended from criminals, but Liam always looked capable of anything, including breaking into a bank vault with his bare hands.

"Liam," he said, grinning back. "I'd say good to see 'ya, but I can't breathe. Stop. You're crushing me."

Liam let go, still beaming. "It's been too long, mate." He took a step back and frowned. "Sorry to hear about your dad. How's he doing?"

Kyle shrugged. "He's doing." He didn't want to talk about it. He wanted to forget about it for tonight and knew Liam was the one to help him with that.

"So?" Liam raised his eyebrows and smiled again. "Are we going to partake of a pint or two, then, Mr. Barada?"

"We're going to partake of many, many pints, mate." Kyle clapped him on the back.

A little later, as they entered the local pub, Liam rubbed his hands together. "Look at all the sheilas!"

Kyle snorted. "Why do you insist on talking like Crocodile Dundee?"

"Because it bugs you, of course." Liam laughed. "And if there are any lady tourists here, they'll eat it up." He added in a falsetto, "And next thing you know, I'll be having a naughty."

Kyle couldn't help laughing. "I missed you, Liam."

Liam nodded. "Me, too. Now, let's get rotten!"

Kyle didn't know if it was Liam's Crocodile Dundee act or his near-giant physique, but he never seemed to be hurting for female attention.

He and Liam were sitting with four, count-em-four, twenty-something women at a table. He never had that kind of play on his own.

Liam pointed at him. "Ladies, Kyle here is a superhero."

Uh oh. How drunk was he? Every once in a blue moon,

Liam drank too much and threatened to tell Kyle's secret. Kyle had told him in a moment of weakness soon after they'd met, both teenagers, new at university. Kyle's dad still didn't know about his mistake, and Kyle wanted to keep it that way.

The women giggled. One said, "Really? What kind of superhero?"

Kyle shot Liam the evil eye. "He's kidding."

The woman closest to him pulled her chair a little closer, touching her knee to his knee. "What's your power?" She smiled enchantingly at him.

He was tempted to spill it. Who knew what she would do for the one-and-only Dreamer of this generation? "I can't really say." But, he might, with the right kind of pressure...

She put her hand on his knee. "Come on. You know you want to tell me."

He wavered.

"My mate Kyle's a time traveler," Liam said.

Kyle couldn't believe Liam had actually said that. It was supposed to be secret.

On the other hand, the women looked like they wanted to believe and would with one more free drink. It would be nice to feel popular for once.

Suddenly, Kyle felt as if the air pressure in the room increased a thousand percent and then whooshed back out again. He had to grab his chair to keep from falling out of it.

"Whoa, baby," the woman next to him said. "Are you all right?"

His stomach rock-n-rolled. "No." He stumbled to his feet and lurched across the room to the can. Inside, he splashed water on his face.

Liam barreled in. "Are you okay?"

"No," he said. "It was like there was some kind of shake-up or disturbance in the universe..."

"A disturbance in the force?" Liam asked. "Seriously?"

"Bloody hell." Still dizzy, Kyle had to hold onto the sink to keep from falling on the floor. "I think my dad just died."

His mobile rang. Caller ID said it was St. Vincent Hospital. Kyle screwed up his courage.

"Yeah. This is Kyle Barada."

Chapter Three
Kairi: Boulder, Colorado, 1999

Kairi couldn't believe it. She was stuck on the side of the road in the middle of nowhere. She didn't have her purse or even her wallet.

What happened? Where was Josh? Her mind couldn't seem to process what was going on.

She gazed at the nondescript highway and the rolling grasslands that surrounded her. Where the hell was she?

When she'd fallen asleep, they were in Oklahoma. Where was she now? Something in her brain nagged her for attention. There had been something wrong... A tornado warning!

Could a tornado have lifted her up somehow and brought her here à la The Wizard of Oz? No. That didn't make any sense. She wouldn't sleep through that, and everything around her looked normal. No tornado had gone through here.

Could Josh have left her by the side of the road? That really didn't seem like something he would do. She glanced at her hand: beautiful, terrifying ring. Check.

She didn't think Josh would leave her stranded in the middle of nowhere.

But where was he? Could he be hurt? She really hoped not. She looked at the dried grass waving in the wind. These thoughts weren't getting her anywhere.

What now?

The late-afternoon sun shone down on her skin. A slight breeze ruffled her hair, and she zipped up her hoodie. All she could hear was the grass rustling in the gentle wind. It was peaceful. She guessed if a person had to be stranded, there were worse places to end up.

But she had to get out of here and back to civilization.

A rumbling sound approached from her right. Kairi turned and spied a truck speeding up the road.

Hitchhiking! She could hitch her way out of here.

She put her right thumb out toward the road and her left hand in the pocket of her hoodie.

Her phone was in her pocket. Thank God. Quickly she turned it on.

The truck roared past, stirring up dust and gravel.

She didn't have any bars. Nothing. "Dammit." She jumped up and down in frustration.

After she'd worn herself out a little from all the jumping and yelling, she realized that was a waste of time. She grimly turned in the direction she thought was northwest and started walking.

As she walked, she kept wondering what happened, where Josh was, and if he was okay. After about an hour of trudging along the highway, with no cars driving by, she didn't have the energy to wonder anymore. In fact, she was starting to feel sorry for herself.

And then she heard a car coming up behind her. She wiped her eyes, stuck out her thumb and stepped into the road.

The car, an old-school station wagon full of people, screeched to a stop. The driver rolled down his window. "What the hell are you doing in the middle of the road?"

As Kairi approached the window, she realized the car was filled with her-age people, skis, coolers, and sleeping bags. They must be college kids on a spring break ski trip. Maybe they were going to Colorado.

"Hey," she said, forcing a smile. "Thanks for stopping. I was on a road trip with my boyfriend, and we got separated somehow. Any chance I can bum a ride? Are you guys going to Colorado?"

The driver, who sported a buzz cut, nodded. "Uh, yeah, we're going to Colorado." He had an odd tone in his voice. "We're going skiing." She could detect a little Texas twang. "But, we're already in Colorado."

How could she be in Colorado? The last she remembered,

she was in Oklahoma.

The woman in the front passenger seat said, "Are you all right, hon?" She had a pug nose and lots of freckles, but much more importantly, she seemed genuinely concerned.

"I've been better." She had to struggle not to tear up at the woman's kindness.

"We've got to help her," the woman said to her companions. "She's stranded here in the middle of nowhere. We can't just leave her here."

The driver shrugged. "Okay. But we don't really have any room."

"I can sit in the back, with the gear," Kairi said, and as she added, "please," her voice broke.

The driver grimaced. "Okay. Get in. And we can trade off who sits where."

"Nice ring," the woman in front said.

"Thanks," Kairi said. She quickly took it off and put it in her pocket. She was confused about Josh and their feelings for each other. How could he leave her by the side of the road? And how the hell had she gotten back to Colorado? It didn't make any sense.

The chubby guy in the back climbed over the seat, love handles jiggling, shoved equipment out of the way and crouched in the bed of the station wagon.

Kairi gratefully opened the back passenger door and got in. "Thank you very much. I don't know what I would have done if you hadn't come along."

As they started on their way north, she said, "I'm Kairi."

The driver in his button-down shirt said, "I'm Mike. The guy in the back is Tom. Next to you is Jim, and this, my little lady, is Lisa."

"It's great to meet you all," Kairi said. "Thanks again."

From behind her, Tom said, "You Mexican? You look kinda' Mexican, but you don't talk Mexican." He had a strong Texas accent.

This ride was not going to be a picnic. Kairi faced him and forced a smile for him and his Texas Rangers t-shirt. "No. I'm not Mexican. I'm American. Lived my whole life in Colorado." As far as she knew, anyway. Those first few years were pretty murky.

Next to her, Jim grinned. "So far." He had a nice, if a bit goofy, grin. It made a person forget about all his acne.

"Huh?" Kairi asked. She realized he was wearing a t-shirt with a big gray sunglasses-wearing head and the words The Dude. The Big Lebowski.

"Your whole life, so far," Jim said.

"Ha. Yeah. Good one," she said. "I don't have any bars."

"Bars?" Lisa shot a look at Mike. "You've been at the bars?"

"Oh. No wonder." Tom mimed drinking. Tom might be an asshole.

Jim snickered. Jim might be an asshole, too.

They did stop for her, though, so they couldn't be all bad. Take a breath, Kair. She did. "So, no one has a phone I can use?"

Lisa and Mike looked at each other again in the front seat. Mike shook his head and said, "Nope."

Breathe, Kairi.

That old hit, The Boy is Mine came on the radio.

As the miles rolled out behind them, the radio treated them to oldies such as You're Still the One by Shania Twain, Together Again by Janet Jackson, and This Kiss by Faith Hill.

Eventually, Kairi dozed off, thinking of Josh again. It must have been all the love songs.

A whispered argument woke her up. "Let's leave her here."

"Don't need a homeless drunk with us." That did not sound good.

As she opened her eyes and looked around, she realized they'd reached a town, and it looked sort of familiar. She couldn't place it, though. "Where are we?"

The fierce whispering cut off abruptly. "Oh, you're awake," Mike said.

Lisa said, "We're in Boulder, Colorado."

"What?" How could they be here already? And if they were in Boulder, why did it look so unfamiliar? Had they come into town from some bizarre direction? On the other hand, the town looking different wasn't the weirdest thing that had happened to her. She had other weird and troublesome things to worry about, like, where was Josh?

"Yeah, Karen," Tom said. "Where did you say you got

separated from your boyfriend? Josh, was it?"

"My name's Kairi." She twisted around to look at him. "I didn't say what my boyfriend's name was. Why do you assume it's Josh?"

"You were talking in your sleep, hon," Lisa said. "You kept mumbling Josh, and Oh, no! Look out! and stuff like that."

"It was kind of freaky," Jim said.

Kairi had to agree. Talking in her sleep was weird. Had she been having a nightmare? If so, about what? What exactly had happened to her and Josh? But she needed to focus on the here-and-now now. If she played her cards right, maybe these folks would take her back to the dorm.

"Forget about Josh. I'm no threat to you." She smiled. "In fact, if you give me a ride over there, you can stay for free in my dorm at the University of Colorado. It's pretty much empty this week."

"You go to CU?" Mike asked.

Kairi nodded.

"Free does sound good," Lisa said.

"Can we get to the slopes from there?" Tom asked. "How long a drive is it?"

"It's thirty or forty miles," Kairi said. "I go up for the day all the time." She didn't mention that the traffic was a bear. So sue her, she really wanted to get home.

Nice and Slow by Usher started up, and she couldn't help humming along. "This oldies station is nice, by the way," she said.

"What do you mean, oldies?" Mike asked.

"Isn't this an oldies station?" Kairi asked."The songs are old."

"Old?" Jim guffawed. "They're practically brand new."

Tom looked at her like she was an idiot.

Kairi wasn't about to get into a music history argument with them. If they didn't know music, that was their problem.

As she directed them to campus, something was weird on the corner of Table Mesa Road and Broadway, but she couldn't quite put her finger on it. In the dark, it was as if the buildings were different somehow--but that didn't make any sense. As they turned up Broadway Street, Kairi realized her foster mom would probably spot her some cash. And she lived just south of campus. "Ooh. Turn here," she said, directing Mike into Pam's neighborhood.

Mike asked, "Why?" but he turned.

"My foster mom lives here. I bet she'd loan me some money. I could chip in for gas."

"That sounds good," Mike said, nodding.

"You have a foster mom?" Lisa asked. At least she didn't ask the next obvious question: What happened to your real mom?

"It's coming up," Kairi said. "Here."

Mike pulled over in front of a small red brick ranch house, pretty much the same as every house on this street.

"I'll just be a few minutes." She popped out and raced up the front walkway. A familiar and sympathetic face would be nice to see after all this weirdness. In fact, she bet Pam would have let her stay on the couch. She shot a regretful look at the Texas crew as she reached the front door. She'd promised them a place to crash tonight, and a promise was a promise, so she'd have to take them to the dorm.

She knocked.

A baby started crying inside. Wow. She didn't know Pam was fostering a baby.

A man she'd never laid eyes on opened the door. He looked super-conservative, except for his big mustache. He had short sandy hair and wore a button-down shirt and khakis.

"Who are you?" she said in surprise.

He scowled. "Who the hell are you, and why are you bothering us?"

As he opened the door wider, she saw Pam--at least she thought it was Pam. She looked twenty years younger, and cradled in her arms was a little brown-skinned baby. Kairi's mouth fell open.

Pam approached the door, saw her, and gasped. "Oh, no. Are you Kairi's mom? Did Social Services send you?" She bounced the baby up and down, trying to comfort her.

The baby quieted, looking up at her with big brown eyes.

Kairi was speechless. She couldn't think.

The man said, "What's wrong with you, lady? Say

something. Who are you?"

Pam said, "John, honey, don't be rude. Maybe we should invite her in?"

He shook his head. "She can't be from Social Services. They would have sent the kid's caseworker, too. She's probably just selling something." He glared at her. "We're not interested." He closed the door in her face.

Kairi stood there, looking at the door.

What just happened?

Chapter Four
Kyle: Sydney, Australia, 2019

Kyle stood at the back of the church, watching people enter his dad's funeral. It was weird seeing everyone, all his aunts and uncles and cousins, in black business clothes, not to mention his younger brother Oliver.

With Dad gone, and Kyle the official Traveler, things were even more strained between Kyle and his brother. They'd only nodded at each other when Oliver came in.

Mom wasn't here, and he wasn't sure she'd even make an appearance.

Even weirder than seeing his relatives was seeing Liam in a suit and tie. Kyle almost didn't recognize him as he walked toward him.

Of course, the weirdest thing of all was trying to wrap his head around the idea that his dad was gone, that he'd never see him again.

"Sorry, mate." Liam frowned and patted him on the back.

"Thanks." At Liam's concerned tone, he was suddenly overcome with a wave of grief.

"Kyle?" Liam said. "Are you all right?"

What is it about a little kindness that breaks down your defenses? "Yeah," he managed to grunt out. "Give me a minute." Kyle focused on breathing and not bawling.

"How about I stand here next to you in the meantime?" Liam asked.

Kyle just nodded, trying to get his act together. He was a leader of the family now. He needed to get it together. After a few long moments, he felt more like himself.

Kyle turned to him. "Thanks for coming."

Liam dipped his chin. "I don't know what I'd do if my dad?" He cleared his throat. "Anyway." He forced a grin. "I had to come. I thought I'd be seeing white body paint, didgeridoos, yirdakis, and clapping sticks. I couldn't miss that."

"Easy there." Kyle knew he was kidding, but he was treading dangerously close to disrespect. He blew out a breath. "We'll have a clan ceremony in the country at my grandparents' place."

"Can I come?" Liam asked.

"No." Kyle had mixed feelings about the old ways. He knew to guys of English heritage like Liam, they seemed like something from another century.

But.

There was something to them, something sacred. When they were dancing, it was as if they were connected in an unbroken line with all those who had gone before and all who were yet to come.

They were connected to all of time itself.

"Our ceremonies are private," Kyle finally said.

"This, here," Liam said, "all seems normal."

"Give me a break. We're Christian, you know we are," Kyle said in a forceful whisper. "Most Indigenous Australians are. Besides," he waved at the crowd, "a lot of these people are clients and business contacts."

"That makes sense," Liam said. "And as a plus, there's more sheilas here than at a Bachelors and Spinsters." Then, he held up his palms as if to surrender. "Okay, even I agree that was too much. I was trying to lighten the mood. Sorry. I'm going to find a seat. Good luck."

As he walked down the center aisle looking for a seat, more than one of Kyle's female cousins checked him out approvingly. Kyle shook his head and almost smiled.

Kyle went and sat in the front pew with his dad's relatives. He zoned out for most of the service. There was some praying and some singing; the pastor said some stuff, and then there was more singing. The whole time Kyle kept thinking, How could Dad be gone? What would he do without him and his guidance? He wasn't ready to lose him.

Kyle's cousin Moira, sitting behind him, had to poke him

when it was time for the eulogy. "Kyle."

He bolted up and stumbled to the podium. He hoped he could do this. He hoped he wouldn't start bawling. And he really hoped he'd do his dad justice.

Kyle cleared his throat and looked out over the sea of faces in front of him, many of them weeping quietly. "Losing someone we love is the most difficult thing we can go through as human beings." He took a deep breath. "But, I don't have to tell you that. No words can really express what we're all feeling right now. No words can do justice to my dad, Riley Barada.

"Dad was always there for me, for you, for all of us, in both body and spirit. He showed us by example how to be a good father, a good friend, and a good man. He wasn't afraid to show and tell us that he loved us.

"We should treasure the time we had with him and focus on the good times we had with him rather than on his absence." Kyle's eyes filled. He had to pause for a moment, too overcome to talk.

"Dad showed me what true love and true partnership were like. I take comfort in that." He tried to blink the tears out of his eyes. "Dad loved us more than he loved himself. He thought nothing of putting himself in harm's way to protect someone else. Ultimately it was this selflessness, this bravery that led us here, today." He looked down at his notes, trying to dampen down his emotions a bit.

"Sometimes, at times like these, families are full of worries and regrets about things left unsaid. Not us. Dad was brave enough to tell us what he felt, and he gave us--he gave me--the courage to do the same. I never doubted that he loved me, and I know you all feel the same. So, in that way, too, we are lucky to have known him."

"Because of his openness, his understanding, and his love, I'm sure he has no regrets. And thanks to him, neither do I."

Kyle looked up at the ceiling. "Dad, thank you for everything. I'll try to live up to your examples. I love you." He looked out at all his friends and family sitting in front of him. "And I love all of you." He finally lost control, and tears coursed down his cheeks. "Thank you." He stepped down.

There were a few moments of silence as the pastor

scrambled back up to the podium.

Kyle's Aunt Jessie handed him a tissue. She was a woman who always seemed to have a hug ready or room on her lap when a kid needed comforting.

Moira patted him on the shoulder.

Sitting next to him, Raymond looked very similar to his dad. He said, "Nice job," in a very gruff voice. Out of the corner of Kyle's eye, he saw his uncle's cheek was wet, too. The pastor said, "And we all rise for the hymn..."

After the service, Liam came up and shook Kyle's hand. "Wow. Good job, mate. Can I get you to do my eulogy?"

Kyle felt the corners of his mouth turn down. "I hope not. I hope that's a long way away, mate."

Liam nodded. "But, seriously, I'm very sorry for your loss," he said. "I always liked him, your dad. He was a good man."

Kyle nodded.

"Are you coming over later?"

"Yeah." Suddenly, Kyle's knees felt weak, and he felt very nauseated.

Liam grabbed his arm before he fell. "Whoa, mate. Are you okay?"

"Not sure." The room spun. "I don't understand what's going on."

Liam helped Kyle to a chair as his relatives started to notice there was something wrong with him.

Uncle Ray strode through the crowd. "Kyle? What's wrong?"

"I'm not sure," he said.

"I, ah, might be." Ray glanced at Liam. "I think I've seen this before. But maybe this is a family matter."

Liam held up his hands, palms out. "No problem. I understand." He started backing away.

"No, Liam's my best friend," Kyle said. "You can talk in front of him."

Ray didn't seem inclined to talk even with this encouragement.

The room continued to spin.

"It's all right, mate," Liam said. "I'll see you back at the flat." He walked towards the exit.

Aunt Jessie shepherded the rest of the non-family members down to the church basement, where food and drink had been laid out for a reception.

Once he was surrounded by family only, Kyle said. "What? What is it? What's wrong with me?"

"I've seen this before with your dad," Ray said. "When he first came into his power as you are now. Someone else is Dreaming. You're feeling it."

Zoom, zoom, the room whirled around him. "I don't understand," Kyle managed to say, head between his knees. "We're all here. We're the only ones who can Dream, and none of us are Dreaming."

"There must be someone else."

Chapter Five
Kairi: Boulder, Colorado, 1999

A hand touched her back, and Kairi whirled, startled. It was Lisa.
"Are you all right? What happened?" she asked.

Kairi was still standing in front of what she'd thought was
her foster mom's house. But upon further reflection, it did look
different than she remembered: the paint was brighter, all the
trees were smaller, and there were no shrubs or flowers.

What. The. Hell.

Lisa sighed.

"Uh, I'm not sure what happened." Kairi paused. "I know this
is a weird question, but ...what year is it?"

Lisa gave her a look like Kairi was crazy, and she couldn't
blame her. "1999."

Suddenly, Kairi felt lightheaded and sweaty. The world spun
around her.

Lisa grabbed her arm. "What's wrong? You got really pale
all of a sudden." Lisa's grip anchored her.

Kairi scooped together her wits, such as they were. She
didn't know what was going on, but acting crazy wouldn't help
anything. If being a foster kid had taught her anything, it was how
to go with the flow in the face of the unexpected. "Uh, my foster
mom said she didn't have any cash. I was just surprised, that's
all." She turned toward the car. "Let's go."

Lisa and Kairi went back to the station wagon. To Lisa's
credit, as far as Kairi could tell, Lisa didn't make any gestures to
indicate to her friends that Kairi was crazy. Kairi wasn't sure she
would have been as restrained in a similar situation.

Mike asked, "Did you get the cash? What took so long?"

The peanut gallery, aka Tom and Jim, didn't say much of

LESLEY L. SMITH

anything. They must have been tired out.

Lisa shushed Mike with a look Kairi couldn't see.

Kairi opened the car door. "No worries, gang. We're off to the dorm," she said in a forced cheerful voice. "Go back out to the main street, Broadway, we were just on."

Mike retraced their route through the neighborhood in the opposite direction. When they got to Broadway, Kairi told him to go north. "We're only a couple blocks from campus." As the asphalt passed below the wheels, she cranked the old-school window down and let the wind blow on her face.

Kairi knew in her bones she lived in 2019. It had definitely been 2019 when she left for spring break. What was this talk of 1999? Was she crazy? Could Lisa be punking her? She glanced at her. Lisa didn't seem the type. And that didn't explain what she'd seen in Pam's house. Pam called the baby Kairi. Was that baby her?

Could it actually be 1999?

"Where to now?" Mike asked as they crossed Baseline.

Kairi stopped her woolgathering. The corner looked different. Where was the strip mall to the south? "To our right is Colorado University. Welcome." In the streetlights, campus looked beautiful as usual with its red sandstone Italianate buildings and rolling green lawns. Too many lawns. The huge new law building was not there. Shit. "Get in the right lane and take the first entrance." As they wound through campus, she couldn't help noticing the buildings that were missing or different. The business building looked different. The big parking garage on the south end of campus was gone. The math building was gone, and the earth science building was gone. "Turn left here onto Colorado Avenue."

As they drove through campus, she wondered if she had been driven crazy. There didn't seem to be any escape from the evidence right in front of her eyes: she appeared to be in 1999. But that was impossible. Right?

"Turn here next to the Physics building," she said.

"The what?" Mike asked.

"Right. Sorry. You don't know what the buildings are," she said. "Just turn here. I live in Baker Hall. We're going to go around back to the parking area." At least Baker was still there.

TEMPORAL DREAMS

Jim sidled closer to her on the seat. "So, what are the sleeping arrangements going to be? I volunteer to share a bed with you if need be."

"What?" This guy was dreaming if he thought she'd share a bed with him. That would be cheating on Josh. Poor Josh. She hoped he was okay.

"What do you think?" Jim nudged her. With his cute goofy grin, she couldn't be mad at him; you couldn't blame a guy for trying.

"Thank you for your generous offer," she laid on the sarcasm, "but I don't think that will be necessary."

"Do you have your keys?" Lisa asked.

"No." Good point. "The door's usually unlocked. And if not, we can knock until someone opens it." She hoped.

"How will you get into your room?" Lisa asked.

What room? Kairi didn't have a room in 1999. "I won't be able to unless I can find my resident advisor. But it's no biggie. The lounge has a bunch of couches, and we can use the bathrooms and stuff." She hoped that would be the case in 1999 anyway.

The parking lot was empty, which she guessed was a good sign.

Mike said, "Hey, that sign says we need a permit to park here."

Kairi waved her hand. "Not during holidays."

"That sounds fishy," Tom said.

She glared at him. "How so? All the student workers who write tickets are on spring break."

"Makes sense to me," Jim said.

She flashed him a grateful smile.

Mike parked in about the same place Josh had been parked at the beginning of this whole fiasco.

They got out of the car, and some of them started unloading bags from the back. Kairi walked over to the back door and tried it. Locked. Crap. She started knocking. "Hello? Anyone there? I lost my keys. Hello?" She knocked harder.

Lisa wandered over. "What's happening? Can't you get in?"

"The door's locked, and no one seems to be home," she said.

The guys had stopped unloading gear and were staring their way.

"What's up?" Mike called.

"She can't get in," Lisa called back.

Kairi continued knocking, but no one came.

Tom snorted. "I knew it. It was a scam from the get-go."

"We don't know that," Jim said.

Lisa walked back to the car. "I believe her. She lost her keys."

Mike started putting bags back in the car. "That doesn't change the fact we need to find a place to stay tonight."

Jim didn't say anything. He just looked at her with disappointment in his eyes.

"I say we call the cops," Tom said. "She scammed us."

Uh, oh. Kairi really hoped they wouldn't call the cops on her. She stopped knocking so she could hear them better.

"Come on," Lisa said. "Cops? That's a bit much, don't you think?" She turned to her. "Come on, Kairi, we'll find someplace else to stay."

"What?" Tom said. "No way we let her scam us some more."

"I appreciate your kind heart, Lis, but I'm done with her," Mike said. "She got a free ride home. That's enough."

Lisa sputtered. "But we can't just leave her here. What's she gonna do? Sleep in the parking lot?"

"Sure, we can leave her here," Tom said. "I don't care where she sleeps. And I say we call the cops."

"Get in the car, Lisa," Mike said, pointing.

Mike must have had a very determined look on his face because Lisa said, "Fine!" with a frown and got in the car.

They finished loading up the rear with their gear and got back into the car.

"Bye, Kairi," Lisa called out as they backed up.

"Good luck," Jim said.

They drove away.

Kairi was left in the middle of campus, pushing ten p.m., with no wallet, nowhere to go, and no one to call.

She walked around the building and tried all the other doors. No luck. She kept an eye open for the cops, but they didn't show; she guessed Lisa talked Tom out of calling. That was fortunate, but unfortunately, all the dorm's doors were locked. Who knew they had such good security in 1999? She walked around the building again and tried all the ground-floor windows. They were all firmly closed, too.

As she stood outside the window of what would be her room in 2019, worn out and cold, she started feeling sorry for herself again. Why had this happened to her? Why was she stuck in 1999? How could she be in 1999?

And then her thoughts turned to Josh again. She wondered where--or when--he was and if he was okay. She imagined how comforting it would be to be wrapped in his arms, to feel his warm breath on her neck and his voice reassuring her that everything would be all right. Would she ever see him again? Would she ever see anyone she knew again? And if she did, would they recognize her? Pam didn't.

As her eyes filled, she blinked rapidly and cleared her throat. "Okay, enough, Kair. Quit feeling sorry for yourself."

And then she did hear a siren coming her way. Tom called the cops after all, the jerk.

She had to hide. She looked at her window--at least the window she'd have in 2019. "Screw this," she said and scooted around the bushes to the window. She kicked out the bottom pane, reached her hand through to the latch, and promptly cut her arm. "Shit!" She checked out the wound, and it was minor, so she tried again and successfully opened the window and climbed in.

She flipped on the lights and saw two unfamiliar but comfy-looking beds, two desks, chairs and dressers, a mini-fridge and assorted college paraphernalia. "That's more like it." She quickly drew the curtains as the siren drew closer. When the flashing lights arrived in the parking lot behind the dorm, she got in one of the beds and pulled the covers up over her head.

Chapter Six
Kyle: Sydney, Australia, 2019

A lot of giggling and whispering woke Kyle up. Honestly, how could Liam and his sheila-of-the-day make so much noise? Kyle stumbled into the living room and found his roommate escorting three giggling women out the front door of the flat.

Closing the door behind them, Liam leaned back against it, wearing only a huge shit-eating grin.

"Mate!" Kyle said. "Put some shorts on. I don't want to look at that."

"You don't appreciate me in the nuddy?" His grin got wider. "Jealous, huh?" He made no move to cover his junk, and it did match the rest of his large physique.

Kyle would never admit it to him, but he may have been a little bit jealous of Liam's lack of shame. And his ability with women. Wow, he had a way with the ladies. "Three women? Doesn't that seem a little greedy?"

"Yeah." He grinned some more. "Oh, buck up, mate. I brought one home for you, but you were working late, so we just had to make do." He turned to the kitchen. "Come on, I'll make you a cuppa."

Kyle wanted to tell him to put some shorts on again, but if he was willing to risk his donger with boiling water, he guessed that was his choice. On the bright side, the counter would block the view. He sat down at the breakfast bar and yawned. "Thanks."

Liam put on the kettle and got out the mugs, tea, and milk. "Were you training again last night?"

Kyle yawned again. "Yeah. In fact," he leaned over the counter, "today's the day."

"What? Your first mission?"

"Yeah." He was pretty nervous.

"So what is it? You going to stop the 2004 embassy bombing in Jakarta? Or the 2002 Bali bombings? Or maybe the 1978 Sydney Hilton bombing?"

"No. And what's with all the bombing talk? Weren't you listening? It's my first mission."

The kettle whistled, and Liam started pouring. "So, what then?"

"I'm going to go back and stop a merger." Kyle poured some milk into his tea.

"A merger? What the fuck, mate?" Liam took a sip and winced at the temperature.

Kyle blew on his tea. "What'd you expect? You know we have a bunch of corporate clients. Gotta' pay the bills." This was something he and his father had disagreed about. He wanted to use their power for good, but Dad said it was too dangerous to make significant changes to the timeline. Maybe that would be something he could change. "This merger was a trick. The other company used it as a ruse to cover up a hostile takeover. I'm going to go back and stop it." He hoped he could do it. He hoped he wouldn't get too dizzy or nauseated. His dad had warned that could happen while Traveling.

Suddenly, Kyle felt nauseated. Was it some kind of bizarre power of suggestion? He slammed down his mug and clutched the stool.

"Kyle? What is it, mate? You don't look so good. Are you going to chunder?"

It felt like it. As Kyle battled his stomach, realization dawned. He was probably feeling himself Travel to his present, to now, from the past. And that's probably what it had been the other times, too. Duh. "I think it's me. Traveling."

Liam whipped his head around the flat. "Here? Where? I don't see you."

"I'm not Traveling here in the room," Kyle said around gritted teeth. "That would probably kill me."

Dressed in one of his new fancy suits, Kyle turned up early at the corporate offices in Sydney.

Uncle Raymond still beat him there. "Kyle! Very spiffy. Professional. You look great. And early. I appreciate your attitude, young man." Possibly he was laying it on a bit thick. Maybe he thought Kyle was nervous.

Kyle was nervous. "Hey, Uncle Ray. Here I am, reporting for duty."

"Okay. We might as well get started." Ray led him to their inner sanctum: The Dreaming Room. It was a fairly small room with lush carpeting, containing only a large dentist-type chair smack dab in the middle. The walls were plain, and the lighting dim. The goal had been to make the room as boring as possible to facilitate Dreaming.

"Ray, I think I felt someone Travel this morning, likely me. That's probably what I've been feeling."

"Oh. Yeah. That makes sense." Ray relaxed his shoulders. "I bet that's it! We should have thought of that. It makes more sense than some mystery Traveler."

Kyle lay back on the special chair. His first mission should be a piece of cake. That was intentional. It was just a quick trip into the past to give a corporate client some business advice. Easy-peasy.

Ray gave him one of their special encoded business cards, and he carefully put it in his inside suit coat pocket. Dad had come up with them. They indicated to the clients that had them on retainer that the possessor was Traveling.

Ray handed him a folder of financial data and the number for their account. Kyle slipped the folder inside the waist of his pants, keeping it inside the all-important four-centimeter buffer.

Ray dimmed the already-dim lights. "Now, close your eyes. Focus on your breathing. Clear your mind."

Kyle focused on breathing for quite a while. When he was totally relaxed, he nodded.

"You can access The Dreaming," Ray said. "You have the power. Feel all of time flowing through you. It's you. You're it. You are The Dreaming."

"I am The Dreaming." All this, the words, the relaxed state, were symbols, triggers that put Kyle in touch with Everything. He'd been training his whole life for this moment, for this eternity.

In his mind's eye, he saw himself putting the card in his

pocket. He entered the inner sanctum and then the building.
He got dressed, drank a cuppa with Liam, saw Liam escort the
women out of the flat, and woke up. He got home last night.
He controlled his breathing. He controlled his mental state. He
trained.

He gave his dad's eulogy.

He hung out with Liam at the pub.

He visited his dad in hospital.

He trained at their compound in the country.

He focused on when he wanted to be.

Kyle emerged one month in his past, still in The Dreaming
Room, and opened his eyes.

An alarm blared.

Kyle winced. That thing was too loud.

A voice on an intercom said, "Just a moment Kyle. We have
to get present-you out of here."

As he cooled his heels, he recalled this incident a month
ago. He'd thought his dad had been the Traveler.

Bloody hell. He didn't know back then how soon Dad would
die.

Kyle wanted to warn him.

But he wasn't allowed.

When Uncle Ray finally let him out, Ray's lips were pressed
into a very thin line, and Kyle knew Ray knew Riley was dead in
Kyle's present. "Is the client in Sydney?" was all Ray said.

Kyle nodded, not trusting himself to blurt out something he
wasn't supposed to say.

When Kyle arrived at the client's offices, some kind of
assistant passed him off to the CEO so quickly you'd think he
had bubonic plague.

As Kyle entered the expansive office, the CEO stood up
behind his desk, frowning. "Kyle Barada? What happened to
your father?" In the morning light streaming through his wall-to-
wall window, the man's silver-gray tie matched the hue of his hair
perfectly.

Kyle made himself smile and reached into the jacket pocket
for the card.

The corners of the executive's mouth dragged down even

further. "You're Traveling? Is it the merger? How bad?"

Kyle handed the card across the desk and waved the file folder at him. "I'd be happy to share all the specifics with you as soon as we receive our bonus."

The man suddenly seemed twenty years older as he sank into the plush chair. He nodded and typed some commands into his computer using two index fingers.

Immediately, Kyle's mobile pinged, and he received a text: Funds transferred.

Kyle handed the man the file. "It's a hostile takeover."

The CEO flipped open the file. "I can't believe it. I've known John for fifty years. I thought we were friends." He looked so sad. Kyle felt a little sorry for him. What would that be like? To be betrayed by a friend of fifty years?

Kyle left him shaking his head and paging through the folder.

Back on the street, it was full-on summer, and he was dressed for much cooler weather, but he didn't want to get back in the car that was waiting for him. This was his first trip into the past. He wanted to drink everything in, to relish it. He walked right past the car.

The driver's door popped open. "Mr. Barada? Is there a problem?"

"No. I just feel like walking a bit." Kyle was In The Past. Everything seemed so real, so vibrant. The sun beat down on them, illuminating everything in surreal Technicolor. Were the shadows always that crisp? Was the sky that blue in his home time? It didn't seem possible.

"Sir, that's against protocol," the driver said. "I'm going to have to ask you to get back in the car, sir. Now."

A wave of queasiness crashed down on Kyle, and he doubled over.

"Sir!" The driver jumped out of the car and rushed over to him as he collapsed on the baking concrete.

Was this what Traveling was supposed to feel like?

Chapter Seven
Kairi: Boulder, Colorado, 2019

Kairi woke, groggy, to the sound of a heavy wooden door opening. Where was she? Who was coming into the room? Shit. When was she? Whoever it was, chances were they wouldn't like finding a stranger in their bed. Quickly, she arranged the blankets over her head and then froze.

The person came in, closed the door, and began puttering around the room. Kairi squeezed her eyes tight and tried to breathe shallowly.

Nothing happened. They didn't notice her.

She heard a dresser drawer snick open, and the person started humming off-key. At least now she knew they were female.

And then she smelled something odd but familiar. Pot.

What? Were all CU students potheads, or was there a chance it was her roommate Dakota? She risked peeking out from under the covers.

As she moved in the bed, the woman screamed. "Who's there? I'm calling the cops!"

Kairi pulled the covers down and started to say, "Please don't call the cops," when she realized it was her roommate Dakota. Thank goodness she was back home.

Dakota screamed again--in happiness--and rushed to the bed. "Kairi? When did you get back? What happened? Josh said you guys were in a car accident. And a tornado! And you were missing!" She threw her arms around her as she sat up. "It's so good to see you. Are you okay? What happened?"

Josh said? That must mean he wasn't injured--at least not seriously.

As Kairi clutched her roommate, she thought she'd never been so glad to see anyone in her life.

They separated, and Dakota said, "Oh, no! You're bleeding."

Kairi glanced at the cut on her arm and then at the unbroken window. Weird. "It's nothing. Superficial."

Dakota sat down next to her and took a toke. Somehow through all the hugging and screaming, she'd kept her grip on her joint. "So what happened? What's a tornado like? How did you get here? And why haven't you been answering your phone?"

"I didn't have any bars," Kairi said, answering her last question, the only one she knew the answer to.

"But Kairi, what happened to you? Where have you been?"

Good question. "I don't know," she said. She glanced down at the bed. "You're not going to believe this: I actually thought I was in 1999 for a little while there. Now I'm thinking maybe it was a dream?" But it seemed so vivid.

"1999? It sounds awesome!" Dakota said. "What was 1999 like?"

Trust Dakota to believe anything. Kairi shook her head. "It really didn't seem like a dream. But being in 1999 doesn't make any sense. Now I'm thinking I had some kind of head injury." She felt her head, but there were no cuts, bumps or sore spots.

"Or, maybe...," Kairi said.

"What?" Dakota asked.

"Maybe I'm going crazy."

Bless her heart, Dakota said there was no way she was crazy. Dakota did talk her into going to the university health center to let them check her head out. Unfortunately, when they got to the health center, it was closed for spring break. Ugh.

"Do you want to go to the emergency room?" Dakota asked her as they stood outside the health center entrance.

Physically, Kairi's head felt fine. She didn't think she'd had a head injury. "No. I guess not. But I'm so confused. What happened to me?"

"What did Josh say?" Dakota asked.

Oh, no! She hadn't called Josh yet. Kairi whipped out her cell phone and hit the speed dial. It went straight to voicemail. "Voicemail." She put her phone away.

Dakota nodded. "Yeah. He's probably still in the hospital in Oklahoma."

Kairi made a little strangled noise. "Hospital? You might have mentioned that earlier! What happened to him? Is he okay?"

Dakota sat down on the bench near the health center entrance. "I thought I did say. He was in a car accident and then a tornado. Or vice versa."

Kairi sank down next to her. "Oh, no." She should have been more worried about Josh. What if he was seriously injured? She'd never forgive herself. She was a horrible person. She was a horrible girlfriend, er, actually, she was a horrible fiancée. She'd make a horrible wife. "Just tell me. How bad is it?"

"Not too bad," Dakota said, waving her hand around. "I think he's supposed to get out of the hospital today."

Kairi forced herself to keep her voice even. "Not too bad? What does that mean?"

"I don't remember," Dakota said.

Kairi had a fleeting urge to strangle her but took a deep breath instead. Calm down, Kair. Dakota's had a tough time of it. Who else might know something? "Pam!" Quickly she dialed her.

Pam answered on the first ring. "Kairi, is that you?"

"Yes," she said. "Did..."

"Thank goodness!" Pam interrupted. "I've been worried sick."

Dakota leaned toward her. "Is that Pam?" She pushed her mouth near her phone. "Pancakes!" Kairi's stomach rumbled.

"Is that Dakota?" Pam asked. "Do you guys want to come over for pancakes? I need to set my eyes on you to make sure you're all right."

"Pancakes, pancakes!" Dakota chanted.

"Kairi?" Pam asked.

"Yes, Pam, thanks," she said. "Dakota and I will be right over for some pancakes."

Dakota chanted, "Chocolate chip, chocolate chip," but Pam had already hung up.

Dakota was inhaling her second helping of chocolate chip pancakes by the time Pam sat down at the table with them.

"What do you know about Josh?" Kairi asked Pam.

"He called here asking if I'd heard from you," Pam said. "He said he was in the hospital. He broke his arm, and they were afraid of a concussion and possibly some internal bleeding, but supposedly it wasn't serious."

"Internal bleeding sounds serious," Kairi said.

"They were worried he might develop internal bleeding, but there was no sign of it so far," Pam said.

"Good." Kairi sighed in relief and took a bite of pancake. It was brown and crispy on the outside and fluffy on the inside. The chocolate chips were molten heaven. She hadn't even bothered with syrup.

She made another quick call to Josh and got voicemail again.

"You truly don't know what happened to you, Kairi?" Pam asked.

Her mouth full, Kairi shook her head.

"Why don't you start at the beginning," Pam said.

Dakota nodded, chewing exuberantly.

"I woke up on the side of the highway. Josh was gone. The car was gone."

Pam grimaced. "That's hard to believe. Josh is a fine young man."

"Yeah, Josh wouldn't abandon you," Dakota said. "Especially considering, you know..."

Pam perked up. "What's you know?"

"Nothing." Kairi glared at Dakota to get her to be quiet.

It didn't work. Dakota barged on, "Josh got an engagement ring!"

Pam dropped her fork. "He what? You've only been going out a few months! It's too soon for that."

"Nine months," Dakota said.

"Eight months and three weeks," Kairi said. "Yep. I guess I'm engaged."

"Where is the ring?" Dakota asked.

"I put it in my dresser," Kairi said. She was uncomfortable wearing something so fancy. And, honestly, she was confused. She needed to hear directly from Josh how she ended up alone by the side of the road.

"Marriage is a big step, Kairi," Pam said. "I'm sorry, but I don't think you're ready for it." Was that a flash of sorrow across her face? "Marriage is really hard."

What did Pam know about marriage? Kairi'd never even seen Pam date anyone. "I don't want to talk about the engagement. Anyway, I hitchhiked back to Boulder," she said, frowning at her.

Pam said, "Oh, Kairi. You should know better than that. Hitchhiking is not a good idea. Something bad could happen to you." She rubbed her forehead. "You're going to be the death of me yet."

Their eyes met.

"Of course, bad stuff can happen in what should be good circumstances, too," Kairi said, her voice small.

"Huh?" Dakota raised her head from her plate. "What are you guys talking about?"

"Nothing," Pam said.

Dakota happily turned her attention back to eating.

"I know hitching is a bad idea, but what was I supposed to do?" Kairi asked. "I didn't have any money or any bars."

"*Hmm*, that is a tough one," Pam said.

"So far, this story doesn't sound crazy to me," Dakota said. "Why did you say you thought you were going crazy this morning?"

"What?" Pam asked. "Crazy?" She glanced at Dakota. "Who's crazy?"

"I haven't got to the weird part yet," Kairi said slowly. "When we got to Boulder, everything looked different. A bunch of buildings were gone. We even came here, and the neighborhood looked different. All the trees were smaller, and the houses looked brighter."

"Why did you come to the neighborhood?" Pam asked. "And why didn't you stop by? You know my door is always open to you."

"I did stop by," Kairi said. "I knocked on the front door, and some man answered it. You were in the living room, right there," she pointed, "with a baby."

"But, Kairi, no one but me was here last night," Pam said. "No man. No baby. And I definitely didn't see you."

"That is weird," Dakota said.

"You looked different, too, Pam," Kairi said. "Younger. And the baby had dark skin like mine. I could have sworn you called her Kairi. And you called the guy John."

Pam gasped.

Kairi shook her head. "Like I said, crazy."

But when she looked at Pam, it was as if all the blood had drained from her face. "Did you say John?" Pam asked in a whisper.

"Yeah," Kairi said. "You definitely called him John. You said something like Don't be rude, John. Invite her inside. Why?"

Pam put down her fork carefully, seemed to gather her wits and finally said, "I had a husband named John."

"What!" Dakota and Kairi said simultaneously as Dakota fell out of her chair.

"You were married?" Kairi said. "I never knew you were married!"

Dakota stood and rearranged herself on the chair. "Why are you so against marriage then?"

"Why didn't you tell me about him?" Kairi asked. "And what happened to him?" She had a bad thought. "He didn't die, did he?"

"No. He didn't die," Pam said wryly. "A few times, I might have wished he would, but no."

"Where is he? What happened?" Dakota asked.

"I don't want to talk about it," Pam said.

"Oh, come on!" Kairi said. "You can't drop a bombshell like that and then say you don't want to talk about it! You wouldn't let me do that."

"Oh? I wouldn't?" Pam met her eyes and was silent for a few moments.

Kairi knew Pam was thinking about Kairi's junior prom. That was the last dance Kairi ever went to, and she did a lot of not-talking about it.

Finally, Pam said, "What's the rest of this crazy story, then?"

"Fair enough," Kairi said. "I came here and saw you, a baby, and some guy you called John. You acted like you didn't recognize me. Then, I left and asked somebody what year it was, and she said it was 1999."

"Awesome!" Dakota said. "I love this part of the story. What was 1999 like?"

Pam was squinting, which Kairi knew meant she was trying to remember something.

"What?" Kairi said to her.

"That's a little weird," Pam said. "As I recall, my troubles with John started in 1999."

"Okay," Kairi said. "Now, you really have to tell us what happened."

Pam looked sad. "I don't think I should. I don't think it would be good for you." She glanced at Dakota. "For either of you."

"Come on, Pam," Kairi said. "You always say honesty is the best policy, and besides, we're both in our twenties now, we can take it, whatever it is."

"Yep," Dakota said. "Honesty. You say it all the time. Tell us."

Pam seemed to be gathering her courage. "Fine. John and I met in college." She looked at Dakota and cleared her throat. "Anyway, I had a huge crush on John as soon as I met him. He was very involved in civil rights. He organized a bunch of demonstrations. I really admired him. We fell in love quickly, and it was very passionate."

Somehow passion and Pam didn't exactly go together in Kairi's mind.

"Passionate?" Dakota asked. "How so? Tell us more!"

Pam cleared her throat again. "Anyway, we got married right after graduation, and John's dad pressured him to get a real job, which he did, to make a long story short."

"Oh, don't do that," Dakota said.

"We grew up," Pam said. "We had some tough times. I wanted to have a baby but never got pregnant." She paused, shaking her head. "I never did understand why. But as the years passed, and we didn't have a baby, I decided I wanted to adopt." She glanced at the young women.

Adopt? Pam never adopted anyone. Kairi used to lie awake at night, wishing Pam would adopt her. And Dakota.

"But John refused," Pam said. "He said he wouldn't adopt. So, I suggested we become foster parents. He didn't want to, but I finally convinced him to do it by saying it would be temporary." She shook her head.

"So?" Kairi asked.

Dakota looked as confused as she was.

"What does all this have to do with me and Dakota?" Kairi asked.

"He made me give you back, Kairi," Pam said. "I fostered you when you were a baby, and he made me give you back."

Kairi felt sick, and she didn't think it was the pancakes. How could a grown man do that to a little baby?

"I fostered several kids over the years," Pam said, "including you for a little while, Dakota. And every time John made me give them back."

Who would be so cruel as to reject little kids?

"But, how could he?" Dakota said. She looked as sick as Kairi felt.

"Finally, I couldn't take it anymore," Pam said. "And I gave him an ultimatum: accept the kids or leave. So he left."

Dakota looked as if someone had kicked her in the gut.

This John was the reason Kairi didn't grow up with a family.

If she'd had a family, all the bad stuff that happened to her wouldn't have happened.

Kairi didn't think she was a violent person, but she was tempted to find this John and make him suffer.

There was a definite lull in the conversation as the three of them pondered the bizarre workings of John's brain.

Finally, Dakota broke it, "So if John lived with you in 1999 and Kairi met John at your house in what she thought was 1999, doesn't that mean she was in 1999?"

Dakota had a point. "You don't happen to have a picture of John, do you?" Kairi asked.

Pam frowned. "I was so upset that I got rid of all his pictures."

"All of them?" Dakota asked. "What about your wedding pictures?"

"Hmm." Pam squinted. "You know, I think I might have a wedding picture or two up in the attic."

Pam retrieved a picture and handed it to them. It featured a beaming young-looking Pam and a man with long stringy sandy hair and a big mustache. The mustache was the same. It was the guy Kairi'd met last night.

"Well?" Dakota asked. "Is that the guy?"
Kairi met her friends' eyes. "Definitely."
Now she was sure she'd time traveled to 1999. But why?
And how?

Chapter Eight
Kyle: Sydney, Australia, 2019

The driver raced Kyle back to the offices of Time Advantages, Inc. The executive secretary, Charlotte, took one look at him and rushed over.

She grabbed his arm and led him over to a couch, setting him down gently. "What's wrong, Kyle? Did something go wrong with the mission? Or did you get injured somehow?"

Kyle lay back on the couch and watched her leaning over him, her short curly gray hair falling around her face, eyes crinkled with worry. Over the years, she'd kept her trim figure, and he could usually still detect the spark of fun in her eyes that he'd seen as a boy. Back then, she'd always been willing to play with him when Dad brought him into the office.

"Kyle? Answer me, or I'm going to call an ambulance."

"Yes, ma'am," he said. "I'm okay now."

She straightened up and put her fists on her hips. "What's this ma'am business? I told you to call me Charlotte years ago. You didn't hit your head, did you?"

"No, Charlotte." While still woozy, Kyle grinned for a second and sat up. "Maybe you could bring me some water?"

Soon, she placed a tumbler of ice-cold water in his hand, and he drank it greedily. The cold water did seem to settle his stomach a bit.

When she took the empty glass back, she still looked worried. She would have made a good mother, but she'd never gotten married.

"I'm okay." He leaned forward. "Are you okay? You seem upset."

She tucked a lock of hair behind her ear, and when it

escaped again, she did it again. And again. He knew that meant she was nervous.

The fact that he was here on a mission meant Dad was dead in her near future, and she had probably just figured it out when he showed up this morning. He leaned back. "I'm sorry, Charlotte," he said softly.

She held up her hands. "Maybe you shouldn't say anything. I don't want any information I'm not supposed to have. I don't want to be tempted to do something against the rules. I don't want to cause a paradox. We've all been warned against that."

She was really upset. For the first time, Kyle wondered if she and his dad had had a relationship. Was that why she never married and had kids of her own? "You and my dad?"

She looked down at the carpet.

"It's okay. I mean, my folks have been divorced a long time. I want you and Dad to be happy." How had he never figured this out before?

When she glanced up at him, there were tears in her eyes.

Rules that just hurt people seemed cruel. He decided to give her a break. "You have a few months," he said softly. "You can make the most of them..."

She nodded and quickly turned away.

He wasn't ready to go back to his time yet. He wanted to figure out why he'd felt so queasy on the street, and maybe there was some information here about what happened to Dad. "Can I go to the records room, or is Uncle Ray waiting for me to return?"

Near her desk, she turned to face him. "Raymond wants you to return ASAP, but he stepped out for a little while." A smile that didn't reach her eyes flitted across her face. "I won't tell him if you don't."

As he went down to the basement where the old paper records were stored, Kyle felt nervous but exalted, too. He didn't have to follow every little rule to the letter. Uncle Ray and Dad were wrong.

Dad. He paused on the stairs. Exactly what rule did he break that killed him? Even though Dad died after this time, maybe the event responsible had already happened? How long did it take to die from Traveling? He should review Dad's mission logs and try to figure that out.

Leave it to Charlotte. The paper files were very well organized, but there was no file labeled 'Queasiness, How to Avoid,' or 'What to Expect When You're Traveling.'

He accessed the most recent records and skimmed his dad's information, standing in front of the cabinet. There were no reports of anything going wrong. That must mean whatever happened to kill him hadn't happened yet. That was good.

He slid the folder back into the cabinet and stood there for a moment.

Kyle really wanted to warn his dad.

But what would he say? Watch out, Dad. You're in danger. But I don't know from what.

That wouldn't work. Plus, Dad wouldn't let Kyle get a word in edgewise if he thought he might be causing a paradox, anyway.

Kyle scanned the drawer again and saw his mom's name. Interesting. He and Mom didn't interact much since the divorce. He had mixed feelings about her.

But he'd always wondered why she'd stopped Traveling. He gingerly pulled the file out, sat down on the floor, stared at the file, and slowly opened it.

As Kyle read the exploits of Temporal Agent Rebecca Barada, his head swam. His mom had apparently been an exemplary Agent. Here it was in black and white. She'd specialized in the kind of corporate gigs he'd just undertaken. And then he looked closer at the dates when she started. They were long before she and Dad got married. They must have met through the company.

So, she wasn't originally a Barada. Duh. He was kind of a naïve idiot. How come he'd never thought about this before? People from the same family couldn't marry and have kids. So how come she could Travel? What family was she from?

And what did it mean that both his parents could Travel? Was that unusual? Did that make him special?

As Kyle turned through the pages, getting closer to the end of the file, he slowed. He read, "...bereft because of her sister's death, an accident on a mission...." Mom had had a sister? Since when? And how many other relatives did she have that he didn't know about?

His uncle's voice rang out, scaring the crap out of him. "What do you think you're doing?"

Standing up, Kyle tried to quiet his hammering heart. "How come no one ever told me Mom had a sister?"

"What about your mom?" Ray said. "Don't change the subject." His voice rose. "Why are you going through the records?"

"What do you mean, why am I looking at records?" Kyle's voice started to rise, too. "I'm an agent, and I can look at the records if I want to." Ray still treated him like a little kid after everything. Kyle was on a mission, after all. He was a Temporal Agent.

"It's dangerous. You might cause a temporal paradox or kill someone!"

Kyle was an adult now. "I thought I was in charge of my actions on my own missions. You don't tell me what to do; I'm responsible."

A strange ulp noise came from the direction of the stairs.

Ray and Kyle both turned that way. It was Dad. "Dad!" Kyle ran over to him. It was great to see him again.

Ray yelled, "No, Kyle, don't touch him." He grabbed for Kyle but missed.

Dad flinched back, but Kyle moved, too. Unfortunately, they tried to move to the same spot, and Kyle's fingers brushed Dad's chest as he stumbled onto the floor.

Kyle drew back. "Oh, no! Are you all right, Dad? Are you okay?" Did he hurt him? The Traveling regulations said Travelers touching each other was fatal.

Dad smiled tentatively. "I'm not sure. I feel okay."

Ray rushed over and grabbed Dad's arm, helping him up. "We need to get you checked out by a doctor as soon as possible, Riley."

Ray turned and glared at Kyle. "What are you even doing here? If you finished your mission, you're supposed to go back. You're not supposed to interact with him." He pointed at Dad. "Especially while you're Traveling."

Dad was staring from Ray to Kyle and back again with a strange expression.

Kyle knew Dad had heard him say he was on a mission.

Bloody hell. He'd just told him he was going to die.

Ray helped Dad up the stairs, and Kyle slowly followed.

When Charlotte saw Dad with Ray, her eyes filled. She glanced at Kyle with regret in her eyes and reached for the phone.

"Get back in that bloody chair and go home, Kyle," Ray said.

"You can't force me. I have to see if Dad's all right?"

Dad said one word: "Please."

Kyle turned and walked to The Dreaming Room.

Had he killed his father?

Chapter Nine
Kairi: Boulder, Colorado, 2019

Kairi and Dakota were back at their dorm room, stuffed to the gills, and she still hadn't been able to get a hold of Josh to find out what happened to him, never mind what had happened to her. "Is it just me, or is time traveling weird?"

"No," Dakota said. "It's weird."

"I don't get it," she said. "Why me?"

"Well, let's figure it out. You time traveled two times, right?" Dakota asked, flopping down on her bed in front of her babies-dressed-as-flowers posters. She called them her flower children--which came as no surprise based on the broomstick skirts and tie-dyed shirts she liked to wear.

"Yes." Kairi nodded, flopping down on her bed. She had posters of the Eiffel Tower and Big Ben on her side of the room. Hopefully, someday, she'd travel outside the U.S. "I time traveled on the road trip to 1999, and I time traveled back here to 2019 in the dorm."

"What did those two situations have in common?" Dakota asked.

Kairi pondered the question. In one case, she was in middle-of-nowhere Oklahoma in an afternoon storm; in the other, she was here in her bed in the middle of the night. They only had one thing in common. "I was asleep."

Dakota nodded. "So, go to sleep and see if you time travel again."

That sounded too weird. Sleeping led to time travel? Kairi's heart started racing. Was she in danger of time traveling every time she went to sleep? That would be horrible.

And if so, why now? She'd slept fine for over twenty years

without going anywhere, er, anywhen. "It can't be that simple," she said.

Dakota shrugged. "You won't know until you try it."

Kairi couldn't argue with that logic. "Okay. I'll give it a try." She stretched out on the bed and started closing her eyes, then jerked them open. "You promise to yell or something if I start time traveling?"

"How will I know?" Dakota asked.

"How do I know how you'll know?" Kairi stopped and considered the question. "Just yell if anything weird happens."

Dakota grinned. "I think we can count on that anyways."

Kairi grinned back. "Okay. Thanks." She settled back on the bed and closed her eyes.

She heard Dakota rustling around on her bed.

She tried to focus on her breathing, and then she heard Dakota get up, open her dresser drawer and fish around inside.

She tried to relax.

Dakota started humming under her breath. Off-key.

Dakota was driving her crazy. She opened her eyes and leaned up on one elbow. "Dakota."

Dakota jerked around, revealing she was about to light up a joint.

"Dakota!" Kairi yelled. "I thought we agreed you weren't going to smoke in our room, and you weren't going to keep pot in here. What if someone finds out?"

Dakota shrugged and moved the lighter closer to her joint.

"Stop." Kairi sat up. "We could both get kicked out of the dorm. And they don't give refunds for room and board when they kick you out."

"But it's spring break," Dakota said. "Nobody's here." She lit it and took in a lungful of smoke.

"We'd be out several hundred dollars!" Kairi jumped up and strode towards her roommate. "And where would we live? We'd be totally screwed." She stood right next to her, glaring.

Dakota exhaled and took another toke.

They both jumped sky-high when someone knocked on the door.

Quickly, Dakota stubbed out the joint in the ashtray on her dresser. Then she waltzed over to the door and opened it before

Kairi could stop her.

Their R.A. Tyler stood there. "If I hadn't heard yelling, I wouldn't have even known you were here. You guys were supposed to register if you were staying. What am I smelling?" Tyler's eyes were drawn to the dresser like a gawker at a traffic accident. He couldn't see anything, could he?

Why did it have to be goody-goody Tyler left in the dorm over the vacation? Dumb question. He had nowhere else to go and no one to go with.

"Is that marijuana I'm smelling?" he asked in a squeaky voice. "Even though it's legal in the state, it's still against university policy. And it's an automatic dorm expulsion and university probation. We have a zero-tolerance policy."

Dakota fluttered her eyelashes. "Oh, don't be that way, Tyler. We're happy to share. Come party with us."

No, Dakota. Couldn't she tell he thought she was the devil right now? Sometimes she seemed to have no sense whatsoever.

Tyler took a step back, sputtering. "I would never..."

Kairi rolled up her sleeve, exposing the large bandage over the cut on her arm. "Would you believe it's medical marijuana?"

"No," he said."You can smoke whatever you want, wherever you want, as long as it's not on campus."

Dakota stepped toward him. "I always liked you, Tyler. If there was anything I could do for you... Anything at all." She stepped even closer. "Anything."

He backed off, looking at the two of them. "Maybe if Kairi was willing to..."

Kairi took a step toward him with narrowed eyes. "If I what?"

He grinned. "We could start with a kiss." He reached for his cell phone. "Or maybe you'd rather I call the CU police?"

Dakota gave her an entreating look. "You're the one who said we couldn't get kicked out."

"Oh, all right!" Kairi said and stepped into the hall.

Tyler leaned in and planted one right on her lips. The next thing she knew, his tongue was trying to find its way into her mouth. She forced herself not to cringe away. But it was pretty horrible. It reminded her of her Junior Prom...

She'd been so excited that Chad-the-hottie had asked her

to go with him to the dance. Looking back on that naïve girl, she didn't know if she should cry or vomit. She'd been living with Pam at the time, and Pam had altered a wine-red dress for her that they'd found at Savers Secondhand Store. Kairi looked awesome; Dakota and everyone else at her group home had said so. Kairi'd thought Chad asked her to the dance because he liked her, but as she tried to fight him off in the back seat of his car, she realized it was because he thought the foster kid would put out. She was so mad at herself. She should have known better. At first, when he got all grabby, she pushed his hands away and tried to laugh it off. "Come on, Chad. Give it a rest."

He pushed the skirt of her dress up. "You know you want it, Kairi. Why else would you be here with me?"

She tried to push her skirt back down, but his hands were in the way. "No, Chad. I don't want to do this. I barely know you."

But he was already reaching for her underwear.

"No!"

"You don't want me to have to hurt you, do you?" His red face scowled down at her.

"No! Stop it!"

"Besides, I'll tell everyone you did it anyway."

Kairi started screaming.

Back in the dorm hallway, Josh's voice rang out, "What the hell is this?"

She and Tyler separated.

Shit. It was Josh. Where had he come from? More importantly, he looked healthy. In fact, he looked better than healthy. He looked great even with a cast on his arm.

Dakota interrupted. "No. It's cool. She just kissed him so he wouldn't have us kicked out."

Josh looked from Dakota to her. "Kairi, is this true?"

She nodded. She was still reeling. Josh was okay. That was a huge relief. But what happened? Why did they get separated?

"Aw, Kair, how could you, with your past?" Josh said. "I thought you said you would treat yourself with more respect."

"Hey, dude, take a chill pill," Tyler said. "It was just a kiss."

Josh turned to him. "For your information, we're engaged."

"You're what?" Tyler sputtered. "You guys were trying to trick me. You are so out of here!" He ran off.

Dakota took a few steps after him. "Tyler, wait."

"Josh, I'm glad to see you're all right," Kairi said. "When did you get back? Why were you in the hospital?"

"Yeah, I'm all right. I was just in the hospital for observation," Josh said. "For some reason, when you say your fiancée disappears into thin air, they don't believe you." He paused, frowning. "I can not believe you were kissing that guy."

Kairi was so happy to see Josh, she'd practically forgotten about Tyler already. "Uh, there's a reason," she said. "Let me explain."

"There's nothing that would make that okay." He shook his head. "I'm disappointed in you, Kairi." Now it was his turn to take off. Every step he took down the hall was a stomp on her heart. In cleats. But she knew going after him now when he was still upset wouldn't work. She had to let him cool off.

Dakota stood staring at the empty space where Tyler, and then Josh, had stood. Finally, she said in a small voice. "I'm sorry, Kairi."

She looked so forlorn that Kairi had to give her a hug. "It's not your fault. Or at least not totally. If I hadn't been yelling at you, Tyler wouldn't have even known we were here." But her mind was racing. Would they be kicked out?

Her first serious fight with Josh was bad enough, but they couldn't get kicked out of the dorms. She didn't have any money for first and last month's rent, never mind security deposits. Neither did Dakota. They were in trouble. They were going to be homeless. She was so mad at herself. How could she let this happen? She really wished she could have a do-over. She knew better than to yell at Dakota--it just made her shut down and turn her brain off.

Chapter Ten
Kyle: Sydney, Australia, 2019

Back in his present, 2019, Kyle needed answers. Did he hurt his dad? Was he responsible for Dad's death? No. That couldn't be true.

He ran out of The Dreaming Room and collided with Charlotte coming out of her office.

"Whoa, there, Kyle," she said. "Where's the fire?"

He stopped. "I want to know why my dad died."

She just stood there looking at him, and then she started tucking hair behind her ears. "Is this about that thing in the basement with you two and your uncle Ray months ago?"

"Is that why he died?" Kyle grabbed her arm. "I have to know. Tell me."

She snatched her arm back. "You know I'm not supposed to tell you."

"Come on." He stared into her gray eyes. Surely she hadn't forgotten he'd bent the rules those months ago. He hoped she'd enjoyed her time with Dad.

She glanced away. "I can't tell you because I don't know."

"I'm going back down to records," Kyle said.

Charlotte shook her head. "Ray says you're not allowed down there again. He locked it up tight."

"What? I'm The Traveler! How can he say that?"

She held up her hands. "You may be The Traveler, but Ray's in charge of the company. It's for your own safety."

"Brilliant. That's really logical. Keep information I need away from me," he said. "Come to think of it, why isn't more of this stuff on the computer?"

"Use your brain, boy. There were no computers years ago

and who knows what we'll have years in the future. It's a format issue. Only paper is independent of technology."

Good point.

"You must be stuffed, Kyle. Why don't you go home and rest?"

Now that she mentioned it, he was exhausted. "Yeah, okay." But there was so much he didn't know. "Can you tell me anything more about how my dad died? Anything?"

Charlotte's eyebrows rose, and she shook her head. "I'm sorry, my hands are tied. Now, you scoot."

There was nothing he could do? That was hard to accept.

When Kyle got back to the flat, Liam was there eating lunch. "What? Back so soon? What happened? Did the mission get canceled?"

It felt as if a week had passed since he'd left the flat that morning. He glanced at the clock. It had only been a few hours. "What yourself. What are you doing here? Don't you work?"

Liam stuck out his pursed lips. Then he said, "Well, someone's cranky, aren't they?"

Kyle sat down at the counter and exhaled. "Sorry." He shouldn't take his bad mood out on Liam.

"Do you want a sanger?" Liam held out one of his giant sandwiches.

"Yeah, thanks." Kyle grabbed it and took a big bite.

"Tea?"

"Does a koala shit in the gum tree?" Kyle forced a grin.

A bark of laughter exploded from Liam. "Yeah, he does. I'd say so." He put the kettle on. "I'll have to remember that one, mate."

Kyle broke out in a genuine grin. "Sorry, I'm cranky. I did go on my mission, and it wasn't what I expected. It was pretty bloody horrible."

"Oh?" Liam turned back around to face him. "Did one of those corporate lawyers challenge you to a duel? Or maybe one of the secretaries hit you over the head with her ancient typewriter?"

"No, nothing like that. The mission, per se, was fine. Went off like clockwork." Kyle was reluctant to tell Liam he might have killed his own dad. He was reluctant to admit it to himself. Surely, there was something he could do? He could Travel, after all!

"It was afterward. I went down to the records room and found out a little bit about my mom. She went on missions. She was awesome."

"So far, so good." Liam nodded.

"And then my dad burst in?"

"Your dead dad?"

Kyle nodded.

"Shite." Liam sank onto his stool.

Kyle nodded again. "Well, first it was Uncle Ray, and we were arguing, and then my dad showed up, and I accidentally touched him, and..."

"And what?"

"And I might have killed him."

"Fuck." Liam's mouth hung open.

The kettle whistled.

Liam got up, poured two cups of tea and handed Kyle one. "How did you kill him?"

"I don't know."

"Shite." Liam took a sip of tea and winced from the heat. "Your life is crazy, mate."

Kyle blew on his tea. "Yeah."

"So, where'd you leave it?"

"Nowhere. I asked for more info and was denied." Kyle shook his head.

"Oh, yeah. That sounds like bullshite. I thought you were a superhero, mate? Are you going to let them bullshite you like that?"

Liam was right. Kyle was The Traveler. "No, I'm not." He sipped his tea. "What do you think about helping me with a little fact-finding mission tonight?" When they'd been in university together, Liam and he were well known for their fact-finding missions after hours in the pub, the girls' dorm, and the professor's office.

"Would this be a fact-finding mission in which we dress in black, occurs after midnight and requires my lock picks?"

Kyle smiled. "You know it."

"Ace!"

Time Advantages, Inc. was very low-tech. This had pluses and minuses. Kyle could use his key on the front door without worrying about some computer recording his entry. On the other hand, they did have a night watchman, Clive.

Clive was a senior citizen and a good bloke. He took his job seriously. He wouldn't care about Kyle showing up after midnight, but he wouldn't be happy about Liam.

But that was okay. They had a plan.

As Kyle unlocked the door, Clive bolted up from behind the front desk. "Mr. Barada, sir. Can I help you with something?"

"Relax, Clive." Kyle smiled at him. "And I thought I told you to call me Kyle."

"Yes, s? Kyle." Clive sat down. "I'm real sorry about your Da, by the way. That speech you made at the funeral was real nice."

Kyle got choked up for a second. "Thanks." It was lunatic the way his grief kept sneaking up on him.

"But, what's this young fella doing here?" Clive pointed at Liam, who'd stayed silent until this point--which was tough for him.

Liam waggled his eyebrows. "We've got a date with some American sheilas."

"Huh?" Clive glanced around, looking for the girls. "But it's the middle of the night."

"They're in America," Kyle said. "It's the middle of the day in America. We're going to play a computer game over the Internet."

"Yeah, it's an MMORPG." Liam shifted the large paper sack he was carrying.

"Eh, okay," Clive said, clearly not understanding at all. "But unauthorized visitors aren't allowed. I don't think?"

"I know visitors aren't allowed because of corporate, shall we say, secrets," Kyle said. "But I promise no secrets will be involved. We're just going to go up to my office," which still felt like his dad's office, "and get on the computer."

"I don't know," Clive said.

"I appreciate your dedication," Kyle said. "I know what a hard worker you are." He hadn't wanted to play this card, but what could he do? "I'm still trying to get over my recent loss, and my mate Liam, here, thought this might help get my mind off it."

"Do you want a tinny, sir?" Liam said as if he'd just thought of it. He opened the bag, stuck his hand in, and came out with a beer. "We have plenty. In fact, have a couple."

Clive looked from Kyle's face to the beers, to Liam's face and back to Kyle. Wow, Clive was reliable.

Finally, Clive said, "Okay, Kyle." He paused. "I assume you don't want Ray to know about this?"

Kyle shrugged casually. "I'd just as soon keep it between us, but if he asks, I wouldn't want you to lie. Do what you think is right." Of course, there was no reason Ray would ask.

Liam piled some beers on Clive's desk, and then the two of them went up the stairs. "That old guy was a tough nut to crack."

"Yeah. Ray should give him a raise."

As soon as they got inside Kyle's office, he closed the door behind them. "Step one complete."

Liam set down the bag, pulled out a beer, opened it and sucked it down in one go. "Ahh."

"Thirsty?"

Liam grinned. "Just maintaining our cover."

Speaking of which, Kyle logged into the MMORPG.

Liam drank another beer.

"Easy there, mate. You need to be able to do your part."

"Do you want a coldie?" Liam held a beer out to him.

He could stand to be a bit calmer. He nabbed it, popped the top, and took a big gulp.

Someone knocked on the door.

Kyle jumped. And when his eyes found Liam's, he must have jumped, too, because they both snickered. They hadn't even done anything yet.

"Eh, Kyle?" It was Clive.

"Sure, Clive." Kyle stepped over to the door and opened it. "What?"

Clive took note of the computer program. "If it's all right with you, I'm going to take my dinner break, then."

Kyle nodded. "Sure. Do what you usually do. You don't have to check with me."

"We're not here," Liam said.

Clive's attention darted towards Liam. "Okay, then," Clive said. "Bye." He stepped away.

Kyle closed the door. "We're not here? What was that? Are you trying to act suspicious?"

"Whatever, mate. Don't spit the dummy."

Kyle opened the door a crack and peeked out. No sign of Clive. "Okay. Let's go." He gestured for Liam to follow him and stepped out into the common area. "Back stairs."

Liam followed him.

As they tiptoed down to the basement, Kyle's heart careened around his chest cavity. Some superhero he was. He got all nervous sneaking around his family's damn company. He hadn't even done anything.

Yet.

What would Uncle Ray do to him if he found out?

At the door to the records room, he pointed.

Liam took a little leather carrying case out of his back pocket, opened it, and raised two picks to the lock with a flourish.

After only a few moments, he said, "There. We're in." He turned the handle and opened the door.

Hurray for low-tech.

Kyle fished a tiny but powerful book light out of his pocket and shined it on the filing cabinets.

He tried to open the drawer he'd been using earlier in the day, but it was locked. "Bloody hell." He pointed at the drawer.

"No worries, mate." Liam brandished his picks again.

Soon, Kyle was extracting the files he wanted. He'd just closed the drawer when he heard the distinct sound of footsteps clomping down the hall outside the room.

The steps approached the door.

Kyle held his breath.

Chapter Eleven
Kairi: Boulder, Colorado, 2019

Back at Pam's house with suitcases, Kairi and Dakota nervously knocked on her front door. They hadn't been kicked out of the dorm yet, but Tyler had been a pain, stopping by the room all the time to threaten them. Asking Pam if they could stay with her was all Kairi could think of. She was avoiding thinking about Josh. She just couldn't deal with the idea that they'd had a big fight.

The door swung open. When their suitcases registered, a huge frown broke out on Pam's face. "What happened?"

Kairi mustered up a smile. "Is there any chance we could stay with you for a while?"

Pam shook her head. "You guys know the rules. You aged out of the system. You have to make it on your own. What happened?"

"I got caught smoking pot in the dorm," Dakota said.

Pam's face fell. "Oh, no, Dakota," she said softly. "I know you know better than that, honey. What were you thinking?"

Dakota shot Kairi a look that said Help.

"It's my fault," Kairi said. "I started yelling at her, and the R.A. came by."

"Your fault?" Pam said, raising her eyebrows.

"Can we come in?" Dakota asked.

Pam looked outside both ways and then stepped out of the doorway. "Of course, you can come inside the house."

They hustled in before she changed her mind. The ratty brown couch and the homemade bookshelves were part of the only real home Kairi'd ever known. She immediately felt a bit better. She put her bag down by the door. "So, can we stay with you for a little while?" she asked again.

Pam looked really sad. "You know I'd love to help you out, but I could lose my standing as a foster parent."

"One night?" Kairi asked. "How about one night?"

"It's spring break," Dakota said. "We're supposed to be having fun on vacation. Woo hoo," she added, but it sounded like she was going to cry.

"I guess one night wouldn't hurt anything," Pam said, looking at her watch. "It's almost dinner time, anyway. What do you guys think of spaghetti?"

Kairi smiled in relief. "We think that sounds great."

The whole evening, from the spaghetti dinner to doing the dishes to watching TV afterward, brought Kairi back to her high school days. Pam had been so sweet to her then. Now she could tell Pam was disappointed she couldn't just let them stay with her.

Her bedroom looked the same and yet different. The two twin beds were still there, and the closet and battered wooden dresser, but all her posters and books were gone--she'd taken them with her when she moved out. Looking back, she was embarrassed about the male beefcake who formerly festooned her room and would now remain nameless.

Nonetheless, Kairi and Dakota settled in as if it was three years ago and they were having a sleepover. The whole experience was very comforting, and Kairi needed it after recent events.

"Kairi?" Dakota asked. "Are you asleep yet?" Her talking when they were supposed to be sleeping was also just like their old sleepovers.

"We went to bed like two minutes ago; how could I be asleep already?"

"I just want to say I'm sorry about what happened."

"I'm sorry, too," Kairi said. "You know you need to quit. You know what happened to your mom." Throwing Dakota's mom in her face was a low blow. Her mom was a drug addict.

"I know. I'm sorry." Dakota sniffled. "I just wish I could undo what happened with Tyler. I totally wouldn't have smoked if I'd known what was going to happen."

Kairi also wished they could undo it. "So, you're going to try to stop smoking?" she asked.

"Yes. Totally." Kairi imagined her nodding in the dark.

"Good night."

"'Night."

As Kairi closed her eyes, she kept thinking if she'd known then what she knew now... In the familiar, relaxing surroundings, she drifted off to sleep almost immediately.

And then she was awake, the room bright behind her still-closed eyelids.

She heard Dakota rustling around on her bed. She tried to focus on her breathing, and then she heard Dakota get up, open a dresser drawer and fish around inside.

She tried to relax.

Dakota started humming under her breath. Off-key.

Dakota was driving her crazy. Kairi opened her eyes and sat up, leaning on one elbow. "Dakota."

She gasped. She, they, were back in their dorm room judging by the posters, and judging by the sunlight, it was daytime.

Dakota jerked around, revealing she was about to light up a joint.

Kairi's mouth started to yell "Dakota," but she stopped it. She remembered saying, "I thought we agreed you weren't going to smoke in our room, and you weren't going to keep pot in here. What if someone finds out?" But she thought that hadn't happened yet if it was going to happen at all. Right now was earlier than that.

She crept across the dorm room, grabbed the joint, stuffed it back into the drawer, and said, "Shh!"

"Why?" Dakota asked. "What are you doing?"

Kairi glared at this Dakota. "Shh!"

Dakota shut her mouth and looked at her in confusion.

In the background, Kairi heard a man, presumably Tyler, approaching, whistling something. He got closer and closer to their door and then walked on by. He continued down the hall.

Kairi let out her breath.

"Can I talk yet?" Dakota whispered. "What's going on?"

Kairi whispered back, "We just almost got kicked out of the

dorm."

"How do you know?"

"I just do."

Kairi remembered the other Dakota talking to the other Tyler in the hall. "I always liked you, Tyler. If there was anything I could do for you... Anything at all." Dakota stepped even closer. "Anything." But that was in the future, wasn't it? Would it happen?

Now, it was just Kairi and Dakota standing alone in the room, looking at each other. This was all very confusing.

And then someone knocked on the door in the here and now.

Kairi was afraid it was Josh, and they were about to have a big fight. She felt dizzy.

"I need to lie down," she said. "Don't answer the door."

She made her way over to her bed and lay down.

She relaxed and closed her eyes.

And then she was awake, the room bright behind her still-closed eyelids.

Someone was pounding on the door.

She was almost afraid to open her eyes. Who knew what she'd see?

Slowly, reluctantly, she opened her lids a tiny bit. She saw the Eiffel Tower. And Big Ben. It was the dorm. She opened her lids the rest of the way and looked at her time and date clock.

It was the morning after they'd been kicked out of the dorm, but they were in their dorm room, not at Pam's house.

Had they been kicked out of the dorm? Her memories were all jumbled. The memories of the fights with Tyler and Josh were still there, but on top of them, mixed around with them, were the memories of her putting Dakota's joint in the drawer and Tyler whistling past their room and her not answering the knock at the door.

What the hell was going on? Why was her brain so addled?

Had Josh and she had a big fight or not? Her heart still felt broken.

She felt like tired crap, too, as if she hadn't slept in a week. That didn't make sense. She was in her bed right now.

The pounding on the door resumed. "Kairi? Are you in

there? It's me, Josh. Open up!"

"Door," Dakota mumbled and threw the covers over her head.

Kairi shuffled over to the door and shoved it open.

It was Josh.

His mouth fell open. "Kairi, what's wrong with you? You look sick."

"Uh, I guess that's what happens when you say you're disappointed in me and act like you want to dump me," she said.

"Dump you?" he asked. "What are you talking about? Hey, wait a minute. Where's your ring?"

"Wait. You didn't see me frenching Tyler?" she asked.

Josh snorted. "You kissed your R.A.? That loser? Yeah, right. And I made out with Jennifer Lawrence when I was in Oklahoma." He paused. "I know you would never kiss someone you didn't want to kiss."

Was Tyler a dream or a memory or somehow an overwritten timeline? She was so confused. "Can we start this conversation over? I'm not feeling so well. Is this the first time we've seen each other since the road trip?"

Josh nodded and immediately stepped toward her. "I stopped by a couple of times yesterday, but no one was here. Are you okay? Where did you go? How did you get back here from Oklahoma?"

Kairi thought she was here yesterday, but she was afraid to answer the door then. So, that meant she avoided their fight. Josh and she didn't fight. They weren't in any danger of breaking up. She dodged a bullet.

"Did you ever get checked out by doctors after the tornado?" he asked when she didn't answer his questions.

"No. But I'm fine. Thanks for asking." He was sweet, and they were apparently still together. Hurray! She grabbed him for a hug. "The doctors said you were ship-shape?"

"Yeah," he said. "Except for this." He held up his cast.

"I'm very glad to hear it." She smiled.

"I'll let you get some rest," he said. "You look like you need it. But, let's get together later so we can talk?"

She nodded. "Sounds good." Everything was going to be okay. Josh and she were all right. She and Dakota wouldn't be kicked out of the dorm.

She paused. She made everything okay. Wow.

What else could she do?

Chapter Twelve
Kyle: Sydney, Australia, 2019

Kyle and his best friend were crouching in the dark in his company's records room in the middle of the night. The night watchman, Clive, was right outside the room. Kyle clutched the pilfered files so tightly the pressboard folder dug into his palms.

Clive walked right on by the door.

Kyle let out a breath.

"Shite," Liam whispered.

"Yeah."

"Did you get what you needed?" Liam asked.

"Yeah. I grabbed my dad's file."

The two of them crept over to the door. Kyle listened intently. Was Clive gone? Very quietly, he cracked the door and peeked through. The coast was clear. They snuck back upstairs and into his office.

The lights were on, the computer was still on, and the beers were still warming in the bag. It was as if nothing had happened.

Liam grabbed a beer and threw himself into a chair. As he opened the beverage, he chuckled. "I can't believe I got so worked up. I haven't felt like that since university." He took a swig. "I think you're a bad influence, mate."

"Uh-huh." Kyle was busy paging through the file. The last page detailed a lot of medical gobbledygook, but the gist of it was Kyle's father was killed because of Traveling. Why hadn't Dad explained what happened to him? All he would have had to do to save himself would have been to say, 'Don't touch me in the file room when you go on your first mission,' or whatever the reason for his death was. Why didn't he do that?

And why wasn't the file more explicit about how Traveling

killed him?

Kyle scrutinized the last page. It was odd to have a single page with a staple. He turned it over, and it looked as if some other pages had been torn off the back. What had been on the missing pages? And who removed pages from the file? Who could remove pages from the file?

What the hell did all this mean?

Clearly, he had no idea what really went on at Time Advantages, Inc.

Then, he had another thought: who did?

Liam opened another beer and slurped it noisily. "What do you want to do now? We could play the game." He yawned. "You know, for our cover."

"I'm too upset," Kyle said. "My dad did die because of Traveling, but I still don't understand how. Or why. I'm starting to think something's wrong at this company. I have to get out of here."

Liam shrugged. "Let's go."

Kyle didn't want to go to work the next morning because he was so tired and agitated. What kind of crap company was this that let his dad die so easily when they could have saved him? It was a bloody time travel company, for Christ's sake.

But, since Kyle'd left the stolen file in his office and he didn't want Charlotte or Ray to find it there, he didn't really have a choice. He had to go in.

When he got there, Charlotte seemed to be lying in wait for him. She jumped up from her desk as soon as she saw him in the common area. She grabbed his bicep, holding it tight. "You owe me, young man," she said very quietly but fiercely in his ear.

He'd only had one triple-espresso, so he wasn't awake yet. "Huh?" He shook his arm. "And ow. Let go."

She dropped his arm but didn't move away. "I know you just went and got the files you wanted last night."

Did Clive squeal? "Uh, why do you say that?"

"Because when I went down to check the information first thing this morning, the files were gone, and the records room door and the file cabinet were unlocked. I know I didn't leave them unlocked. Are you trying to get me fired?"

Unlocked? He and Liam were really out of practice with their fact-finding missions. "No, ma'am." He noticed she didn't tell him not to call her that.

"I covered for you, although I don't know why."

"Thank you." At her glare, he added, "I appreciate it, Charlotte. You're great. I owe you."

She looked slightly mollified.

"Can I ask you a question about the file?"

"I guess."

"It looks like some of the pages have been removed," he said. "Did you do that?"

She frowned. "No. No one is supposed to remove information from the files."

Working in his office, Ray glanced out at them, grimaced, and then got up from his desk and took a step in their direction.

Charlotte and Kyle quickly moved apart.

"So, ah, stop drinking so much, young man," she said loudly, "if you know what's good for you."

"Yes, Charlotte," he said equally loudly.

Ray shook his head slightly and nudged his door closed.

All morning, Kyle sat at his dad's desk fuming. What was on the missing pages from the file? Who took them? Why? What really happened to his dad? Why shouldn't they Travel back and save him?

Finally, he reached a decision. He was going to Travel back and find out exactly what happened to his dad and then save him.

It couldn't be a sanctioned time travel trip because there was no client. There was no way Uncle Raymond would agree to the trip. It would have to be top-secret. Hopefully, Liam would help him again.

At lunchtime, he was too antsy to stay at the office, so he went back to Liam's flat.

At Liam's place, he was very surprised to find him home. "Why aren't you at work?"

From one of the stools at the kitchen counter, Liam glanced at him and yawned. "I chucked a sickie."

"Why?" Kyle loosened his tie.

"Duh. I was up late last night, helping you, mate. But what

are you doing back here so early? Did you get sprung? Did they find out about our mission and fire you?" Liam threw his shit-eating grin Kyle's way.

"No. They didn't find out." Kyle paused. "Actually, somebody did. But, no, that's not why I'm back." He put the maddeningly vague file on the counter and sank onto one of the stools.

"So?" Liam raised his eyebrows. "Are you gonna tell me? Or make me guess? What happened?"

"Charlotte found out that we, er, I, broke into the records room. But that doesn't matter. Traveling definitely killed my dad." Kyle shook his head. "The whole thing's a mess."

"So, when are you going to time travel back and save him?"

Kyle looked over at Liam. He'd been wondering the same thing since he'd made his decision. Uncle Ray would stop him if he knew what he was planning.

He had to go back and try to save his dad. But he wasn't supposed to go back. Kyle kept going around in circles.

"Kyle?"

"What?"

"Zone out much? I asked if you could go down to the pub and get me some fish and chips for brekkie."

It was early afternoon, and Liam still hadn't had breakfast? "Why would I play waiter for you?"

There was that annoying grin again. "You're gonna ask me to help you break into something at your office again tonight, aren't you?"

Damn. Liam was right. Kyle was going to need his help to get into The Dreaming Room. "Yeah. All right." He stood up. He was hungry himself anyway.

"Don't forget the coldies!"

That night Clive didn't even bat an eyelash when Liam and Kyle showed up again after midnight. "Good evening, Mr. Barada, Mr. Bowes."

"Good evening, Clive." Apparently, getting Clive to call him Kyle was a lost cause.

Liam nodded. "Can I offer you a tinny?"

Clive checked Kyle's face.

"It's fine with me," Kyle said. He was teaching Clive some

bad habits.

Clive smiled fleetingly and reached into Liam's large paper sack. "Those American girls must be something."

"You know it, mate," Liam said, grinning.

In Kyle's office, Liam set down the bag, pulled out a beer, opened it and sucked it down in one go. "Ahh."

At Kyle's slightly annoyed look, Liam grinned. That was getting annoying, too.

"Set up the game, mate, and I'll play while you're otherwise occupied."

That wasn't a bad idea. Kyle sat down at his computer and logged into the MMORPG. Then he said, "I just need you to open The Dreaming Room for me."

Liam shrugged. "Okay. Piece of piss."

As they walked across the common area to The Dreaming Room, Liam asked, "What kind of equipment is in there, anyway? A time machine?" He grinned. "Could I use it to time travel?" He knelt and applied his picks to the door's lock.

Kyle glanced around, keeping watch for Clive--although he didn't know what they'd do if he showed up. Claim there were sheilas or beers in The Dreaming Room? "No. There's no time machine. It's just a distraction-free room with a special chair. The Traveling depends on me." He tapped his head.

Liam turned the handle on the door, and it snicked open. "Then why do you need a special room?"

"It's just the way it's always been done."

"Always?" Liam quirked his eyebrow as he stood up. "I thought your grandfather and a bunch of other ancestors could time travel. You can't tell me your family has always had this room."

Liam raised some good points. Now Kyle had something else to ask his dad when he saw him. "You just don't understand because you can't Travel," he said huffily.

"Whatever, mate." Liam turned to go back to Kyle's office. "How long will you be gone?"

It wouldn't be good to run into himself when returning from this trip. Kyle peered around. He wasn't back already, was he? "I plan to be gone about five minutes."

"Take your time. I want to actually play the game this time."

Inside, Kyle lay back on the special chair in the middle of the room and tried to calm his mind. Why did he need this chair and this room anyway? Could he just Travel whenever he wanted? Maybe he didn't need the company at all. His mind wouldn't settle. Damn that Liam for raising all these questions when he needed to concentrate.

Eventually, because of his many years of practice, Kyle calmed his mind. He focused on his breathing. "I can access The Dreaming," he said. "I have the power. I can feel all of time flowing through me. I am The Dreaming."

In his mind's eye, he saw himself talking with Liam outside the door and with Clive down at the front desk. He saw himself breaking into the records room with Liam.

He tried to speed things up.

He trained. He gave his dad's eulogy. He visited his dad in the hospital. He trained.

In his dream, he finally saw past-Kyle's day a few months ago when present-Kyle accidentally touched Dad. He dreamt of standing on the sidewalk right before that. He concentrated on that when.

He forced himself out of The Dreaming and landed on the street a few yards away from himself.

The other version of himself was dressed for much cooler weather, but he didn't want to get back in the car that was waiting for him. He walked right past the car.

The driver's door popped open. "Mr. Barada? Is there a problem?"

"No. I just feel like walking a bit," the other Kyle said.

"Sir, that's against protocol," the driver said. "I'm going to have to ask you to get back in the car. Now."

Kyle took a few steps closer to the other Kyle. If he talked to him now and told him not to touch Dad in the file room, maybe he could nip the whole thing in the bud. So far, the other Kyle hadn't seen him. He wasn't very observant.

A wave of queasiness crashed down on Kyle, and he doubled over. The other Kyle also doubled over.

"Sir!" The driver jumped out of the car and rushed over to the other Kyle as he collapsed on the concrete.

Chapter Thirteen
Kairi: Boulder, Colorado, 2019

Since Kairi was so worn out, she'd gone back to bed after talking with Josh. When she and Dakota finally got up, Dakota believed every word she said about rewriting the timeline.

"You traveled back in time again and saved us from getting kicked out of the dorm?" Dakota said. "Awesome! That rocks." She got a funny look on her face. "Do you have a time machine? Or did space aliens or ghosts or something help you?"

"What?" Kairi said. She wasn't as kooky as Dakota, was she? Aliens? Ghosts? "Come on, Dakota. That doesn't make any sense." Come to think of it, time travel didn't really make any sense. She needed to get more information about dreaming and time travel from somewhere. Reliable information. She was determined to focus on time travel and get the hang of it. If she could control it, who knew what she could do? She grabbed her computer and started typing.

"Then how do you do it?" Dakota asked, completely reasonably.

"Uh," Kairi said. "That is a good question." She pondered the situation. The only thing she knew for sure was all the times she time traveled, she was sleeping. "It happens when I'm asleep."

"Cool! Can you teach me?"

"I don't know how I do it," Kairi said. "Somehow, I need more information about sleeping and what happens when I'm asleep."

"Ooh," Dakota said. "I know who knows about that stuff--my transcendental meditation guru. She knows all about meditating and sleeping. All that."

Kairi'd been surfing the web while they were talking. There was entirely too much weird information out there, most of which was obviously crap. Since she didn't have any better options at the moment, she decided to consult Dakota's guru. She needed to get a better handle on what the hell was going on.

They stopped on The Hill for lunch, and afterward, Dakota brought Kairi to her transcendental meditation teacher.

The woman's name was Mary, and she lived in a big house on The Hill. Apparently, transcendental meditation was lucrative. She got them all settled in on her spacious patio with herbal iced tea. They were lucky it was a very warm sunny afternoon for March.

"So, Kairi, Dakota tells me you've been on some kind of spiritual journey?" Since Mary looked like a preppy soccer mom with her blonde bob, oxford shirt and khakis, these words sounded a bit odd coming out of her mouth. "Why don't you tell me about it?" She took a sip of iced tea as the wind rustled the leafless branches of the mature trees surrounding them.

Kairi wasn't sure how much of this woo-woo stuff she even believed in, but why not see what this woman had to say? Her house and patio sure seemed nice. She must be doing something right.

"I seem to have developed the ability to time travel."

Mary's forehead wrinkled. "Time travel? Why do you say that?"

Kairi shrugged. "I think I've literally traveled in time. I went to 1999 and came back, and on another trip, I went back twenty-four hours and came back."

"Could it be something like astral projection?" Mary asked.

"Sorry," Kairi said. "What's that?"

"It's an out-of-body experience," Dakota said. "Your spirit visits other places."

"No, I don't think it was astral projection," Kairi said. "My spirit went to another time, and my body went right along, too."

"Really?" Mary asked, looking at Dakota.

Dakota nodded energetically.

Mary leaned back in her puffy-cushioned teak chair. "Interesting. Tell me more."

Quickly Kairi gave her a rundown of her bizarre experiences.

"So, every time it happened when you were asleep?" Mary asked.

Kairi nodded.

"Interesting," Mary said. "And what did you mean by you developed this ability?"

"I used to be normal, sleep normally." Kairi shrugged. "I just started this time traveling stuff a couple of days ago."

"And what do you think triggered it?" Mary asked.

"The tornado, right?" Dakota said. "You time traveled first to avoid the tornado."

Mary frowned. "There haven't been any tornadoes here."

"No," Kairi said. "But Dakota is right. I was on a road trip through Oklahoma. I did seem to time travel to avoid a tornado. It must have been some kind of self-preservation thing. I did it to protect myself." She didn't protect Josh, though. Him, she abandoned. Quickly she quit that train of thought. It was too mortifying and confusing.

Mary drank some tea. "So, what do you want me to do?"

"I guess I wanted to learn more about what happens when I sleep and when I dream," Kairi said.

Dakota interrupted. "I thought maybe we could try something with lucid dreaming. An experiment or something."

"Interesting," Mary said. "Yes. A lucid dream experiment could be very informative. Kairi could at least tell us what she perceived during her dream. What do you know about lucid dreaming, Kairi?"

Kairi held up her hands. "Nothing, really. I'd be happy to learn whatever you have to teach me."

Mary nodded. "A lucid or conscious dream is a dream in which the sleeper is aware they're dreaming," she said. "Since the dreamer is lucid, they can actively participate in and manipulate the experiences in the dream environment."

"It's cool," Dakota said.

Mary smiled at her. "There are three ways a lucid dream can begin, dream initiation, wake initiation, or mnemonic initiation."

"I must admit, you lost me there," Kairi said.

"In dream initiation, the dreamer just figures out they're

dreaming inside the dream," Mary said. "In wake initiation, a dreamer goes directly from the waking state to the dream state. In mnemonic initiation, the dreamer uses affirmations or signs to force themselves into a lucid dream."

"Uh, okay," Kairi said. "So, you want to try one of those, now?" It all sounded complicated, but Mary seemed to know what she was talking about.

"Not now," Mary said. "Without balancing your levels of acetylcholine, serotonin, dopamine and norepinephrine, natural methods are a little iffy if you're well-rested."

What the heck were all those chemicals?

At Kairi's blank look, Mary added, "I'm a neurophysiology professor at the university. Didn't Dakota tell you?"

"No." Kairi glared at Dakota. If she'd mentioned it, Kairi would have been much more enthusiastic about coming.

"I have something in my lab on campus that I'd like you to try," Mary said. "Dakota's tried it, my lucid dream induction device."

"Yeah, it's awesome," Dakota said.

"Seriously?" Kairi asked. "You have a machine that makes people have lucid dreams?"

Mary smiled and nodded. "Yep. It's based on mnemonic initiation. It detects when you've entered REM sleep and triggers an auditory tone, flashing lights and a small vibration. Whichever triggers you detect are incorporated into your dream and thus remind you to dream lucidly."

"I guess I'm game," Kairi said. It couldn't hurt, right?

"Ooh. Tell her about reality testing," Dakota said.

"Reality testing is used to determine if you're dreaming or not," Mary said.

Somehow, that didn't seem like it would be a tough problem.

"You can try to stick your finger through the palm of your hand or hold your nose closed and see if you can breathe without using your mouth," Mary said.

"Or, even just pinch yourself," Dakota said and reached over and pinched Kairi.

"Ouch," she said.

"See, you're not dreaming," Dakota said, grinning.

"Gee, thanks," Kairi said but couldn't help grinning back at her.

"You can also flip a light switch," Mary said. "They usually don't work in dreams. Or look inside a book--they're usually blank in dreams."

"I do reality tests all the time," Dakota said.

Kairi bit back a comment that Dakota probably needed to do reality tests all the time. "So, what do you want me to do?"

"How rested are you?" Mary asked.

Considering they'd been up a whole hour or two, Kairi's answer was: "Very."

"Why don't you guys come to my lab tonight at, say, ten p.m.?" Mary said. "Dakota knows where it is."

At ten o'clock, they showed up at Mary's neurophysiology lab. They'd been drinking a little to prime the pump. And because Kairi was nervous. She admitted it. What if this didn't work and she didn't learn anything? And even more nerve-wracking, what if it did work?

Mary put a helmet with a bunch of wires on Kairi's head and had her lean back in a big dentist-type chair. And then Kairi was supposed to go to sleep.

But every creak and rustle in the room conspired to keep her awake. After several minutes, she finally said, "I'm sorry. I don't seem to be going to sleep."

"I have a mild sedative, a herbal supplement, I can give you," Mary said. "Just a sec."

"Can I have some, too?" Dakota asked.

Mary sighed. "No. I thought you were going to help me observe."

"Oh, yeah, right," Dakota said.

Kairi took the pills and leaned back again. Eventually, she must have drifted off because she became aware of a beeping sound.

There was something important about the beeping.

Something she was supposed to remember.

Oh, yeah. Lucid dreaming. She was supposed to have a lucid dream, right? "Hey, is anyone there?" she asked.

As if from far away, she heard Mary's voice say, "Are you dreaming, Kairi?"

"I think so," she said. She tried to open her eyes, but everything was still dark. "Hello? Is anyone there?"

"We're here," a woman said. "What do you see?" The voice was getting farther away.

"I don't see anything," she said. "Just darkness."

From a great distance, she heard, "Focus."

She concentrated and saw herself in the lab getting into the big dentist-type chair. "I'm in the lab." Then she saw her and Dakota walking across campus to the lab. "I'm walking to the lab."

Kairi could barely make out Mary's words, "Keep going."

She was in her dorm room. "In the dorm." And then she was in her dorm room, and then she was in her dorm room some more. Boring. She needed to speed this up. She was sleeping in her dorm room.

She was fighting with Josh and Tyler. But overlaid on it, she wasn't fighting with them. It was as if she was reliving the whole confusing mess and once had been more than enough. "Josh and Tyler." She didn't hear Mary say anything in response. She sped past that.

At Pam's house. Things started moving past her even more quickly. It was as if her life was rewinding.

In the car with Lisa and company driving back to Boulder.

In the car with Josh on spring break. Everything was becoming a blur.

Finding the engagement ring in the dorm parking lot.

Packing for the trip.

Going to class, walking around campus. It was all too much. She needed to stop.

Kairi focused on a planter outside the University Memorial Center. It was filled with cigarette butts and dirt.

Then a cool breeze blew over the skin on her hands and neck. She was standing. She took off the helmet and noticed the wires were all severed.

She pinched herself. "Ouch!"

She tried sticking her finger through the palm of her hand. It didn't work.

Kairi stood outside the University Memorial Center, holding the weird helmet, getting colder by the minute.

Chapter Fourteen
Kyle: Sydney, Australia, 2019

Months in his past, on an illicit time travel trip trying to save his dad's life, Kyle lay on the sidewalk. The driver had taken the other Traveling Kyle away in his car. Kyle should have stopped the other Kyle because what he was about to do would probably lead to Dad's death, but Kyle felt so awful right now he was worried he might die.

With difficulty, he got his mobile out of his pocket. Who should he call? Hospital? And tell them what? He couldn't think. By instinct, he called his mom.

"Kyle?" she asked. "Why are you calling? What's up?"

"Mom?" He couldn't remember the last time he heard her voice.

"Yes. What?" She sounded worried.

"Mom, I don't feel so good. Can you come to get me?"

She paused for a few seconds before answering. "Yes. Give me your address. I'll be right there."

His mother was as good as her word and arrived soon, pulling up in her car. Kyle was glad to confirm she would help him, no matter what their past.

She got out and rushed over to him. "Kyle? You don't look so good." She leaned over him. "What's wrong?"

He jerked back. "Don't touch me!"

Her eyes narrowed. "Are you Traveling? Oh, no." Her hand flew in front of her mouth. "Your dad is dead. What year are you from? Wait. Don't tell me."

How did she get all of that out of just seeing him? "There's something wrong with me. I feel very sick. Should I go to hospital? Can they help Travelers?"

"Is this your first mission? It's not unusual to feel a little nauseated."

Kyle groaned. "It's more than a little." He'd never felt so sick.

Mom glanced around. "Why don't you have a car and driver?" She stood up straight. "Are you on an unsanctioned mission?" She took a step back. "Wait. Ray warned me. Have you gone rogue like your father? Are you helping him? I'm not telling you anything about that reporter Lachlan Harris."

She took a breath. "Was that Lachlan why Riley died? He said something about a car accident." She held up her hands. "Don't answer that. It's better if I don't know how he dies."

"Why would this Lachlan guy kill him?" Could that be what was on the missing pages? The world stopped spinning in circles around Kyle.

"Riley!" Mom said. "That man drives me crazy! He never listens to me. He doesn't care at all if he causes a paradox. That's why we had to split up, you know."

"No, I didn't know." They never really explained their divorce. And none of that was in Dad's file. Kyle sat up. He didn't feel quite so badly. The other Kyle must be fairly far away by now. Could that be why he felt better? "What are you talking about?" He stared at his mom.

"If you don't know what I'm talking about, what are you doing here?"

"I'm trying to save Dad!"

"Dad?" She seemed surprised.

"Why? Who else would I be saving?"

She leaned back against her car, crossed her arms, and looked steadily at him.

"You?" Kyle said. He scrambled to his feet. "Why would you need saving? Tell me what's going on."

She backed away. "I've said too much. I got carried away. Forget everything I just said." She got in her car. "You look okay to me." She started the car. "Take care of yourself, Kyle," she said more softly through the open window before she drove away. The whole exchange had only taken a few minutes.

Kyle watched her drive away, confused. What paradox?

Why would she be in danger? Since she was still alive in Kyle's present, did that mean Dad saved her once already?

But she seemed to be implying that's why she divorced Dad and broke up their family. The divorce had been years ago, so did Dad do something years ago? And who would divorce someone for saving their life?

Kyle got in a cab.

He needed to find his dad so he could warn him about his impending death. While he was at it, he was going to ask him a few questions about Mom and that Lachlan guy and about going rogue.

But first, he needed to stop the other Traveling Kyle from touching Dad in the file room. He wracked his memories, but he couldn't recall exactly what time he'd run into his father.

Riding through Sydney, as the buildings flew by the cab's windows, Kyle knew he was running out of time. He took out his mobile. Maybe he could call someone. Who? He realized he couldn't call himself. The other Traveling Kyle had the exact same mobile number as him. Bloody hell. But he could leave himself a voicemail. He dialed himself. "Kyle, this is Kyle. Stay out of the records room." But who the hell knew if the other Traveling Kyle would get the message in time?

He could call his dad, but he didn't always carry his mobile around with him. He often left it on his desk in his office. And exactly what would he say to him?

Maybe he should just try to Travel back to earlier in the day? Or even an earlier day? But the idea of starting over, after having nothing to show for today, exhausted him.

Charlotte. Maybe Charlotte would help him.

"Kyle?" She answered on the first ring tone. "Are you calling me from the file room? Are you feeling sick again?"

"I'm in the file room?" Kyle asked. "Already?" That meant the other Traveling Kyle could touch Dad any second.

"You don't know where you are? How sick are you?"

Kyle's mind raced. "Pull the fire alarm, Charlotte! Get everyone out of the building!"

"Fire alarm?" she asked. "Why? I'm not pulling a false alarm. People could panic and get hurt."

"I put a bomb in the bloody building! It's going to go off in seconds! Forget hurt! Everyone will be blown to bits! Pull the bloody alarm!"

"What?" She sputtered. But then, over the phone, he heard the siren shriek.

A few minutes later, as the cab pulled up in front of the Time Advantages building, the siren was still blaring, and business-suit-clad people streamed out. Charlotte followed Ray and Dad out the front doors. They all looked nervous. Most of the people kept turning around to look up at the building, presumably for flames and smoke.

Dad saw him jump out of the cab. "Kyle? What are you doing there? I thought you were downstairs?" He turned around and saw the other Traveling Kyle step up behind him.

Kyle started feeling nauseated.

The cabbie said, "You're a twin, huh?" Then, his eyes widened, and he said, "No, a triplet? Wow."

The Kyle of this time must have come out of the building, too.

Dad's eyes didn't seem to know which way to look, darting from one Kyle to another.

In the meantime, Kyle clenched his stomach.

Then, Dad keeled over onto the sidewalk in front of the Time Advantages building.

Kyle didn't see why. He was too busy trying not to puke.

Charlotte focused on Dad. "No! You can't die! I was trying to save you!"

When Kyle Dreamed his way back to his present and came to in The Dreaming Room, dizziness and nausea washed over him in waves. "Bloody hell." He clutched the arms of the chair as his memories were overwritten. In the current timeline, his dad died months earlier during a fire drill, collapsing on the sidewalk. "Bloody fucking hell."

When the waves finally subsided, Kyle lurched out of The Dreaming Room, looking for Liam. He was playing a video game in Dad's office as if nothing had happened.

"Kyle! You look like shite, mate."

"Gee, thanks." It was a struggle to speak. How could things

have gone so wrong? He barely even did anything. "Can you take me home?"

"Yeah," Liam said. "Now?"

"No, bloody yesterday. What do you think?"

"So..." Liam grabbed his gear. "The mission didn't go well?"

Kyle didn't answer him.

The one positive thing that had come out of his recent Traveling fiasco was the clue he'd gotten from his mom about the reporter Lachlan. He clung to that until he could Travel back and fix everything.

The offices of The Daily Telegraph were just south of Belmore Park, near the CityRail-Central Station. Kyle went over there after downing two triple espressos. He hadn't been sleeping well.

The woman in reception seemed surprised someone would want to look at old clippings from Lachlan, but she showed him to an ancient microfiche machine and gave him some pointers on how to use it.

It took him a while, but eventually, Kyle was staring at a photo of a huge car pile-up from 2004. That was the only photo that seemed to have anything to do with a car accident. He had to get the receptionist to help him print it out, and she made him pay for the copy.

"Why are you interested in some old accident, anyway?" she asked when she gave him his change.

Kyle glanced down at the printout. It was a bit grainy, maybe too grainy. Maybe if he garnered some sympathy from her, she'd help him out some more. A little white lie couldn't hurt, right? "I'm sorry to say I had a relative who was in this accident." Maybe he did in an earlier timeline? He paused. Could that be true? It was weird to think there might be a timeline he didn't know about. What would that mean? That someone else had changed things?

"Oh, dear." She put her hand in front of her mouth. "I'm so sorry."

"I'm trying to understand what happened." He peered at the picture, squinting. It showed a bunch of pixelated mangled cars with a bunch of pixelated people standing around.

"It's going to be difficult to get much out of that old copy."

She looked down at the printout. "I can try to get you in touch with the photographer, Lachlan Harris. He probably took several pictures of the, ah, event. And they'd be better quality than that."

"Really? That would be great. I'd appreciate it. Thank you."

She turned to her computer and typed. "I'll try calling his extension. He might be in his office."

She got on the phone. "Lachlan? This is Ruby. I'm glad I caught you. I have a young man..." She stared at him.

"Kyle Barada," he said.

"Kyle Barada, who would like to meet with you about an old story from 2004. Do you have a few minutes? Great." She hung up and smiled. "He said you could go up."

Kyle clipped his visitor badge to his collar on the way up the stairs. He needed to understand what Mom had been talking about if he could. How did it affect his dad? Did Dad do something? And how could the accident have something to do with their divorce?

As he entered a big room of cubicles, a skinny older man stood up and yelled, "Kyle. Down here."

He picked up his pace but still noticed most of the cubicles were empty.

When he got to Lachlan's cube, he held out his hand. "Hi, Mr. Harris. I'm Kyle Barada. It's nice to meet you."

Lachlan popped again up from his desk and grabbed Kyle's hand, enclosing it in both of his. "Kyle. Call me Lachlan. Have a seat." He pointed at a battered chair. "You're lucky you caught me. Unless I'm on assignment, usually I work at home nowadays, like everyone else." He waved his hands, indicating the empty room.

"Yes, thanks, Lachlan." Kyle sat down and wiped his palms on his thighs. For some reason, he was getting nervous. "The reason I'm here is?"

"Oh, I know why you're here. Ruby told me." He gestured at his computer. "You want to know about the accident, right?" he said more softly. "That was a bad one."

Suddenly, Kyle was embarrassed by his lie. People had died in that accident. "Uh, yes, sir. Anything you can tell me, especially any photos, would be great."

89

Lachlan clicked around with his mouse. "I do have a number of photos from that day. Looking them up jogged my memory. It happened pretty close to here, at the corner of Eddy Avenue and Elizabeth Street. That's why I was able to get there so quickly. It was kind of a crazy accident. Bystanders said a woman seemed to appear out of nowhere right in the middle of the street."

"Oh?" Kyle couldn't trust himself to say any more than that.

Lachlan brought up a picture on his large monitor. "Say, that fellow there in the crowd looks a bit like you." He pointed. "And that guy looks sort of like you, too, but older."

But Kyle wasn't paying attention to the photographer anymore. Here, the grainy people in the photo were in sharp focus.

The guy did look like Kyle. But it wasn't Kyle. It was his dad as a young man. He was at the scene. Bloody hell.

And Dad, as an old man, was at the scene. In fact, he looked very similar to how he looked just before he died.

And there was Mom right next to old-Dad.

Dad, what did you do?

It looked as if Kyle was going to have to Travel back to 2004 and find out.

Chapter Fifteen
Kairi: Boulder, Colorado, 2019

Kairi stood like an idiot, freezing to death, outside the student center. Students streamed past her, a few giving the metal helmet in her hands or her lack of jacket an odd look. When did it get so cold again? She decided to go back to Mary's lab. Hopefully, Mary wouldn't be too upset about the helmet getting damaged. And hopefully, she could help Kairi interpret what happened.

She deliberately did not think about the possibility that it might not be the same day.

Her jog to the neurophysiology lab turned into a full-out run as the cold wind sliced through her clothes. Soon, she was gliding through the open lab doorway.

"Can I help you?" Mary asked politely.

Kairi held out her helmet.

"Is that my L.D.I.D?" Mary asked. "How did you get it? What have you done to it? Who are you?"

Kairi said, "You don't know me?"

"Know you?" Mary asked. "No. I've never laid eyes on you before. That helmet is a proprietary device. Where did you get it?"

Kairi put the helmet down on one of the lab tables. "You wouldn't happen to know what day it is, would you?"

"I asked you a question. Where did you get that helmet?" Mary said.

"Actually," Kairi said, "you gave it to me."

"Nice try, but I don't know you. I didn't give it to you. Tell me what's going on here, or I'm calling campus security." She reached for her cell phone.

Kairi didn't hang around to see what happened next.

She ran back to the UMC to check the date on the newspapers on the shelves inside near the doors. It was twelve days before she'd met Mary. It was also mid-afternoon and blessedly warm inside. She patted her pockets to determine her resources: no phone this time and no wallet again, but she did have her keys. Note to self: start keeping more helpful stuff in your pockets.

She ran back to her dorm room. At least she could get a jacket there.

As she unlocked the door, she smelled a distinct sweet odor that Dakota promised she wouldn't smell in their room anymore. Or was that promise in her future? Their future? Thinking about time made her head hurt.

When Dakota saw her, she gasped and waved her hand through the smoke in the room. "What are you doing back so soon? Did you forget something?"

Kairi didn't know what to say, so she just opened her closet and rummaged around for a jacket. Her winter jacket wasn't there. Damn.

Duh. The other her, the-her-of-the-present, must be wearing it. She pulled out her raincoat and zipped it up, shivering.

"Come to think of it, Kairi," Dakota said, "how did you change your clothes? You weren't wearing that outfit when you left a few minutes ago."

Kairi sat down on her bed in front of Big Ben. Dakota always seemed to believe everything she said, so why not tell her the truth? "I'm a time traveler. I'm from your future." And she was tired. It was around midnight her time. She debated just laying down on her bed and taking a nap. No. She needed to save her sleepiness to hopefully time travel home.

Dakota gasped. "Wow. Do you have a time machine? Where is it? What's time travel like?"

"I don't have a time machine," Kairi said.

"How do you do it then?" Dakota asked.

A reasonable question from Dakota. "I don't know, totally." She held up her forefinger. "But I do happen to know that in about ten days you will get us kicked out of the dorm for smoking pot, so stop it."

Dakota stubbed out the joint in the ashtray on her dresser. "I can't believe I've known you all these years, and you're only now telling me you can time travel. What neat stuff have you seen? Where did you go in the past? Have you met Jesus? Ooh! Have you been to the future? What's it like? Do they have flying cars?"

She raised a very good question. Could she go into the future? That would be awesome. It would make all this trouble worth it. If she could ever learn to control it.

"Kairi?" Dakota asked.

"I, uh, haven't met Jesus or gone to the future," she said. "I only just figured out how to do it on spring break. Which reminds me, you have to tell Josh and me not to leave for Texas on the Saturday before spring break. We're going to hit a tornado in Oklahoma."

"A tornado! That doesn't sound good. Okay, I'll tell you," Dakota said and smiled.

Kairi couldn't help thinking Dakota might believe what she said, but she rarely believed what Dakota said. If Dakota told her there was going to be a tornado, she probably wouldn't believe it. "Uh, maybe you should take a picture of me, or us, with your phone."

"Okay." Dakota quickly sidled over to her and snapped a pic. "What else?"

"Be quiet a sec and let me think," Kairi said. She was twelve days in her past, which could work out well. She knew what questions she'd get on her midterms.

She wished she knew what the winning lottery numbers had been. That would be another good thing to carry around with her.

On the minus side, there already was one of her here. If she hung around, where would she sleep? What would she do? She'd have to make some kind of arrangements with the other her. That just seemed too freaky.

Kairi grinned. "I guess I need to go back to my present, which is your future."

"Neat," Dakota said. "But, how?"

"That is the question," she said. Mary and her helmet got her into this mess. They were going to get her out of it. "I need your help. Tell me about your transcendental meditation guru."

"My T.M. guru? But how do you know about her?" Dakota

asked.

Kairi just raised her eyebrows at her.

"Oh, from the future," she said. "Right. Mary has a class at three o'clock, so I can't take you to meet her right now."

That sounded perfect to Kairi. "Will her lab be open?"

"Yes," Dakota said. "I think her lab assistant Topher will be there." She giggled. "I think he's hot for me."

Better and better. "Do you think you can distract him while I try out Mary's lucid dreaming helmet?"

"You know about that? How? Oh, right." Dakota seemed to relish the prospect of distracting Topher, so the two of them took off for Mary's lab.

Sure enough, the lab doorway stood open and Dakota, and she went right on in.

A male voice called out, "Dakota! Hey, how's it hanging, chickadee?" As Kairi should have expected, Topher was a twenty-ish college guy, hot in a blond dreads, lots of tats kind of way. In other words, totally Dakota's type.

"Hey, Topher," Dakota said, giggling.

They walked toward each other, and even Kairi could feel the sexual tension crackling between them.

"So, Mary wanted my friend to try out the lucid dreaming helmet," Dakota said.

"Cool." Topher nodded, and his dreads barely moved. "Hey, we had a bizarre thing happen earlier. Some chick brought in another L.D.I.D. Mary thought it was ours, but ours is right here."

"Weird." Dakota shot her a glance. "So, can Kairi try it out?"

"Kairi?" Topher asked. "Cool name. Sure. Let's fire up this bad boy."

He handed her the undamaged helmet, and she put it on as she sat in the dentist's chair.

"So, do you know how it works? You're 'sposed to..." His voice faded away as she drifted off. She was tired.

Everything was black.

She and Dakota walked to the neurophysiology lab.

She sat on her bed in her raincoat.

She was in the lab.

She stood outside the UMC, holding the weird helmet, getting colder by the minute.

She was in the lab.

Mary put a helmet with a bunch of wires on her head and had her lean back in a big dentist-type chair.

Everything was dark. Again. This must be it! "Wake up! Wake up! Wake up!" she screamed and started pinching herself. "Ouch!"

Chapter Sixteen
Kyle: Sydney, Australia, 2004

Kyle'd Traveled back to 2004, emerging from The Dreaming near his past self in his childhood home. His dad had Traveled back here from 2019 to some big car pileup in an attempt to save Mom or reconcile with her or something, and it had somehow led to his death in 2019--at least that's what Kyle thought.

    The kitchen looked amazing, just the way he remembered it from his childhood: the brown and yellow linoleum floor, the sunbeams shining in through the handmade blue and yellow drapes, the breakfast dishes drying on the dish rack, the old kettle on the stove.

    Sitting at the kitchen table, a little boy sucked in a big breath. "You're a Traveler. But you're not my daddy. Who are you?"

    Kyle froze. Don't ever interact with your past self was an important rule from training. It was supposed to be very dangerous. Clearly, he needed to be careful.

    "Uh, nobody, kid. I wasn't here. You never saw me." He turned and walked quickly towards the back door.

    "Daddy!" the little boy wailed. "There's a nobody in the kitchen!"

    Kyle opened the door, stepped out into the garden, and closed the door behind him.

    Standing on the stoop, he tried to calm his hammering heart. Bloody hell. That was a close one. For the first time, he wondered why, if it was so dangerous, a Traveler always appeared near their past self when they emerged from The Dreaming.

    Through the closed door, Kyle could hear Dad enter the

kitchen. "What's wrong little man?"

"Nobody was here!" Kyle could imagine the little boy pointing at the back door.

Very quietly, Kyle crept down the steps, through the back garden, and out the back gate. He walked all the way over to the park a half-block away and parked himself on a bench. He needed a plan of action.

From Lachlan's photos, he thought Dad might have interacted with another version of himself, a Traveling version of himself, which eventually killed him in 2019 (in the original timeline).

He hoped Dad hadn't died because he touched him in the file room. Could it be that Kyle hadn't done anything to him in the file room? Dad had already been hurt somehow from being here, now?

Hopefully, whatever Kyle did here would also wipe out that horrible new timeline when he killed his dad on the street during a fire drill.

Furthermore, it appeared the car accident was caused when his mom popped into the middle of the road while she was Traveling. What was she doing?

Why would his mom and his dad both be Traveling? There was only supposed to be one Traveler at a time.

And where was 2004-Mom, young Mom? She had been the one in Lachlan's photos, right? She didn't appear to be home just now. Usually, she made little-boy Kyle breakfast.

Focus Kyle. He could only think of two possible 2004 courses of action: warn 2004-Mom not to Travel into the middle of the street or warn 2004-Dad not to interact with his future-self at the accident.

2004-Mom was M.I.A., so option two it was. At least he knew where 2004-Dad was. Kyle turned around and went back to his childhood home.

Unfortunately, when he got back there, there was no sign of 2004-Dad or 2004-Kyle, for that matter. He crept around the house, peeking in the windows. No one was home. The garage was empty of cars. Bloody hell. He missed his chance.

An elderly gentleman interrupted him, yelling from across the street. "Say, you there, young man. What are you doing?"

He was dressed conservatively in an elbow-patch tweed jacket and a flat cap. He ran the fingers of one hand down his neatly trimmed white goatee. "Are you going to rob those nice Baradas? Or are you a Peeping Tom? I saw you creeping around, looking in the windows. You stay right there. I'm calling the police." The man turned and opened his front door.

Bloody hell. Kyle took off while he still had the freedom to do so. Unconsciously, he ran back to the bench in the park. Probably because it was the only familiar thing in the here and now.

As he sat and tried to catch his breath, he wished he had a cell phone, a car, and a driver like he'd had on his authorized trip. How did Charlotte arrange all that?

Was his money even any good? He pulled out his wallet, and sure enough, all his money was from after 2016. His credit cards were no good either. Well, crap. How was he supposed to accomplish anything with no money or anything?

Cars rushed by the park, the occupants on their way to work or school. As he watched them, he realized the day was passing him by. His best chance to save his dad was counting down.

Time was ticking away. The irony of a time traveler running out of time wasn't lost on him. Kyle glanced at his watch. That was it. He could pawn his watch. He got up and started making his way to the pawnshop he vaguely remembered from his childhood.

Kyle loitered outside the offices of Time Advantages, Inc. His plan was to wait for either the Dad or the Mom of this time to come out, and then he'd pounce on them and warn them.

His attention may have wavered a bit.

"Young man! I say, young man!" a strident female said from down the sidewalk. Kyle knew it wasn't Mom, but nonetheless, the voice sounded familiar.

With some dread, he turned to face the music. It was Charlotte; fifteen years younger, she was almost hot. "Yes, ma'am? Can I help you with something?" There was no way she'd know who he was, right?

She grabbed his bicep. Huh. The more things change, the

more they stay the same. "I know you're waiting for someone to come out of Time Advantages, Inc."

Kyle froze. She'd touched him. Was she going to die now? When she clearly didn't die, he relaxed a bit.

How could she possibly know he was waiting for someone from Time Advantages? "No, ma'am. Time what?"

"Cut the act," she said quietly but fiercely. "I know you're a member of the clan. You look just like one." She squeezed his arm. "Are you Traveling? I don't recognize you. You must be from further in the future. What's wrong?"

"Uh."

She pushed her face in his face. "Is something wrong? Is a disaster looming?"

Kyle jerked his arm away. "Yes, Charlotte."

"How do you know my name?" She tucked her hair behind her ear.

"What's important is I need your help."

She drew her hand over her mouth and gasped. "I knew it! A hurricane? A huge fire? Some other big natural disaster? Or war? Oh, no. It is World War Three?"

She reminded him of Liam. "No," he said. "Nothing like that. My parents?"

"Don't tell me you're here for personal gain!" she said. "I'm not helping you."

"Shh," he said. "Keep it down. Unless time travel is common here in 2004?"

"No." Her eyes narrowed. "So, what about your parents? Who are your parents? What's wrong with them? Or what's about to be wrong with them?"

Kyle recalled that she had some kind of relationship with his dad in her future. If she already had feelings for his dad, and he suspected she did, would she let him proceed?

She looked into his eyes. "Your dad isn't Riley Barada, is he?"

He had to convince her he was official. The best way to lie was with part of the truth. "All right. You caught me. I'm here on a mission. I'm looking for the Baradas."

Her eyes narrowed again. "Why didn't you say that before? And why haven't I heard anything about it?"

"You're not in the loop."

"But I'm Mr. Barada's personal secretary."

"Sorry," Kyle said. "It's above your pay-grade. If you won't help me, please leave me to it."

Reluctantly, she strode to the door and grabbed the handle. She glanced back at him.

"And you didn't see me," he said.

Going in, she nearly collided with his mom. Charlotte pointed at Mom and mouthed, "There's one."

Mom stumbled and dropped her purse. Lipstick, pens, tissues and assorted female paraphernalia spilled out onto the sidewalk.

Kyle took a step forward to help Mom, but Charlotte was still looking his way, so instead, he shooed her away and leaned back against the exterior brick wall, feigning nonchalance.

This was before the divorce. He was getting distracted from his mission. Kyle and Oliver and their parents were still one big happy family.

As Mom scooped up the contents of her purse, he couldn't take his eyes off her. She was the same as he remembered and yet not the same. She was so young. And pretty. Her brown skin was smooth and clear, her curls bounced, and her eyes shone with warmth and intelligence.

She finished getting her things together and walked past him. He heard her mutter, "That Charlotte's a menace," as she passed by.

He waited for a beat and then followed her.

The foot traffic on the sidewalk was heavy. He had to hustle to keep her in sight.

And then he lost her. He craned his neck. She had to be somewhere in front of him, but he couldn't see her.

He picked up his pace, searching the crowd.

Until a woman accosted him from a doorway. "Why are you following me?" Mom said in that stern tone he recognized from when he didn't clean his dinner plate.

He lost his voice for a moment, mouth totally dry. He swallowed.

"Are you a detective?" she asked.

The word Mom was on the tip of his tongue.

"No. I don't think you are." She examined his face. "Wait. I know you, don't I?"

"Mom, it's me, Kyle. Your son. You're in trouble. The family is in trouble."

The blood seemed to leave her face. "Kyle? You're all grown up. How can you be here?" She paused. "Are you Traveling?" Then, she whispered, "Oh, no. Riley's dead, isn't he? And me. We're both dead." She seemed to deflate into herself.

"Please, calm down. You guys don't die for years."

She straightened a little. "How much Traveling have you been doing?" Her voice rose. "And more importantly, what are you doing here? Wait. I'm in trouble? The family's in trouble? What trouble?"

The doorway they blocked was the entry to a coffee shop. Kyle pointed inside. "Let's go in and talk."

After a moment of consideration, she nodded.

They sat at a tiny cafe table a little while later, sipping coffees.

Surprisingly, Kyle was enjoying himself. It had been years since he and his mother had just hung out. He'd never understood why his dad got custody of him after his folks' divorce. Why didn't she fight for him? He resisted the urge to ask her. "It's good to see you, Mom," he said. "I missed you."

"How long?" She raised her hand. "Maybe you shouldn't tell me too much."

"I need to tell you some things." He started to reach for her hand but stopped in time. All he needed was to accidentally kill Mom now by touching her. "It's important. You're in trouble, and Dad's in trouble."

"You said that before. Is that part of your mission? What is your mission? I'm supposed to help you?" She shook her head. "I must admit this seems odd, a Traveler enlisting the help of another Traveler. I've never heard of that before."

Kyle placed his coffee on the table. "Technically, I'm not on a sanctioned mission."

She gasped and put down her cup too. "What? What are you doing here then? How did you even get here?"

"I'm on a mission. It's just a personal mission."

"Oh, no, Kyle!" She stood up abruptly, knocking her chair

behind her. "That's not allowed."

He jumped up, too. "Mom, I had to come. You're going to cause a big car accident, and Dad's going to die!"

"No!" She placed her hands over her ears. "I can't hear this. I'm not supposed to know!" She ran for the door. "It'll cause a paradox!"

"Screw paradoxes!" He took off after her.

She ran across the street.

Kyle tried to chase her, but the traffic light changed, and cars streamed in front of him. He yelled after her, "Whatever you do, be careful today!"

But she was gone.

The crowd on the sidewalk jostled him as he stood there, staring in the direction she'd gone. "Oh, Mom." Why was she so uncooperative?

When Kyle finally turned away, the coffee shop employees were all in the front window staring at him. That could have gone better.

Chapter Seventeen
Kairi: Boulder, Colorado, 2019

"Thank God you're back, Kairi!" Mary said. "What just happened?" Mary stood over her as she lay in the big dentist's chair.

"That was so cool," Dakota said, approaching them. "Wait a minute... Something about that raincoat you're wearing..."

Kairi sat up, drawing attention to the helmet's severed wires.

"Oh, no," Mary said, face turning red. "What happened to the L.D.I.D.?"

Kairi took off the helmet and handed it to the professor. "Gosh, I don't know. Sorry."

"Tell us what happened," Dakota said.

"The short answer is, the helmet thing totally worked," Kairi said, jumping up. "It worked. We did it. I time traveled to about twelve days ago. What did you see? Did I disappear? How long was I gone?"

"You lay in the chair for a few minutes, and then you disappeared for about two hours, and then you reappeared," Mary said, waving her hands around. "It was like magic--which doesn't make any sense, I know."

"Cool," Dakota said. "And I think I remember something about the raincoat. About two weeks ago, you showed up at our room without your winter coat when you were supposed to be at the library. And you put on your raincoat, and then you told me about time travel!" Her voice got louder and louder. "And I was supposed to tell you something about spring break. But I don't remember what. Sorry."

Kairi suppressed a sigh.

"It was the tornado!" Dakota said. "I was supposed to warn

you about the tornado. But I sort of hooked up with Topher, and I forgot."

Mary turned to her. "My lab assistant Topher? I hope you didn't do any actual hooking up here in the lab. He should know better. We have delicate equipment in here."

"Ah, no," Dakota said. "It was a different Topher, Topher Smith."

Good thinking, Dakota. Kairi smiled at her. They might need Topher's help again. "When I traveled back in time, I interacted with both of you. Mary, I came to the lab, and you didn't know me and threatened to call campus security. Do you remember?"

Mary squinted. "We did have an attempted robbery in the lab." She leaned over her, staring. "It was you. You were here. You dropped off an L.D.I.D. and ran off. And then we had two L.D.I.D.s. I wonder if we still do." She walked over to a cabinet and rummaged through it. "It's not here." She sat down on the floor. "This is all too weird. It's mind-boggling."

Dakota went over to her. "Maybe it'd be a good time to meditate?"

Mary nodded. "I think you're right. I'm not myself." She leaned back against the cabinet and closed her eyes.

Dakota tiptoed back. "We should go. She's too boggled."

Kairi yawned. Despite all her napping, she was exhausted. "What time is it, anyway?"

"A little after midnight," Dakota said.

"It's late," Kairi said. "Thanks for waiting."

"Mary was worried when you disappeared," Dakota said. "She didn't know what to do. If she called the cops, what would she say? I was doing an experiment on a student, and she disappeared?" Dakota grabbed her arm. "C'mon. Let's go home."

When they got home, though, Josh was camped outside their door, waiting. He scrambled up when he saw them.

Kairi was wary. She thought she'd fixed the fight, but all the different timelines were running together in her mind.

And then he smiled at her, the corners of his eyes crinkling.

Hurray. They weren't fighting. She smiled back.

And then they were kissing. His warm lips pressing against hers felt like heaven. The longer they kissed, the warmer she got.

Somewhere in there, Dakota went into their room and closed the door, leaving them alone in the hall.

When they separated, he said, "So you do still like me." He grinned. "I was starting to think you were avoiding me. After I stopped by this morning, you never called. We haven't really talked since I got back. What's going on with you?"

Kairi gathered her thoughts. What had she told him?

"Notice how nice I'm being not asking you why you're not wearing the ring?" His grin seemed a bit forced now.

"I appreciate that," she said, smiling herself. "You're right. We have to talk. Should we go over to your place?"

Josh agreed, so they went. He lived in the dorm apartments for upperclassmen, and since it was spring break, they had the place to themselves. The full kitchen and bathroom, not to mention the privacy, seemed luxurious. She sank onto the empty couch in the family room where Josh's roommate was usually camped playing video games. "Got anything to drink?" she asked.

Josh was already at the refrigerator. "In honor of spring break and our engagement?"

"I'm not wearing the ring because I'm afraid I'll lose it," she blurted out. Was that the reason? "I've never owned anything so fancy."

Josh looked relieved, but she knew what else he wanted to hear.

"I still consider us engaged if you do," she said.

"But, of course." He smiled.

"Do you want to talk about what happened with the tornado?" she asked. She was a little afraid Josh wouldn't believe her when she told him she could time travel. But it felt like telling him was the right thing to do. Engaged people shouldn't have secrets between them.

"No. That can wait. We haven't properly celebrated our engagement yet. In honor of it, I was considering a bath of champagne."

Whew. Kairi was glad to postpone a possible fight. "Aw. A bath? That would be a waste of champagne," she said, smiling.

"But then I decided it would be a waste of champagne." He closed the refrigerator, and she heard a clinking noise, a soft pop, and fizzing.

He handed her a filled champagne flute.

"You bought fancy glasses?" she asked and took a sip. It tasted great. "Mmm. I don't know much about wine, but this seems really nice."

Josh sat next to her on the couch and leaned in for a kiss.

So much for talking. Her lips sought his, and other body parts soon sought each other. Earlier in their relationship, Josh helped her work through some issues she had around sex. He taught her making love could be great with someone you trusted.

Much later, naked on the couch, she couldn't help yawning.

Josh chuckled. "Am I boring you?"

"No," she said. "Not at all. That was great. And we've never done it in the family room before. Why did we plan to go out of town for spring break again? We could have just stayed here all week." She yawned again. Her eyelids felt very heavy.

Josh chuckled again and said something.

She jerked her eyes open. "Sorry. What?"

"Nothing," he said, shaking his head. "Let's go to bed."

They managed to make their way to the bedroom.

She was too tired to worry about the possibility of time traveling while she was asleep and nodded off immediately.

Kairi was awakened by the sound of pots and pans clanking together. Judging by the familiar furniture and bachelor decor, she was in Josh's bedroom. The real question was: when was she? She looked at the clock. Noon. But what day? Her sleep cycle was really messed up. Reluctantly she dragged herself out of the nice warm bed and into the kitchen to see what day it was.

"Morning, sleepy-head," Josh said. He looked adorable in his holiest jeans and a gray-blue t-shirt that matched his eyes. "I was wondering when you were going to get up." Hurray, she hadn't time traveled!

She plopped down on a stool at the breakfast bar and let a slow smile spread over her face. "You must have worn me out last night."

He grinned back. "What would you say to a mimosa? We didn't finish the champagne last night. We got distracted somehow."

"I'd say, hello, mimosa," she said and held out her hand. Then, she took a nice deep sip of frothy orangey goodness and sighed. "Yum."

Josh looked at her with approval in his eyes. "What would you say to pecan pancakes?" He quickly added, "And don't say hello, pancakes."

"Greetings, pancakes?" Before he could groan, she quickly added, "That sounds great. Do you want me to make them?"

He pointed a spatula at her. "No. You'd probably have to get dressed for that, and I'm enjoying the view."

Kairi looked down and realized she was naked from the soles of her feet all the way up. She shrugged. "Your call. But I'm cleaning the kitchen afterward."

"Okay." He tried to leer. "Watching you clean the kitchen naked could be fun."

After the lovely brunch, she accidentally, of course, spilled maple syrup all over her. Josh just had to lick it off, and one thing led to another...

Suffice it to say, it got to be mid-afternoon, and she hadn't cleaned the kitchen, much less talked about time travel.

Once they were all squeaky-clean après shower and decent, or at least as decent as they were going to get, she sat down on the couch and bit the bullet. She said, "So, you're a physics expert, right?"

Josh grinned. "Yeah. Duh. You know that. Why do you ask?"

"I was just wondering what physics says about time travel," she said.

"Seriously?" Josh asked. "You want to talk physics? You've never been that interested in it before."

Kairi nodded. "I seriously want to talk about physics." She wanted to find out as much as she could about time travel so she could control it.

Josh grinned. "Of course, we all time travel every day."

That statement had her baffled. As far as she knew, she was the only time traveler. "Huh?"

"We travel into the future at a rate of one second per second all the time," he said.

"Ugh." She punched him on the arm.

Josh smiled. "Time travel is a fascinating topic. For

one thing, there's time-reversal invariance, which says that processes like particle collisions have equal rates going forward or backward in time."

He leaned forward on the couch. "And then there are tachyons, the particles that travel faster than the speed of light. When that happens, according to special relativity, there would be a reference frame in which the particle was moving backward in time."

"Huh?" she said. "Why?"

"Well, to be honest, I don't understand that yet," he said. "Special relativity also says time dilation would let us travel into the future. But, anyway, to make a long story short, theoretically, there are lots of possible time travel mechanisms into the future or the past. There are also wormholes and other general relativity methods."

None of these things sounded like what she'd been through. But she was encouraged that actual scientists didn't think the idea was crazy.

"So, about the tornado..." She took a deep breath and screwed up her courage. "I'm pretty sure I time traveled away from it to save myself."

Josh just looked at her.

She heard a drop fall from the kitchen faucet and smack into the dirty dishes.

"Say something," she said.

Chapter Eighteen
Kyle: Sydney, Australia, 2004

Kyle was back in 2004 trying to stop his dad from dying in 2019. So far, he'd tried to warn his mom not to Travel, but she hadn't listened at all.

He staked out the Time Advantages, Inc. offices the rest of the morning and the beginning of the afternoon, but Mom never returned. He never saw Dad either.

About an hour before the car accident, he decided he couldn't wait anymore. He had to go to the intersection of Eddy Avenue and Elizabeth Street, just south of Belmore Park.

He'd loaded Lachlan's photos onto his phone. On the sidewalk, he held it up to look at the photos and figure out exactly where 2004-Dad, 2004-Mom, and 2019-Dad had been during the accident.

After a lot of holding up the phone, squinting, and shifting around, he thought he'd pinpointed each person's location. Now he just had to wait until they appeared.

Kyle tried to come up with a plan. The goal was to save 2019-Dad, but what was the best way to do that? He considered that as the traffic zoomed along, oblivious to its impending problem.

Probably the best way would be to warn 2019-Dad off. Whatever he'd done here and now while Traveling hadn't been good and must have led to his death. Yes. That was the ticket. He'd warn off 2019-Dad.

Kyle carefully made his way over to 2019-Dad's location in the pictures of the accident. Okay, Dad, where are you?

The first hint that something was happening was the squeal of brakes, followed quickly by honking horns.

Then, crunching metal.

Where was Dad? Kyle looked around. And was that Lachlan guy here somewhere? Kyle didn't see him either.

He immediately heard more squeals, honks, thuds, and crunches. It all happened so fast. Who knew accidents were so noisy? The sound of a full-sized automobile crashing into another, metal screaming, and glass shattering was as uncomfortable as the sound of fingernails on a chalkboard.

Kyle's instincts were telling him to run away. He smelled petrol.

Then, the screams started.

"Oh, my God!" Dad said next to him.

Kyle whipped his head around, and his 2019-Dad had appeared on the sidewalk.

"I'm too late," 2019-Dad said. "Rebecca!" 2019-Dad didn't seem to see Kyle.

What was going on? And what did 2019-Dad think was going on?

Before Kyle could say anything, 2019-Dad ran into the street, right into the thick of the crashed cars and debris.

Kyle thought he saw 2004-Dad running to the same location. What did they know that he didn't? There was only one way to find out.

He ran after 2019-Dad. The petrol smell grew stronger, along with the stench of something burning.

Kyle ran around the first of the crunched cars, which still emitted pings and squeaks. He caught sight of 2004-Mom, 2004-Dad, and 2019-Dad trying to make their ways towards each other around all the debris.

Why were they doing that? Didn't they know it was dangerous?

A man in one of the cars near Kyle called out, "Help me."

Kyle barely spared him a glance. "I'm sorry, I can't."

As he approached the trio, he heard 2019-Dad yelling, "Rebecca!"

2004-Mom stared at 2004-Dad, yelling, "Riley!"

2004-Dad saw both of them and had momentarily stopped. He whipped his head back and forth, looking from one to the other.

Kyle picked up speed. Surely, he could outrun 2019-Dad. He jumped up on a car, running from car to car until he reached 2019-Dad. "Dad, stop! What are you doing?"

None of the trio seemed to notice him.

Sirens approached.

Kyle jumped down from the car.

2019-Dad had his arms outstretched and continued staring at 2004-Mom.

They were surrounded by broken glass, moaning people, and twisted metal.

The sirens got closer.

2004-Mom had finally noticed 2019-Dad.

He was still running towards her. "Rebecca!"

2004-Mom stopped. "Riley? What happened to you?"

"Don't touch her!" Kyle said. "Don't touch him! He's dangerous!" He reached 2019-Dad, but at the last second, he pulled back. Kyle couldn't touch 2019-Dad either.

2004-Dad must have been caught up in the moment. "Don't worry. I'll get him." He grabbed for 2019-Dad. "Stop, Riley."

"No!" Too late, Kyle tried to stop 2004-Dad from touching 2019-Dad but didn't succeed. Then, he deliberately took a step back. Touching them would only make it worse, right? They needed to stop touching each other.

With 2004-Dad still clutching 2019-Dad's arm, the two Riley Baradas looked each other in the eyes. 2004-Dad said, "What are you doing?"

2019-Dad looked for his wife. "Rebecca?"

"Quit touching!" Kyle stepped closer.

2004-Mom grabbed for Kyle's arm. "Kyle! Why are you here? What did you do?"

Instinctively, Kyle shook her off. "No! Don't touch me! It's dangerous."

Both Dads were now staring at Kyle.

2004-Dad said, "Kyle?"

2019-Dad seemed to come out of some kind of trance. He looked down at 2004-Dad still touching him, and at Kyle and 2004-Mom, who had just been touching. The light left his eyes. "Oh, no. God, no," he whispered. In seconds he collapsed onto the pavement and began shaking.

Moments later, 2004-Dad and 2004-Mom followed him, falling on the pavement and shaking.

On the ground, 2019-Dad grimaced and clutched his chest; blood trickled out of his ear.

2019-Dad stopped moving.

What was happening?

2004-Mom said, "We forgive you, Kyle. It's not your fault we died here." On the ground, she started shaking uncontrollably.

On the ground, 2004-Dad said, "We love you. Never forget." He grimaced like he was in a huge amount of pain.

Kyle stared down at all of them. "Dad? Mom? Dad?"

What was happening? They couldn't all die. They just couldn't.

He stared at them, lying motionless on the ground.

After Kyle didn't know how long, a man in a uniform touched his arm. "Sir? Where are you hurt?"

Kyle jerked away and looked at the uniformed man. Then he turned and pointed at the two men and the woman lying on the ground between twisted cars.

The man kneeled down, quickly taking their pulses. He glanced up at Kyle, shaking his head. "I'm sorry sir. Nothing we can do for them now." He stood. "What about you? What hurts?"

They couldn't be dead.

In a fog, Kyle said, "I wasn't in the accident."

Kyle found himself standing on the sidewalk.

They forgave him?

But he didn't do anything.

More time passed. Most of the ambulances had driven away. Some of the cars had been towed away. The sun had started to set.

"Sir?" a man in a uniform asked him. "Are you all right?"

Was it the same guy from earlier? Kyle didn't even know. "I'm fine," he finally said. "I wasn't in the accident."

"Maybe we should check you out anyway." The man pointed at one of the few remaining ambulances.

Kyle realized he was clutching his phone in his hand. The pictures. What would the pictures show now? "No. I have to check my phone."

"Sir, I need to check you out. What's your name? Let me

help you."

"No! Leave me alone!" Kyle turned and walked away, quickly accessing the pictures Lachlan had given him. They were all the same as before. There was 2004-Mom, 2004-Dad, and 2019-Dad right after the accident, and there they were after more time had passed. All of them. And they weren't dead.

That meant everything was still okay, right? It hadn't really happened, right?

All Kyle had to do was try to calm down and Dream his way back to 2019, and everything would be back to normal.

His shoulders unclenched.

He could breathe again.

He could think again.

He just needed a kip.

Chapter Nineteen
Kairi: Boulder, Colorado, 2019

Kairi and Josh sat on the couch in his apartment. "I want to believe you can time travel, babe," Josh said, frowning. "Can you show me?"

She paused. "I'm not sure. Maybe. I have done it on my own. But Dakota's guru Mary, a professor here, has this helmet thingy, an L.D.-something that seems to help me time travel with lucid dreaming."

"Lucid dreaming?" Josh said. "What does that have to do with anything?"

"Oh. I time travel in my sleep. Didn't I mention that?"

"No." He gave her a long measured look. "Is that what happened in the car?"

She nodded.

He jumped up. "I knew I wasn't crazy. You did disappear from the car." He paced around the small family room. "The doctors didn't believe me."

She winced. "I apologize about that. What happened from your perspective?"

"We were driving along," he said. "You were sleeping. There was a tornado warning over the radio."

"I remember that," she said.

"Do you want to hear the story or not?" He seemed a little peeved.

"Yes, of course," she said. "Sorry."

"You were napping. The weather got worse and worse, with black clouds that turned sort of greenish."

Kairi wanted to say I told you so but knew better. She just nodded.

"It started hailing," he said. "There was a loud noise like a freight train."

She remembered that.

"There was a weird roundish horizontal cloud in front of us," he said. "And it started bending, and then it was vertical, and I could tell it was a tornado. I screamed, 'It's a tornado!' but you were gone." He shook his head. "And then I pulled the car over and jumped out into a ditch, or something. It's kind of a blur. The wind was whipping around; the noise was deafening. I'm not sure what all happened. I think I was screaming, 'Kairi, where are you?' over and over again."

"It sounds scary," she said.

"I lay in the ditch covering my head for a while, and the wind and roaring sound eventually went away. I was debating getting up and looking for you when a sheriff's car stopped. The deputy made me go to the hospital to get checked out. I don't even know when I broke my arm. When I told them my girlfriend disappeared, they made me stay for observation."

"It sounds frustrating," Kairi said. "You have to know, I didn't deliberately desert you. It was accidental, a self-preservation thing, I think."

Shaking his head, he sat back down on the couch next to her. "I knew there was something weird going on that day. I'm glad to get some kind of explanation. But what were you saying? Something about lucid dreaming?"

"I have time traveled more than once, but on my own, it doesn't seem to be reliable. On the other hand, Mary invented this helmet that helps you do lucid dreaming. Last night, it enabled me to time travel to about two weeks ago."

Josh was scowling, which she knew meant he was thinking deep thoughts. "Time travel would be awesome. Neat stuff like time travel was one of the reasons I got into physics." He looked at her. "But, if it's true, we should be able to reproduce it. Can we try this helmet thing out again?"

Kairi pondered. "When I used it the first time to go to twelve days ago, the wires got cut."

"So, how did you get back here?" Josh asked.

"I sort of swiped the undamaged helmet from twelve days ago," she said.

Josh started to say something that she knew would be, Aw, you shouldn't have done that, Kairi.

"But I left the helmet from now in its place. It wasn't that big a deal. If Mary built the helmet in the first place, she should be able to fix it."

"I guess." Josh shrugged. "But, wait a minute. Both times you used it, it broke?"

"Yeah. It's pretty much broken right now. I don't think Mary is too pleased with me. Plus, she freaked out when I disappeared for two hours and then reappeared. I don't think she would go along with another time travel experiment."

He was quiet for a few moments. Finally, he said, "What about going to the lab when she's not there?"

"You're suggesting we break into a professor's lab and use her equipment without her permission?" She grinned. Usually, Josh and she had different philosophies about following the rules. "Who are you, and what have you done with my boyfriend, er, fiancé?"

He ignored her attempt at humor. "I can probably fix some wires. Is there any way we can get into the lab?"

She had a strong feeling Topher was in for another date with Dakota. She knew she should feel guiltier about pimping out Dakota, but Topher was the best guy Kairi'd ever seen Dakota date. As far as she knew, he didn't do drugs and had an actual j-o-b.

Topher let Josh and her into the lab, and she sent Dakota and Topher off to dinner, her treat.

Josh was eager to get a look at the mysterious helmet. He'd brought his electronics lab toolbox. He turned the helmet around in his hands. "It should be no problem to splice this back to a power cord." He got right to work.

"Hmm," he said loudly.

"What?" she asked.

"What you're wearing travels with you, right?"

She had a flash of imagination in which she showed up naked, in the snow somewhere, and shuddered. "Yeah."

"Apparently, you travel with a little buffer of air or whatever around you." He held up the severed wires. "But not a big enough buffer to take these wires with you."

Hmm, indeed. She wondered why it worked that way.

Josh finished fixing the helmet, and soon she was lying back in the big chair.

He handed her the helmet. "So, how does it work?"

"The helmet?" she asked. "I don't know."

"No. The time travel."

"It's like my life flashes before my eyes," she said.

"I don't get that." He frowned. "To be honest, I'm not sure if I get any of this."

"Fair enough," she said. "One of the times I went back, I saw myself in the neurophysiology lab. Walking to the neurophysiology lab. Sleeping in my dorm room. Uh, fighting with you. And then some other stuff. Anyway, I fixed things so you didn't get mad at me." She froze. She actually fixed things. Relationships-between-people things.

He quieted. "But I don't have any memory of being mad at you. What did we fight about?" Josh said something else, but she wasn't paying attention.

What if she could fix more stuff? Saving-lives stuff?

"Babe," he said with a hint of steel in his voice. "I'm talking to you. Here I am sort of breaking into a university lab for you. The least you can do is pay attention to me when I'm talking."

"Sorry. What did you say?"

"I asked what we had a fight about in the other, ah, situation."

What did we fight about? It was kind of fuzzy; the first timeline was becoming vaguer. In the first timeline, Josh interrupted her kissing Tyler, right? But telling him that would make him mad now, too. "Uh."

"I thought we agreed relationships were based on honesty," he said with more steel.

"Yes." Ugh. "Okay. You got mad at me for disrespecting myself. I sort of made out with our R.A. Tyler so he wouldn't kick Dakota and me out of the dorm."

Josh didn't say anything at all--which she knew meant he was counting to fifty in Spanish before he said something he'd regret.

Finally, he said, "I'm disappointed in you, Kairi."

Wasn't that what he said in the timeline in which they broke up? She started getting very nervous. "I'm sorry," she said. "It was wrong. I made a mistake. But I make mistakes. I'm human."

He didn't say anything back to her.

"But, actually, I went back and fixed it. I learned my lesson and didn't do it." She paused, looking into his eyes for forgiveness and not finding it. "So, do you want to do the experiment or what?" she finally asked, heart pounding.

He jerked his head down. "Fine. But we're not done talking about this."

"I hear what you're saying," she said.

"Where are you going to try to go?" he asked.

"I know exactly where I'm going to try to go." She started to put on the helmet.

Josh's nose creased. "Where?" He stared into her eyes and must have read the quiet determination there. "Oh." He figured out she was going to stop her rape after Junior Prom.

She turned on the helmet and closed her eyes.

"Wait!" Josh yelled. "Stop."

She opened her eyes and turned off the helmet. "What's wrong?"

"How will you get back?" Josh asked. "The wires will get cut again."

He was right. Blood thundered in her ears. She was almost trapped in 2014 with her worst nightmare, Chad-the-rapist. "Oh, my God." She sat up. "You could teach me how to fix it, couldn't you?"

Josh flattened his upper lip and tapped it with his finger. "I guess we could try that. You'd have to bring the tools and supplies in your pockets."

She thought she detected a hint of skepticism in his voice. It made her a little mad. "I can totally learn how to fix it!"

He held up his hands. "Okay. Okay."

After her electronics for dummies session, she leaned back in the chair wearing the helmet and with full pockets. She closed her eyes. She opened her eyes and looked at Josh. "Are we forgetting anything else?"

He shook his head. "I don't think so. Of course, I don't know what's going on here."

She turned on the helmet and closed her eyes. She tried to breathe slowly and regularly. She thought she had gone to sleep. In her mind's eye, she saw Josh, her, Dakota, and Topher talking. She saw Josh and her walking to the lab. She saw brunch in Josh's apartment. She saw Josh and her making love. After lingering a little while on those images and feelings, she tried to speed things up.

Josh waiting for her at their room.

Her adventure in Mary's lab.

Starting out on the spring break road trip.

Going to class.

Graduating from high school.

Going to class.

She pinched herself awake when she came to the day Chad asked her to the Junior Prom.

She stood outside Pam's house. It was a beautiful April morning. The sun shone, the breeze blew, birds chirped, and flowers bloomed. She didn't remember the neighborhood being so pretty.

She planned to stop herself on the way to school. She sat on the neighbor's bench near the sidewalk, stashing the helmet underneath.

Past-Kairi didn't even slow down as she zoomed by on her way to school. Her brown curls were askew, her face was smooth, and her features were even and symmetrical. Past-Kairi was pretty. She hadn't even realized it.

Past-Kairi also appeared to be trying to do her homework as she walked down the sidewalk. She had a pencil and her notebook and was trying to write something on a piece of paper.

"Kairi," she said.

Past-Kairi looked up, squeaked and dropped her notebook. Her math homework almost blew away. Suddenly her bad math grades started to make a whole lot more sense.

As past-Kairi leaned down to get her homework, she asked, "Who are you? Are you a relative?" Her voice got kind of squeaky. "Are you my sister?"

"No," she said. "I'm you."

"No, you're not me. You're too old. Get away from me, freak."

Kairi couldn't believe her past self was being so bratty. "For your information, I'm only about five years older than you."

"As I said, old," past-Kairi said. "And I don't believe you're me. That's crazy."

She tried to remain calm. "Whatever. I'm here to tell you not to go to the dance with Chad."

"Chad's going to ask me to go to the dance?" A huge smile broke out on the younger woman's face. It made her look even prettier. "Great!"

"No." She paused and stared into her eyes. "It's not great. You don't want to go to the dance with Chad."

"Yes," past-Kairi said. "I do."

Kairi sighed. Geez, past-Kairi was annoying. She gritted her teeth. "Chad's going to date-rape you after the dance."

"I don't believe you. I don't know you. Besides, Chad wouldn't do that."

She pushed her face into the other woman's face. "I'm you, and I'm telling you to say no." She started feeling a little sick to her stomach.

Past-Kairi took a step back and opened her mouth. She closed her mouth. "Fine. Can I go now? I have class."

Kairi didn't know what else to say. It hadn't occurred to her that past-Kairi wouldn't believe her. She let her go on her merry way.

She went back to the bench and sat down. Did it work? She didn't feel any different. She tried to remember this morning five years ago...

All she could remember was rushing to the bus stop and riding the bus to school.

"Dammit. It didn't work."

Kairi was going to have to go to the Junior Prom.

Again.

And the first time had been bad enough.

Chapter Twenty
Kyle: Sydney, Australia, 2019

Kyle came to in hospital. When was he?

Wave after wave of conflicting memories washed over him. He clutched the bed railings as his lives passed before his eyes. He went to his parents' funerals, and at the same time, life went on as usual: he and his brother went to school, and his parents started having knockdown drag-out fights. An orphan, he floundered in school and got a counselor, and alternately his parents got a divorce.

In the real world, someone talked to him.

Kyle tried to ignore all the memories, to shut them out, but he couldn't. So much loneliness versus his parents going to battle over his brother and him and everything else.

He leaned over the edge of the bed and heaved, but his stomach was empty.

He felt a presence hovering nearby and looked up. Gradually, a man's face, tired and needing a shave, appeared. He finally focused on the face clearly and realized it wasn't Dad. It was his Uncle Raymond. "Hey, Ray." His eyes felt heavy.

Ray's eyes narrowed. "How do you feel, Kyle? You had us worried there for a while." He paused. "What happened? You haven't been Traveling, have you?"

Kyle was glad to see his uncle, even if he did look suspicious and disappointed.

One of the nurses, a gray-haired old-timer, bustled in. "Let's have a Captain Cook." She looked Kyle over, nodded, and adjusted the pillows behind his back. "There we go. That's better."

Ugh. She was the one that called him a no-hoper before. He

must have grimaced.

"What's that?" she asked. "Are you in pain?"

"I just don't appreciate being called a no-hoper."

"Huh?" Her mouth fell open.

"Before. When Dad was here."

"Your dad wasn't here before," Ray said.

Kyle's memories were all jumbled. But Ray was right. In the new timeline, Dad didn't go to hospital because he was already dead. And apparently, Ray didn't recall the overwritten timeline. That was interesting. That meant only the actual Traveler remembered an overwritten timeline.

"Should I send the doctor in, then?" the nurse asked.

"Uh, no," Ray said. "We're fine for the moment. Thanks."

Once she left, Ray closed the door firmly behind her and dragged the chair up near the bed, but not too close. "What's going on, Kyle?"

Kyle tried to shrug, but another wave of nausea overtook him. When it settled, he said, "I don't know. Is my mobile here?"

"I think so." Ray rummaged around in a drawer, extracting Kyle's mobile. "Here."

Kyle accessed the photos, and there were none there from Lachlan. None there from the accident. Nothing.

"What's wrong?" Ray asked.

"Hypothetically, when does a timeline change?" Kyle asked slowly. "Say, I was in 2018 and did something. Would it immediately change the rest of 2018 and all of 2019 and so on?"

"No." Ray shook his head. "We think the timeline doesn't change until you return to your present. What's this about?"

Kyle couldn't breathe. He should have stayed back there in 2004. He shouldn't have come back.

He killed them. He killed his parents.

He wished he was dead.

After several moments, Ray said, "Kyle?"

"I may have changed the timeline."

Ray pressed his lips together in a thin line. Then, he said, "How?"

"I don't want to talk about it," Kyle said.

Ray's face looked thoughtful as he leaned back in the chair. "I don't care what you want. You need to tell me. Your life may depend on it."

Could that be true? Could his life be in danger? Did he care? "Back in 2004, I killed my parents."

Ray just looked at him. Finally, he said, "Really?"

Kyle nodded, setting off another wave of nausea.

After a few more moments, Ray said, "I don't remember that. I thought they died in a traffic accident. What could you have to do with it?"

"Whatever." Maybe Kyle's life being in danger wasn't such a bad thing.

As his memories settled, Kyle realized it was good to see Ray, to see he still had living relatives. In this timeline, Ray and his wife Jessie had raised Oliver and him along with their daughter Moira. They'd had some good times. Kyle reached his hand out to him.

Ray shrank back.

Kyle couldn't blame him. He'd forgotten for a second that they weren't supposed to touch.

This whole situation was unacceptable.

Ray's eyes narrowed again. "I don't know what you're thinking, but I'm sensing it's not good."

"When can I go back and fix things?" Kyle asked.

Ray jumped up. "You can't! You have to leave this event alone. The absolutely most important rule is that you cannot Travel to the same event more than once. It just makes things worse and worse."

"I don't recall that from my training," Kyle said.

"That's because it's never supposed to happen." Ray leaned over and reoriented the chair. "Never." He sat down. "In fact, you should never mention this again to anyone. And, I hate to say it, but you aren't The Traveler in this timeline." Tradition dictated that there could only be one Traveler at a time. Now, Kyle was starting to realize it had to be because a Traveler could change the timeline. He could overwrite another timeline. What would happen if there were two Travelers and two new timelines tried to come into existence at once? Nothing good.

The full implications of what Ray said finally hit Kyle. "Right. You're The Traveler." His nausea was fading as this timeline's memories clicked into place. "I understand." He understood more all the time. One Traveler at a time seemed like a really good idea, now that he thought about it.

Ray dipped his chin. "Good."

"So what about Oliver?" Kyle asked. "When can I see him?"

Ray's face stilled. "I have no idea. He's at university in the U.S. Don't you remember?"

But they were interrupted by a voice from the doorway. "Kyle! There you are!" Liam smiled widely, came right over to him, and gave him a big bear hug.

Kyle could barely catch a breath. "Liam," he said, grinning back. "I'd say good to see 'ya, but I can't breathe. Stop. You're crushing me."

Liam let go, still beaming. "It's been too long, mate." He took a step back and frowned. "Sorry to hear about your illness." He pointed. "What's wrong exactly?" He looked at Ray. "Hi, Mr. Barada."

Ray forced a smile. "Food poisoning. But he's over the worst of it."

Kyle did feel significantly better, almost normal. It was as if once the new timeline was fully stable, his body calmed down, too.

Ray stood up. "I'll go and let you boys catch up."

Catch up? Kyle'd been hanging out with Liam for days. No, that was in the other timeline. Kyle searched his memories of this timeline: he'd been training and doing corporate busy-work.

Ray walked towards the door. "I'll talk with you later, Kyle."

"Yeah, Ray," Kyle said. "Count on it."

Once he left, Kyle said, "Close the door."

Liam did so and came back over to the bed. "So, do you truly have food poisoning?"

Kyle gestured him closer and then said softly, "No. I went Traveling."

"No shite?"

He nodded.

"You little Ripper!" Liam sat down, pulling the chair closer to the bed and leaning towards him. "I thought that wasn't allowed."

"It's not," Kyle said.

"What! Then how'd you do it?"

"It's a very long story," Kyle said. "But you helped me."

Liam leaned back. "Shite. I don't remember that."

"It was another timeline."

"Another timeline? You're a superhero!"

If Liam only knew how not-a-superhero he was. He was a killer.

"I'm buying," Liam said. "When do you get out of here?"

At Liam's massive enthusiasm for liquid refreshment, Kyle couldn't help smiling. At least Liam was the same; he still loved partying. "I'd love to get out of here, but I don't know when I can leave."

"No worries, mate." Liam stood up. "I'll go check with the nurse."

A little later, as Liam and Kyle headed out the hospital door, Liam raised his eyebrows and grinned. "Are we going to partake of a pint or two, then, Mr. Barada?"

"Does a koala shit in the gum tree?" Kyle managed to grin. "But first, I need to make a stop."

Liam snorted as he led the way to his car.

Kyle's nerves stretched to the breaking point as they drove out to the cemetery. He started to wonder if he was going to be sick again. He'd never been here before, and at the same time, he remembered the double funeral. For that matter, he remembered his dad's overwritten funeral. So many funerals. This whole situation was bizarre. And horrific.

"Kyle?" Liam asked as he turned off the engine. "Are you okay? You look a bit crook, mate."

Kyle forced the weirdness away. "Yeah. I'm okay." He opened the car door. "Do you want to come?"

"I think this is a big moment for you. I'll wait here. Take your time."

Liam was a good mate. "Thanks." Kyle walked nervously up the gravel walkway to the gravestone, seeing every bush, flower, and blade of grass on the grounds as if he'd never seen a plant before. He breathed in the sweet scent of flowers and newly mown grass. It was all so green and alive. How could that be? Here in this place of death?

Finally, he paused in front of the grave, gathering his wits. Okay, Kyle, just look at it already. What's the hold-up? He glanced back at Liam in the car.

Liam nodded and waved at him.

Kyle turned back to the gravestone.

Barada. Riley and Rebecca. Beloved parents. They left us too soon.

The year of death was given as 2004. Oh, God.

That wasn't right, not the way it was supposed to be. His mom was supposed to still be alive, for Christ's sake. And his dad was supposed to live until 2019. He stared at the engraved number.

He did this.

It felt to Kyle as if his heart had stopped. He fell to his knees, scattering gravel. The sound of shifting gravel boomed in the quiet of the cemetery. The quiet of death.

He felt his eyes fill and leaned his forehead on the ground. He didn't have the energy to rail against this, to curse.

He wished he was the one buried here.

After a few moments, he heard footsteps approach from behind. "Kyle?" Liam asked. "Are you okay, mate?"

He lifted his head. Not sure he could talk, he just nodded.

"Do you want me to go back to the car?"

Kyle shook his head.

"Okay. I'll just wait here with you until you're ready."

Kyle looked back at the huge hunk of stone with his broken heart spelled out on it.

He would make this right.

Chapter Twenty-One
Kairi: Boulder, Colorado, 2014

Kairi was five years back in her own past the day before the Junior Prom, standing outside Pam's house.

In hindsight, she couldn't help thinking she should have been more suspicious about being asked to the dance on the day before the dance.

Having just seen past-Kairi, however, she also recalled how excited she'd been about her first dance. She sighed, feeling sorry for that poor naïve girl. Her life was about to be changed forever unless she stopped it. Because of Chad, she was totally messed up about guys. Josh was the first real boyfriend she'd had, and he'd helped her work through a lot of stuff.

Then she paused for a second. If she did stop it, would it change her life? How? Would she be the same Kairi? Would she still be engaged to Josh and best friends with Dakota? Or would she be someone different?

Pam drove past, interrupting Kairi's reverie and prompting her to remember the key Pam kept hidden under the front flowerpot. She could hang out at her house today. Surely she could talk past-Kairi out of going to the dance when she got home from school, right?

At Pam's house, she managed to reconnect the power cord to the helmet. She stashed it under some plastic tarps in the old shed in the backyard. Other than that, she just watched TV and got more and more nervous. What if she couldn't talk past-Kairi out of the dance?

At three o'clock, past-Kairi waltzed through the front door and stopped dead when she saw her sitting on the couch. "How the hell did you get in here?"

"I'm you. How do you think I got in here? I used the spare key under the flowerpot."

Past-Kairi opened and closed her mouth. Had she rattled her? Was there a chance she was starting to believe her? "Get out of here, whoever you are," she said. "You're not supposed to be here. You're not invited."

"You can't go to the dance with Chad."

"Get out."

Kairi stood up. "You can't go."

"Get out! Get out! Get out!" past-Kairi screamed.

Did that mean she believed her and didn't want to?

"I'm serious," past-Kairi said. "I'm going to call the cops if you don't leave right now." She reached for her phone.

"Oh, come on," Kairi said. "You wouldn't call the cops on yourself."

"You're not me! I'm dialing."

Kairi crossed her arms. "I don't believe you."

And then past-Kairi said, "Help, police. There's an intruder in my house," and gave the address when asked. She put down her phone and crossed her arms. It was like looking in a left-right-flipped mirror. "They're on their way."

Immediately, they heard a siren.

The stubborn look on past-Kairi's face faded. "Wow. That was fast."

Kairi was caught off guard. Should she run away or what? "If I get arrested, it'll be your fingerprints in the system."

In no time at all, someone was pounding on the front door. "Open up. Boulder PD"

Past-her shuffled to the front door and swung it open.

Two middle-aged white men in uniforms stood on the front stoop. "Did you call 911?" the fatter, older of the two said. "Are you all right, Miss?"

The younger cop said, "Can we come in?"

Past-Kairi nodded and stepped out of the doorway.

The officers approached Kairi. "Are you the intruder?" the younger one said.

She shook her head, "No."

"Can we see some ID?" the older cop said.

She felt in her pockets, but all she had were wires and other electronic paraphernalia. "I don't seem to have my ID with me right now."

"They look just like each other. Clearly, they're related," the fatter one said. "They've got to be sisters."

Past-her said, "That's not my sister. I'm way better looking!"

Both officers turned to past-Kairi. "Yeah, right. Calling 911 for no reason is a serious offense. What's your name? Do you have ID?"

"I don't have my driver's license yet. My name is Kairi Johnson, but the last name is made up. I don't know my last name," past-Kairi said. "And I didn't call for no reason." She pointed at her. "I don't know her."

The younger officer took his phone out of his shirt pocket and scrolled through it. "Is this the home of Pam and John Taylor? We've been called here several times for domestic disturbances. Is it this John? Is he your father or guardian? Did he threaten you? Has he hurt you?"

John? That must be the guy she met here before. Did he hurt Pam?

Past-her looked confused and shook her head. "No. I don't know him. I don't know any John. He doesn't live here."

The older officer wagged his finger at them. "Wait a minute. Kairi no-name! You're the baby I found in the middle of the street when I was a rookie. It was back in 1999."

She'd been found in the middle of the street? Kairi felt dizzy and grabbed the arm of the couch.

"It was the darnedest thing," he continued. "No one was looking for you. No one came to claim you. It was like you popped in out of nowhere. And you were the cutest little thing."

"You found me in the street?" past-Kairi asked, looking dizzy, too. She sat down on the couch. "I never knew that."

The rest of what the officer said finally registered: Kairi'd popped out of nowhere! She collapsed on the couch next to the younger Kairi. Had she time traveled as a baby? Why? Had she been in danger? Did she have parents somewhere in time looking for her? She felt woozy.

The older officer said, "I know you've had a hard time. I guess we can let this one false alarm go." He raised his forefinger in admonishment. "But don't do it again."

Past-her looked dazed.

She probably looked dazed, too; she certainly felt dazed. "Yes, sir. Yes, officer," she managed to say.

They left, shaking their heads, and shutting the door behind them.

Past-Kairi's eyes shone with unshed tears. "No one wanted me?" she whispered.

"I'm sure someone wanted you," Kairi said. "You're a good person." Who was she trying to convince? "They wanted you. They just couldn't find you." She hoped that was true. She wasn't sure what else to say. She paused.

"Please leave," past-Kairi said quietly.

She looked so pathetic that Kairi couldn't argue with her anymore. She left.

Back at the bench, she tried to regroup, still reeling from the possibility that she'd time traveled as a baby. What happened back then? She realized she could probably go back in time and find out. She was just wondering if it would be safe to go back to Pam's house and retrieve the helmet from the shed when Pam drove up. Right after that, Pam and past-her drove away. Oh, yeah. She remembered shopping with Pam for a dress for the dance.

She still had the flowerpot key in her pocket. She returned to the house, got the helmet, plugged it in, turned it on, put it on and lay back on the couch. She was going to find out what happened to baby-her. Why didn't anyone look for her?

She closed her eyes and tried to go to sleep. "Go to sleep, Kairi." She slowed her breathing. She tried to think calming thoughts.

She must have drifted off because she heard a tone ringing. The tone was important... Oh, yeah, it meant she was dreaming. She tried to focus on her past. In her mind's eye, Chad asked her to the dance. She tried to speed things up.

She was in class. She was in class. She met Pam for what she thought was the first time. She was in class. She met Dakota. She was in a group home. She was in class. Things started getting more indistinct. She was somewhere with some other kids; they played on a red rug. She was in a high chair. She was in a crib. There were noises and lights. It was dark.

There was a loud blaring noise. Two very bright lights got closer and closer. "Wake up! Wake up!" She woke up, standing on the side of the road in a residential neighborhood. It was cold and pitch dark except for a police car stopped in the street, headlights shining on a tiny brown baby wrapped in a fuzzy pink blanket.

Her.

She crouched down in the bushes, not wanting to draw attention to herself. She stared at the sad tableau in the middle of the street.

The cop got out of the car, walked over, and picked her up. "Aren't you a little cutie? What are you doing here? You shouldn't be here in the middle of the street. Where's your momma and daddy?" He got back in the car and started talking; it must have been on his radio. Eventually, he drove away with her.

Now what? She couldn't follow him; she had no transportation. And there were no cars on the road. She couldn't hitchhike. It must be two or three a.m. Crap. And she was freezing. It felt like a whopping thirty degrees or so out here. This was a total bust.

She decided she might as well go back to 2014. She looked around for a place to lie down and decided to just do it in the grass--the sooner she got out of here, the better. She lay down and shivered and closed her eyes. She slowed her breathing and thought calm thoughts.

All that happened was she shivered some more.

She opened her eyes and noticed the wires from the helmet were severed, and besides that, there was no power source out here on someone's lawn. Duh. She stood up.

Judging from the design of the houses, small brick ranches, and sizes of the front yards, small, she was in Pam's neighborhood. She felt for the flowerpot key in her pocket. It was still there along with the wire-stripper and extra plugs. She had to get back to Pam's house.

How cold did it have to be to freeze to death? She started running.

Eventually, after checking street signs, she found Pam's house. Very gently, she unlocked the front door. Hurray. The key worked. And thank goodness it was warm inside. Was Pam home? And what about that John guy? She'd have to be super quiet not to wake them up. She turned on the table lamp in the family room and silently spliced the wire back together. She was getting good at it. She turned off the light, put on the helmet, turned it on, lay down and closed her eyes. She slowed her breathing and thought calm thoughts.

There was a tone, and then two bright lights and a loud noise. It was dark. There were noises and lights. She was in a crib. She was in a high chair. She was somewhere with some other kids. They played on a red rug. Things started to get clearer. She was in class. She was in a group home. A bunch of classes. She tried to slow things down.

Chad asked her to the dance. She went shopping with Pam for a dress. Saturday, Chad picked her up for the dance. She was in the gym, and it was filled with teenagers, blue balloons and streamers and fish made of poster board and construction paper.

"Wake up!" She woke up, standing in the corner of the gym.

A big banner hanging over the stage in the gym said: Enchantment Under The Sea.

She scanned the crowd for past-Kairi. She was dancing with Chad near the stage but didn't look happy. Kairi edged closer to the stage through the crowd and stashed the helmet underneath it.

The band stopped playing, and the lead singer started talking. "Thank you, Boulder High. You guys rock."

The crowd cheered.

"For our last number, a new hit from Mariah Carey. Grab your honey and make it last. Mine. Mine. Mine.Mine. You're mine...

Ready for a slow dance, Chad reached for past-Kairi, but she pushed him away and took a step back. She scowled and said something unpleasant, judging by his reaction.

He frowned and shook his head. Kairi saw him mouth, "No," something.

She snuck closer, trying to hear them.

Past-her seemed to be yelling at Chad. The other couples near them were all staring.

She couldn't hear anything over the music.

Past-her turned on her heel and stomped away from him through the crowd. Then she saw her and stomped her way.

When she got to her, Past-Kairi said, "Well, I hope you're happy. You ruined the whole dance for me. I kept worrying that he might attack me, and I didn't have any fun!"

Kairi felt very odd. Her head broke out into a sweat. The room started spinning. It was hard to breathe.

The floor tilted.

Chapter Twenty-Two
Kyle: Sydney, Australia, 2019

Back at Liam's apartment after the cemetery visit, Kyle leaned back on Liam's couch and sighed. How could trying to save people be wrong?

"Are you sure you're not sick?" Liam asked.

"No. I'm okay." Kyle's memories of the aborted timeline were fading. They weren't gone, but they were easier to ignore.

"To the pub? Ready for some pints? I want to hear all about time traveling. Don't leave me hanging, mate."

Kyle glanced at him. Liam was a big, pasty white guy, but one who was always there for him. "I'd love a pint or two, but I don't think I'm up for the pub."

"No worries," Liam said. "I'll pop out to the shops and get us a slab." He grabbed his car keys and headed for the door. "You hang out here; I'll be right back." He turned around, facing Kyle. "Where are you staying?"

Where was he staying? Suddenly, Kyle got dizzy. He grabbed the arm of the couch and accessed the revised memories. He'd been staying out at the family compound in the country, training, and doing scut work for Time Advantages, Inc. Ugh. How many years was he supposed to keep doing that? "Can I stay here in the city with you for a few days?"

"Sure. No problem. In fact, sounds fun." Liam flashed him a grin. "Be right back." He went out the front door.

While he was gone, Kyle lay back on the couch and closed his eyes. He was exhausted.

What the hell was he supposed to do now? Going back out to the country and doing nothing did not appeal. Too much had happened. Too much that he needed to change.

Then images flashed through his mind: a gravel walkway, surrounded by bushes and flowers, every plant, every blade of grass, lush. Their verdant scent overwhelmed his nose.

Why was it so smelly? It was odd. It gave him a weird feeling.

Kyle focused. He was on Liam's couch; he was supposed to be on Liam's couch. Why didn't he feel the couch? It was evening. Liam went for beer. He was in Liam's apartment.

The smell disappeared, and he felt the scratchy couch under his body again.

He heard Liam say, "Fuck me!" followed by a loud thunk.

Kyle opened his eyes and looked over at him. "What?"

Liam was staring at him, mouth open and eyes bugged out. "You weren't there, and then, Bam! you popped out of thin air."

Kyle swung his legs around and sat up. "Really?"

Liam nodded and leaned down. "Good thing I got tinnies." He scooped the case of beer up off the floor, tore open the box and started guzzling one.

Kyle's mind and pulse were racing. What just happened? It seemed as if he'd Traveled. But how could that be? He didn't use The Dreaming Room. Plus, his uncle was The Traveler, and only one Traveler was allowed at a time.

But, he must have Traveled. That was the only thing that made sense.

When Liam came up for air, he said, "Phew," and wiped his mouth with the back of his hand. "Want one?"

Kyle held out his hand, and Liam passed him one. Kyle popped the top and gulped some down.

"So, what the hell was that?" Liam pointed at Kyle and the couch as he sat down.

"Ah." Kyle grinned. Despite being a so-called superhero, it wasn't often he had the upper hand over Liam. He wanted to make the most of it. "Beer hits the spot."

"Kyle! Talk."

Kyle took another swig. He felt weird, excited, and more alive than he'd ever felt before. Could he Travel whenever he wanted? "You said it yourself--why do we need a special room to time travel? Apparently, we don't."

Liam was frowning. "I don't remember saying anything like

that."

"Oh, right. That was the other timeline. It still applies."

"Other timeline!" Liam shook his head. "Shite. If you say so, mate. Say, what else happened in this other timeline, besides, you know, that bad stuff with your folks?"

Kyle couldn't resist saying, "Among other things, you had a foursome with three sheilas."

"Brilliant!" Liam showed off his shit-eating grin. "That sounds about right. And you? You didn't partake in the fun with the young ladies? I bet I would have shared."

"What?" Kyle narrowed his eyes. "Are you saying you would want me to partake with you?"

Liam laughed. "Whatever, mate. I'm flexible."

Kyle couldn't tell if he was joking or not. And what did he mean by flexible, exactly? He flashed back on that image of Liam's junk he'd gotten in the other timeline. He shook his head to shake the picture out. "No. For the record, I'm not partaking of anything with you. If I stay here with you, no orgies."

"Aw." Liam pretended to be disappointed. Then he finished off his beer. "Relax, mate." He patted Kyle's knee. "We lived together for three years at university; I think I know you a little. I'm just pulling your chain." He paused and smiled. "It's so damn easy." And like that, Liam had the upper hand again.

Kyle's good feeling was evaporating. "So, yeah, I time traveled, just now. I'm pretty sure."

"That's fucking awesome, mate!" Liam did seem happy for him. "Tell me about it."

"I only went back a little while, but I saw and smelled the plants and stuff at the cemetery. I think I was there." As if once hadn't been enough.

"Brilliant." Liam popped two more beers and handed one to Kyle. "But why can you do it?"

"You mean, why can my people access all of time through The Dreaming?"

"No. You already explained that part. It's crazy and amazing, but I believe it. I mean, now, I've even seen it for myself." He took a swig. "Why can you time travel now, just lying on the couch, when you couldn't before? And could your parents do it whenever? And your brother?"

His brother. Kyle hadn't thought about him since he got back, and now tons of new memories slammed through his consciousness. Mom and Dad had fought over him and Oliver, inadvertently pitting them against one another in the old timeline. In this timeline, Ray and Jessie had raised them, but they'd been hollow shells of their former selves. "Oliver." Kyle sighed. "I should call him."

"Isn't he over in the U.S. at university? In Colorado or something? What time is it there?"

"I don't know." Kyle already had his phone out and was looking through the numbers. Oliver's number was there. He dialed.

Oliver answered. "Kyle? What's wrong? Did someone die?"

Kyle flashed back to Dad's funeral in the other timeline, and how broken up Oliver had been. "No. I just wanted to call and say hi, see how you're doing?"

"Since when do you?" Oliver said. "Never mind. Actually, I've been feeling weird. A few minutes ago, I was feeling kind of woozy, and when I woke up in the middle of the night a few hours ago, I felt dizzy. Is something up?"

Woozy? Dizzy? Could Kyle's Traveling affect Oliver? "I'm not sure."

"You're not sure if something's up? Why are you calling me, then? It's four a.m. here."

"Bloody hell. Sorry, Oliver. I guess I forgot about the time difference."

Liam snorted.

"I'll investigate the dizziness thing and get back to you," Kyle said. "Call me back when it's convenient."

"Okay. That would be nice." Oliver paused.

"Anything else up?" Kyle asked. He wanted to ask Oliver if he'd been Traveling, but he didn't want to give his little brother any ideas.

"Actually," Oliver said. "It's interesting that you called now. There's something else weird. I saw a girl on campus yesterday that reminded me of Moira."

Kyle remembered Moira at the funeral in the other timeline, crying quietly, like a grown-up. It had been heartbreaking.

"Kyle?" Oliver said.

"Ah, what?"

"Did you hear what I said? Spitting image of Moira."

"That is a little weird," Kyle said. "I didn't know there were any other members of the Families over there."

"Me neither," Oliver said.

It seemed as if everywhere Kyle turned these days, there was something weird. "So, sorry about waking you up. I'll get back to you about the dizziness." They hung up.

"How's young Oliver?" Liam asked.

"Weird."

Liam nodded.

Kyle and Liam drank in companionable silence for a few moments.

"So?" Liam asked. "Are you going to answer my earlier questions? Why can you time travel so easily now? And what about the rest of your family?"

"I don't think Oliver's been Traveling. As far as I know, Uncle Ray still uses The Dreaming Room." He sipped his beer. "Maybe I can Travel now because I did it before? It was some sort of paradigm shift?"

"Paradigm? That's a big word." Liam grinned and fished another beer out of the worse-for-wear box. "I'm going to have to go get more beers at this rate." He turned to Kyle. "The question is: what are you going to do now that you can time travel any time you want?"

That was indeed the question.

Chapter Twenty-Three
Kairi: Boulder, Colorado, 2014

Kairi got a flash of gray eyes and bushy eyebrows.

"Kairi?" a man asked.

"Josh?" she asked.

And then she seemed to boomerang somewhere else.

She came to lying on a hard wooden floor. An earnest man in an EMT uniform knelt over her. "Can you tell me your name, Miss?"

What just happened? She felt woozy. It was good she was lying down. "Uh, Kairi Johnson," she said.

The EMT turned his head to look at someone else. "I thought you said your name was Kairi Johnson."

"Yeah, I did," the other Kairi said.

Memories roiled over her like breakers over churning sand. She tried to fight off Chad in his car, and at the same time, she stood in the near-empty gym with some EMTs. She was crying in Pam's arms and wouldn't tell her what was wrong, and at the same time, she didn't experience a felony. She stayed home from school for days, hiding out, and at the same time, she went to school and got an A on her English test. And on and on. It was nauseating. If she'd been standing up, she would have fallen down.

A man she couldn't see said, "So? What's the truth? Who's the real Kairi?"

The other Kairi said, "We both are. We have the same last name because we're cousins. My folks and her folks both liked the name Kairi. What can we say?"

The man kneeling over her said, "Your color isn't so good. Can you tell me the date?"

What was the date? Kairi looked into his eyes. They were blue with flecks of brown. "No," she whispered.

He shot a look at his fellow EMT.

In the gym, the blue streamers and balloons finally registered. "Wait. It's Enchantment Under the Sea!"

The EMT nodded. "Good."

The EMT she couldn't see said, "I think we should take her in."

"No," she said. She couldn't remember why but that seemed like a bad idea.

The other Kairi said, "She doesn't have any insurance."

Wave after wave of conflicting memories washed over her. She stayed home in bed so many days that they ran together, and at the same time, she brought her grades up and went out more on the weekends with friends. Pam said she was worried about her and wanted to take her to a psychologist, and at the same time, she said she was proud of her and bought her an old clunker car.

She barely passed the eleventh grade, and she finished in the top twenty percent of her class.

In the real world, someone put her on some kind of gurney, but she couldn't focus on what was happening to her physical body.

She tried to ignore all the memories, to shut them out, but she couldn't. She graduated high school in the top twenty percent, and she graduated in the top one percent. She socialized only with Dakota and some other foster kids, and she was Homecoming Queen. That couldn't be right, but she could clearly recall going up on stage, hot and sweaty from dancing, people clapping, someone putting a plastic crown on her head, and joking around curtsying and thanking her subjects. Who was she?

She went to CU, paying in-state tuition and sweating every dime, and overwriting that she went to CU on a full scholarship. She roomed with Dakota, and she roomed with chubby Jessica from Minneapolis. She met Josh, and she didn't meet Josh.

She, at least one version of her never knew Josh. It was too much.

Everything went black.

Kairi came to this time lying on a white-sheeted bed, surrounded by pistachio green walls and sundry electronic equipment. It must have been the hospital.

"I think she's awake," Kairi's voice said, but Kairi didn't say it.

She tried to lean up on an elbow and spied Pam getting up from an uncomfortable-looking plastic molded chair. Her hair was rumpled as if she'd gone to bed and gotten up again.

"Hi, there." Pam smiled. "You had us worried."

Someone who looked like her stepped near the bed. "Hi. Are you feeling better?" She glanced at Pam.

Who was that other her? Then, it all came back to her, and she shuddered. That Kairi was past-her. She was in the past. And if her drastic memory changes were any indication, somehow, she'd totally altered her life. The nausea threatened to come back, but she pushed it down.

Pam put a fist on her waist. "You would not believe the story this one has been telling me. You're her, Kairi, from the future." She forced a smile. "I'm starting to think she needs some psychological attention."

Past-her shook her head.

Kairi opened her mouth. She closed her mouth. She didn't know what to say.

"So you're saying time travel is impossible, Pam?" past-her asked.

Pam turned to her with a scowl. "Of course."

"Okay. In that case, I happened to run into, Kair? er, Karen, here," past-her pointed at her. "And we immediately noticed our resemblance and wondered if we were related. It turns out Karen doesn't know about her family, either. Isn't that right, Karen?"

Who knew she was such a convincing liar? Kairi opened her mouth. "Yeah. So, we might actually be related, don't you think?"

"Wow," Pam said. "That would be amazing. Thank you for finally telling me the truth." She turned to past-her. "You've always wondered about your family."

"Can she come home and stay with us?" past-her asked.

Pam turned back to Kairi. "Well..."

"Please, Pam," past-her said. "What if she's my sister? I

have to get to know her."

"Don't you have family looking for you?" Pam asked. "Somewhere else to stay?"

Kairi shook her head. "Not that I know of."

Pam narrowed her eyes. "How old are you?"

"Twenty-one," she said.

Pam looked from one to the other. Finally, she sighed. "It's so late, I guess so. The docs said physically, you seem okay. I'll send one of the nurses in here with the paperwork and go get the car." That was the Pam she knew and loved--always taking in strays.

Once she was out of earshot, past-her said, "You're welcome."

"Thank you," Kairi said. "Why are you being so nice to me now?"

Past-her looked at the floor. "I believe you now. I think you're me from the future. And I guess I owe you for saving me from Chad."

"You're welcome," she said.

"Just because I believe you doesn't mean I think you hanging around would be good for me. I hope you'll be able to go back to the future or whatever if you get out of the hospital. Can you get back?"

She wasn't sure. While she was talking, she started to get dizzy again. She didn't think being in the hospital was helping her. Carefully, she nodded her head. "Sure. I can get back." But to what? How much had she changed her life?

They all slept late Sunday morning. It turned out preventing felonies, having one's memory rewritten and ending up in the emergency room until the wee hours of the morning made a person tired. When Kairi woke up, she hoped she was back home in 2019, but such was not the case. She was with past-her and past-Pam, still in 2014.

Pam tried to be nice and made them pancakes for brunch, but Kairi could tell she was kind of conflicted. Was the strange woman related to her Kairi? If so, what would that mean for her relationship with Kairi? If not, what was her scam? Pam said she had errands to do and went out after they ate.

Kairi was doing the dishes when she brought up an issue

that had been bothering her. "So, uh, Kairi."

Past-Kairi grinned. "Yes, Kairi." She stepped towards her.

It felt as if the room was spinning. She had to grab the edge of the counter to keep from falling. "Anyway, I left something important in the school gym last night, at least I think that's where I left it. I need this important something to get back to the future. What do you think? Will you help me get it back?"

"I guess," past-Kairi said. "We need to get you back where you belong. But, breaking into the gym sounds like a big job. I think we need reinforcements."

"I think the fewer people that know about me, the better. Who were you thinking of?"

"Dakota."

"Ooh, a caper," Dakota said on the phone a little later. "Count me in."

Soon Dakota was at the front door. Her eyes opened wide when she took in the two of them, two Kairis. "Awesome." She pointed at them. "Are you guys, like, clones or something? Or maybe one of you is an android?"

Both Kairis couldn't help smiling. Leave it to Dakota to come up with an outrageous explanation.

"No," Kairi said. "I'm from the future." How many times had she explained this to Dakota?

Dakota gasped. "Wow. Do you have a time machine? Where is it? What's time travel like?"

Kairi remembered multiple versions of this discussion. It was overwhelming. She sank to the couch before she fell down. "I sort of have a time machine. I left it in the gym at the Enchantment Under the Sea dance."

"Ooh! The dance." Dakota turned to past-her. "How was the dance? How was Chad? Did you kiss? What happened? Was it wonderful?"

Past-her shrugged. "The dance was pretty fun. But it turns out Chad is an asshole." She glanced her way.

Kairi could still faintly remember screaming and crying and trying to push him off her in the back of his car. She shuddered.

Past-her continued. "Anyway, we need to get into the gym and retrieve this time machine thing."

Dakota nodded. "Okay. What's the plan?"

They both looked at the older woman. "Don't look at me," Kairi said. "It's your school. What do you think?"

They shrugged.

Past-her said, "There are supposed to be tunnels under the school, but I don't know where the entrance is." She turned to Dakota. "Do you?"

Dakota said, "Ooh. The tunnels. That's a great idea."

"Great," Kairi said. "Where's the entrance?"

"I don't know," Dakota said.

Had she ever been so immature? Kairi resisted the urge to sigh. "Let's wait until dark and go down there to the high school and see what we see," she said.

On Sunday night, Boulder High seemed to be deserted. More importantly, the doors were locked. Crap. She'd picked nighttime, so they could caper without being detected, but now she was realizing that had been a bad idea.

"Now what?" past-her asked.

Kairi shook her head. If memory served (and that was a big if at this point), generally, security was pretty pathetic. "I guess let's walk around and see if any of the windows are open."

As they circled the building, Dakota started asking questions about the future. "Are we still friends in the future? Where do I go to college? Do I go to college? What about Kairi? Where does she go to college? Do we get married?"

Kairi shot her a look. "To each other?"

"Of course not," Dakota said.

"Maybe it's better not to know these things," past-her said.

"Okay," Dakota said. "But you'd tell us if something really bad was going to happen, right? You'd tell us?"

Kairi and past-Kairi looked at each other.

Past-her nodded and said, "Yes, she'd tell us."

In the back of the building, they did find a window open and climbed in. With all the lights off, the school was kind of spooky.

They made it to the gym with no trouble. This so-called caper was turning out to be boringly easy. They flipped on the lights, and the gym was still in full under-the-sea mode.

Kairi hurried to the stage and tried to find the helmet. Where had she left it? She got down on all fours and crawled under the stage.

"What are you two doing here?" a man's voice asked. "And how did you get in?"

"Ah," Dakota said.

"We're on the cleanup committee," past-her said.

"Yeah, the cleanup committee," Dakota said. "We're totally on the cleanup committee."

"It's about time someone started to clean this mess up," he said. "But, where's your faculty sponsor? And why wasn't it on the schedule?"

"Ah," Dakota said.

"Ah," past-Kairi said.

"I'm going to have to escort you ladies out," the security-minded guy said.

Soon, he'd frog-marched them out of the room and turned off the lights.

In the dark, Kairi heard him lock the doors behind him.

Craptastic.

Chapter Twenty-Four
Kyle: Sydney, Australia, 2019

After a night of drinking and philosophizing at Liam's flat, Kyle woke with a pounding headache. When he stumbled into the living room, he found Liam sitting on the leather couch, flipping through the channels on TV, wearing only a shit-eating grin.

"Mate!" Kyle said. "Put some shorts on. I don't want to look at that."

"You don't appreciate me in the nuddy?" Liam's grin got wider. "Jealous?" He made no move to cover his junk, and it did match the rest of his large physique. Then he stopped grinning and said, "Huh."

Kyle would never admit it to him, but he may have been a little bit jealous of Liam's lack of shame. He wasn't jealous of Liam's junk. It practically made him a circus freak, or whatever the porn equivalent was. "Huh, what?"

Liam got up and sauntered to the kitchen. "Come on, I'll make you a cuppa."

Kyle averted his eyes. He wanted to tell him to put some shorts on again, but if he was willing to risk his donger with boiling water, he guessed that was his choice. On the bright side, the counter would block the view. Kyle sat down at the breakfast bar. "Thanks." He yawned.

Liam put on the kettle and got out the mugs, tea, and milk. "I'm getting that feeling where you feel like you've done something before. What's that called?"

"Déjà vu?" Kyle finally started waking up. They had done this all before--in the other timeline. In fact, this was very similar to the scene the morning after Liam's foursome. Ugh. He wasn't going to bring that up again; Liam enjoyed it too much.

"What's wrong, mate?" Liam asked.

"What?"

"You're making a funny face, like a grimace."

"Sorry," Kyle said. Don't mention the foursome. Don't mention it. "Guess I'm hungover." Come to think of it, why was it Liam never seemed to get hungover no matter how much he drank?

Liam just grinned. The kettle whistled, and he started pouring.

"Why aren't you?" Kyle poured some milk into his tea. "You drank more than me last night."

"C'mon. I'm twice your size. Ergo, I can drink twice as much as you."

Kyle couldn't help laughing as he blew on his tea. Little droplets spewed onto the counter. "Ergo? What, did you sleep with a dictionary last night? Or a librarian?" But laughing made his head hurt more. Ow.

"Don't try to change the subject," Liam said.

"What subject? The hangover subject?"

"You said you were going to Travel back to the 2004 embassy bombing in Jakarta and stop it," Liam said.

Jakarta? What about saving his parents? "I don't remember that." It did sound cool, though. Kyle succeeded in getting a sip of tea. "Do you have any aspirin?"

Liam rummaged in a drawer, pulled out a bottle of aspirin and threw it at Kyle.

Kyle managed to catch it. Barely. "Thanks." He popped three into his mouth and chased them down with some more tea. "Don't you have to go to work?"

"Don't you?"

Kyle was sick of work, aka doing nothing, aka waiting for Ray to die. "I need a new job."

"What? You'd stop working for your uncle Ray? How? Aren't you the crown prince or something?"

Kyle nodded. "Yeah, or something. And being the prince sucks."

"Sounds awesome to me."

"Think about it."

Liam shut up and sipped his tea for a moment. "Oh, yeah.

You're waiting for your uncle to cark it. That does suck." He paused and then grinned yet again. "So, Jakarta?"

Kyle considered it for a moment. "I said I was going to go on a mission? I said I was going to accomplish something?" He was starting to remember the conversation last night and several others over the last weeks and months in this timeline. With Ray, they tended to involve requests like 'Can't I go on a mission?' With Liam, they tended to involve whinging, 'The company is stupid with its little corporate missions. Why can't we do something important?'

Liam nodded.

Kyle did need to practice Traveling if he was going to go back and successfully save his parents--as opposed to making everything worse and worse, which was all he'd done so far.

Screw Time Advantages, Inc. He was ready to branch out on his own. "Jakarta is problematic because it requires an actual airline ticket to Jakarta. Remember, despite the name, Traveling doesn't actually involve moving geographically."

Liam shrugged. "So? You've taken trips before."

"But they were on the company. I can't get the company to pay for an unauthorized mission. Do you have the dollars lying around to buy the ticket? I know I don't."

Liam shook his head and took another slurp of tea. "What about the 1978 Sydney Hilton bombing?"

Kyle didn't remember much about the conversation last night, but saving the Hilton did sound familiar. They must have discussed it. And staying in Sydney sounded easy. "Did we talk about it last night?"

"You know it, mate. You can do it, too. You're a superhero."

Kyle didn't feel like a superhero, but the idea of Liam thinking he was a superhero did sound good. And the idea of some sheilas, er, women, thinking he was a superhero sounded even better. He knew Liam would brag and tell them all about it.

He was sick of waiting for his life to start. He wanted to do something. "I'll probably regret this, but okay."

Kyle leaned back on the couch. "I am The Dreaming." All this, the words, the relaxed state, were symbols, triggers that put Kyle in touch with eternity. He'd been training his whole life for this moment, for this eternity. Images flashed before his mind: in the car with Liam after seeing the graves, walking up the gravel walkway, seeing and smelling every bush, flower, and blade of grass in the cemetery.

He tried to speed things up and saw days of training that blurred into weeks and months, and before that university and hanging out with Liam, and before that more training and secondary school, training and primary school, pre-school, and then things got weird. Everything was sort of blurry; there seemed to be random colors, lights, shapes, and noises. Then there was a period of darkness with a loud drumbeat.

Then, blackness. He couldn't push back any further. It was like a colorless impenetrable wall.

He moved forward in time, back to the darkness with the drum and tried to focus on that. He forced himself to wake up and open his eyes.

A woman screamed. "Where did you come from?"

Where was he? Kyle tried to understand what was going on. The screaming woman was wearing all white. "Please stop screaming," he said. She must be a nurse.

"But you popped out of the air, out of nowhere," she said, face red, chin trembling and finger pointing.

"What's the date?"

"What do you mean what's the date? That's not right. You're not right." She looked around wildly in what Kyle now saw was a hallway in hospital. "Security! Help! Security!"

As soon as Kyle moved, he felt very dizzy, but he stumbled away. It wouldn't do to get in trouble here, wherever, er, whenever, it was. He lurched to the stairs and blundered down towards the ground floor. As he moved around, he began to feel less dizzy. By the time he was tramping down the ground floor hallway, he felt almost normal. He strolled out the front doors, and no one tried to stop him.

He stopped at the newspaper machines outside and leaned down. The front of The Sydney Morning Herald heralded the date: November fifteenth, 1994. "Huh." Kyle straightened up. It was not 1978. Obviously, he was not going to stop the Sydney Hilton bombing.

It was the day he was born. "What the hell?" he said.

"That's my line," a deep male voice said behind him.

When Kyle turned around, it was the nurse from upstairs, accompanied by two hospital security guards.

"That's him, officer!" a woman said. "He popped out of thin air. There's something wrong about him. He was around the delivery ward and the babies, asking weird questions and acting crazy. He's not a father or relative of a baby. I know all of them. He doesn't belong here."

"Whoa." Kyle held up his hands. "I just got lost. I wasn't doing anything. I wouldn't hurt any mothers or babies."

"Yeah, kid," one of the guards said. "That's what they all say."

"But, seriously?" Kyle was about to say his mother was upstairs right now giving birth to him, but he realized that wouldn't help his case.

"We're calling the cops," the other guard said. "You can sort it out down at the police station."

"I swear, I wasn't doing anything wrong," Kyle said as another wave of dizziness broke over him.

"Maybe you were trespassing; maybe you weren't. We'll figure it out." Within moments the cops pulled up in a squad car, siren blaring, and Kyle was shoved into the back seat.

As they pulled away from the front of the hospital, he could only clutch the door and mutter, "How am I going to get out of this without getting into more trouble?"

Chapter Twenty-Five
Kairi: Boulder, Colorado, 2014

Locked in a high school gym, in the dark, in the past, Kairi was starting to feel sorry for herself.

Get a grip, Kairi! You can get out of here. First things first: find the helmet. She crawled under the stage, only smashing her head against the supports a few times before running into the helmet. Helmet, check.

The helmet was damaged, wires severed. Crap. Was it getting hard to breathe? No. It was just nerves.

Calm down, Kairi. You can do this.

Second things second: fix the helmet. She patted her pockets. She didn't have the tools. Duh, she was wearing different clothes. Where had the tools gone? She had no idea. Josh was going to kill her for losing his tools. Or maybe he wouldn't. Maybe he wouldn't remember giving her the tools. Maybe he wouldn't even remember her.

Her heart hurt. Was this what a heart attack felt like?

Breathe in, breathe out. Okay, the second thing is: get tools. This is a school. They must have some kind of tools here in the physics lab or something, right?

She very carefully walked to the doors of the gym in the dark. They were locked. They wouldn't budge.

Breathe.

Okay, the second thing is: get out of the gym. She looked around the dark room. Some windows let in a little illumination from the streetlights, but they were twenty feet off the ground. She couldn't tell for sure in the dim light, but it didn't look like they even opened.

She sat on the floor, leaning against one set of locked

doors. What now?

She stood up and pounded on the doors. "Help! Security guy! I'm trapped in the gym! Come let me out!" She pounded some more. "Help!" This had to be against the fire code. Eventually, she got tired of pounding.

No one came.

Breathe in, breathe out. Kairi yawned.

On the plus side, she was getting sleepy. If she couldn't get out of the gym through the doors, maybe she could get out another way. She did time travel without the helmet before.

She lay down and got right back up. The gym floor was very uncomfortable. She walked over to the stage, yanked off a big piece of its decorative skirt, wadded it up, and lay down again, using it as a pillow.

So, she wanted to go to sleep. And she wanted to have a lucid dream. She closed her eyes and focused on breathing and relaxing. Gradually her breathing slowed and evened out, and she dipped into dreamland.

In her mind's eye, she saw herself sneaking into the gym with past-her and Dakota, and Dakota saying, "Ooh, a caper. Count me in." That was the wrong way. She needed to go back to the future, not the past.

She saw herself getting an A on her English test. She saw herself graduating high school with honors and attending a big party. In the background, there was a weak memory of hanging out at Pam's house and toasting graduation with sparkling cider.

She saw herself attending the University of Colorado with a full scholarship but feeling very nervous about not knowing anyone. At the same time, she faintly remembered scraping the money and student loans together to go to CU.

She remembered meeting Jessica, who also was very nervous and how they initially hung out together out of desperation but eventually became true friends. She sat in lots of CU classes, did homework, took tests, and worried about keeping up her GPA. She went on dates with various guys, often double-dating with Jessica and her boyfriend Hank, but didn't really hit it off with anyone.

And she very faintly remembered Dakota introducing her to Josh and the two of them hitting it off immediately.

She saw herself staying at CU to study for spring break to maintain her grades and keep her scholarship.

And then nothing. It was as if a black curtain hung across her memory. "Wake up! Wake up!" She pinched herself, and it hurt. "Ow."

She sat up in bed. It was nighttime, but the drapes let through a little light, and she could see a poster of the Eiffel Tower and of Big Ben over her bed. Thank goodness she was home. Someone stirred in the other bed. "Dakota, what's the date?" she asked.

"Geez, Kairi," a female voice--not Dakota's--said. "Do you know what time it is?" The woman sat up. "And which Dakota? North or South?"

Kairi flipped on the reading light over her bed.

Her best friend Jessica rubbed her eyes. "What's with you?"

She'd been expecting to see her best friend from high school, Dakota. But she knew that wasn't right. She felt dizzy. Jessica was her roommate. Not Dakota. She lost touch with Dakota. The room was spinning.

Jessica got out of bed and leaned over her. "Are you okay? You look funny. Your skin's kind of grayish."

She'd just come back from time traveling, right? The room spun. She knew how to time travel, didn't she?

"Seriously, Kair," Jessica said. "You're starting to scare me. Say something."

"Uh, Jessica, you haven't noticed anything weird with me lately, have you?" she said.

"You mean besides you waking me up in the middle of the night and asking me the date and about weirdness?" She sat down on her bed. "Besides that?"

"Yeah," she said. "Anything else?"

"No," she said. "Go back to sleep." She lay down. "And turn out the light."

When Kairi woke up again, Jessica was gone, but she was definitely still in their room. Same two beds, two desks, two chairs, two dressers, same Twins and Vikings posters Hank had gotten Jessica over her bed. Logically, she knew it was their room. She could remember moving in, joking with Jessica and

Hank, but it didn't feel like home.

She missed Pam and Dakota. And especially Josh. But how could she miss a guy she'd never met? It was all very confusing.

She tried to call Dakota, but her number wasn't in her phone.

Neither was Josh's.

She called Pam.

"Kairi!" she said. "How's spring break going? Are you doing anything besides studying?" It was great to hear her voice.

"Spring break's okay," Kairi said.

"What's wrong?"

"I guess I'm a little homesick. I miss you and Dakota."

"Aw, that's sweet. I miss you guys, too."

"How are you doing? How are things going on the foster parent front?"

Pam updated her on all her doings.

"So, I don't seem to have Dakota's number," Kairi finally said. "I must have deleted it or something. Is she still in the dorm?"

"The dorm?" Pam asked.

"Yeah. The dorm. At CU."

Pam didn't say anything.

"The University of Colorado."

"Dakota's going to go to CU?" Pam asked. "That's great. That's wonderful. I'm so happy for her."

"What do you mean, going to go?" Kairi asked. "Doesn't she go to CU now?"

"No," Pam said. "Wow. You guys have lost touch, haven't you?"

"I don't get it. If she's not going to CU, what's she doing?"

Pam sighed. "Supposedly, she's working at a coffee shop, but every time I stop by, she's not there. All I know is she's living in a house on The Hill with a whole bunch of people. My guess is she's mostly getting high."

Kairi knew Dakota liked to party, but that sounded extreme. "What's her phone number?"

"I don't think she has a phone," Pam said. That wasn't good.

"If I get in touch with her, can we stop by your house?"

"Sure!" She could hear Pam smile. "Come for dinner. I'd

love to see you two."

Kairi had a very bad feeling about Dakota.

The bus dropped Kairi about a block from Dakota's purported digs, and she started walking. She wasn't familiar with the neighborhood, but the sweet scent of marijuana led her right to Dakota's house. The front door was wide open, and considering it was about forty-five degrees outside, that didn't seem like a good thing. "Hello?" she said as she walked right in. "Anybody home? Dakota?"

The living room sported a mismatched array of couches no doubt found on the side of the road. Everything reeked of pot. She was guessing there were a lot of drugs and drug users in this house. She hoped it was the wrong place, and Dakota wasn't here. "Hello?"

She heard some giggling coming from the back and walked through the kitchen. It had three ancient refrigerators, all broadcasting loud hums. It sounded like an airplane hangar. "Hello? Dakota?"

Dakota popped her dread head out of a doorway. Confusion morphed into delight on her face. "Kairi? Is that you? I haven't seen you in years! What are you doing here?"

Taking in her stained skirt and t-shirt combo and her bloodshot eyes, Kairi said, "I'm on spring break. What are you doing here?"

Dakota rushed to her, holding out her arms, and a wave of body odor spread out in front of her.

They hugged while Kairi managed not to breathe in. As soon as she could, she stepped away. "How's it going?" She waved her hand around the house.

"Good," Dakota said. "We're partying. Do you want to join us?"

Behind the refrigerator hum, she could hear more giggling from the bedroom. She peeked her head in and saw two twenty-something guys laying on a rumpled futon. The air was gray with smoke. "Uh, gosh, thanks, Dakota. I'm going to pass for now. I was going to go over to Pam's and get something to eat. Do you want to come?"

Dakota smiled brightly. "I could eat."

"Great. Let's go."

Dakota nodded and headed for the front door.

"Uh, do you have a jacket?"

"I think so." Dakota stepped back into the bedroom and rummaged around on the floor. She came out wearing a man's stained down coat. Kairi was just glad she had some kind of coat.

They headed for Pam's place, taking a shortcut through campus. As they walked along, Dakota kept up an almost nonsensical monologue, "Have you ever noticed how lonely trees look without their leaves?"

Kairi couldn't help worrying about her. What happened to her? Was she high all the time, now? How was she supporting herself? Thinking about those two guys, how was she paying her rent? What kind of future could she have?

Campus was pretty empty since it was spring break. Every once in a while, they'd see someone hurrying between buildings, probably faculty or maybe a grad student. Taking in the homogeneous red stone buildings, she felt strangely homesick. There, outside the UMC, near the fountain, she had a hazy memory of her first kiss with Josh. But it hadn't happened in this timeline.

But why did she still remember it? And why did she miss him so much? It was as if there was a hole in her soul where he used to be.

She and Dakota strolled around the chemistry building, past the art building and ATLAS Center, and crossed eighteenth street. As they passed the Laboratory for Atmospheric and Space Physics, she started to get a feeling...

Dakota said, "Are you even listening to me, Kairi?"

Kairi turned to look at her and smacked right into someone. "Sorry," she mumbled. When she looked up, she saw Josh, complete with his gray-blue eyes and unruly dark-brown hair.

"Josh!" she cried. Her arms rested on his warm chest, and she didn't want to extricate herself from him, ever.

He took a step back and frowned. "Do I know you?"

Chapter Twenty-Six
Kyle: Sydney, Australia, 1994

Stuck in his past, on the day of his birth, things went from bad to worse when Kyle got to booking at the police station. The police demanded his ID and, still dizzy, he gave them his driver's license.

At first, he didn't understand why the officer started laughing so hard. For that matter, he didn't understand why he was in 1994. He didn't understand any of this.

"What?" Kyle asked.

"It says your date of birth is today, and the license was issued in 2014!" The officer started guffawing again. "Didn't you even check the date, mate?" He held it up to the light, tilting it up and down. "This doesn't even look realistic. Why does it have two pictures? And what's this shiny bit?" He laughed again. "Hey, Peter, come see. It's the worst fake ID yet."

Fake ID? He didn't need a fake ID. How could they think he was seventeen or younger? He was twenty-five, for Christ's sake. But giving the cop his ID from the future was a stupid mistake.

A second officer came over, looked at Kyle's ID and started laughing. "You're right, Clive." He glanced behind him. "John, take a squizz at this."

Clive? Kyle knew their Time Advantages security guard had started as a police officer, and he did work in Sydney back in the day. Could it be the same guy? He stared at the first officer. His blue eyes did look very familiar.

A third officer came over and started laughing.

Kyle's irritation turned into a plan. If they thought he was underage, he might as well play it up. Eventually, they'd have to put him in a cell, and then hopefully, he could Travel as soon as he nodded off.

After all the chortling petered out, Clive said, "So, what's your real name, son? Is it even Kyle?"

Kyle tried to sound like he was lying, "Yeah, Kyle, ah, Baroda, er, Barada. Yeah, that's it."

"Come on, son," Clive said. "Tell the truth."

"That's the truth."

"Give us your name and your folks' phone number."

Even if Kyle had known his parents' phone number back in 1994, he knew they weren't home. They were at hospital at his birth. "I'm Kyle Baroda, and I'm, ah, twenty-five."

They went back and forth a few more times, but Kyle stuck to his hopefully unconvincing story, and Clive put him in a cell by himself--protecting him from the adult offenders, no doubt. That was fine with Kyle. It meant he got the cot, its pillow, and scratchy blanket all to himself in relative peace and quiet.

He lay back and closed his eyes. He tried to calm his mind. He focused on his breathing. "I can access The Dreaming," he whispered. "I have the power. I can feel all of time flowing through me. I am The Dreaming."

In his mind's eye, he couldn't focus. He kept wondering, why did he Travel to 1994 rather than 1978? According to theory, he should have access to all of time when he was in The Dreaming. What was that colorless wall he couldn't pass? How much more didn't he know about Dreaming?

And why did he run into Clive? Was there some weird Traveling rule that caused you to run into people you already knew? If so, why hadn't they covered it in training?

After many minutes, he opened his eyes and sat up. He wasn't going anywhere. "Bloody hell."

Clive was standing next to the cell, staring at him through the bars. "Did you have a nice nap?"

Kyle shrugged. "Not really."

Clive nodded and rubbed his chin. "Yeah, a guilty conscience will do that to you."

"Whatever."

"Whatever, what?" he asked, squinting his eyes.

Apparently, Kyle's twenty-first-century slang was confusing

the man. Kyle just shrugged again.

"So, we called all the Barodas and Baradas in the phone book," Clive said. "A David Barada was very alarmed and then confused when we said we had a Kyle Barada in custody. He seemed to think we were the hospital at first."

David Barada? That must be his dad's dad. Kyle had never met his grandfather. "Oh?" This couldn't be good.

"Yeah. And then he said he'd be right down. Immediately or sooner." Clive grinned. "Someone's in trouble."

Kyle didn't like the sound of that. According to Dad, his dad David had been a strict disciplinarian. "Are you sure you can't let me go? I learned my lesson. I made a mistake with the fake ID. I'm sorry. It'll never happen again. Maybe I could pay a fine?"

Clive laughed. "Are you sure your money isn't from 2014, too? You better check your wallet." He leaned back and crossed his arms. "Your dad was mad as a cut snake. I think I'm going to enjoy seeing your reunion." He ambled out back towards the front of the station.

An officer yelled, "Barada," and approached Kyle's cell, jingling some keys. "Your dad's here, and he's spewin'." He grinned.

Yeah, his grandfather was mad. Kyle got it.

The officer said, "I wouldn't want to be you. He was ropeable when we showed him your fake ID." He opened the cell door.

Kyle wasn't entirely sure he wanted to leave. His grandfather would know he was Traveling for sure. And he'd be pretty suspicious that it wasn't a sanctioned mission.

"Come on, kid."

Very slowly, Kyle trailed him to the front of the station.

When they got there, Clive was manning the front desk and grinning a mile wide. "Here he is, Mr. Barada. Kyle Barada--born today." He started laughing.

The other officers joined in.

David Barada resembled his son, Riley: skin the same shade of warm brown, same haircut close to the scalp, similar flat nose. But Kyle had never seen his dad look so angry. David's forehead and the bridge of his nose wrinkled, and his teeth were visible behind his tense lips.

"Ah, hi, ah, Dad," Kyle said. "I'm sorry," he added before David said anything.

"Hi, son," David said as if holding in a raging inferno. "I paid your fine. Get your stuff. We're going."

Kyle scooped his wallet and phone up from the counter. "Ah, yes, sir." Based on his dad's stories and David's obvious anger, Kyle was careful to stay out of arms' reach.

The policemen hooted as they exited, and Clive called out, "I better not see you here again, Kyle."

Kyle didn't answer him. He was too worried about what David might do.

David didn't say anything further as they walked a dozen yards from the entrance. The silence was overbearing. As he walked down the sidewalk behind him, Kyle felt like he was trying to pick his way between landmines. "I'm sorry for the trouble, Grandpa. I'm your grandson, Kyle, by the way. Thanks for coming to get me."

David whirled around, glowering. "Don't thank me, you little shit. You're a bloody problem. You could have ruined everything with your little joy ride. You're not supposed to be Traveling. Our whole business, our whole legacy, depends on discretion. And now the cops know about us." David breathed heavily.

"They don't know anything," Kyle said. "What do they know?"

"We're on their radar, you little shit." David lunged toward him.

The next thing Kyle knew, he was lying on the concrete sidewalk, gravel cutting into his hands, having trouble seeing. He shook his head. Big mistake. Pain pierced his left temple. What happened?

When his mind finally cleared enough for things to make sense, Kyle looked around and was surprised to see David lying on the concrete next to him.

He wasn't yelling anymore.

Face pale, David stared from his right hand to Kyle to his hand and back to Kyle. "I don't bloody believe it." He clutched at his stomach and puked onto the sidewalk. Shaking and sweating, he said, "The bloody rules are true."

"Grandpa?" Kyle patted his pockets for his mobile to call an ambulance. When he found it, it said, No signal. Duh.

David's eyes closed as he flailed on the ground.

"Help!" Kyle said. "Somebody help him! He needs a doctor!" But there was no one passing by. With difficulty, Kyle got to his feet and lurched towards the police station. "Help!"

When he was a couple of feet from the door, Clive poked his head out. "What? What's wrong?"

Kyle pointed at his grandfather lying on the ground. "My grand, er, my dad's hurt."

Clive ran over to David, leaned down, and checked for a pulse. His face stilled, and he gazed over at Kyle, shaking his head slightly. He stood up and walked to Kyle. "I'm sorry, son. He's gone."

"Bloody hell." Kyle stared at the ground, eyes filling.

Clive asked, "What happened, son?" He seemed to be staring at Kyle's temple. "How are you feeling?"

Kyle was dizzy, and his head hurt. "I?" Now was not the time to get into that. "I'm okay." He looked up at Clive and then down at David. "He was yelling at me. He got all worked up. The next thing I knew, he was lying on the ground, groaning and clutching his chest." That was sort of what happened. Bloody hell. He killed his grandfather.

Even after everything that had happened, Kyle hadn't truly believed Traveling was so dangerous. The brief contact of David's fist with Kyle's Traveling head had apparently made David drop dead. He'd heard Grandpa David died on the day he was born, but he'd had no idea it was all his fault.

What would have happened if he hadn't Traveled here? Would Grandpa still be alive? But that contradicted family history.

"Son?" Clive was still talking to him. "Are you going to be okay here for a few minutes? I have to do some things."

"Yeah." Kyle contemplated David. "Are you sure he's gone?"

"Yes." Clive nodded. "I'm sure. I'll be back in a few minutes. You stay right there, son."

Like that was going to happen. As soon as Clive stepped inside, Kyle quickly crossed the street and ducked into an alley. There was no scenario where him sticking around was going to be good. The next thing you knew, he'd be touching and killing his grandmother, dad, or mom here in 1994. Kyle had to get away, far away.

He had to get far a-when. He had to get back to his present. Hopefully, he could still Travel.

Chapter Twenty-Seven
Kairi: Boulder, Colorado, 2019

Kairi found herself standing in front of Josh outside the Physics Building in 2019, but he didn't seem to recognize her. She definitely recognized him: they'd dated for months, and he asked her to marry him. He was the love of her life. But, wait, she felt dizzy. None of that had happened even though she remembered it. Her heart was breaking, and her knees buckled.

Josh caught her. "Are you all right?"

Did he feel their special connection, too? Maybe she hadn't ruined everything between them with her time traveling.

"Seriously, say something," he said. "Or I'm going to have to call an ambulance."

"Josh, it's so good to see you again," she said, still in his arms.

He pushed her upright. "How do you know my name? What do you mean, see me again?"

Dakota snickered.

This was not going well. Kairi stood up straight. "I'm just saying, thank you for your help here." She made a little circle with her finger. "And, uh, I make it a point to know all the handsome guys on campus." Yikes, did she actually say that?

"Handsome?" He peered at her and Dakota in turn.

Dakota nodded at him.

"Ah, okay." Josh took a step away from them. "Whatever." He took another step. "You should watch where you're going." He started walking away.

That was it? What happened to their connection? It was like they were strangers. And then it hit her they really were strangers--at least from his perspective.

He didn't even look back as he continued on with his life. Kairi couldn't help wondering where he was going and who he was going to. As she stood there and watched him walk away, her heart broken into a million teeny-tiny pieces.

After a few moments, Dakota poked her. "Are we going to Pam's or what?"

Was that where they were headed? "Yes. Off to Pam's. Here we go. It'll be fun to see her, huh?"

Dakota nodded.

As they walked the rest of the way across campus, Kairi reviewed her memories of Josh that had never happened, from Dakota introducing them, to him handing her a filled champagne flute as they toasted their engagement. It had been amazing; they felt such a connection. In that timeline, Josh helped her work through her relationship issues; he'd been the first guy she really loved.

In this timeline, she never had any issues to work through, but she was still waiting for love. That didn't seem fair.

Back in real life, dizzy, she stopped short, and Dakota ran into her. "What?" Dakota asked.

Kairi could feel the earth spinning on its axis. "I need to sit down."

Dakota led her to a bench. "What's wrong?"

In this timeline, she never had any issues with sex because she stopped Chad before anything bad happened. How could doing the right thing lead to the wrong thing? Why was she so unsuccessful in love now? None of this stuff made any sense.

Dakota said, "Hey! Kairi, you're starting to scare me."

Everything spun around, and she clutched the bench. "I'm starting to scare me, too."

"Maybe that Josh guy was right about the ambulance. Should we call one?" Dakota asked. "Or should we call Pam?"

"Just give me a minute." She breathed deeply. "It's March 2019, right?"

Dakota nodded.

"I'm fine," she said. "It's just a minor freak-out. It's March. I'm on spring break, just like any other normal college kid. I'm totally fine. There's nothing weird going on here."

Dakota scrunched up her nose. "If you have to say nothing

weird's going on, it's probably not a good sign, Kair."

High Dakota was making more sense than her. Something weird was going on here. Breathe, Kairi. She took a deep breath and let go of the bench. She carefully stood up. "Okay. Here we go. To Pam's house." She started walking, and after a couple of seconds, Dakota followed.

A little later, Pam opened her front door as they came up the walk. "There you are!" She beamed like she was happy to see them.

Kairi felt a spark of joy. She was with people who cared about her, Dakota and Pam. They were like a family, even if technically they weren't one.

She reached out to Pam's ample form and hugged her. "Thanks."

Pam looked a little uncertain. "Thanks for what?"

"Just thanks for being you," she said. "I appreciate you letting us come to visit. This feels right."

"Me, too," Dakota said. "I agree with Kairi. Thanks."

"You're welcome. Come on in." Pam stepped out of the doorway and gestured them in.

The whole evening at Pam's, from the spaghetti dinner, to doing the dishes, to watching TV afterward, was delightfully familiar. At about ten p.m., when they should have gone their separate ways, Kairi couldn't bear the thought of Dakota returning to that drug house.

"Pam, what would you say to a sleepover?" she asked.

Pam's gaze passed over Dakota's homeless appearance, and she made herself smile. "Sure. It sounds fun."

And so the familiarity continued as Dakota, and she got ready for bed. Her bedroom looked the same and yet different.

"Kairi?" Dakota asked. "Are you asleep yet?" This was just like their sleepovers when they were girls.

"We went to bed two minutes ago; how could I be asleep already?"

"I wanted to thank you for coming to get me. This is, like, my best spring break ever."

Hanging out with her and Pam was the best? Briefly, she considered saying, You have to be going to school to go on spring break, but instead, she said, "Good. I'm glad."

"That Josh guy was cute, huh?"

"Do you think so?" She longed to see him again, which was crazy. She barely knew him.

Dakota was silent.

"Dakota?"

She yawned. "I was nodding."

Nodding is pretty hard to see in the dark. Kairi grinned. "Night."

"Night."

She lay there stewing for a while. Why didn't Josh and she hit it off today? Or alternately, why did they hit it off in that other timeline when Dakota introduced them? She'd thought they were soulmates, destined to be together no matter what, but now her faith in them was badly shaken.

This whole time travel thing was crazy, but she couldn't believe stopping a rape was a mistake.

Finally, Kairi got out of bed and went back into the living room to think. Her memory of meeting Josh about a year ago in that other timeline was overwritten by her current timeline. A year ago in this timeline, she'd just been hanging out with Jessica and Hank and studying.

She could still remember the other timeline, but it was fainter than her current timeline. In the now-obsolete timeline, she'd gotten a freak-out phone message from Dakota saying she was going to drop out of school. But a little later, when she found her outside the Math building, she seemed fine. She was with Josh and introduced the two of them. Then the three of them went for coffee. Josh asked her out, and the rest was history. She sighed. Or at least it had been history.

Maybe the key was meeting Josh a year ago?

If she got the hang of this time travel stuff, she should be able to arrange that, shouldn't she?

She went back to bed, determined to time travel back to a year ago and meet Josh. She closed her eyes and willed herself to sleep. In her lucid dream, she rewound back to March seventeenth, 2018 and then pinched herself awake in the morning of the day she met Josh.

Ouch. She woke in her dim dorm room, curtains drawn, apparently in bed with herself. Gingerly, she lifted the covers and started slipping out of bed. As past-her stirred, she froze. But past-her just turned over.

Lacking a better plan, she decided to go to the spot where she'd first met Josh and wait for him there.

Then, she realized she was only wearing the big t-shirt she'd worn to bed at Pam's. Ugh. Note to self: get dressed before future time jaunts. She grabbed some sweatpants and a sweatshirt out of her laundry and her jacket and tennis shoes out of the closet, threw them on and snuck out the door.

She parked herself on the famous-to-her (where she'd met Josh) bench. After many very long uneventful minutes, she felt as if she was freezing to death.

Eventually, she saw him exit the Physics Building and start to head her way. She stood up as her heart labored in her chest. As he approached, she plastered her best smile on her face-- perfected from years of trying to entice foster parents to adopt her.

As he passed by, he glanced over at her, but he didn't smile back or even slow down.

She opened her mouth to say, Josh, it's me, Kairi. We're supposed to meet now and fall madly in love. But if she said that, he'd think she was some kind of crazy stalker. She closed her mouth. There was nothing she could say that wouldn't sound crazy or stalker-y.

She watched in silence as the love of her life walked away. Her heart broke again.

When she couldn't see him anymore, she sat back down on the bench.

This was going to be harder than she thought.

The timing was important, but the circumstances had to be right, too.

Just going up to him wouldn't work. She needed to get Dakota to introduce them. But how did she do that? And where was past-Dakota? Shouldn't she be here now?

Step one was to find Dakota in this time. She wracked her brain but had no clue where Dakota might be in March 2018.

Presumably, past-her would know where Dakota was, but she'd been anything but cooperative back in 2014.

Maybe Pam would have an idea? She needed to call Pam.

But she didn't have her cell phone. And would her calling plan even work now? Doubtful.

Okay, she needed to go back to past-her's room and talk to her or use her phone.

Unfortunately, when she got to the dorm, the building was locked, and she couldn't get in.

She tried to squelch her feelings of frustration. She could time travel. Surely, she could overcome one measly locked door.

A very tall guy walked up to the front door.

"Hey, stilts." She grinned.

He scowled.

"You on the basketball team?"

He unlocked the door.

She tried to sneak through.

"Do you live here?" he asked.

"Uh, yeah."

"I don't recognize you." He pulled the door shut behind him. So much for her charm.

Locked outside in the past with no friends, family, or phone, Kairi shivered in the cold.

Chapter Twenty-Eight
Kyle: Sydney, Australia, 1994

On the street, on his literal birth day, Kyle could still hardly believe he'd killed his grandfather just by coming in contact with him.

And if that wasn't bad enough, his temple still throbbed where Grandpa punched him. He touched it gingerly, and his fingers came back bloody.

Someone nudged his shoulder. "Are you all right?" a woman asked.

Kyle jerked away. "Don't touch me! I'm dangerous!"

She frowned at him. "You don't look dangerous. You look hurt. Please let me help you. Let me take you to hospital." She started to reach for him again, but he lurched away.

"Go away. I don't want to hurt you, too."

She backed up, holding her hands in front of her. "Okay. I'll leave you alone if you promise you'll go to hospital on your own."

Kyle stared at her. He'd first assumed the woman was around his age, but her crow's feet made him revise upwards to middle age. But she seemed genuinely concerned for him. "Okay," he said. "I'm going."

She dipped her head. "Thank you." She turned away but then turned back around. "God bless you." After hesitating for another moment, she turned and walked away.

Kyle frowned. She wouldn't say that if she'd known what he'd done. Then, since he'd promised and since he didn't have any better ideas, he went back to hospital, where he was busy being born.

The front entrance still bustled with people coming and going, but the security guards that had ratted him out earlier were gone. Kyle marched inside the emergency room, wiping blood from his face. He approached the admissions desk.

The nurse sitting there looked alarmed when she saw him. "Sir, are you all right? What happened?"

"Ah." Kyle wasn't sure what to say. *I just killed my grandfather, but he got in a good punch to my head before he died? Or, I'm Kyle Barada, being born right now upstairs? Or I'm a time traveler?* "I don't know?"

The nurse stood up. "You better come back at once." She pointed at him over the counter, and another nurse came out through the swinging double doors. The new nurse started to reach for his arm.

Kyle jerked back. "Don't touch me!" He paused. He knew he was in trouble and needed to be more careful about what he said. "Ah, don't touch me, please. It hurts."

"Come on back, young man." She led him through the doors. "Let's have a Captain Cook. We'll get you sorted."

Kyle stared at her. Something about her was familiar.

She led him to a bed and then pulled some flowered curtains around it. "Get on, young man."

He did. When he leaned back in the relatively private bed, he felt himself relax.

"Now, what's your name, young man?"

There was no good answer. "Ah, I'm not sure."

"Oh, dear," she said. "I'd better go get the doctor right away."

When Kyle came to, his head didn't hurt as much. He touched his temple gently and ran his finger across coarse stitches. He was still in bed, surrounded by the same floral curtains. In the distance, a man yelled, slurring his speech. Since he was lying down and relatively comfortable, now was as good a time as ever to try to Travel home.

Kyle calmed his mind. He focused on his breathing. "I can access The Dreaming," he said. "I have the power. I can feel all of time flowing through me. I am The Dreaming."

In his mind's eye, he saw himself talking to the kind middle-aged woman on the street. He saw his grandfather clutching his stomach, puking, shaking and sweating. "The bloody rules are true."

He was in jail. He was in hospital. The events of his life blurred together until he found himself leaning back on Liam's couch.

"Bloody hell!" Liam said. "Where did you go?" He approached the couch. "And what happened to your head, mate? Ouch. Did you come a gutser?"

"Yeah, I had an accident." Kyle sat up. "What day is it?"

"It's the same day you left to fix the 1978 Sydney Hilton bombing." Liam's eyebrows drew together. "Hey, wait, I remember that. So, it didn't work? Why didn't it work?"

"I accidentally killed my grandfather instead."

Liam sank to the couch, and his mouth fell open. Finally, he said, "Shite. You did come a gutser."

Kyle nodded. "Yeah."

"What happened?"

"I met my grandfather; he bailed me out of jail. Then we got into a fight, and he died. Because he touched me."

"Shite."

"Yeah."

Liam held up his finger. "But how does that work? How did you think your grandfather died before?"

"I always heard he died of a heart attack on the day I was born. I just didn't know time traveling-me was the reason. Until now."

"Fuckin' shite."

"Yeah."

"What are you going to do?"

Kyle rubbed his hands together. "The first thing I'm going to do is get a cup of tea and something to eat, and then I'm going to stop myself from going on the mission I just went on."

"Okay," Liam said. "I guess I'll put on the kettle."

Kyle drank a cup of tea, ate a sandwich, and then didn't have any more excuses. He had to try to put right what he'd put wrong. He had to at least try to save his grandfather.

He went back over to the couch and lay back.

Liam followed him into the family room. "So, what are you going to do?"

"I'm going to go back to right before I left and stop myself."

"What will I see? Two of you?"

"Yeah." At least Kyle thought that would be what happened.

"Okay." He paused. "So, then, will we have this conversation? Or will it be wiped out somehow?"

"I think it'll be wiped out. You won't remember this."

In his mind's eye, Kyle saw himself leaning back on the couch. He saw himself say, "I am The Dreaming."

He went back a little further and saw himself say, "I'll probably regret this, but okay."

He saw Liam say, "You know it, mate. You can do it, too. You're a superhero."

Now! He appeared next to himself in the living room.

Liam stumbled over his own feet and fell to the floor. "Fair suck of the sav! There's two of you." He pointed at Kyle and Kyle.

Kyle said to his past self, "Kyle, don't go! Don't Travel! You're about to kill your grandfather."

Past-Kyle said, "What? Kill? I'm not trying to kill anyone. How? Why? What are you doing here?" He took a step toward Kyle.

Kyle was unsteady and trying to take a step back, instead lurched towards Past-Kyle, his fingertips brushing his hand.

Suddenly, it felt like he was being turned inside out. The pain was excruciating. His last thought before everything went black was: so this is death.

When Kyle came to, his whole body ached, especially his head. He must not be dead. Death couldn't hurt this much.

He brushed his temple, and his stitches had disappeared. Did that mean he'd undone the fight with Grandpa David?

He was in a bed in some kind of private room. Where the hell was he? When the hell was he? He'd lost track.

Something squelched in the corner of the room. His uncle leaned forward in an uncomfortable-looking chair. "Ah. So, you didn't die after all."

"Uncle Ray? What are you doing here? What happened? How long have I been here?"

"You've been here, in a coma, for about three weeks. It's

2019, by the way. I know you've been Traveling. As far as we can tell, you touched your past self. I've been terrified you were going to die and at the same time furious that you did this to yourself. You know the rules about personal Traveling and interacting with yourself. I didn't know you could even Travel without The Dreaming Room. You're lucky to be alive. Frankly, I'm not sure why you survived."

"I almost died? Why didn't I?"

Ray shrugged.

What the heck had he been up to? It was something about his Grandfather. "What about Grandfather? Is he alive?"

His uncle got up out of the chair, scowling. "No." He paused as Kyle's words registered. "Wait. What do you mean is Grandfather alive?" Blood rushed to his uncle's face. "He's not alive. Did you try to save him? Is that what caused this whole mess?"

Kyle drew back from his uncle's wrath. Ray had more in common with Grandfather than he'd thought.

"Did you do something?" His uncle clenched his fists. "What did you do?"

Lying seemed like a good idea at this point. "I didn't do anything. I'm not sure what's going on, Ray," Kyle said. "But I'm glad to see you. You look good. Are you good?" He paused. "I love you." It couldn't hurt to lay on the charm.

Ray gave him a long look. "I love you, too, Kyle." He took a breath and sank back down in the chair. "I'm glad you're alive." He sighed and rested his head in his hands. After a few minutes, he lifted his head. "Since you can't be trusted not to interact with yourself, I think we have to get you out of town. I don't want you to die. In fact, the farther, the better."

What about his training and the company? What about his friends and family? How could he leave it and them all behind?

On the other hand, Traveling seemed to be nothing but trouble.

"I'm exiling you to the other side of the planet."

Exile? Bloody hell. That didn't sound good. Not good at all.

Chapter Twenty-Nine
Kairi: Boulder, Colorado, 2018

Kairi couldn't believe she was having so much trouble getting into her own dorm. Granted, it was a year in her past, and she didn't have her key, but still.

Eventually, she slipped into the dorm when someone was slipping out.

The door to her room was locked. Of course. She pounded on the door. "Is anyone there? I locked myself out." She really hoped someone was home.

Kairi heard the lock turn and saw the door swing open.

Past-her stood in the doorway. Her kinky hair was askew, and she looked grumpy. "I was wondering when you'd show up again," she said. "What's about to go wrong?"

She glanced nervously down the hall. "Are you going to let me in? What if someone sees us together?"

"Then I guess I introduce them to my twin sister," she said, but stepped out of the way, gestured her inside, and closed the door after them. "So, what's wrong?"

Kairi plopped down on the bed in front of her Big Ben poster.

"Are you wearing my clothes?" past-her asked.

"Uh."

"No wonder I couldn't find my jacket. And here I'd been cursing Jessica for borrowing it without asking."

"Sorry." She sighed.

"What's wrong? Why are you here?"

There was no help for it; she just needed to plunge in. If she didn't ask her to help find Dakota, she'd never hook up with Josh, and she'd never be happy. "You just missed meeting the love of your life."

"Seriously?" She stared at her. "Not meeting someone is the problem that made you travel through time?"

Kairi nodded. "Yes. So, I need your help to get things back on track."

Past-Kairi stared at her some more. She knew past-Kairi was torn because she knew what she would think. On the one hand, she thought she was being melodramatic, and she prided herself on being practical. On the other hand, she secretly wanted a family of her own more than anything. She watched past-Kairi's thoughts battle across her face. The tension grew.

Kairi wondered if maybe she could just remember what she'd done instead of waiting here and now in anticipation. She turned her memory back to a year ago, and the room started spinning. She clutched the bedspread as her stomach roiled. She leaned over the bed.

"What's wrong with you?" Past-her stood over her.

"I'm not entirely sure."

"Does time travel injure you?"

"I don't think so," she said. "It's more like it makes me dizzy and nauseated."

"When? All the time? Afterward, or during, or what?"

"I don't know." She tried to concentrate on the bedspread instead of her past. "Are you going to help me or not?"

"Okay," past-Kairi said.

Kairi carefully sat up. "Really?" She hadn't been too helpful back in 2014. She couldn't talk her out of going to the dance with Chad, and then she'd been trying to help her, to save her from being raped.

"Yes. Really." She scowled at her. "You did save me from Chad."

This was too easy. Kairi narrowed her eyes. "What's the catch?" She'd called the cops on her in 2014.

"I'll help you if you teach me how to time travel."

Kairi's mind raced. She didn't know that much about time travel, but this did not sound like a good idea. What would happen to her if some other version of her changed her past? "Uh."

The other Kairi frowned. "Does time travel make you

stupid?"

She glared at her. "Nice." Behind her, on the dresser, she spied past-her's phone. That was all she needed to track down Dakota. She stood up. "No. Time travel doesn't make me stupid." She took a step towards the dresser. "I'm just here to try to help you." She took another step towards the dresser.

Past-her sat down in her desk chair. "No. You're here to help you. If you fix something here, it will be magically okay when you return to your time, right?"

Kairi took another step towards the dresser. "This will help you. Josh is a great guy, kind and smart." She lounged against the wall next to the dresser. "You need to meet him." The phone was within reach. All she needed to do was grab it and bolt out the door.

"Kind and smart? He sounds ugly."

"No." How could she say that about him? "He's totally hot." She thought about his long-lashed gray-blue eyes, his perfect smile, and his oh-so-firm pecs. In that now-gone timeline, she'd spent a lot of time with all his firm parts...

"Are you blushing?" Past-her glanced away from her. "Whatever."

But Kairi could tell she was intrigued.

"I want you to teach me to time travel," past-Kairi said again.

Kairi grabbed the phone, threw open the door, and ran down the hall, out the exterior door and across the parking lot. She crouched down behind a car, panting, peering at the door. Was past-her chasing her? Apparently not.

She sat on the curb and looked through the phone's stored numbers. No Dakota. Darn it. There were a few numbers of people she knew in high school. She started dialing.

Unfortunately, no one knew for sure where Dakota was. The only lead she'd gotten was disturbing. Somebody said they'd heard through the grapevine she'd been begging on The Hill. That had to be wrong, but it was the only lead she had, so she walked to the nearby business district.

On The Hill, at the first street corner, a guy wearing a filthy down jacket held up a piece of cardboard that said, Vet. Hungry. Please help. God bless America.

She walked up to him. "Hey, buddy."

"Hey." He held out his hand.

"Uh. Sorry. I don't have any cash." Crap. She didn't have any cash. Her stomach rumbled. She was really going to have to start doing a better job of planning her time travels. "I'm looking for a friend of mine, Dakota. She's white, twenty years old, and has blonde dreads. Usually high. I heard she hangs out around here." Dakota had been such a cheerful, sweet girl. Kairi remembered the way her eyes lit up when they'd giggled together. Could she truly be reduced to begging on street corners?

"Kota! Yeah, I know her." He rubbed his gray-stubble-encrusted cheeks. "She always shares her herbs." He grinned.

Crap. That did sound like her, generous to a fault. "Do you know where she is now?"

He shook his head. "Haven't seen her today. But she's usually down by the piercing and tattoo place."

"Thanks." Kairi wished she had some food or money to give him. But she didn't. "Thanks. Uh, God bless you."

He nodded. "God bless."

Now she was depressed. How did a sweet girl like Dakota end up begging outside a tattoo parlor? Was she too sweet? Had life beaten her down? Life didn't deal her a fair hand, that was for sure, what with no dad and a drug-addict mom.

As she came up on the tattoo and piercing parlor, it looked as if someone had dumped a bundle of rags in front of it. When the bundle moved, resolving into Dakota's too-thin figure and smiling face, Kairi's heart broke. She couldn't help thinking she'd failed her. How could she lose touch with her like this?

"Kairi!" Dakota beamed and struggled to get up. "Long time no see. How's it going?" Up close, she reeked.

"It's going okay." Kairi's voice caught in her throat. "Uh, how's it going with you?" Obviously, Operation Meet-Josh was derailed. She had to help Dakota.

"Good." As Dakota nodded her head, she resembled a too-skinny bird. "What'cha doing here?"

Kairi led her to a bench. "I heard you were here, and I thought I'd come by and say hi." Where had she gone wrong? She'd have to get all the info she could about Dakota now and then time travel back and fix it. "I apologize for losing touch with you. That was wrong of me."

"I missed you, Kairi."

"I missed you too, Dakota." Her eyes stung. "So, let's catch up. What have you been up to?" From Kairi's perspective, she'd just seen her in 2019 and back in 2014 when they'd had their caper with past-her. "Do you remember that time in high school when we snuck into the gym after the Enchantment Under the Sea dance?"

Dakota wrinkled her nose. "I thought there were two of you that night. But no one believed me."

Was that the beginning of her troubles? "I believe you, Dakota. I'm sorry about that. I want you to tell me everything that has happened to you since then." They settled in on the bench.

After a couple of hours, their stomach rumbles threatened to drown out their conversation. But Kairi couldn't buy the two of them anything to eat; she didn't have any money. All she had was past-her's phone.

She figured she might as well call past-her on their room phone and offer her the cell in return for lunch. So she did.

When she arrived, past-her's grumpy face transformed into horror before settling into fake cheerfulness. "Dakota! Wow. It's so good to see you."

"So, there are two of you?" Dakota said. "I knew it. I knew I wasn't crazy."

"You're not crazy," Kairi said.

"Who wants some lunch?" past-her asked and pointed at the pizza and burger joint, The Sink, on the corner.

Dakota looked around as if this question was too good to be true and then raised her hand. "I do."

Kairi and the past version of her followed Dakota to The Sink. "What happened to her?" past-her whispered.

"I think we happened to her."

Chapter Thirty
Kyle: Denver, Colorado, 2019

Newly arrived in Denver and in a wheelchair, Kyle was surprised to see his younger brother Oliver when the elevator doors opened at the airport. He was also surprised at how different Oliver looked. His too-big jeans sagged down, showing off his boxers. He had on pristine white sneakers, a spotless black hoodie with a logo-covered t-shirt poking out, and a too-small baseball cap was balanced on the top of his head. He looked like one of those American rappers.

The airline employee stopped the chair just outside the elevator. "Can you take it from here, sir?"

Kyle could tell the man wanted to get on with his day. "Yeah. Thanks for your help." He carefully levered himself out of the chair and struggled to keep his balance.

"Bro!" Oliver beamed. "You look like shit! Welcome to exile." He grabbed Kyle's carry-on bag from the employee. "You must have seriously fucked up to end up here!"

Kyle'd been awake for over twenty-four hours and had barely made his connection in L.A., so he wasn't at his brightest. On top of that, he was still feeling the physical effects of his coma. "Oliver? Why are you so cheerful? And what are you doing here?" As he took a step away from the elevator, everything hurt.

"Uncle Ray ordered me to pick you up, so here I am reporting for duty." He smiled and mock-saluted. "Sir. He said you were messed up from some accident, and he wasn't kidding. What happened?"

"I'm not supposed to tell you about my accident." Kyle was under strict orders from his uncle, and he wasn't about to disobey this one. He had a newfound respect for all the rules and regulations of Traveling.

"Come on, give me a hint," Oliver said.

Kyle ignored him. "What time is it? Is it day or night?"

Oliver glanced at his watch. "It's about two-thirty in the afternoon."

It felt like two-thirty in the morning. "Why are you in such a good mood? You can't be glad to see me." They weren't close. It had all stemmed from Mom and Dad's divorce. Oh, wait, that was the old timeline. In this timeline, Ray and Jessie raised them. Because Mom and Dad died when Kyle and Oliver were boys. Kyle froze as a wave of grief and guilt broke over him.

"Au contraire, bro." Oliver smiled again. "I'm very happy to see you. The crown prince is in disgrace. You're practically a mere mortal now. What'd you do?"

Crowds of people streamed around them to points unknown. Kyle had no intention of telling his brother about his Traveling mishaps. Oliver might want to try it for himself and, in the process, maybe get injured or even killed. He wasn't going to let that happen. "I can't tell you." They might not be super close, but he wasn't going to be responsible for his brother's coma or death. "In fact, let's just say, if I told you, I wouldn't have to kill you--you'd probably be dead already."

"Really? How so?" Oliver looked puzzled. "It's got to be something to do with Traveling, right? But you're not allowed to Travel. Uncle Ray's the designated Traveler." He paused, and then his eyes bugged out. "No way! Did you do some unauthorized Traveling? How? I didn't even know that was possible. Tell me!"

How did he get all that out of I can't tell you? Clearly, Kyle couldn't say another word about it. "Do you know where my luggage is? I wasn't paying attention."

"Yep. Right this way, sir." Kyle had never seen Oliver so happy as he led him towards the baggage carousels.

Kyle woke up as they pulled into a tiny driveway in front of a tiny brick ranch house. "Where are we?" Behind them towered the hulking Rocky Mountains. "Whoa. Mountains. Where'd they come from?"

"You snore, dude," Oliver said, turning off the car. "We're at my house, of course."

"Your house? How did we get here?"

Oliver snorted. "Shit. You're really out of it. I drove you here to my house from the airport in my car. You fell asleep."

"Asleep?" Kyle did feel slightly less exhausted. "I didn't go anywhere, did I?"

"Go anywhere? What are you talking about, dude?" Oliver popped the trunk and grabbed two of Kyle's bags. "Get the last one."

Kyle got his smallest bag and trudged after Oliver into the house.

Inside, Oliver dropped the bags in the tiny family room. "You get the couch." He pointed at a worn brown couch that had seen better days. "What do you want to do now? Do you want something to eat?"

"Actually, I'd love to just go to bed," Kyle said.

Oliver stared at him for a moment. "Yeah, okay. That trip is a bitch. For tonight, one night only, you can use my room." He walked down the hall a few steps and pointed inside an open door. "Here."

"Thank you, Oliver. I owe you one." Kyle made his way to the bed and collapsed.

When Kyle woke again, it was light outside, and he felt better. He stumbled to the bathroom and then out to the family room.

"Ah. Sleeping Beauty awakens!" On the couch, Oliver put down his video game controller. "I can't believe you slept so long. It's been twenty-four hours."

Kyle rubbed his face. Everything still hurt, but at least he didn't feel tired. "You, ah, didn't check on me, did you?" He didn't think he'd Traveled in the last twenty-four hours, but who the hell knew?

Oliver snickered. "Well, yeah."

"You didn't see anything strange, did you?"

"No. Why? I was starting to get worried you were dead or something."

Kyle felt the blood drain from his face. Did Oliver know something? How? And what did he know?

"Relax, dude," Oliver said. "No need to look so dire. I was just kidding about the dying thing."

Kyle was determined not to tell Oliver anything about Traveling that might put him in danger. If Oliver knew how easy it was to Travel, he might try it and die.

Oliver must have seen something in his face. "I was kidding about dying, wasn't I? Travelers don't die, do they?"

"Travelers do die," Kyle said. "I don't think I'm in any significant danger of dying. But, you never know." All it might take was one more episode of Traveling.

"Okay, dude."

"When you checked on me, I was there, in the bed, right?"

"Kyle? I'm starting to seriously worry about your mental state."

Since Oliver wasn't the first-born, he knew very little about Traveling, and he certainly didn't know it could be done without The Dreaming Room and The Dreaming Chair or without permission. He probably didn't know anything. "Sorry. I guess I'm still out of it, jet-lagged."

"So, what happened back at home with the company? I know you did something to piss Uncle Ray off. He wouldn't have sent the heir apparent away without a good reason."

"I can't tell you." Because I don't want to put you in a coma or kill you. Poor Grandpa. Kyle shuddered. Poor Mom and Dad.

"Come on, Kyle," Oliver said. "Ray's thousands of miles away. He'll never know." Being excluded from Time Advantages business all these years must have made Oliver feel left out.

"It's not that I don't want to tell you. I can't tell you," Kyle said. "It's for your own safety."

Oliver's face shut down. "Whatever." He picked up the game controller and turned his attention back to the TV, muttering, "Fuck you, too."

Kyle stared at him. Things were not going well. But he understood; he'd be pissed in Oliver's shoes. "I'm sorry I can't tell you. If I could, I would."

He needed to change the subject. He'd been thinking about what he'd do while he was in this strange town. "Have you ever investigated time travel at university? I heard they've got some crazy-smart science professors here."

"No," Oliver said. "I'm not supposed to study Traveling, remember?"

Yikes. Hostile much? "Okay. Right." He paused. "How's school going?"

Oliver deigned to glance at him. "What do you care?"

Defensive, much? "Okay. Do you want to go out to eat? My treat."

"Can't. I have to leave for a meeting in a few minutes."

"A meeting? For school?" Kyle lumbered to the kitchen area. "Is it okay if I get something to eat here, then?"

"If you can find something, help yourself."

Kyle opened the refrigerator, and all it had in it was some cans of beer, a jar of pickles, and some steak sauce. He closed the door and glanced at Oliver. "So, you don't have any food?"

"I was going to get something on the way to my meeting."

"What's the meeting?"

"Black Student Alliance."

"What kind of group is that?"

Oliver shrugged. "It's mostly African Americans. We hang out and support each other and try to get stuff done, change stuff."

Change stuff? Kyle would never have guessed Oliver was political. "But you're not African or American."

"What?" Oliver threw the controller down on the sofa. "You don't think someone like me would want to empower the Black community?"

Apparently, Kyle didn't know Oliver at all. "No, I'm not saying that. It sounds good. Good for you."

"Now you're being condescending."

Kyle held up his hands. "What do you want from me? I'm trying to be nice here. Obviously, we don't know each other very well, and I'm sorry for that." He put down his hands. "Maybe now that I'm here, we'll finally get to know each other. I hope so."

"Well, okay, I guess," Oliver said. "Do you want to come with me to the meeting? It's at the UMC, and we can stop and get something to eat there."

What's a UMC? "Sure. Sounds good."

A UMC turned out to be the university's student union. As they walked into a cafeteria, Oliver said, "Welcome to the Alferd

Packer Restaurant and Grill."

"Thanks," Kyle said. "Who's Alferd Packer? A famous chef?"

Oliver guffawed. "Kind of. He was a cannibal."

Kyle stopped short. "What?"

Oliver laughed outright.

There was no way the cafeteria actually served cannibal meat, right? "Good one, Ollie. So, what's the story?"

At the grill, they ordered burgers and fries and helped themselves to sodas.

"It was around 1870," Oliver said. "This guy Alferd Packer was looking for gold, silver, and stuff in the mountains, but his group got trapped in a bad snow storm and ended up eating each other. It was cool."

It was pretty cool the university named its cafeteria after such a bizarre historical episode. He pointed at the El Canibal sign and grinned. "How come we're not eating there?"

Oliver shrugged. "You can. It's Mexican. I just felt like a burger."

"You're right. Burgers sound good." Kyle couldn't remember the last time he'd grabbed a bite and hung out with his brother. Or the last time he'd seen him laugh. Maybe living here would turn out to be a good thing after all.

"Oliver, my man!" one of the guys in the meeting room called out as they entered. "How's it hanging?"

"I can't believe it," another one said. "You found another brother on campus?"

Oliver set his food down on the table. "Not exactly. This is my real brother, Kyle. He's visiting."

"No way! You have a brother?"

"I didn't know you had a brother."

"I thought you said he was an asshole." At least one of Oliver's friends knew he had a brother. "He came to check up on you, huh? Are you still on academic pro?"

Oliver interrupted. "Say hey, to my friends, Kyle." He sat.

Kyle put his food down on the table and waved. "Hey. Nice to meet you." He sat down.

"Whoa. What an accent. He sounds Aussie."

"Put another shrimp on the barbie!"

"G'day mate!"

"How come you don't sound as Aussie as him, Oliver?"

Oliver smiled. "I've been here in the U.S. hanging out with you losers." He took a big chomp on his burger.

Kyle followed his lead and started eating, too.

Eventually, the guys calmed down.

"So, Oliver, I think I saw that hot girl you mentioned," one of the guys said.

"I told you, DeShaw!" Oliver put down his burger, licking ketchup off his fingers. "There's another hot woman of color on campus. Where'd you see her?"

"I spied her in your neighborhood," DeShaw said. "And look, I got her picture." He held out his phone. "I'm a regular double-o seven."

Kyle glanced at it. The woman looked very like his cousin Moira, just a little older. "What the hell?" How was that even possible?

Chapter Thirty-One
Kairi: Boulder, Colorado, 2018

Past-Kairi was surprisingly cooperative about letting Dakota shower, borrow clothes and crash at her place.

Past-Jessica was not. "I can't believe you're letting a homeless person stay in our room!" she said while Dakota was in the shower and past-her had gone to the laundry room with Dakota's clothes. Past-Jessica thought the time-traveling Kairi was her roommate.

"Dakota is my best friend from high school," Kairi said.

"She reeks!"

Kairi couldn't disagree with that. They'd gotten some funny looks at the restaurant, but in Boulder, Dakota's appearance wasn't that out of the ordinary. "Not for long. She's cleaning up now," she said. "She's a good person. She's not going to do anything to you or your stuff."

"She's a bum."

Jessica had veered into dangerous territory. Kairi wasn't sure she was the friend she'd thought she was. She'd expected her to be a little surprised, but she hadn't expected her to act like Dakota wasn't a person. "She's a human being. If you can't see that, I'm very disappointed by your behavior."

"Don't judge me! I have the right to pick who stays in my room." Jessica marched to her closet, grabbed a bag and started throwing stuff into it. "I'm going to stay at Hank's place. And I'll be contacting the R.A. This is not cool."

Kairi couldn't agree more. Her behavior wasn't cool.

Jessica finished packing and stormed out.

Kairi was a little relieved. She hadn't quite figured out how to handle the two Kairis issue yet. Now, they wouldn't have to.

Past-her stuck her head in. "Is the coast clear?"

"Yeah," she said, sitting at the desk. "Jessica left."

"You say that like it's a bad thing." Past-her dropped an empty laundry basket on the floor.

"I mean, she had a fit, packed a bag, and left. She said she's reporting us, er, I guess, you, to the R.A."

"Well, shit." Past-Kairi sighed and glanced at the door. "Couldn't you stop her?"

"I tried." One of these days, Kairi would have to quit living under the control of the R.A.s. "Frankly, she was acting like a bitch. I'm not sure she's actually your friend."

"Are you sure you didn't provoke her?" Past-her's tone was decidedly snippy.

"No, I didn't provoke her. I was nice and polite. Even though she was yelling at me and calling Dakota names."

"Oh," past-her said in a little voice.

"Maybe she'll apologize when she calms down." Kairi hoped so. She thought Jessica was a true friend, someone who would stick by her through thick and thin, no matter what. Since she didn't have a family, her friends were very important to her.

Past-her had a hollow look in her eyes, and Kairi knew she was thinking the same thing. "So, what's the plan now?"

"Now that I've got lots of Dakota intel, I'm going to travel back in time and try to nip her problems in the bud." But first, she needed to travel back to her present and get some decent clothes, money and supplies. She needed to quit doing this time travel stuff so half-assed.

"Are you sure you don't want to teach me how to time travel?" past-her asked. "Maybe I could help."

"To be honest, I haven't totally gotten the hang of it myself yet." She gestured at her sweats. "I mean, I didn't even bring any clothes with me."

"You need to quit doing this time travel stuff so half-assed," past-Kairi said.

"Gee, thanks for the advice."

"Don't you take a snippy tone with me. I'm cleaning up your mess here." She pointed at the laundry basket. "And I'm going to get in trouble for it. And you're wearing my stuff. And you stole my phone. I'm like a saint compared to you."

"Saint?" Kairi snorted. "Don't get carried away."

As Kairi time traveled back to her present, she was nervous about what she'd find. When she'd left, she and Dakota were staying in Pam's guest room. How much had her recent jaunt changed things?

She lucid-dreamed until she got to the black curtain that hung across her memory. "Wake up! Wake up!" She pinched herself, and it hurt.

She sat up in bed. It was nighttime, but the drapes let through a little light, and she could see the empty walls over the twin beds in Pam's guest room. Someone stirred in the other bed. "Dakota, what's the date?" she asked.

"Beat's me," Dakota said, lifting her head. "Is it morning yet?"

"No. Go back to sleep." It was weird. She didn't feel dizzy at all. And nothing seemed to be changed. Wait. Maybe there was a relationship between those two things? She was too tired to think about it now. Exhausted, she leaned back and went to sleep. She didn't dream.

In the morning, Kairi quizzed Dakota about what she remembered from a year ago. Dakota said she'd had fun staying on campus with her for a couple of days during spring break but that her roommate Jessica eventually kicked her out. Grrr. She and Jessica needed to talk, but it would have to wait.

She also quizzed Dakota about her life story to see if it jibed with her earlier intel. It did. According to Dakota, her troubles started after their caper to the high school gym back in 2014 when Dakota met future-her. When she'd told folks about time travel at her group home, no one had believed her.

It was pretty obvious what Kairi needed to do. She needed to go back to 2014 again and stop past-her and past-past-her from calling Dakota and asking for her help with the caper.

So, after they had brunch and visited some with Pam, Kairi bid them adieu and went to assemble her time travel supplies. She bought a jacket with a ton of pockets at the second-hand store. She went to the bank and got a bunch of cash from 2006, seriously depleting her account, and yes, the teller thought she was weird. Her driver's license was old enough to be good all the way back to 2006. She couldn't figure out how to get a cell phone or credit card now that would work back in 2014. If she had to have one of them, she'd just have to steal, er, borrow it from past-her. Her stuff was her stuff anyway, right?

Kairi lucid-dreamed to Sunday morning, April twenty-fourth, 2014, the morning after the junior prom. She crouched in the bushes outside Pam's house. If she recalled correctly, Pam went out to do errands after they all ate pancakes.

Sure enough, Pam came out the front door with her purse and got into her car. Instead of starting it up, however, she stared at the house for a few minutes. Then, she shook her head and finally drove off.

Kairi ran up to the front door and pounded on it.

Past-her opened it.

Past-past-her was picking up the phone.

"Drop that phone!" She pointed at past-past-her. To her credit, past-past-her did put down the phone immediately. But she said, "Ack. It's another one."

As Kairi took a step toward past-her, she started to feel dizzy. She took a step back. She felt less dizzy. Interesting.

Past-past-her approached them, and Kairi started to feel dizzy again. "What's wrong with the phone?" past-past-her asked.

"Maybe you should stay away from me. Don't get any closer," Kairi said. "The caper doesn't work out well for Dakota. Don't call her. She gets in trouble for talking about time travel. The two of you can go. You'll be fine." Actually, one of them probably would be caught by security, and the other wouldn't repair the helmet and have to time travel home on her own, but she thought they'd manage.

Past-past-her said, "We could tell Dakota not to talk about it." Then she shook her head. "Yeah, that probably wouldn't work."

Past-her said, "Is that it? Don't call Dakota?"

"Yep."

They both shrugged and said, "Okay."

Kairi went back to 2019. She had a dizzy spell but immediately went back to March 2018 to check on Dakota and to see if she would introduce her to Josh. It was the day before she'd been here recently, at least she thought it was. She'd have to start keeping notes about all this.

Again, she didn't know where Dakota would be. Again, she didn't have a phone. Again, she decided to use past-her's phone. She hustled over to the dorm. Again it was locked. She lounged nonchalantly near the dorm's front door.

A very tall guy walked up to the front door.

She smiled and nodded. She did not say Hey, stilts.

He unlocked the door and held it open for her.

"Thanks." She stepped inside and went over to her room. The door was locked. She pounded on the door. "Jessica, are you in there? I locked myself out." She really hoped someone was home.

Kairi heard the lock turn and saw the door swing open.

Jessica stood in the doorway. "You just left. And I could have sworn I saw you take your keys." She shrugged. "Whatever. I have to get to class." She took off.

Kairi searched her side of the room, and her cell phone wasn't there. Of course. But luckily, the only phone number she had memorized was a useful one. She called Pam on the archaic landline.

"Kairi," Pam said. "How's it going?"

"Okay."

"What's wrong?"

"I guess I'm a little homesick," she said. "I miss you and Dakota."

Pam didn't say anything.

"Pam?"

"Wow." Pam expelled a burst of air. "Dakota. That's a name I haven't heard in quite a while. She had such a sad life. I still blame myself for not doing more for her."

Kairi had a very bad feeling about Dakota and started feeling dizzy again. "Uh. What?"

"What do you mean, what?" Pam sounded irritated. "I still feel bad that Dakota overdosed in high school."

Dakota overdosed? A wave of vertigo swept over her, and

she fell onto the bed.

Pam paused for a second. "I thought you blamed yourself, too," she said more gently.

Oh, God. The room spun around her. Now, she remembered the funeral. It had a pathetically small turnout, only her and Pam and a couple of people from the group home. Kairi's eyes overflowed. Dakota didn't deserve that. She was so warm and generous. How could people not realize that? How could people not come to her funeral?

How could Dakota be dead?

And what did Kairi do to cause it?

Her heart shattered.

Chapter Thirty-Two
Kyle: Boulder, Colorado, 2019

When Kyle and Oliver got home from the meeting, every muscle in Kyle's body ached, and he couldn't stop yawning. In the car, he'd tried asking Oliver about school but got shut down again. That was suspicious.

"Bro, I think you need to go to bed." Oliver sat down on the couch and grabbed his game controller.

"I'm not gonna argue with you. Couch?"

"Well, that's a problem because I was going to kick back and play some Syndicate. I gotta hack the world and invade some enemy minds."

"So, what do you want me to do?"

Oliver sighed. "I guess you can have my room again."

"Thanks." Kyle stumbled down the hall.

"Sleep tight." Back in the living room, Oliver booted up his game. "I gotta kick me some ass and slow down time..."

Kyle entered the bedroom. His goal, the bed, was in sight. He unbuttoned his shirt as he lumbered towards it. Ah, bed, beautiful bed. He sat.

Back in the family room, Oliver screamed, "Fucking fuckedity fuck!" He ran down the hall and burst into the bedroom. "I figured it out! You did Travel, and you do it when you sleep! That's why you kept asking if you went anywhere when you were asleep! Fuck! This is huge! Fuck!"

This was hugely bad. How did Oliver figure it out? Kyle dropped his shirt on the floor and turned to his brother. "Quit saying fuck."

"That's all you have to say? This is huge! So, can anyone do it? I can do it? Can I do it?"

Kyle grabbed Oliver's arm and dropped it abruptly. "Listen to me very carefully, Oliver. You know we are not the designated Travelers. Ray is. But even if you were allowed to Travel, you absolutely should not Travel. I practically killed myself when I Traveled back in time to stop myself from Traveling. I was in a coma for three weeks. Ray almost pulled the plug on me. And before that, I did kill someone." Oh, God, his parents were still dead in this timeline. His breath caught in his chest. "I killed more than one person. This is not a game. It's dangerous. Are you hearing me? Don't try it." The one thing keeping Kyle from freaking out was he didn't think Oliver could do it without any training.

"How do you do it? How do you Travel?"

"You're not listening. Traveling is, it can be, fatal." Kyle rubbed his scar. "I don't want you to die, Oliver. Please listen to me."

Oliver frowned at him. "Okay. I won't try it." He pointed at him. "If you answer my questions."

Oliver's imagination would probably be worse than reality at this point. "What are your questions?"

He sat down next to him on the bed. "Who did you kill?"

Kyle pressed his lips together, not wanting to admit any of it. Maybe he could tell Oliver a little. Finally, he said, "I think I killed Dad's dad, David Barada." It was pretty fuzzy at this point.

Oliver's mouth fell open. "That's so freaky. I mean, the dude's been dead for twenty-five years. And I thought he died of a heart attack."

"He did," Kyle said. "Sort of." It was difficult to tell this story without telling all the backstory about how he tried and failed to save their parents' lives. He only started Traveling in the first place because Dad died. And if he told Oliver about Traveling, he might try to Travel to save Mom and Dad, or who knew what. Kyle still didn't know what he was going to do about his parents.

Oliver poked his shoulder. "You said you'd answer my questions."

"I said maybe. So, I Traveled to 1994 and got arrested."

"Why did you Travel back to 1994, and why did you get arrested?"

"Honestly, 1994 was an accident." He definitely was

not going to mention the harebrained scheme of stopping a bombing.

"So, even with all your training, you don't know what you're doing?" Oliver grinned.

"Basically. A bitchy nurse said I was harassing her or some babies or trespassing. Who knows what the rules were back in 1994? Anyway, I got hauled down to the police station, and the cops called Grandpa Barada, and he came down to bail me out."

Oliver shook his head. "This is so freaky. He was young then. What'd he look like? What was he like?"

"He was harsh. Actually, he was an asshole. He knew I was Traveling, and he basically punched me out. And then he had a heart attack and died."

"Fuck." Oliver shook his head some more. "Why'd he have a heart attack?"

Oliver hadn't had training. He didn't know any of the laws for Traveling. "There are a lot of Traveling rules, and it turns out they are very, very important. One of them says touching a Traveler is fatal."

Oliver jumped up off the bed. "Whoa. You might have mentioned this before."

"Relax. It's only fatal if you touch them when they're Traveling. I'm not Traveling. And I think it's only clan members, our genetic group, that are affected."

"Is this why Uncle Ray never touched us?"

"Yeah. He was just being extra careful."

Oliver sat down on the bed again but a good three feet away from Kyle.

"I must admit I don't get the touching thing. What's the story?"

"Do you know The Dreaming mythology?"

Oliver snorted. "Duh. I am a Barada."

"Okay. We each have access to The Dreaming, the true reality. When we Travel, a Traveler is in contact with all of reality, all of time, at once. If a Traveler comes in physical contact with another one of our clan, it's as if different realities come into contact." Kyle looked into Oliver's eyes. "And there can be only one reality."

"So, the realities fight it out?"

Kyle nodded. "Yes. That's a good way to put it. Grandpa's body couldn't deal with conflict and gave out." Surely, a young, healthy Traveler would always overpower an older Traveler? That wasn't in the rules, was it? Why not? Poor Grandpa didn't stand a chance.

"If Grandpa knew all this, why'd he touch you?"

"He was pissed I was there because it was against the rules. That's how I got this scar." Kyle touched his temple but didn't feel any scar.

"What scar? How did you end up in a coma? Was it when Grandpa touched you?"

"No." Kyle really didn't want to admit this part. He didn't want to give Oliver any ideas. "I went back to try to stop myself from Traveling to 1994."

"What do you mean you tried to stop yourself?"

"I Traveled back to a few minutes before I left on the trip to 1994, and I confronted my past-self."

"No way!" Oliver's eyes opened wide. "But what about the dueling realities thing?"

"I didn't say it was a good idea." Kyle shook his head. "It was a stupid idea. I would undo it if I could."

"Well?" Oliver lifted his hand, palm up. "Couldn't you? You're a Traveler, after all."

"Haven't you been listening to a word I've been saying?" Kyle jabbed a finger in Oliver's direction. "I almost died! I killed Grandpa! This stuff is not a game! I'm telling you all this, so you don't do it!" Kyle couldn't bring himself to tell Oliver about their parents.

"So..." Oliver stood up. "I could do something like this?"

Bloody hell. He didn't understand how dangerous it was. "No. You couldn't. You haven't had any training. You don't know how to do it." And thank God for that.

The next thing Kyle knew, it was light outside. He was in Oliver's room, check. So he was in his present. Check.

He stumbled to the bathroom and then out to the family room.

Oliver was still zonked out on the couch.

Kyle looked at the clock. It was one p.m. "Oliver? Don't you have any classes?" Maybe he wasn't on academic probation. Maybe he'd flunked out?

Kyle walked over and stared at him. He didn't look good. Kyle hesitated but reached out and shook him.

Oliver's body was as cold as ice.

"Oliver!" He tried to find a pulse in his neck and wrist, but there was nothing there.

"No!" He leaned over him. Oliver wasn't breathing. "No way!"

He stared at the body. "What the bloody hell did you do, you idiot? You bloody idiot! I told you not to try to Travel! I warned you! But once you get something in your damn head, you never give up on it." His voice trailed off.

It was just like when they'd been little, and Oliver kept stealing his favorite cricket bat and hiding it in his closet. Kyle'd had to keep retrieving it and was late for practice. "Why do you keep doing this?" he'd finally asked.

Oliver had replied, "I thought you'd teach me how to play." And Kyle had; he'd taught Oliver cricket.

Shit. Now they'd never play cricket together again. Ever.

Now he'd never patch things up with him.

Kyle's eyes felt heavy. He blinked the tears back. Fucking fuckedity fuck.

His mind went back to those times they spent together on the pitch. Oliver had been horrible when they started, with no hand-eye coordination, but he got better. A lot better.

He wasn't better now. "Bloody idiot!"

Eventually, Kyle carefully tucked the blanket around Oliver's body. "I have to call someone. Who do I call? The police? What's the number here?" He wiped a tear out of the corner of his eye. "I have to call Uncle Ray. But I can't call him. He'll blame me for Oliver's death." He paused. "He should blame me."

He took a step back, staring at his little brother's still form. "I don't accept this. There's no way I'm killing my brother. I'd rather die than let that happen. I'll just have to Travel back and stop him."

From the office in Oliver's spare bedroom, Kyle could hear Oliver and another version of Kyle arguing in Oliver's bedroom.

"Haven't you been listening to a word I've been saying?" the other Kyle said. "I almost died. I killed Grandpa! This stuff is not a game. I'm telling you all this, so you don't do it!"

"So..." Oliver said. "I could do something like this?"

"No," the other Kyle said. "You couldn't. You haven't had any training. You don't know how to do it."

Kyle had to duck back into an empty room as Oliver stormed out of the bedroom and down the hall.

Then the stupid past version of him just went to bed, oblivious to what was about to happen.

Kyle crept down the hall and peeked into the family room.

"Fuck him," Oliver muttered. "I can Travel. He thinks he's so damn important. He thinks he can boss me around. I'm not a little kid. I'm an adult. I can do whatever the hell I want!" He lay back on the couch. "Little does he know how many times I spied on him during his training. I bet I'm a better Traveler than he is!" Oliver closed his eyes.

Bloody hell. This didn't look good. This looked like Oliver was trying to Travel. Kyle reluctantly stepped into the room. "Stop. You have to stop what you're doing. Now."

Oliver jolted up. "I thought you were going to bed?" He swung his legs over the side of the sofa. "You look different. Your face is all red and blotchy. Fuck. You haven't been crying, have you?"

"No," Kyle said. "I don't cry. Besides, what would I have to cry about? Nothing. Nothing's going on."

"Something's going on." Oliver got up off the couch. "Wait a minute. Are you Traveling now?" He pointed at Kyle. "You are! You're Traveling right now!"

"No, I'm not," Kyle said.

"Traveling doesn't look so dangerous to me." Oliver took a step toward Kyle. "Are you really doing it?"

"No, I'm not doing it. But, stop," Kyle said. "Don't come any closer!"

"Quit bossing me around!" Oliver took another step toward Kyle. "If you're not Traveling, why can't I come any closer?" Oliver stepped closer.

Kyle jerked away but tripped on a throw rug, falling on the floor.

And he came in contact with his brother.

Oliver fell back onto the couch, shaking. "Augh." He clutched at his mid-section and puked onto the floor. The shaking intensified.

"Oliver?" Jesus bloody Christ. What had he done? He had to get him some help. "Oliver?" But who could help? Nobody, that's who.

EMTs couldn't do anything for Oliver. No one could do anything.

Already, Oliver had stopped puking and shaking. He was barely moving. He was barely breathing. His skin had taken on a grayish cast. Then, he stopped breathing.

Kyle couldn't take any more. He'd killed his little brother.

He collapsed onto the floor. "No. No. No."

Chapter Thirty-Three
Kairi: Boulder, Colorado, 2019

Kairi wanted to crawl into bed, cower under the covers and cry for about a year, but that wouldn't bring Dakota back. Dakota's death was on her hands. She didn't have any illusions about that. Something she'd just done had caused her best friend to overdose.

She was a killer, but not for long if she had anything to say about it, and she did.

The only question was, should she undo what she just did, or should she try and stop the overdose? Kairi decided the simplest thing would be to undo what she just did. There was no telling what the hell would happen if she started mucking about any more than she already had.

Again, Kairi lucid-dreamed to Sunday morning, April twenty-fourth, 2014, the morning after the junior prom. She crouched in the bushes outside Pam's neighbor's house, waiting for past-her to appear. When she did, Kairi sidled up to her in Pam's bushes and started to feel dizzy. "Hey," she whispered.

Past-Kairi jumped sky-high. When she came back down, she said, "What the hell? Don't sneak up on me like that." She scrutinized her outfit. "Is that my new jacket? Are you wearing the same clothes as me?" She examined her hair. "Are you me from later today?"

Kairi nodded. "Good catch. Yes. And I know you're here to stop the me's, us'es, whatever, from calling Dakota in on the caper because you're trying to help her, but forget it." As she leaned toward the past version of herself, she had to take a step back to avoid the dizziness.

"Why would I forget it after going through all the trouble to come back here?" Past-Kairi put her hands on her hips. "I want to help Dakota."

Kairi debated what to say. The truth, while brutal, seemed like it would be the most effective. "Okay. Listen closely. I was just here. I stopped the past-me's from calling Dakota and then stopped to check on things in 2018?"

Past-her gave her an expression that said, Yeah, right. It had nothing to do with Josh.

She ignored her. "And found out Dakota died of a drug overdose in high school."

Past-her gasped, and her hand flew in front of her mouth. "But when I left 2019, she was fine, not great, but alive." She paused, and her eyes moistened. "Oh, my God."

"Abort this mission," Kairi said. "We'll have to think of something else."

The other Kairi frowned. "All right."

Then Pam bustled out the front door with her purse.

"Hide!" Kairi whispered. They smashed themselves into the bushes until Pam got in her car and drove away. "That was a close one." She was starting to wonder how many hers would have to come back here before somebody caught them. And she was going to have to come up with a better naming convention than past-her and past-past-her, etc. Ugh.

"Thanks." The past-her-in-the-bushes touched Kairi's shoulder, and she shuddered. Kairi fell to her knees and vomited her 2019 brunch.

From the retching sounds next to her, evidently, the past-her-in-the-bushes was similarly incapacitated.

After they finished vomiting, by unspoken agreement, they crawled away from one another.

"What the hell was that?" past-her asked, looking like death-warmed-over.

Kairi shrugged, which wasn't so easy to do from all fours. "I'm beginning to think it's not good for different versions of us to interact."

"Gee, ya think?"

"There's no need to be snarky."

"How come they aren't having the same problem inside?"

She jerked her shoulder towards the house.

"I don't know." Sadly, there was an awful lot she didn't know, and apparently, more and more of it all the time.

Kairi lucid-dreamed to her present. "Wake up! Wake up!" In the growing light of sunrise, she could make out her posters of the Eiffel Tower and Big Ben on the wall. So, she was in her own bed. Thank goodness. She didn't feel dizzy. What did that mean?

Exhausted, she turned over and went back to sleep.

When she finally got up at a more reasonable hour, she had no idea what day it was. Time traveling really scrambled your brain. The computer said it was March twenty-fifth, 2019. Find out the date, check. She was still smack-dab in the middle of her spring break. Spring break this year seemed as if it was lasting forever. Yay.

On the other hand, it wasn't as if she was doing anything fun. Boo. She had no time for fun. The irony wasn't lost on her.

Next, Kairi needed to find out if Dakota was okay. If she recalled her present correctly, Dakota was living in a run-down house on The Hill with a bunch of guys--at least that's what she'd been doing the last time she was here and now. Dakota's number wasn't in her cell. Did she even have a number? But Kairi did remember where she lived. Hopefully, she still lived there in this timeline. Or remembering how horrible the house had been; hopefully, she didn't live there? She was confused.

The bus dropped Kairi about a block from Dakota's digs, and she started walking. She was a little familiar with the neighborhood from being here a couple of days ago. Again, the sweet scent of marijuana led her right to a house. The front door was wide open, and considering it was about forty-five degrees, that didn't seem like a good thing. "Hello?" she said as she walked right in. "Anybody home? Dakota?"

The living room still sported a mismatched array of couches no doubt found on the side of the road. That was a good sign because that's what she'd seen before? Everything reeked of pot. "Hello?"

She heard some giggling coming from the back and walked through the kitchen. It had three ancient refrigerators, all emitting loud hums. It sounded like an airport runway. "Hello? Dakota?"

Dakota popped her dread head out of a doorway. Confusion morphed into delight on her face. "Kairi? Is that you?"

Thank goodness she was okay. Things were back to normal. Kairi grabbed her old friend for a hug. "Dakota. It's good to see you."

"I saw you a couple of days ago, right?" Dakota said. "What are you doing here?" Taking in her stained skirt and tie-dyed t-shirt combo and bloodshot eyes, Kairi felt like they'd done all this already. Because they had.

"I'm still on spring break. I stopped by to say hi. How's it going?"

"It's going good." She giggled. "You wanna party?"

Kairi wasn't totally against partying. She'd done some partying in her day. She considered it but decided it would just slow her down. She was on a mission, and part one, save Dakota, was on the right track. She was starting to think, too, that partying was worse than she'd thought. Did it play a part in Dakota's death in that aborted timeline? "No, thanks. Okay?"

Dakota nodded. "Sure."

"So, Dakota," she said. "Is there anything I can do for you?"

"What do you mean?" she asked, scrunching up her nose.

"Are you okay living here? Do you need me to help you find a place to live? Or a job?"

"You're acting like I'm some kind of loser." She frowned. "Or charity case."

"No, I'm not. I don't think you're a loser or a charity case." Or did she? Based on the aborted timeline, she did think there was a chance she'd overdose.

"Whatever. If you don't want to party, I'm busy with my peeps." Dakota pointed back at the bedroom.

"Maybe..." Kairi started to try to talk her out of partying, but Dakota was already giving her an angry look, and she'd hardly said anything. She changed gears. "Okay. Do you want my phone number? You can call me if you need anything. Do you have a phone? What's your number?"

But Dakota just walked back to the bedroom at the back of the house.

Kairi was left in the kitchen surrounded by whirring refrigerators. "Okay, Dakota. Take care." It was pretty tough to help someone who didn't want any help. But the way Kairi was acting, she couldn't really blame her. She was sort of treating her old friend like a charity case.

Frankly, Kairi was stumped. How would she help her without treating her like a charity case? She went back out the front door of Dakota's house and sat down on the couch on the porch. For someone who could travel through time, she was surprisingly ignorant. The only thing she could think of was to go to Pam's house and ask her for advice.

Kairi showed up on Pam's doorstep with a pepperoni pizza and a bottle of Pam's favorite wine.

When Pam opened her door and saw the refreshments, her frown turned upside down. "Wow. Twice in one week. What an honor."

"Yeah, sorry for eating so much of your food, the spaghetti and all the pancakes."

"Pancakes?"

Oh, right, some of those timelines were overwritten, and some of those pancakes were years ago to Pam. "You know, over the years."

Pam smiled. "Don't just stand there. Come on in, already."

Kairi waited until they'd polished off the pizza before broaching what was on her mind. "So, I'm worried about Dakota."

Pam nodded. "Yeah. Me, too." She glanced up at her. "But why the sudden interest? You guys haven't interacted much in the last few years, have you?"

Kairi wracked her memory. In the now-current timeline, she'd lost track of Dakota in high school when she started to get more popular. In fact, in her memories, it all started when future-her came to stop the rape.

Weird. She still recalled doing that just a few days ago. And she recalled future-her coming and interfering in her life years ago.

"Kairi?" Pam asked. "You look odd. Are you okay?"

"I think so." She nodded.

"You know, you seemed to grow apart from Dakota after that weird woman, what was her name, Karen, showed up at that dance. Did you ever find out anything about her? Was she a relative?"

Considering she looked exactly like Karen now, Kairi was a little worried about the direction this conversation was headed. "She disappeared. Don't know anything about her. Back to Dakota."

Pam sighed. "Right. Dakota. What I'm about to say wasn't your fault. You were a teenager. You had to live your own life. But you were the only good thing Dakota had going for her. When you dropped her, she never really was the same."

"I didn't drop her." Kairi knew she was a good person. She didn't drop people.

Pam stared at her with her yeah, right look.

"I didn't drop her." Did she? She tried to recall those years. After the dance, she'd had more confidence. When Chad bad-mouthed her one day in the hall, she totally shut him down in front of everyone. She thought it was after that she was invited to eat with some more popular girls in the cafeteria. Things just went uphill from there until she was basically too busy to hang out with Dakota.

Shit. She did drop her.

But more importantly, what was she going to do about it?

Chapter Thirty-Four
Kyle: Boulder, Colorado, 2019

The room spun around Kyle. He moaned. "No. No. No."

After the room stopped spinning, he realized he didn't know where or when he was. He lay on the floor on an ugly blue shag carpet next to a bed. Why was he on the floor? He lifted himself on his elbow in preparation for getting up.

"Haven't you been listening to a word I've been saying?" another version of him said.

He was back at his argument with Oliver. Right. That was the plan. He had to stop himself from Traveling to stop Oliver. But that hadn't worked at all. Oliver had ended up dead.

That meant in the meantime, there was a version of him on the bed and another version of him skulking around in the hall. Bloody hell. He lay back down and slid partway under the bed.

"So..." Oliver said. "I could do something like this?"

"No," the Kyle-on-the-bed said. "You couldn't. You haven't had any training. You don't know how to do it."

Oliver stormed out.

Kyle popped up immediately.

The version of him on the bed looked at him, made a strange ulping noise, and then said, "You can't be here."

On his way to the door, Kyle glanced his way. "I'm not here." In the hall, he saw the retreating back of another Traveling Kyle. "Kyle!" he whisper-shouted at himself.

The other Traveling version of him turned around, and his mouth sagged open.

Kyle motioned the other Traveling Kyle into the bedroom.

The other Traveling Kyle glanced Oliver's way and tiptoed into the bedroom. "What are you doing here?" As the other

Traveling Kyle approached Kyle, he started feeling nauseated.

"What are either of you doing here!" the not-Traveling Kyle on the bed said.

Neither Traveling Kyle answered the Kyle-on-the-bed.

Kyle backed up against the wall and said to the other Traveling Kyle, "It doesn't work. You end up killing Oliver."

"Killing Oliver?" the Kyle-on-the-bed said. "Bloody hell!"

The Traveling Kyles said, "Shh," together.

"So, what do we do?" the other Traveling Kyle said. "You can't expect me, er, us, to do nothing, to just let Oliver die."

Ding, ding, ding. That was it. They did need to do nothing. Stopping Oliver from Traveling was too difficult. He needed to avoid Oliver, stay away from him entirely. Then, Oliver wouldn't know more about Travelling and wouldn't try it. "Yes! We have to avoid Oliver altogether." Kyle pointed at the Kyle-on-the-bed. "You too. Stay away from Oliver."

"I don't feel so good," the other Traveling Kyle said.

"Me neither," the Kyle-on-the-bed said. He fell back as if he'd fainted.

Kyle didn't feel so good either, and it wasn't just the mental whiplash of so many Kyles being in the same place and time. "We need to get out of this time ASAP."

The other Traveling Kyle nodded, waved, and staggered back into the hall, presumably on his way back to the empty room.

Kyle knelt on the ugly carpet in preparation for lying down.

"You have to tell me what's going on," the Kyle-on-the-bed said, voice shaking. "Why do we feel so sick?"

Kyle lay down. "I don't know. This is confusing. Just stay away from Oliver." He heard something in the hallway. "And run interference if Oliver comes in here now."

Kyle needed to Travel back to a time before he met up with Oliver at the airport, but the spatial constraints on Traveling were a huge problem. He hadn't realized it before. He could only materialize in the approximate spatial location of himself at the desired time--which meant on the airplane--if he wanted to stop his past self from interacting with Oliver at all. And he didn't think the airline employees would take kindly to a person appearing out of thin air on a plane in thin air. But there was no help for it.

As he recalled, there were some open seats in first class on the flight from L.A. Kyle materialized there and crept back to the other Kyle's seat in coach. As he closed the distance to the other Kyle, he started feeling sick again.

The kid sitting across the aisle from the other Kyle noticed him first. "Hey, you look just like him."

The other Kyle blanched. "You can't be here."

"I know. I'm not here," Kyle said.

"You're here," the boy said. "I see you." He pointed.

"You can't let Oliver pick you up at the airport." Kyle grabbed one of the seats to avoid wobbling. "He learns about, uh," he glanced at the boy, "Traveling and dies."

The boy gasped. "Dies!"

Kyle did not feel well. "Stay away from Oliver. Okay?"

The other Kyle's color was not good. "I guess I have to trust you. Okay. Message received. Now, get out of here before I faint or worse."

Kyle nodded, almost causing himself to fall in the aisle. Very carefully, he made his way back to first class and lay down in the reclining seat.

When Kyle woke up, he didn't know where or when he was. He looked around the room and saw a bed, nondescript artwork on the walls, a wooden dresser, table and chair, a flat-screen TV, and a mini-fridge. Bland. He must be in a hotel room.

He sat up and swung his legs over the side of the bed and was overcome with dizziness. He grabbed the headboard as waves of nausea rolled over him along with new memories.

He remembered another version of himself appearing on the plane and telling him not to interact with Oliver. He remembered the little boy sitting next to him causing a brouhaha when he kept asking where the other Kyle was. The boy's parents hadn't known what to make of his behavior.

When he got off the plane, he told the airline employee not to bother with the wheelchair.

He'd hobbled slowly to the baggage carousel with his carry-on, stopping to rest often in his weakened state from the coma. When he got within sight of the carousel, he noticed Oliver with his checked bags, scanning the crowd. Dammit.

He was disappointed by this whole turn of events. He'd hoped his exile would give him a chance to reconnect with his brother and get to know him again. But, he knew his future self wouldn't have contacted him without a very good reason.

He slunk away to ground transportation and got a taxi to the nearest hotel.

And here he was in his present. In this timeline, he'd slept and ordered room service for two days.

Kyle checked his phone. Oliver had left twenty messages, and Uncle Ray had left five. He didn't bother to check them.

He called his uncle and got voicemail. What time was it at home? "Sorry, Ray. I know you planned for me to see Oliver. But believe me when I tell you--it's not safe for him. I can't interact with him. You need to call him and tell him."

Kyle lay back down on the bed. Oliver would be hurt and pissed. He'd think Kyle didn't want to see him. He'd think Kyle didn't want to be his brother.

Kyle'd probably never be able to mend their relationship.

But better a pissed Oliver than a dead Oliver.

Kyle pulled the covers up. What the hell was he supposed to do now?

When Kyle heard his mobile ringing, he didn't know where he was. He didn't know when he was. He flipped on a light next to the bed. He looked around the room. Bland. Oh, yeah, he was in a hotel room.

According to his phone, he was in his present, a few hours later than the last time he'd used his phone.

"Kyle? It's Ray. What's going on? Where are you? Why can't you interact with Oliver?"

Even from eight thousand miles away, Kyle could tell Ray was worried.

"Kyle?"

"I apologize, but I had to rewrite the timeline," he said.

"That's what I felt! You know that's not allowed, Kyle."

"I had to," Kyle said. "Oliver died. He tried to Travel. I swear I didn't tell him how to do it. In fact, I told him not to do it."

Ray didn't say anything. He'd already warned him repeatedly about Traveling.

"Ray?"

"Are you absolutely positively sure about staying away from Oliver? This is the only way?"

"Yeah. As soon as he saw me and my injuries, he started asking questions. I only gave him the sketchiest of answers and told him not to try Traveling. But I guess he couldn't resist."

Ray asked, "How many times did you go back?"

Kyle knew he needed to lie. "Just the once." Traveling was evil.

"At least you're learning something from your many mistakes. I don't want Oliver to get hurt. I guess it can't be helped--but I'm not happy about this."

"Can you patch things over with Oliver?" Kyle didn't want his only sibling to hate him.

"I'll try. But, Kyle, you have to move. Go to New York or somewhere else. You can't stay there. If your statement is true, you're putting Oliver in danger."

"I know enough to avoid Oliver! I'm not an idiot." Even though they couldn't interact, Kyle still wanted to keep an eye on Oliver from afar and make sure he didn't Travel. And figure out what else was going on with him. What was that crack Oliver's friend had made about school? "I'm staying."

"No," Ray said. "You're not."

"I am, and there's nothing you can do about it." Kyle had had it.

"If you stay, I'm not supporting you."

"Then it's bloody lucky I've got money in my bank account!"

"Don't call me again until you come to your senses!" Ray hung up.

"Well, fuck you, too," Kyle muttered.

Chapter Thirty-Five
Kairi: Boulder, Colorado, 2019

All the way back to campus, Kairi pondered how to un-drop Dakota. She must have had dozens, if not hundreds, of opportunities to interact with Dakota in high school. Did she need to time travel back to all of them? How was she supposed to even remember them all?

She was cutting across Farrand Field when she smacked right into someone and fell on her ass. Good grief. The campus was practically deserted. How could she manage to find a person on campus to run into?

On the other hand, hadn't she just run into Josh a couple of days ago? Maybe it was him again? Maybe it was fate pushing them back together? She turned her gaze up hopefully towards the man's face.

"Are you all right, chica?" It wasn't Josh.

Damn. She struggled to get to her feet. Why was she so clumsy these days? "Yeah. I'm okay."

"Good." He grinned. "I'd hate to take out one of the few Chicanas on campus. Maybe it's fate that we ran into each other. We Chicanos have to stick together, am I right?" the (apparently) Chicano guy said. "Hi, I'm Diego." He stuck out his hand, and they shook.

"Kairi," she said. "But, to be honest, I don't know that I'm Chicana or Chicano or whatever." And even more honestly, she didn't believe in fate anymore.

Diego checked her out. "Your hair is a bit curly for a Chicana. But wait, hold the phone. How can you not know your heritage?"

She was in a bad mood, still feeling guilty about Dakota,

and this guy's nosy questions weren't helping. "I'm an orphan, okay. What's it to you?" She wasn't bitter about being alone in the world, not having any info about her family, or not having a boyfriend. About not having Josh in her life. Yeah, right.

Diego opened his big brown eyes wide. His lashes were amazing. "Sorry, chica. I didn't mean to upset you."

"And quit calling me chica." She turned back to her dorm and stormed off.

"You've got grass stains on your butt," he called after her. "Cute jeans, though."

Back in her room, there was no sign of Jessica. Just as well, she had unresolved feelings about her. On the bright side, the one glass of wine she'd had with Pam had made her sleepy. So, as soon as she figured out how to un-drop Dakota, she was good to go.

She surveyed her memories. Clearly, at the time of the Enchantment Under the Sea dance, they were still friends. What about going back to then and telling past-her to stay friends with her?

Then, she remembered how sick she'd been when she ran into past-her-in-the-bushes on the morning of April twenty-fourth, 2014. She shuddered. She didn't know what made her so sick, but she was not going back to that morning.

What about going back to the next morning, April twenty-fifth, 2014? She must still be friends with Dakota then. She could stop past-her on the way to school and give her the instructions to stay friends with Dakota. It sounded like a plan.

Kairi lucid-dreamed to Monday morning, April twenty-fifth, 2014, two days after the junior prom, and sat on the bench near Pam's house.

At the usual time, past-her came out of the house, yawning. She saw her right away and frowned. As she approached the bench, she said, "Oh, no. It didn't work? You couldn't get back?"

"Huh?" What was she talking about?

"You couldn't find your time machine in the gym? I'm sorry Dakota, and I left, but that security guard, well, you saw him. He was scary."

Gradually, it hit her. Past-Kairi was talking about the so-

211

called caper. Even though it had been only a few days ago to her subjectively speaking, it seemed like forever ago. "No. I got back to my time fine. Thanks for your help." Such that it was. She hadn't actually done anything, had she?

"If you went home to your when, what are you doing here now?" She put her hands on her hips and took a step towards her.

Kairi moved away from her. She didn't know what caused that nausea before, but she didn't want to experience it again. Past-her shouldn't touch her. "Oh, yeah. That. I came back."

Past-her jerked backward. "Back? What the hell for? Why can't you leave me alone for once?"

Kairi held up her hands. "Relax. I just wanted to tell you to make sure you stay friends with Dakota."

"And why the hell wouldn't I stay friends with Dakota? She's my best friend. She's like family."

"I know she's like a sister to you. Now." She paused. "But you are about to get a bunch of new opportunities. I'm just saying don't forget about her. It's important."

Past-her said, "Is that it? Don't forget about Dakota?"

"Yep."

She shrugged and said, "Okay." As she turned in the direction of school, she muttered, "As if I would drop my BFF. Future-me's an asshole."

Kairi didn't have the heart to stop in 2018 to check on things. She sped right on through to her present, late at night on March twenty-fifth, 2019. After she woke, she sat up in bed. It was nighttime, but the drapes let through a little light, and she could see posters of the Eiffel Tower and Big Ben over her bed. Thank goodness she was home.

She felt dizzy and disoriented. That was a good sign, right? Memories in her mind shifted and rearranged.

Someone stirred in the other bed. "Dakota? Is that you?" she asked hopefully.

The person in the other bed turned over. "Yeah? It's me. Who else would it be?" It was Dakota.

"Yes!" Kairi pumped both hands into the air. She jumped out of bed and onto Dakota's bed. She grabbed her for a hug. "It's you. It's you." In the dim light, she saw Dakota grin.

"What's up with you?" Dakota asked. "Have you been partying?"

Kairi laughed. "Not exactly. Bear with me. You go to CU?"

"Yeah. Why else would we be roommates in the dorm?"

"And you're doing well? No serious problems?"

"I did get a D on that quiz, but I can drop it, so no. No major probs." She scrunched up her face. "What is this about?"

"Do we know a guy named Josh?" Kairi held her breath, waiting for her answer. Please, please, please say yes.

"Who?"

Her heart sank. "Josh Williams, my boyfriend?"

"You have a boyfriend? Awesome!" Dakota obviously didn't know who she was talking about.

It felt as if Big Ben was parked on her chest. "Never mind. Go back to sleep. I'll see you in the morning."

Dakota nodded and closed her eyes as she got back under the covers.

Kairi didn't get it. She and Dakota were friends again, just like in that first timeline. Why wasn't she with Josh?

Dakota started breathing regularly, back to sleep already.

Kairi glanced at her in the murky light. She was relieved she was back to normal, still like a sister to her. Thank God. She resolved to put a moratorium on going back to 2014. She didn't want to screw up Dakota's life again.

In the morning, Dakota was gone by the time Kairi woke up. That was a little odd. She'd never known her to get up early.

She lay in bed and relaxed for what seemed like the first time in years. Dare she say Operation Save-Dakota was successful? Dare she restart Operation Meet-Josh?

What did she remember about that day back in 2018 when she met Josh anyway? She focused her recollections of 2018 in this timeline and found she couldn't remember anything of note.

From her original timeline, the date March seventeenth was burned in her brain as The Day She Met Josh. But in her current timeline, apparently, nothing special happened that week. All she could remember was being jazzed about spring break coming the following week.

What happened that day in this timeline?

Kairi decided going back for a little recon couldn't hurt

anything. She closed her eyes.

Whoa. She bolted up out of bed. Didn't she do this exact thing before? Show up in 2018 in her pajamas? Hadn't she learned anything?

She got geared up and tried it again, being careful to arrive before pajama-clad time traveling her arrived.

She woke on March seventeenth, 2018, in her dim dorm room, curtains drawn, apparently in bed with herself. Gingerly, she lifted the covers and started slipping out of bed. As past-her stirred, she froze, but she just turned over. She snuck out of bed and out the door.

She went to a spot where she'd be able to see Dakota exit the Math Building (hopefully) and Josh exit the Physics Building (hopefully) and where none of them, including time traveling past-her, would see her.

Okay, she was hiding in the bushes again. Why did it seem she was getting to know a lot of bushes intimately lately?

Soon, time traveling past-her arrived, planted herself on a bench, and started shivering and staring at the Physics Building.

Kairi shook her head. The other version of her did not appear attractive. In fact, she looked like a crazy stalker. That was not good.

She sidled up and stood behind the bench, pulling up the hood of her jacket. "Psst."

The other her jumped. "Shit." Then, she glared at her. "What are you doing here? Get out of here. You're going to ruin it."

"You're going to ruin it. You looked like shit. You look like a stalker."

"I do not." She glanced down at her ensemble and frowned. She ran her hand along her hair. "Okay, I've looked better. But, you know how important this is."

Kairi felt kind of sorry for her. She was so desperate and clueless. "Yes?" She touched her shoulder, and then it felt as if her body was turned inside out. She fell to her knees and started vomiting.

In the meantime, past-her fell off the bench and started vomiting. When she was finished, she said, "What the hell did you do to me?"

Kairi still writhed on the ground, wishing she was dead. Her body spasmed uncontrollably. Tears ran down her cheeks.

Past-her got up and stood over her. "Are you okay?"

She couldn't answer her.

"I'm serious. Should I call an ambulance?" Why were people always asking her that these days?

Past-her started to lean over her but quickly put a hand to her stomach and stood up straight. "What the hell?"

"Don't touch me," Kairi managed to grunt. "Move away."

Past-her took a couple of steps away. "I don't get it. What's going on?"

Kairi started to feel like a human being again. She rose to a sitting position. "It's bad when we interact."

"No, it's not. I've interacted with past-me's before."

That was true. What was different now?

Past-Kairi glanced at her watch and the Physics Building. "You have to get out of here, or you're going to wreck everything."

"I've got news for you, sister. Whatever you think's going to happen here isn't. And shut up. I'm thinking." Kairi also felt sick when she returned to Sunday morning, April twenty-fourth, 2014 and interacted with past-her-in-the-bushes.

"Duh." She smacked her forehead. Both times she interacted with past-hers that were time traveling themselves.

"What? What is it?"

"It's the time travel. We're both time traveling right now."

"So?"

"So, apparently, it's not good for us to come in contact with each other."

Past-her looked at her watch again. "Seriously, you need to get out of here."

"How long do we have?"

"Less than ten minutes."

Kairi got on all fours and started crawling towards the bushes. She turned back to her. "Are you coming?"

She sighed. "All right. I guess I'm not poised to make a good first impression." Carefully keeping her distance, she followed her. "Why are you here?"

"I just wanted to see what happened here and now."

The other version of her frowned and turned around to look

at the Math and Physics Buildings.

Dakota exited the Math Building with two other girls, smiling and laughing. Hurray. Dakota was in school. That had to be good.

Josh exited the Physics Building, engrossed in thought.

Dakota and company and Josh walked straight toward each other. Kairi held her breath.

And they walked right on past each other. They never interacted or even looked at each other.

What the hell?

Past-her glanced at her and said, "What the hell?"

Kairi shrugged. "I don't know."

Chapter Thirty-Six
Kyle: Boulder, Colorado, 2019

In the now-overwritten timeline, when Kyle had gone to the student union with Oliver, he'd noticed the UMC had an old-school bulletin board with rooms for rent and job openings. That was as good a place as any to start looking for a place to live and a job.

All he had to do was avoid being seen by Oliver. To that end, he shaved his head and got some fake glasses. With his hoodie pulled up, he didn't think Oliver would recognize him. It had been a couple of years since they'd interacted in person in this timeline.

In his disguise, in the UMC, he got some good leads for a room. That was the beauty of a university town. He stood in front of the bulletin board, and students streamed around him as he input the contact numbers into his phone. He went over to the Alferd Packer Grill. Feeling a little melancholy, he sat down and started making calls. Soon, he narrowed it down to two options in Oliver's neighborhood south of campus. That might be a little dangerous in terms of being discovered by Oliver, but he wanted to keep an eye on him, and that was also where that DeShaw guy had said he'd seen the Moira look-alike.

The two places were close enough to walk to, so that's what he decided to do. As he rambled south through campus, he checked the map on his phone and noted the building signs, trying to get his bearings. Even in early fall, er, spring, the campus was appealing with its red sandstone buildings, numerous basketball courts, and lush green sports fields. He still hadn't gotten used to the abrupt change of season due to moving from the Southern to the Northern hemisphere. Back home, the leaves were changing, and it had only just started staying cool during the day. It was a lot like Traveling to instantly go from fall to spring.

As he approached the tallest buildings on campus, he looked them up on his phone. It was the Duane Physical Laboratories Complex. Hmm. He should go into the Physics Library. They might have books there on time travel. Maybe someone in there could help him understand Traveling better. That might be an appropriate use of his time--no pun intended.

Kyle walked up to a door, opened it and smacked right into a man coming out of the door. "Sorry."

The man, about Kyle's age, took a step back, frowning. "Hey! What's your hurry? You got a physics emergency?"

Kyle smiled in spite of himself. "Sort of. I need to learn more about time travel."

The man lost the frown and raised his bushy dark-brown eyebrows. "More?" With his voice relaxed, he reminded Kyle of his fun-loving buddy Liam. "What do you know?"

"What do you know?" Kyle asked. "Do you know something?"

The man nodded. "I know a bit. It's a hobby of mine."

Jackpot. "I know a bit, too. It's a hobby of mine, also. Hi, I'm Kyle."

"Hi, I'm Josh."

"This may sound weird, but I'm new in town and don't know anybody," Kyle said. "Do you want to go for a beer or drinks later? Maybe I could pick your brain about time travel?"

Josh frowned. "Are you asking me out? Cause I don't swing that way."

"No." Kyle chuckled. "But I see how you could get that idea. Sorry. You remind me of my best mate back home in Australia."

"Mate?"

"Sorry." This was not going well. "No, I meant?"

"I'm messing with you, dude." Josh grinned. "I knew what you meant." He nodded. "Sure. I like drinks. You said you were buying, right?"

"Yeah." He reminded Kyle of Liam. He wondered when or if he'd see Liam again.

"I know just the place, The Rio. Seven o'clock? If you give

me your number, I'll text you the address."

"Sounds great," Kyle said. He gave Josh his number, and they went their separate ways.

In the Physics Library, which turned out to be in the Math Building, Kyle couldn't make heads or tails of any of the technical books there. Maybe that Josh guy could translate for him.

When Kyle walked up to the Rio, Josh was already standing outside waiting. "Sorry. The bus was late," Kyle said.

"The Skip? Yeah, there's no telling when that thing will show up. If you'd told me you were taking the bus, I would have warned you." He grabbed hold of the restaurant's massive door's massive handle and pulled. It was the biggest door Kyle had ever seen. "But, no worries. I just got here."

As the door opened, a wave of noises and spices flowed over them.

"Wow. It's crowded," Kyle said over the din of conversation. "The food must be good here."

"The food is good here." Josh grinned. "But people come for the margaritas."

"I like margaritas." It seemed as if it had been forever since Kyle'd kicked back and had a drink with a friend. "And I didn't drive, so who knows how many I'll have?" He smiled.

"The limit is three." Josh picked his way through the crowd to the bar.

"Limit?" Kyle said. "I'm Australian! I can drink any Yank under the table."

A few minutes later, at a table in the bar, they took their first sips of margaritas. Kyle said, "You're right. That is good."

Josh held up his glass. "Cheers."

They clinked glasses and took another sip.

"Do you go to the university?" Josh asked.

"Not exactly," Kyle said. "Let's say I'm pursuing independent studies. In fact, I just recently got to town, and I think I found a place to live this afternoon." One of the leads from the bulletin board looked like it would pan out--at least it'd better, he'd put down a deposit.

"So, you mentioned time travel earlier," Josh said. "What's your interest, if you don't mind me asking?"

Kyle didn't know what to tell him. He wasn't supposed to reveal family secrets to outsiders. On the other hand, Liam had been a great help over the years, especially lately, harebrained schemes notwithstanding.

A saucy male voice interrupted them. "Now, that's what I like to see, two fine strapping young men out for a romantic night on the town." The speaker was Latino and in decent shape.

"Romantic? No, mate," Kyle said.

"Hello, there. I'm Diego." Diego opened and closed his eyes quickly a few times. Was he trying to flirt? Kyle'd never had to deal with this back home. This was the second time today. Were a lot of Americans gay?

"Hi, Diego. I'm Josh, and this is Kyle," Josh said. "We're not gay."

"Such a pity," Diego said. "Ta ta, then." He waved goodbye with one finger.

"So, back to time travel." Josh grinned. "Of course, we all time travel every day."

What did he know? "We do?"

"We travel into the future at a rate of one second per second all the time." Josh smiled. "Time travel is a fascinating topic. For one thing, there's time-reversal invariance, which says that processes like particle collisions have equal rates going forward or backward in time."

He leaned forward over the table. "And then there are tachyons, the particles that travel faster than the speed of light. When that happens, according to special relativity, there would be a reference frame in which the particle was moving backward in time."

"Why is that?" Kyle asked.

"Well, to be honest, I don't understand that yet," he said. "Special relativity also says time dilation would let us travel into the future. But, anyway, to make a long story short, theoretically, there are lots of possible time travel mechanisms into the future or the past. There are also wormholes and other general relativity methods."

Josh raised his eyebrows and took a sip of his drink. "I feel weird right now. I'm getting a really strong feeling of déjà vu." He peered at Kyle over his drink. "Are you?"

Kyle shrugged. "No." He searched his memory. He was pretty sure he'd never interacted with this Josh guy in any timeline. And this was the first time he'd talked to anyone who actually knew scientific facts about time travel.

Two margaritas and a huge platter of grilled steak fajitas later, Kyle was feeling very chatty. He pushed his decimated plate away. "I didn't answer you earlier. The reason I'm interested in time travel is it's part of my spiritual heritage. My people believe The Dreaming was a sacred time when the world was created."

"Who are your people?" Josh asked.

"Native Australians."

"Okay?" Josh said. "But, what does that have to do with time travel?"

"The Dreaming is eternal, and our people exist eternally in The Dreaming. There is no time, no past or present or future. Everything exists at once."

"So," Josh held up his finger. "Are you saying you can access all of time, any time, via this Dreaming?"

"Yes." Kyle nodded. "Exactly."

"That's so cool," Josh said. "But is it metaphorical? I mean, you can't truly access other times, right? It's not like you can physically go to the other times?"

"I can," Kyle said. "It's real. I'm a time traveler. I Travel through time." Maybe he shouldn't have said that.

Josh's eyebrows rose almost to his hairline. "Are you serious? Or is it the margaritas? I told you you shouldn't have had that third one."

"But it's weird," Kyle added. "Bad stuff keeps happening. And I keep running into the same people when I Travel. Why do I do that?"

Josh leaned back in his chair and laughed. "That's what's weird? Not time traveling itself, but seeing the same people?"

"You don't think it's weird?"

Josh was silent for a moment. "Okay, that is kind of weird. Actually, time itself is kind of weird. It's a man-made construct. We impose the concept of time onto our reality and force it to evolve at a rate of one second per second. Physics shows time should be on the same footing as space. And we can move any

221

direction in space, so why not time?" He looked at Kyle. "What do you think?"

"What was that again, mate? You lost me."

Josh smiled and stood up. "Come on; it's time to get you home."

Kyle stood up, too. Where did he live now? "I wrote down my hotel address here. Is there any chance you can help me get there?"

"Sure, I'll give you a ride," Josh said.

As they threaded their way through the still-crowded entryway, Kyle thought he saw Moira. "Moira!"

But when he looked back through the crowd, she was gone.

Chapter Thirty-Seven
Kairi: Boulder, Colorado, 2018

Kairi and past-Kairi were cowering in the bushes on campus on the day in 2018 they were supposed to meet Josh. But it didn't happen. They were very confused.

The other Kairi asked, "What now?"

Kairi blew out a big breath. "I don't know." Looking at past-her, she added, "What do you remember about this day in the first timeline?"

Past-her said, "It's difficult. That timeline has been overwritten so many times."

"Dakota called from math class, crying, right?"

"Yes." Past-her nodded. "And I came over here. And Dakota was sitting on that bench," she pointed, "with Josh."

"And she was glad to see us," Kairi said. "She introduced us to Josh, saying something like Kairi, this is my good friend Josh. Josh, this is my good friend Kairi. even though she'd just met him."

The two Kairis smiled at each other. That was so Dakota.

"And Josh said, Nice to meet you. and smiled," past-her said. "And we shook hands."

"Then Josh asked if he could buy us a cup of coffee," Kairi said.

Past-her looked sad. "And the rest is history."

She was sure she looked sad, too. "The question is, what did Dakota say to him before we got there?"

Past-her shrugged. "I don't see how we can know that now. We didn't see it personally, and that timeline is gone."

"So, the thing to do is to get Dakota to introduce us to Josh, hopefully saying something like what she said before."

"I guess," past-her said. "How do we manage that?"

The two of them looked at each other for a while.

"And what's going on here, with us?" Past-her pointed back and forth.

"You mean the dizziness and nausea?"

"Duh."

"I'm guessing it's like I said--it's not good for us to interact too closely when we're both time traveling. But how do I know? I'm only a couple of days older than you."

The other version of her sputtered. "A couple of days? That's all?"

"Yeah. What did you think?"

"I don't know. But I thought you were more advanced than that."

"I seem wise, do I?" Kairi grinned. This was more like it. Past-her should treat her with respect.

"Well, no."

Good grief.

But past-her shot her a weak grin. "All this is confusing. I'm going home."

Kairi nodded. "Probably a good idea." She decided to go home, too.

Back at home in 2019, it was still spring break. Thank goodness for that. Kairi was worn out from all the timelines, time trips, and whatever the hell was going on. She couldn't face any more. She went back to sleep. She didn't dream.

Dakota woke her up by banging the door open and clomping around the room. Judging by the Big Ben and the Eiffel Tower posters, she was still home. Good. Judging by the sunset, she'd slept the day away.

"You're still in bed?" Dakota asked. "Are you sick? Do you want me to go get you some soup?" She knew how to procure soup?

Kairi lifted herself on an elbow and examined her. She'd never seen Dakota look so good. She didn't have dreadlocks and wasn't as skinny as she remembered. Her clothes were clean, her skin was clear, and her eyes practically sparkled. "You look good, nice, I mean, healthy. I'm glad." She still felt giddy with relief that Dakota wasn't dead.

Dakota chuckled. "Okay." She took a step toward her. "So, that's a yes on the soup? You're feverish?"

Kairi sat up. "No. I'm fine. I guess I was just tired."

"Okay." She turned away and opened her closet, pondering her clothes.

"What are you up to tonight?" Kairi wanted to get to know this new, more self-sufficient Dakota.

Dakota reached into her closet and took out a blouse, holding it up in the dimming light. "Nothing much. Some friends and I were thinking about hanging out, but there's nothing definite yet."

This Dakota didn't hang out with her? "What do you think about going out to dinner with me?"

Dakota didn't answer right away.

"My treat. Come on. We never hang out anymore." Kairi was guessing.

"Where?"

"The Sink?" Kairi said.

Dakota wrinkled her nose.

Not fancy enough for her now? "The Rio?" The Rio Grande was the hippest, most popular restaurant in downtown Boulder.

"Ooh. Some margs would be excellent! Do I have time to change?"

"Yeah. I'm gonna take a shower."

An hour later, they were waiting in the bar for a table at the university student hot spot, famous for its margaritas. They each sipped one. Kairi smacked her lips after a sip. They were justifiably famous. Cold. Tangy. Mmm.

It felt really good to relax and do something normal again. Now that Operation-Save-Dakota was a success, maybe she should leave well enough alone.

On the other hand, she still missed Josh. She sighed. Maybe she should try to forget about him.

The bar was jam-packed with people and noise-packed, as usual. You'd think the food and drinks were free it was so crowded.

Dakota surveyed the eye candy. Kairi was guessing neither one of them had a boyfriend in this timeline. "Ooh, he's cute."

225

Kairi stared across the crowd at a familiar-looking Latino. How did she know him?

Whoever he was, apparently, the two of them staring at him made him want to come over. He sashayed through the crowd.

"Oops. Gay," Dakota said. "Really cute, though."

As he approached, Kairi remembered his big brown eyes and gorgeous lashes. He was Diego, the guy that knocked her on her ass in Farrand Field the other day. "Diego, right?" she said. "How's it going?"

He drew his eyebrows together. "How do you know my name?"

Crap. They hadn't met in this timeline? She was going to have to start taking notes or something. "Uh, I make it a point to know all the handsome guys on campus." Yikes, did she actually use that bad line again?

Diego moved his forefinger in a circle. "We're not on campus."

"I must have seen you on campus and uh, asked around." Dakota snickered.

He grinned. "I am fine, so I can see that. But, too bad, so sad for you, we don't play on the same team."

Dakota turned back to the crowd, scanning it for cute straight guys.

"Yes." Kairi nodded solemnly. "Too bad for me. Can I buy you a drink, anyway?"

He pursed his lips. "I wouldn't say no to one of those fabulous margs."

She tried to get the waitress's attention, waving at her like a fool. In the meantime, she said, "I'm Kairi, and this is Dakota."

"Pleased to meet you, ladies. Kairi, are you by any chance a Chicana? We have this group on campus?"

She wasn't about to go down that road again--admitting she didn't know who she was. And why did people keep thinking she was Latina? "I, uh, don't think so, Diego. Sorry." To distract him, she added, "So, what's your major?"

"I'm pre-med. In fact, I work at the local hospital."

"Ooh, he's hot." Dakota stared across the crowd at another guy and gave him a big smile.

The hot guy smiled back at her and walked their way.

Diego glanced at him and said, "You are wrong, girlfriend. He's not hot. He's hottie-hot-hot."

As the mystery hottie approached their table, he spied Diego checking him out and bee-lined straight for him.

Dakota shrugged and gave Kairi a look that said, what are you gonna do? "Hi, I'm Dakota," she said to the hottie. "This is Kairi." She pointed at her.

He mumbled something that sounded like, 'Alex,' as he stepped up to the table.

Dakota piped up. "Alex, this is my good friend Diego. Diego, this is my good friend Alex."

The men beamed at each other. This was similar to what Dakota said when she introduced her and Josh originally. Very interesting.

"Nice to meet you," Diego said, smiling like the cat that owned a cat-food factory.

Diego and Alex's handshake lasted a little too long.

"Can I buy you a drink?" Alex asked, staring into Diego's eyes.

"Sure," Diego said. "I enjoy drinks."

"Me, too." Alex smiled. "We have so much in common." They walked off without even a backward glance.

"What was that?" Kairi asked Dakota. "The way you introduced them? Why did you do that?"

She shrugged again. "I could tell they had chemistry. I just tried to help it along a little."

That must be what she did for her and Josh in the now-overwritten timeline. "That was really nice of you. You're a really nice person, Dakota."

She bobbed her head. "Yep."

And then the waitress finally deigned to make an appearance. "Yes? Did you want something else?"

She had been going to buy that Diego a drink. He missed the boat there. What the heck? She pointed at the table. "Another round for us girls, please."

Eventually, they called them to their table in the dining room. It was a good thing, too, because she was buzzed.

When someone put warm chips and homemade salsa on their table, she attacked them. Before she knew it, most of the chips were gone. When was the last time she'd eaten, anyway?

"Easy, there, chippy," Dakota said. "I think you may have had too much to drink." She moved the basket across the table, away from her.

This Dakota was responsible. That took some getting used to. "You may be right. 'Kota, if I asked you to do a favor for me, would you do it?"

"Probably--unless it involved a felony." She cocked her head to the side and then straightened it. "No, I'd probably still do it. What's the favor?"

"Will you introduce me to a guy?" Kairi asked.

She smiled. "Any guy, or did you have someone specific in mind?"

"Specific. But not now. Another time. His name is Josh."

Chapter Thirty-Eight
Kyle: Boulder, Colorado, 2019

The morning after a night of drinking and talking time travel, Kyle
had a pounding headache. At least he was still in his present.
He stumbled to the little kitchenette and put the kettle on. He
remembered waking up at Liam's place after a similar night
of drinking and then joking around with him. This new life in
America was going to be lonely without him. He should call Liam.
What time was it at home?

When he grabbed his mobile, though, there was a voicemail
from Josh. "Some of my buddies and me are gonna play
basketball later. We need another guy." Maybe the U.S. wouldn't
be so lonely after all. "I still don't know if it was the margaritas
talking or not when you mentioned time travel, but I want to
discuss it more. Call me when you get over your hangover.
Cheers, mate!" Kyle could hear the teasing in his voice when
Josh said, 'mate.' It seemed as if he'd made a friend here. Good.

The kettle whistled, and he made himself some tea. As
he sipped, he thought about what he had to do for the day. He
should call his new landlord, a crusty senior citizen named John
Taylor, and see if his check cleared yet so he could move. Based
on John's reluctance to take Kyle's Australian check, he needed
to get an American bank account. And he needed to call Josh
back.

He sipped and tried to recall the night before. Something
important had happened at the end of the night, something to do
with his family... Something related to what DeShaw had said in
that other timeline. As he sipped, the caffeine jump-started his
brain. Oh, yeah, he'd seen a woman who looked like Moira.

Maybe if he talked to Oliver's friend DeShaw he could get

more information. Of course, the current timeline overwrote the timeline where he'd met DeShaw, so that could be a problem. He had no way to contact him. And it wasn't like he could call Oliver for help. Damn.

Kyle knocked on his new landlord's door. He'd just finished shopping and had a laptop and a bunch of wifi cameras for surveillance in the trunk of his rental car. If that Moira-lookalike was in the area, he'd find her.

Slowly, the door swung open. The older man scowled out at him. "What do you want?"

"I want to move in. Did my check clear? Can I get my key?"

The man rubbed his white-stubbled chin. "No. The check didn't clear. Now, go away. Quit bugging me."

Kyle suppressed a sigh. "Can you give me an estimate on when I might be able to move in?"

John wrinkled his brow. "No. And quit bossing me. The last thing I need is a bunch of uppity colored university students thinking they're better than me and bossing me. You can move in when I say you can move in and not before!"

Kyle couldn't believe what he'd just heard. He grabbed the doorjamb to steady himself. "Excuse me? Colored? What century do you think this is, old man?"

"Old man! How dare you call me old man! You're a little punk. That's what you are. A little colored punk."

Kyle could feel the blood rushing to his head all the way to the tips of his ears and his nose. "Punk! I'm no punk! I'll tell you who's the punk. You're the punk, an old racist punk!"

"Screw you, you colored punk!" John slammed the door.

Kyle barely moved back in time to avoid smashed fingers.

"You're out! You're not living in my apartment!" John yelled through the closed door. "And I'm keeping your check!"

That didn't sound legal. "Oh, no, you're not!" Kyle yelled back.

As he stomped down the walkway to the street, he dialed his bank. Unfortunately, his bank told him the funds had already been transferred. There was no way to stop the check. "Bloody hell!" For someone who was unemployed, the eight hundred dollar check was a serious chunk of change. Kyle fumed as he sat in his rental car, staring bullets at John's house.

Finally, he turned the key in the ignition and drove back to his hotel. He knew it was wrong, but he was going to Travel back and undo the scene with John.

Kyle knocked on his new landlord's door. He'd been careful to arrive well before the other version of him was here. He didn't want to run into the past version of himself. His stomach couldn't take it. He'd had enough trouble avoiding himself at the hotel.

Slowly, the door swung open. The older man scowled at him. "What do you want?"

"Hello, Mr. Taylor." Kyle forced himself to smile. "I'd like to move in. Did my check clear? Can I get my key?"

John rubbed his white-whiskered chin. "No. The check didn't clear. Now, go away. Quit bugging me."

Kyle suppressed a sigh. "My bank says the funds did transfer. Is there any chance you could check with your bank?"

John wrinkled his brow. "No. And quit bossing me. The last thing I need is a bunch of uppity colored university students thinking they're better than me and bossing me. You can move in when I say you can move it and not before!"

"Sir, I've been nothing but respectful to you." Kyle gritted his teeth. "I'm not trying to boss you, sir, and I'm not an uppity colored university student." He stepped into the doorway of John's house. Now John wouldn't be able to slam the door.

John's mouth hung open for a moment. "Why did you come in? I didn't say you could come in."

"I just want to move into my new apartment--which I paid for, sir."

"Get out. Get out of my house! Get out!" John was practically jumping up and down.

"Please, calm down, sir." Kyle reached for John's arm, hoping to steady him.

"Don't touch me!" John jerked his arm back, unbalancing himself, and fell to the floor. "Oh, Ow!" He clutched his hands to his chest. "It hurts."

Kyle was bewildered for a moment. What was going on? John wasn't a Traveler. Touching him shouldn't have any effect. Was John having a heart attack? How could that be?

231

"Ohh. Call 911!" John said, writhing on the floor.

Kyle shook his head clear and grabbed the phone on the table by the door, dialing the number.

The operator said, "911. What is the nature of your emergency?"

Kyle stared at John, still writhing on the ground, moaning, and clutching his chest. "I'm with someone who's having a heart attack."

Kyle gave the operator the address and tried to follow her instructions on how to help John.

Within a few minutes, an ambulance drove up, and two men in uniforms jumped out and ran up the walkway to the still-open front door.

Kyle was somewhat dazed by the turn of events. "Over here." John wasn't writhing anymore, and his color had phased from reddish to grayish.

The men rushed up and knelt over John. One man touched his neck. The other was messing around with a blood pressure cuff. Their eyes met over the prone man.

The first one stood up. "I'm sorry, sir, but he's gone."

Kyle just shook his head from side to side. What the hell had he done? He knew Traveling was dangerous. He knew he shouldn't do it anymore.

"Sir?" The second emergency worker was now standing next to him.

"Sorry. What?"

"What's the deceased's name?"

"He's John Taylor. And I just met him. I don't know him," Kyle said.

"What's your name?"

"I'm, uh, John Smith." Kyle's gaze drifted back to the street and his rental car. Then he realized they could run the plates on his car and find out who he was. And that he did know the old guy. His bank records would show that. Bloody hell.

"I'm sorry about this guy, but I didn't have anything to do with it. He just fell screaming and clutching his chest." Kyle turned and ran for his car.

Once in his car, he raced for his hotel. He had to get away from this whole horrible episode.

When he returned to his present, opening his eyes in his hotel room bed in mid-afternoon, the room spun around him. He grabbed the bedspread as new memory washed over him. He seemed to have killed his elderly landlord. "Bloody hell."

When the room stopped spinning, he got up and made himself some tea. He could try to Travel back and undo his latest Traveling. But the timelines were turning into a tangled disaster. And every time he went back, things seemed to get worse.

Maybe he should just stop Traveling. He'd considered that before but hadn't obeyed his own rule.

Kyle made up his mind. That was it. Absolutely no more Traveling. At least until he figured out how to save his folks.

So, what did non-Travelers do with their days?

He needed to get an American bank account. And he needed to call Josh back.

He sipped and tried to recall what he'd been thinking first thing this morning.

The beginning of an idea was percolating in his brain. What had that DeShaw said? Something about double-o seven...

Chapter Thirty-Nine
Kairi: Boulder, Colorado, 2019

Hangovers were hell. Kairi was never drinking again. She spent her last official day of spring break in bed. She didn't know what Dakota did. She kept coming and going and snickering at her.

At dinnertime, Dakota said, "I'm going to meet some friends. Do you want me to bring you back something to eat?" She grinned. "Or someone?"

Kairi pulled the covers away from her head. "Huh?"

"Maybe this mysterious Josh would make you feel better?" She grinned some more and wiggled her eyebrows.

"You remember that from last night?" Responsible Dakota was a little hard to get used to.

"So, you got it bad, huh?" She dropped down on her bed.

"Never mind," she said. "It was all a dream. Forget about it."

Dakota's forehead got all wrinkly. "Are you sure? You seemed pretty interested in this guy."

"Yes. Forget it." She needed past-Dakota's help, not this Dakota.

March 2018 was about the way she remembered it. Cold. The sixteenth was even colder than the seventeenth, but luckily, she'd dressed appropriately in warm nondescript clothes. She'd snuck out of their room first thing in the morning and was now waiting outside the dorm for Dakota to emerge to get something to eat.

If her revised memory served, responsible Dakota actually got up on Sunday morning to eat breakfast.

Dakota emerged from the dorm, and she pounced. "Hey, Dakota."

She startled. "How'd you beat me out here? I could have sworn you were still in bed."

"I woke up, and you were gone, and I wanted to ask you a favor, so I rushed out here."

"Okay." She stamped her feet. "Can't you ask me in the cafeteria? It's cold."

At the mention of food, Kairi's stomach growled. "Yes. Let's go inside."

When they passed the work-study guy at the door who was supposed to check their IDs, he was sound asleep. Good. She didn't think her 2019 ID would pass muster. She'd been planning on holding her thumb over the date.

They got some food and went to sit down.

"So, what's this favor?" Dakota asked.

"I want you to introduce me to a guy," she said. "His name is Josh, and he's going to be coming out of the Physics Building tomorrow at the exact time you'll be coming out of the Math Building." She gave Dakota all the details, and she was very agreeable.

As Dakota was finishing up her breakfast, Kairi stood up and prepared to rush out. "Wow. I'm super-sleepy all of a sudden. I think I better go back to bed."

"Wait a couple of minutes; I'll walk back with you."

"No. I have to go back now." She started walking away and then turned back. "Did I ever tell you I have a bit of a problem with sleep-walking?"

"No," Dakota said. "And I've known you a long time, so I think I'd know something like that."

"I guess we all have our surprises. But if I act like I don't remember this conversation, that's what happened. I really want to meet this guy Josh no matter what else I say." She zoomed out of there before her roommate could catch up.

Kairi debated going home to 2019 and just living her new happy life, but she couldn't resist popping over to tomorrow and watching the meet-cute.

She carefully avoided any benches or bushes where other hers might be loitering. Vomiting was not on today's agenda if she could help it. Instead, she chose to peek out from between the Earth Sciences Building and the Math Building. At the appointed time, Dakota came out of the Math Building, and past-her dashed up to Dakota, looking concerned.

It looked like Dakota was reassuring past-her.

In the meantime, Josh exited the Physics Building and walked toward the two women. He looked even better than she remembered him, strong, kind, loving. And then she couldn't help remembering him handing her a filled champagne flute and then one thing leading to another...

Get a grip, Kair. None of that has happened.

Yet. But now it might. Her heart beat a little faster.

As he passed the Earth Sciences Building, Dakota spied him and turned past-her in his direction.

Past-her seemed intrigued.

When Josh walked by, Dakota said something to get his attention.

He turned to them.

Dakota and past-her smiled brightly at him.

He smiled back.

Dakota seemed to be introducing past-her and Josh.

Past-her and Josh shook hands and stared into each other's eyes.

Score.

He pointed north and said something.

Kairi pressed against the building and tried to look nondescript to avoid being seen.

The women nodded, and they all started walking her way.

Quickly, Kairi walked back around the north side of the Earth Sciences Building and into the bitter March wind.

The three of them stepped onto Colorado Avenue.

And a blue Prius plowed right into them.

Dakota flew into the air, landing in a heap in the middle of the road.

Oh, God!

Past-her and Josh, on the pavement, struggled to get up. At least they were alive.

Kairi ran towards them. Dakota wasn't moving.

The driver of the car, a fifty-ish woman, got out, looking dazed. "I didn't see them. They stepped right in front of me."

"Call 911!" Kairi screamed, leaning over Dakota. She peered

into her face. She seemed to be breathing. She opened her eyes. "How do you feel?" Kairi asked. "What hurts?"

Dakota looked into her eyes. "Kairi, how did I get here? Why am I in the street?"

"We called an ambulance." Her eyes shot over to the driver, and she nodded.

Dakota's eyes widened. "Why can't I move?"

Past-her, head drenched in blood, jostled her out of the way. "Dakota? Thank God you're alive. Don't try to move."

Kairi felt sick but didn't think it was only because of her contact with past-her.

"I can't move," Dakota said. "Why can't I move?"

Josh leaned over her, his left arm and torso saturated with blood, his face white. "Hang in there, Dakota. It'll be okay. Just try to breathe through the pain."

"But I don't feel any pain," she said.

Past-her and Josh glanced at each other with faces that said, Uh, oh. Not good.

Eyes heavy with moisture, Kairi took a step back.

Focused on Dakota, past-her and Josh didn't even notice her.

The driver did, though. "How is she?" she asked.

"Not good." Kairi shook her head, eyes overflowing. She couldn't believe she had hurt Dakota again. Jesus fucking Christ. How could this happen again? Shit, shit, shit.

"You saw it, though, didn't you?" the woman asked. "They just stepped right in front of me. They were distracted, talking. They weren't paying attention. You saw it, right?"

Cars streamed around them. Pedestrians encircled them. "What happened?" someone asked.

What did happen next? They were in her past. She should be able to recall it, right? Kairi staggered back against the car, trying to remember.

Unfortunately, everything was very fuzzy. She recalled her current timeline, where she never met Josh, but she didn't seem to know what would happen here next. Shit.

"Are you okay? You look woozy or something," the driver asked her as the ambulance siren approached.

She shook her head.

The ambulance pulled up, and the EMTs jumped out. One of them called, "Don't move her," and ran to Dakota.

The other EMT approached Josh and past-her. "What hurts?"

Before they could answer, the first EMT came over and said something quietly in the other one's ear. The second EMT said, "You guys will have to wait for a moment. We need to take care of your friend here."

A police car approached.

Kairi took a step towards the Earth Sciences front door. And another.

The squad car stopped.

The driver of the Prius said, "I'm so sorry. It was an accident."

Kairi slipped through the crowd and walked into the Earth Sciences Building.

The EMTs must have loaded everyone up quickly because soon, she heard the ambulance siren retreating.

She felt horrible. This whole thing was her fault. Time travel was a curse. It kept putting people she cared about in danger.

She had to know what was going on with her friends.

Was Josh injured?

And Dakota couldn't really be paralyzed, could she?

Chapter Forty
Kyle: Boulder, Colorado, 2019

Kyle went shopping and purchased a laptop and a bunch of wifi cameras for surveillance. He returned to his hotel room and plugged the laptop to charge it.

Then, based on the recommendation of the teenager manning the hotel's front desk, he went to lunch at the local pancake house. It was packed. As he looked unsuccessfully for a seat in the waiting area, he debated leaving. He heard a loud 'woo hoo,' and then someone tapped him on the shoulder.

"Hola, cutie," the man said.

"Are you talking to me?" Kyle pointed at himself.

"Aw." The strange man frowned. "You don't remember me. And here I thought I always made a good impression."

Kyle shook his head. "Sorry? Have we met?"

"At the Rio last night, silly. You were with your boyfriend, that hottie-hot-hot guy."

Last night? So much had happened since then. "Boyfriend?" Kyle searched his Swiss-cheese memory. Today had been overwritten with a new dead landlord. Last night, however, the problem wasn't Traveling. The problem was margaritas. "Oh. Margaritas."

"Oh, yeah." The man nodded. "The Rio's margs are the bomb. I guess I'm not too insulted you don't remember me." He grinned. "I'm Diego. I'm here with my special friend from last night. Do you want to join us?" He pointed at a table where a fraternity-looking guy waved.

That sounded like a third-wheel situation. But Kyle was feeling kind of lonely. "I wouldn't want to intrude."

"Don't be silly." Diego hooked his arm around Kyle's and led him to the table. "There aren't that many gay men of color in this town."

As they sat down, Diego said, "This beautiful man is Alex. Alex, say hi to ...?"

"Hi, I'm Kyle. Nice to meet you, both of you."

The waitress dropped off another menu.

"But I should probably say I'm not gay," Kyle added. Didn't he already tell this Diego guy that?

"We won't hold it against you." Alex smiled.

"Unless you ask us to!" Diego said, and Alex laughed.

After a moment, Kyle joined in. Once they all calmed down, he said, "So, what's good here?"

"What isn't?" Diego said.

The waitress came back, and they all ordered various forms of pancakes.

Once she'd left, Diego leaned back and said, "So where are you from, Kyle? I'm hearing a very sexy accent."

Kyle glanced at Alex, who had stopped smiling. "I'm from Australia. But I want to hear about you guys and your town. I'm new to the area, and I don't know anything or anyone. I'm guessing the Rio is one of the local hot spots."

The two men smiled and looked at each other.

"Oh, yeah," Alex said.

"And the pancake house seems popular," Kyle said. "Thanks for letting me jump the line. Actually," he pointed at Diego, "it's weird that I ran into you again."

Alex stood up. "I'm going to the john." He stalked off.

"It's not that weird. It's a small town," Diego said. "In fact, I'm betting I'll run into you again."

"Quit flirting," Kyle said. "I'm not into guys. And what about Alex?"

Diego sighed. "Alex is a good guy, but he's not the one. He's not my true love."

"You can tell that after one night?"

"Sí, señor."

Kyle asked, "But how do you know?"

Diego frowned. "I know because I met my true love once."

"And? What happened?"

"I don't want to talk about it," Diego said. "It's too

240

depressing."

They were silent for a few minutes. As Alex returned to the table, Kyle said, "Maybe you have more than one true love."

Diego didn't answer.

When Alex sat down, Diego smiled and put his arm around him. "There you are, beautiful Alex. We were missing you."

Alex smiled with what appeared to be relief.

Their food came, and they all dug in.

After Kyle and Diego were finished and Alex was still eating, Diego leaned back on his side of the booth. "So, Kyle, what are you up to the rest of this fine day?"

Kyle leaned back, too. "Believe it or not, I'm on a quest to find a woman."

"Oh, we believe it, Kyle," Diego said. "We believe."

Alex grinned. "Are you looking for a special woman, or will any woman do?"

Kyle grinned back. "It's not what you think. I'm looking for a relative in town. We lost touch, but I heard she was living here." Close enough.

Diego got an odd look on his face. "You know, we met a woman last night at the Rio that did look like you." He turned to Alex. "Remember?"

"At the Rio?" Kyle said. "I knew I saw something!"

Alex nodded.

That sounded like a lead. "This is important. Do you remember her name?"

"Was her name Karen?" Alex asked.

"No," Diego said. "The chica was Carrie."

"Yeah! Carrie, that was it," Alex said.

"Basically, she just introduced herself and her friend Dakota," Diego said.

"That's it?" Kyle asked. This was tantalizing, but he needed more information. "Did you get her last name? Or her friend's last name? Or where she lives? Or her phone number? Anything?" So close to finding her, and yet so far.

"Hmm. Sorry," Diego said. "Yeah, that's pretty much it. I guess she also mentioned she went to the university."

"Sorry we couldn't help more," Alex said.

"No, you guys helped a ton. I know way more than I knew

an hour ago. Her name is Carrie, and she goes to the university." It was frustrating to think he'd been in the same place at the same time as the mystery woman last night and hadn't realized it.

"Who is she?" Alex asked.

"Yeah," Diego said. "How come you know so little about her? Didn't you say she was a relative?"

"Ah, yes," Kyle said. "She's a long-lost relative. She's from a branch of the family that we lost track of." That was as good an explanation as any.

After lunch, Kyle went back to his hotel room. He'd been planning on picking up his now-charged laptop and driving around Oliver's neighborhood to see where he could plant the cameras.

But instead, he made himself a cup of tea and tried to talk himself out of Traveling back to the previous night and looking for this mysterious Carrie at the Rio.

Traveling was very dangerous. He killed his parents. He killed Grandpa Barada. He put himself in a coma. He killed Mr. Taylor, maybe. He shouldn't Travel.

But, he had unkilled Oliver. That had stuck. And how else was he going to find this woman? She was important. He could feel it.

But after killing John Taylor, he'd decided he wouldn't Travel anymore. Period.

But maybe if he didn't interact with anyone, it would be okay.

No, he wasn't gonna do it.

Nope.

No way.

As soon as he finished his cup of tea, he lay down on the bed.

Kyle grabbed hold of the massive restaurant door's massive handle and pulled. As the door opened, a wave of noises and spices flowed over him. An hour earlier, the place was still packed. Keeping an eye open for the mysterious Carrie, he elbowed his way to the bar, got a Coke and went to the seating area upstairs that overlooked the entire bar. He planned to nurse his Coke for as long it took to find Carrie, and then he wasn't sure what he'd do.

He knew he wouldn't interact with his past self under any circumstances. He didn't want to end up in another coma.

At seven o'clock, he saw himself come in with Josh. Josh put their names in at the hostess counter, and then the two of them went into the bar and got margaritas.

If anyone spotted him up here and down there simultaneously, it could mean trouble. Kyle put his sunglasses on and pulled his hood up.

Still no sign of Carrie.

On the plus side, both Josh and the other Kyle seemed to be having a good time down there on the first floor. On the second floor, Kyle was on edge.

Eventually, Josh and the other Kyle went into the dining room.

Finally.

Kyle took off his sunglasses and peered more intently down into the bar.

After another half hour or so, the Moira-lookalike came in with a blonde girl who looked like a sorority girl, Dakota, presumably. They found a table in the bar and got drinks.

Kyle couldn't believe how similar she looked to Moira. But she was clearly older. It wasn't Moira. Unless... There was an outside chance it was Moira-from-the-future. But many family members would have to die for Moira to become the designated Traveler. He shut down that line of thought quickly.

Diego walked over to their table, followed closely by Alex. Dakota seemed to introduce them. Diego and Alex sashayed off together.

Kyle needed more information about Carrie.

When Carrie got up from the table and walked towards the restrooms, Kyle saw his chance to pump Dakota for info. He jumped up, rushed down the stairs, and ran up to Dakota.

She smiled broadly when she saw him. "You're not gay, are you?" she asked.

He positioned himself so he could see the restrooms. "No." Why did people keep thinking that? Was he giving off a gay vibe or something? "I, ah, was sitting upstairs, and I couldn't help noticing you and your friend."

"Hi, I'm Dakota," she said.

Kyle restrained himself from saying, 'I know.'

"And you are?" she asked.

Hell. He should have come up with a cover name. "Ah. Hi. I'm John Taylor."

She wrinkled her nose. "Why is that name familiar?"

He shrugged. "Common name? So, what's your last name?" Jeez, he was rusty at flirting. He decided to try to do what Liam would do.

She smiled again.

"Come on; I told you mine." He smirked and leaned in.

"Moore."

"See, that wasn't so hard, was it?" He grinned. "It's a real pleasure to meet a sheila like you."

She giggled. "Oh, you're from Down Under, aren't you?"

"Yep, mate. And how about your friend? Is she from Down Under?"

"Carrie? No. She's from right here, born and raised."

Bloody hell. Could that be true? "Carrie is a pretty name. C-a-r-r-i-e?"

"No. It's K-a-i-r-i."

"And what's her last name?"

"Johnson."

That didn't make sense. Johnson wasn't an Australian name. "And where do you guys live?"

Dakota leaned back. "Wait a minute. You're acting like a cop or a stalker or something. Why do you want to know all this stuff?"

"I just appreciate some fine sheilas when I see them." He forced another grin.

"I don't know," Dakota said. "I'm getting a weird vibe. You need to leave now."

"Aw, sheila, don't be like that."

"I'm serious. Leave us alone."

"Come on..."

"Get out of here before I call the bouncer."

He forced another smile, but he could tell she was serious. "Your wish is my command, Dakota. It was lovely meeting you."

He bowed, whirled, and walked away.

"Are you sure you're not gay?" she called after him.

As Kyle yanked the giant door open and stepped out into the night air, he mumbled, "Okay, time for plan B."

All he had to do was think of it.

Chapter Forty-One
Kairi: Boulder, Colorado, 2018

Dakota, Josh, and past-Kairi had been flattened by a car, and it was all Kairi's fault. If they died, she'd never forgive herself.

As she walked into the hospital emergency entrance and over to admissions, she couldn't stop the tears from rolling down her cheeks.

At the desk, a gray-haired nurse was typing something into a computer. Kairi wiped the tears off her face with the backs of her hands. How was she going to get any info out of her?

Then, she saw a hot guy wearing pink scrubs sashay behind the nurse. "Diego!"

Diego swiveled her way, looking puzzled. He approached the counter. "Do I know?" His expression cleared. "Oh, you must be Kairi's sister. Come on around." He gestured at the swinging doors that led to the emergency treatment area. "She's okay," he said to the nurse, pushing a big button on the wall.

Kairi quickly slipped through the opening doors before the admitting nurse wised up and asked her for ID.

"You must be wondering how Kairi's doing?" Diego stepped in next to her.

"Yes," she said. "And also the friends she came in with, Dakota and Josh. How are they?" Please be okay.

Diego walked her to a treatment bay, where past-her lay on a hospital bed.

Past-her jerked up when she saw her. "How's Dakota? How's Josh?"

"Easy there," the nurse who was treating her said. "Please lay still." The nurse turned towards Kairi. "You must be her sister?"

Kairi nodded and asked, "Is she going to live? There's so much blood." She was guessing if past-her died, present-her also died. She could barely breathe.

"Yes," the nurse said. "Her wounds are all superficial. All head lacs bleed significantly, even if they're not serious."

"Thank God," Kairi said. She turned to Diego. "Can you take me to the others so I can report back to my, uh, sister about them?"

Diego looked at the nurse, who nodded.

"The hottie, Josh was it, went up to X-ray, so I can't take you to him right now. They think he broke his left radius and ulna."

"His what?"

Diego flashed her a perfect set of pearly whites. "He broke his arm. He'll be okay."

"What a relief." She had a stray thought, why did Josh always seem to break his arm?

"Right this way to Dakota." He directed her to the other end of the large room and another treatment bay filled with people.

The two of them watched the grim-faced medical staff rush around Dakota's bed.

"What about her?" Kairi was almost afraid to ask. Dakota looked dead lying there, not moving.

Diego shook his head and looked at the floor. "They're still doing tests. But it's not good?"

"What do you mean? Is she dying? Is she paralyzed?" It felt as if the Rocky Mountains were crushing her chest.

"They aren't saying anything official," he whispered, "but I think she's paralyzed." Then, more loudly, he said, "Does she have any other family to call?"

Dakota was paralyzed? Because of her? Kairi staggered. This was all too much.

Diego grabbed her by the arm. "Are you okay, honey?"

"Not really," she whispered. "This was all my fault."

"Here," he said. "Why don't you sit down?" He led her to a chair by the nurses' station.

She sank into the chair. "I'm a horrible person. It would have been better if I'd never been born." She buried her face in her hands.

"Honey," Diego said. "It's not your fault. A car hit her." He handed her a tissue.

She lifted her head to dab at her eyes. "But it is my fault."

"You weren't driving the car, were you?" he asked in a matter-of-fact tone.

"No. But it was my fault she was there on campus with past-er, I mean with my sister Kairi and Josh."

"Come on, chica," he said, frowning and crossing his arms. "That doesn't make any sense. Dakota is a grown woman; you can't control her."

"You don't understand." Kairi wished she was dead.

"Why don't you explain it to me?"

"I can't. You'd never believe me."

"Sure I would. I see a lot of crazy stuff working in an ER."

She shook her head. "Not this crazy. You wouldn't believe this."

"Try me."

She was a wreck. She didn't care about anything anymore except undoing the car accident and helping Dakota. "Fine. I'm a time traveler. I manipulated things so she'd be at that time and place so she could introduce me to that guy Josh. I think Josh is my soulmate." That was a laugh. She didn't deserve a soulmate.

"Oooh-kay." Diego took a step back from her.

"I know it sounds crazy, but I'm serious."

He smirked, and she could tell he wanted to say Yeah, right, but he was restraining himself, probably because he felt sorry for her.

"If I'm lying, how did I know your name?" she asked. "According to you, we never met before, did we?"

He glanced back in past-her's direction. "Kairi told you."

"How? Did she use her cell phone?"

"No. But?" He shut up. He looked her up and down. "You do look an awful lot like Kairi, now that the blood is off her face."

"I'm her from the future." This was hopeless. Everything was hopeless.

"Are you saying that you and that chica, there," he pointed behind him, "can actually time travel?"

"She hasn't figured out how to do it yet." Kairi paused. "Do you believe me?"

He said, "No," but he smiled gently while he said it.

She had an inspiration. Maybe Diego could get her a sleeping pill so she could go to sleep and undo this whole thing now. "I admit time travel was a mistake. But haven't you ever done anything crazy for a guy?" Or maybe he could bring her a whole bunch of sleeping pills so she could put herself out of her misery.

He tensed up as if he wanted to say something but wouldn't let himself.

"Or maybe you wish you'd done something crazy for a guy?"

He held his body very still.

"You can help me undo this, Dakota's injuries, if you find me a place to lay down and maybe a sleeping pill."

"How would that help anything?" He crossed his arms again.

"I time travel when I dream." That sounded crazy to her, and she knew it was true.

He sighed. "Chica, please get a hold of yourself. I'm getting concerned. Were you in the accident? Did you hurt your head? Maybe you need to see a mental health professional."

A counselor might give her drugs so she couldn't dream, so she couldn't time travel, and that would be unacceptable. She had to save Dakota if it was the last thing she did. "I'd be willing to help you if you help me," she said. "Are you sure there isn't something a time traveler could do for you?" She squashed the voice inside her that said, No! It always turns out very badly. "I promise to help you if you help me."

He opened his mouth. He closed his mouth.

"Please, Diego. I can't live with what I've done to Dakota."

He grabbed her arm. "I'll take you to the break room where you can lie down, but I'm not getting you any drugs." He led her down the hall and into an empty room with cots. "Here."

She sat down on one of the cots. "What can I do for you, Diego?" He'd held up his part of the bargain.

He scowled and plopped down on another one of the cots. "It's not that I believe you. But, if there's even a ghost of a chance you could do something..."

"Yes?"

"Do you remember Ethan Jones?" He looked at her with sad

puppy-dog eyes.

"I'm sorry. No."

"That freshman who was beaten to death here in town?" She shrugged.

"Because he was gay." His voice hardened. "He was brutally killed just because he was gay."

She did vaguely recollect something horrible. "A few years ago? Did you know him?"

"Sort of. I'd seen him around freshman year. He was hot. I always thought if I'd gotten up the courage to ask him out, maybe he wouldn't have..." His voice petered out.

"Okay," she said. She had to get to dreamland to save Dakota. Maybe she could save this Ethan guy. She'd never know until she tried.

"Okay, what?"

"Okay, I'll try to save Ethan. Tell me everything you know about what happened to him."

Kairi time traveled back to late afternoon on November eighteenth, 2009. It was the Friday before Thanksgiving week, and the campus was clearing out quickly. She loitered outside the main entrance of the University Memorial Center--the last place anyone (except the killers) had seen Ethan alive. She had no idea what she would say or do when she saw him.

And then Diego came out of the building. Ah, reinforcements. "Diego!"

He turned around and approached her. "Sorry? Have we met?"

Think fast, Kair. "Uh, yeah. Through the LGBT Center." She pointed back at the Union. "Uh, there was a party..."

Diego grinned. "There's always a party. Which one? Halloween?"

"Yes! Halloween. That was awesome." Still upset about Dakota being paralyzed, she had to force a smile.

He checked her out. "I must admit I don't remember you, but that's not saying much. It was a really good party. Are you bi? Or, wait, I know." He may have smirked. "I bet you're transgender."

What the heck was that supposed to mean? "Anyway, what do you remember about the party if you don't remember me?"

"That's kind of a random question, but there was a really cute guy there..."

"Right!" She held up her index finger. "Ethan. You said he was hottie-hot-hot."

"That does sound like something I'd say." He checked her out again, trying unsuccessfully to place her.

"Anyway," she said, "you left the party before you heard Ethan say you were hottie-hot-hot. Did you guys ever get together? I thought you made a really cute couple."

"Seriously?" He dropped a shoulder and crossed one leg in front of the other.

"Oh yeah. I can see you guys as a couple. And I have a feeling he can use a friend about now." Then she had a horrible thought. What if, instead of saving Ethan, two freshmen were beaten? She guessed she could always come back and try again. But still, the thought of Diego and his friend getting hurt... She froze in sudden indecision.

"Ah, you..." Diego said. "I'm sorry, I don't know your name."

What if her actions killed both Diego and Ethan?

And then, Ethan came out of the UMC. He said, "'Scuse me," as he brushed past them. She thought Diego's big brown eyes were beautiful, but Ethan's baby-blue eyes and symmetric features were dazzling. He could have been a model, he was so pretty.

It was now or never. "Ethan!" she said.

"Yes?" He turned to them. "It's Diego and...?"

"He knows my name," Diego whispered to her. "Hi, Ethan," he said more loudly.

"Hey," Ethan said, adjusting his messenger bag.

"Hey. We don't really know each other," Kairi said. "But Diego here was just saying I wonder what that hottie Ethan is doing for Thanksgiving and if he'd want to come over to my place?"

"You were?" Ethan turned a thousand-watt smile on Diego, who melted.

"Ah, yeah," Diego stammered.

She nudged Diego, who added, "So, ah, do you want to come over to my place?"

"It just so happens I am free for turkey-day," Ethan said. "I'd be delighted."

They beamed at each other.

From what Diego told her in the hospital, Ethan died within the next couple of hours, so Kairi was determined to stick to him like glue. "So, maybe we should all go grocery shopping now?"

"I do need to go grocery shopping," Diego said. "And I wouldn't mind some help."

Diego and Ethan gazed into each other's eyes. She wasn't sure they even realized she was still standing next to them.

"So, it's settled, then," she said. "We're going grocery shopping."

Diego looked at her. "I think we can handle it, chica."

"Are you sure?" she asked. She didn't want to let them out of her sight. "Let me help."

Ethan gave her a look that said, 'she seems kind of lonely and desperate.' He poked Diego with his elbow. "I never turn down help."

Diego shrugged. "Fine"

"Come on, then, girl," Ethan said. "I need to stop by my dorm first and dump my books."

As the three of them tramped across campus, night fell.

Baker Hall came into sight, and Ethan said, "Shit," under his breath when he saw a group of guys hanging around one of the back doors. "Let's go around to the front door."

"Is this your dorm?" Diego pointed. "Why don't we just go in here?" He kept walking.

"I'd rather go around to the front," Ethan said.

Diego shrugged. "Okay, whatever," and turned to go around the building, but it was too late.

"Ethan?" one of the guys called out in a singsong voice.

"Come on," Ethan said, ignoring the taunting guy and pointing around the side of the dorm.

"Hey, faggot," one of the guys yelled.

Ethan stopped and turned. "I told you not to call me that."

The four guys flowed away from the stoop towards them. They were all scrawny-looking Caucasians.

Diego had an interesting expression on his face as if he couldn't quite believe what was happening.

One of the guys pointed at Diego. "Lookit. The faggot's got

a little faggot friend."

Diego scowled and clenched his fists.

Ethan put his hand on Diego's arm. "We don't want any trouble."

"Faggot."

What year was this? 1950? "Why don't you losers just fuck off," Kairi said before she realized it.

They looked shocked for a second but then walked towards them. She had probably just antagonized murderers. Shit. Did she make things worse?

"I should pound you, faggot," one of them said.

She stepped in front of Ethan and Diego. "If you're going to pound anyone, pound me."

The next thing she knew, she was on the ground, dazed.

And then the pain hit. It felt like her cheek had been flattened. She couldn't focus on anything else.

In the background, she heard a lot of scuffling and grunting noises.

Trying to get up, she pressed her hands onto the parking lot blacktop. The grit dug into her palms. She flashed on an image of a tiny velvet box lying on the same blacktop. She shook her head. With great difficulty, she got back to her feet.

In the distance, she heard a siren.

In her peripheral vision, something came toward her head. She turned to look at it...

Chapter Forty-Two
Kyle: Boulder, Colorado, 2019

Still one day in his past, Kyle crouched behind a newspaper machine every time the door to the Rio opened with an accompanying breeze of chipotle peppers, beer, and mole sauce. He couldn't believe it had come to this. He was, as Dakota said, a stalker. What he was going to do when the women came out of the restaurant, he still didn't know. Stalk them for as long as he could, apparently.

No, he wasn't a stalker. He was a spy. That was it. He was on a mission to discover who Kairi was and how she fit into the family. He was really helping her; that's what he was doing.

Eventually, Kairi and Dakota did emerge. Kairi seemed quite drunk, stumbling and giggling. Dakota seemed sober and sensible. How did those two end up friends, anyway? They seemed like night and day. The women strolled south and turned the corner at Walnut, traveling east.

Kyle hurried to catch up with them.

They walked down the sidewalk to Broadway, then stopped at the bus stop about half a block down.

Hell. If he got on the bus with them, surely that Dakota chick would notice him. If he didn't get on the bus, he'd lose them. While he was still making up his mind, the bus rumbled behind him. He ran for the bus stop.

Ahead of him, the two women and another couple got on.

Kyle kept running. Just as he approached, the driver started closing the doors. But Kyle waved and caught his eye.

The doors opened, and he jumped on. The bus immediately drove away.

He faced front and slouched down while putting his money

in the machine. He looked for Kairi in the driver's mirror. The women were engrossed in conversation and oblivious to their surroundings.

He slunk over to one of the front seats and sat down, still facing forward, keeping an eye on the women in the mirror. He hummed the Mission Impossible music to himself. He wasn't a half-bad spy.

The women stayed on the bus all the way down Broadway until Euclid, when they pulled the string and stood up. Kairi swayed back and forth as the bus stopped. Dakota had to help her get out the back door.

Kyle waited until the last possible second and darted out through the front door.

When he saw the women turn and head towards the underpass, he acted as if he was waiting for another bus. Dakota still hadn't noticed him. Kairi seemed too drunk to notice anything.

The two women sauntered under the underpass.

Kyle followed them.

They walked through campus, past the UMC, past a big parking lot, past the Music Building, and Kyle followed.

The women walked up to the back door of a big stone building. Dakota got out her key, slipped it in the lock, and helped Kairi through the door. The door snicked closed behind them.

Kyle hid behind a dumpster, grimacing at the smell of greasy old pizza boxes and stale skunky beer, checking the map on his phone. The two women had gone into Baker Residence Hall. Judging from their key, they must live there. That was something. That was a discovery. He practically was double-o-seven.

The cool March wind whipped past the dumpster, clearing out the stink. Kyle put his phone back in his hoodie pocket and shivered. Now what?

Flashing lights reflected off the building's windows. What the heck? He glanced around and realized a campus police car had pulled into the parking lot behind the dorm.

"Bloody hell."

He tried to sneak around the dumpster towards the sidewalk without being seen.

"Hey, you!" a man yelled. "What are you doing? Let's see some ID."

Kyle ran.

"Stop!"

He didn't look back.

Back home safe and sound in his normal place and time, Kyle was surprised when no dizziness or nausea accompanied his return. What did that mean? He hadn't changed anything?

But he felt ashamed. What happened to his resolve not to Travel again? He knew he shouldn't do it. Why couldn't he stop himself?

It was like Traveling was a bloody addiction. What did addicts do to stop?

He decided to call Liam. Didn't he have some experience with addictive behavior? "Liam, hey, mate."

"Hey, mate," Liam said. "You're up bright and early. Things must be going well there in the States." It felt really good to hear Liam's voice.

Kyle didn't want to admit what was going on, didn't want to say he thought he might be addicted to Traveling. "Not exactly." He paused. "So, do you know anything about drug addiction or alcoholism?"

"Whoa! Have you been doing drugs? Drinking?"

"No," Kyle said, "or at least no more than usual. Just answer the question."

"Depends. Do you want to be an alcoholic or a drug addict, or do you want to get over it?"

"Let's say I want to get over it."

"That's easy, mate. You need a twelve-step program and a sponsor to call when you're about to slip."

Hell. There wasn't any twelve-step program for Travelers.

"Kyle?" Liam asked. "What's going on out there?"

"I'm not sure," Kyle said. "I can't seem to stop Traveling."

"Shite."

"Yeah."

"I have to leave for work, but I'll tell you what. Why don't you call me when you feel the urge to Travel, and maybe I can talk you out of it? I'll be your time travel sponsor."

That sounded good to Kyle. "Thanks, Liam. Yeah, let's try that."

After he hung up, Kyle found himself in the middle of the afternoon in a hotel room with no emergencies.

He decided to run some errands, buy some clothes and other supplies. He was almost optimistic as he headed towards downtown Boulder.

He was waiting in line at the grocery store when he suddenly started feeling nauseated. The room spun around him, faster and faster. At the same time, his head felt light, and he broke out in a sweat all over his body.

The walls closed in on him, making it difficult to tell up from down. As he vaguely perceived he was falling, he muttered, "Bloody hell."

His head throbbed in synchronicity with the beat of his heart. Then a stabbing pain pierced his forehead. Kyle focused on breathing and not wishing he was dead. When the pain finally faded enough for him to focus on something else, he heard a loud but indistinct argument. When he opened his eyes, he was lying on a high narrow bed, surrounded by flimsy curtains. A machine next to him beeped regularly. A blood pressure cuff was on his left upper arm. He wore a hospital gown and was covered by a thin cotton blanket. "Bloody hell."

When was he?

The argument on the other side of the curtain escalated. "Don't touch me!" an elderly man said.

"Now, honey, you have to calm down," a young man said. "I'm just trying to help you."

"Don't call me honey!" the old man said.

The blood pressure cuff on Kyle's arm suddenly filled with air, squeezing his arm, and Kyle jerked away from it. What the hell? There was no one here. It must be automated somehow.

"Get away from me," the elderly man said. "Don't touch me!"

"Please, sir."

The blood pressure cuff deflated.

The conversation was muffled on the other side of the curtain.

Suddenly, a man, dressed in pink scrubs, pulled back the

fabric. "Now, who do we have here? Kyle, was it? My name is Diego. What happened to you?"

"Nice to meet you, Diego," Kyle said. "I'm not sure what happened to me." He paused. He had a very strong feeling of déjà vu.

The room started spinning again, and Kyle broke out in a sweat again. The fabric walls closed in on him. At least he was already lying down...

When Kyle came to, his whole body ached, especially his head. What happened? Where was he? When was he? He seemed to be in a hospital bed in some kind of private room. "Hello? Is there anyone there?"

A young woman in pink scrubs bustled in. "It's good to see you awake, Mr. Barada. We were worried about you. Your ID says you're from Australia?" She smiled, showing off dimples in her very round cheeks. "I must admit I played a bit of detective. There's only one other person in town named Barada, an Oliver Barada. I called him, and he said he was your brother. He's on his way." She showed off her dimples some more.

"No!" The last thing Kyle needed was to put Oliver in danger. The last time Kyle interacted with Oliver, he'd ended up dead. "You shouldn't have done that. You had no right to do that."

The dimples disappeared. "I'm sorry, sir."

Even in his diminished state, Kyle could tell he'd offended her. "It's just that, I, uh, don't know the guy. He's not my brother."

"Oh, okay." The dimples reappeared. Her shoulders relaxed. "How do you feel?" Kyle couldn't tell if she believed or was humoring him.

"Could I get something for the pain? My head's killing me." Then Kyle had a horrible thought. Could his head be killing him? Could all the Traveling have taken too large a toll? Why did Dad die in that first timeline? He needed to leave now, but if he didn't get some painkillers, he wasn't sure he could even walk.

The nurse scanned the chart at the foot of the bed. "Yes, sir. I'll get you something for the pain in a jiffy." She scurried out.

While she was gone, his mind raced. What was going on with him? He'd been taught the dizziness was a result of the timeline being reset when he returned to his present. But he hadn't done anything to affect the timeline on his most recent trip.

And surely he hadn't been doing anything to the timeline at the grocery store. It didn't make sense for it to reset after he'd been back for over an hour. He tried to scan his memories of recent days to see if there'd been any changes in the timeline, but his headache was making it difficult.

The nurse bustled back in with a hypodermic. "Here you go." She grabbed the IV and quickly injected the drug.

"What's wrong with me?" Kyle asked.

The nurse picked the chart up again. "We're not sure. The doctor examined you when you were out. We're waiting on some test results. I'll get him. Is there anything you'd like to tell us?"

He wasn't sure what to say. He was suffering from time travel?"No." The pain in Kyle's head started to diminish, enabling him to think a little more clearly. "What day is it?" He needed to leave before Oliver got here.

"What day is it? Oh, honey, you may be worse off than we thought."

Not helping. "Is my mobile around here somewhere?"

The nurse rustled around in a drawer and pulled it out. "Here you go." She handed it to him.

He quickly checked the date. He was still in his present. He looked through his voicemails.

There was a new message from Uncle Ray at the time of Kyle's collapse. "Kyle, I just felt you come back from rewriting the timeline again. Stop it, or I may have to take more significant action."

Ray also forwarded a message from Oliver from the same time. "I feel dizzy and weird. Is there something wrong with me? Call me as soon as you get this."

But Kyle knew he hadn't rewritten the timeline then.

What the bloody hell was going on?

Chapter Forty-Three
Kairi: Boulder, Colorado, 2018

Somebody was screaming like a little girl. Kairi opened her eyes. It was Diego. She was back in the hospital break room with him. He sat on a cot near the door. She wasn't entirely sure what day or time it was. She felt slightly dizzy and a lot achy.

"Diego, what's wrong?" she asked. Her entire face ached, and she had a monumental headache. She touched her cheek gently. It was very tender. Her fingers came back with blood on them.

His brown eyes were open wide, and he was breathing heavily. "You, you just appeared." He sputtered. "From nowhere." Then, he crossed himself and whispered something that sounded like diablo. "But you're hurt. Are you looking for the ER?"

She was starting to get annoyed. "You didn't just call me the devil, did you? After all, I've done for you?"

His breathing slowed, and he scowled at her. "Okay, chica, maybe you're not the devil, but I do not know you, so quit acting like you know me." He wagged his forefinger back and forth. "And all you've done for me? You haven't done for me."

Was that a good sign or a bad sign? The timeline must have been rewritten. Did she stop the car accident? When was she? But what did he mean, she hadn't done anything for him? Was Ethan still dead? "Are you saying Ethan's not okay? I time traveled for nothing?" She lowered her voice. "He was still beaten to death?"

Diego jerked back and narrowed his eyes. "Time travel? Beaten? You know my Ethan? Did you do something to him?" His mouth tightened. "Who are you?"

"I'm Kairi. I didn't do anything to Ethan. I saved his life back in 2009 just now and introduced the two of you." She grinned. "I'm the reason you two are together." Her grin faltered. "You're still together, aren't you?"

"Maybe." He pursed his lips. "What are you even doing here? Not that you don't look like you need medical treatment," he continued. "But this area is for staff only."

"In the ER, were you just treating victims of a car accident? Dakota, Josh, and Kairi?" she asked. When was she? "What's the date?"

Before he could answer, the door opened. "I'm here, D. Sorry, I'm late." It was Ethan, complete with his still-gorgeous baby-blues, and he stopped dead when he saw her. "Who's this?"

Diego jumped up off the cot. "I don't know who this chica is. I swear. There's nothing going on here. She just popped out of thin air."

Ethan grinned. "Relax. I don't think anything's going on. I know you're crazy about me."

"Speaking of loco," Diego said in a falsetto voice. He circled his finger near his head and nodded towards her.

Ethan was staring at her. "Wait a minute. Kairi? I almost didn't recognize you with your injuries. Where did you go after the fight that day? You just disappeared."

"Hi, Ethan," she said.

Diego's mouth fell open as he looked from Ethan to her and back again. "You guys know each other?"

"Aren't you the woman that made Diego ask me over for Thanksgiving years ago?" he asked. "And got in a fight with those bullies?"

She gave Diego her so there! look. "As a matter of fact, I am."

Diego wrinkled his nose. "What are you talking about? I asked you over for Thanksgiving, Ethan. No one made me."

"Yeah, right, D," Ethan said, chuckling. "You know your memory is notoriously unreliable. Back then, you'd been eyeing me all semester without managing to screw up your courage enough to talk to me."

Diego glanced down at the ground and bit his lower lip.

"Come to think of it, I do remember something." He glanced at her. "I said you looked like you were transgender?"

Geez, of all the things to remember. "Yes," she said. "And thanks for that, by the way." Speaking of remembering, how was Dakota? Was this even the right time? "What's the date?"

Ethan grinned. "You should know, Kairi, that Diego only acts prickly when he's nervous."

Diego glared at him. "I do not!"

"You do, honey. It's one of the things I love about you." They started kissing.

"Okay, so..." She suddenly realized why Diego and Ethan had a meeting set up in a room full of cots. She stood up and took a limping step towards the door. "Guess I'll see you 'round." She felt a little woozy but shook it off.

"Hey, not so fast, Kairi," Ethan said. "You need to go over to the ER."

Dakota was in the ER but only if this was the right date and the timeline hadn't been rewritten. She turned to Diego. "Did we meet recently in the ER?"

He shook his head.

"And maybe we can give you a lift somewhere afterward?" Ethan said.

They did owe her, although they didn't fully appreciate it.

Diego twisted one side of his mouth. "I'm not sure that's a good idea."

"Why ever not?" Ethan asked.

"I'm not sure she's all there," Diego said in a loud whisper.

Great. She started limping away again. It hurt to breathe.

"Why in the world would you say that?" Ethan asked.

"She said something about time travel and?"

"And what? Spit it out."

Diego sighed loudly. "She said she saved your life. She said she saved you from being beaten to death freshman year."

Kairi'd stopped walking since it was difficult to eavesdrop from far away.

Ethan didn't say anything. She risked a glance back at him. His face was pale, and there was a wrinkle between his eyebrows. Finally he said, "That is entirely possible."

"What?" Diego asked.

"Some guys from the dorm were really hassling me that first semester. Some of the things they said." He shuddered. "And then they jumped us." He turned to her. "You were just there, weren't you?" He took a step closer. "Is that how you got the injuries you're sporting right now?" He stared at her.

"Huh," Diego said. "It seems I do remember something about a fight. But that was years ago. How could she have injuries now?"

Kairi felt woozy. She sank back down on one of the cots.

"You do look kind of grayish-green," Diego said. "And not in a good way."

What would be a good way to look grayish-green?

The two men exchanged a look.

"You need to let me take you to the ER to get patched up, chica," Diego said.

She did need to go to the ER to check on Dakota and the others in the car accident--if this was the right date. She quickly stood up and promptly almost fell over.

"Whoa," Diego said, grabbing her arm. "You're in worse shape than I thought. Come on." He led her out of the room, with Ethan following.

They swayed on over to the ER. "Is Kairi here? Is Dakota here? Are they all right?" She peered into the bays, but they were empty. She turned to Diego. "What's the date? Please, what's the date?"

Diego turned around, raising his eyebrows at Ethan. "I thought you were Kairi."

Ethan turned the corners of his lips down but said, "March sixteenth, 2018."

She wracked her brain. March 2018 was the key. But, yes, she thought the accident happened on March seventeenth. She sighed in relief. "Good." She still had time to save them.

A nurse approached the three of them. "Diego, honey, what've you got for me?"

"That's a good question," he said, face blank.

"She was in a fight," Ethan interrupted. "She got beat up."

"Sí," Diego said. "We found her wandering around outside." In a falsetto, he added, "You better check her head."

The nurse grabbed Kairi's arm and led her to a bed. "Don't

worry; we'll check everything, hon."

They cleaned, stitched, bandaged and iced her up. When the nurse tried to give her some pain meds, however, she shook her head, bringing on another bout of wooziness.

"Come on, chica," Diego said. "Take the medicine." The two of them were still hanging around the ER, watching over her. Ethan had made Diego stay.

"Why don't you want the medicine, Kairi?" Ethan asked.

Her eyes darted to the nurse. The last thing she needed was to get stuck on some psych hold for twenty-four hours or more.

The nurse took in her expression and said brightly, "Gosh, I have another patient to check on," and walked away.

"What's up?" Ethan asked once she was gone.

"I'm here right now because I have to save some people from a car accident tomorrow. If I take these pills, they might zonk me out, and I might be too late."

Diego snorted.

Ethan turned to him. "You're the one who said she popped out of thin air. Were you speaking metaphorically?"

"Well," Diego glanced at the floor, "no. I thought she popped out of thin air, but I must have fallen asleep and not noticed her walk into the room."

"You don't believe your eyes?" Ethan asked. "Now, who's crazy?"

Hey, did someone say she was crazy?

"Kairi, we'd be happy to help you with your mission," Ethan said. He poked Diego with his elbow. "Wouldn't we, D?"

Diego bobbed his head. "Yeah, I guess."

"What do you want us to do?" Ethan asked.

She tried to think. Tomorrow the Kairi, Josh and Dakota of this time would step in front of a car. She needed to stop that. That was the mission.

She caused the accident by talking to Dakota early in the morning of March sixteenth. She looked at her watch. She already missed her opportunity to stop that.

Shit.

What could she do?

If she told the her-of-this-time or Dakota not to go to the

meeting with Josh tomorrow, that should work--if past-her or Dakota listened.

But experience had shown she shouldn't let Dakota know about time travel, right? Didn't that cause problems before? Her head hurt, and it was not entirely because of her injuries.

"Kairi?" Ethan asked.

"I'm thinking," she said. If she called past-her, there was a definite possibility she might not listen. She'd have a better chance in person.

She faced Ethan and Diego. "Can you give me a ride to campus? I need to talk to someone."

"And then you'll take the drugs?" Diego asked.

"Yes. Then I'll take the drugs."

When past-her saw her battered face, she gasped and reached for her own face. "Oh, no! What happened?" Kairi'd waited until Dakota went to class to knock on the dorm room door.

In the meantime, Ethan and Diego gaped at her and past-her standing next to each other in the hallway.

Cheered a little by the thought that her injuries might help make past-her obey her, Kairi tried to grin. Ouch. "All you need to know is what I'm about to tell you is very important. You cannot go with Dakota tomorrow afternoon to meet cute Josh outside the Earth Sciences building. If you do, Dakota will be paralyzed." She stared into her eyes. "Do you hear what I'm saying?"

The past version of her nodded. "Don't go meet cute Josh tomorrow afternoon. Keep Dakota away."

"Yes," she said. "Do you hear what I'm saying?"

"Yes!" Past-her frowned. Kairi could tell she was starting to get annoyed. "I hear what you're saying. I'm not going to do something that will end up making Dakota paralyzed."

She sincerely hoped not.

Chapter Forty-Four
Kyle: Boulder, Colorado, 2019

In hospital, as soon as he could walk, Kyle grabbed his clothes and ducked into a nearby restroom. There was no way he could investigate anything effectively from a hospital bed, and he had to avoid seeing Oliver. He quickly shucked the gaping gown and slipped on his clothes. In his street clothes, he walked nonchalantly right up to an exit door. Unfortunately, when he opened it, an alarm started blaring.

"Jesus." He covered his ears. The last thing he needed, the way his head ached, was deafening noise. Kyle loped across the parking lot towards the bus stop.

Once he got to the bus stop and out of the alarm range, he sank to a bench. There must be something going on with Traveling. Someone unauthorized was Traveling. But who?

Back at his hotel room, Kyle called his uncle. "Hi, Ray. Before you say anything, I didn't rewrite the timeline."

His uncle didn't answer him. That was a bad sign. Ray was only quiet when he was trying not to yell.

"Ray? Are you there?"

"Yeah," he said. "I'm here. I'm very angry with you, but before I get into that, where were you? Why'd it take you so long to call me back?"

Now, it was Kyle's turn to pause.

"Kyle?"

"I was in hospital," Kyle said. "I'm not sure what happened. I was minding my own business in the middle of a store, and it felt as if the timeline was being rewritten. I didn't do it."

"In hospital? Are you all right?" his uncle asked.

"I guess," Kyle said. "It's hard to say since I don't know what the hell happened."

"I felt the timeline being rewritten," Ray said. "If you didn't do it, I don't know what to think. I know I didn't rewrite the timeline, and I talked to Oliver, and he definitely didn't rewrite the timeline. He doesn't know anything about Traveling."

Kyle doubted Oliver knew nothing. He knew something. "Oliver probably doesn't know what he felt was the timeline being rewritten."

"Probably not," Ray said. "Are you going to call him?"

Kyle's mind flashed back to Oliver, cold and dead, and he shuddered. "No. I don't think that's a good idea, do you?"

"Probably not."

"Did you reassure him?"

"Yeah. I think he's all right," Ray said.

"That's good, at least." Now, Oliver could focus on whatever normal problems he was having. Was he flunking out of school? Kyle wasn't going to rat out his brother to their uncle, at any rate.

Kyle needed to focus on his own problems. "So, what do you think happened with the timeline?" he asked.

"I honestly don't know," his uncle said. "As far as I know, this is the first time in history that two experienced Travelers, us, have both been alive and potentially Traveling at the same time."

But Kyle's mind flashed back to his father's funeral in that overwritten timeline, his dad dressed up and lying like a mannequin in the casket. The funeral was weird to the point of surreal: everyone dressed up, Kyle having to sum up his father's life in a few sentences, and that gaping ragged ache in his heart. That had started this whole thing--Kyle Traveling.

"Maybe we've done something to time itself," Ray said.

Bloody hell. "Is that even possible?" Maybe saving Oliver had been the wrong thing to do if it was unraveling time itself. Traveling was so bloody complicated.

And he still had to save his parents.

"I don't know."

"If you don't know, no one does." There was something else, though, from that service in the overwritten timeline. What had happened at the end? Kyle had felt dizzy, and Uncle Ray hypothesized that someone else was Dreaming. Now that he thought about it, Dad had said something about someone else

Dreaming when he was in hospital before he died. That's why he'd made Kyle call all the relatives and ask about illegitimate kids. That had been an embarrassing job. Kyle wasn't about to do that again. "Let me know if you think of anything to explain it, Ray."

"I will. In the meantime, take care of yourself, Kyle. I'm starting to get pretty worried about you. You've been in hospital a lot lately."

But Kyle hadn't knowingly done anything. It wasn't as if he tried to end up in hospital. "Yeah, okay," Kyle said. "Bye, then." They hung up.

After the phone call, Kyle wasn't sure what to do. He decided to make a cup of tea. That always helped him clear his mind and think. Going through the motions of filling the kettle with water, turning it on, and getting out a mug and tea bag calmed him.

"So, let's assume our hypothesis is correct," he said to himself. "The timeline was rewritten. I didn't do it. Ray didn't do it. No one I know did it."

Once he finished making his tea, he sat back down. "Someone else can Travel." He took a sip. "Weird. How would they learn how? And how could they? I thought it was just our genetic group."

There was a knock on the door, and Kyle jumped. Who in the world could that be? He got up and answered the door.

A sweaty Josh stood there in athletic gear. "Dude, you're home. Why didn't you meet me at the basketball court? Weren't we going to play hoops?" He walked into the room. "Who were you talking to just now?" He glanced around the room. "There's no one else here."

Kyle was glad to see him. He could compare notes with Josh and see if any of their memories of the timeline differed. "The talking must have been on the TV." Kyle pointed at it.

"The TV isn't on." Josh sat down. "Got any beer?"

"I, ah, just turned the TV off." This guy reminded him of Liam. "Yeah. I got beer." Kyle got Josh one of the beers he'd stocked in his mini-fridge.

"What's up? Why'd you miss the game?"

"I was in hospital."

"No shit?" Josh opened the bottle. "I came over to give you grief. But, hell, if you were in the hospital, that sucks." He took a swig. "You okay now?"

"Close enough." Kyle got himself a beer and took a swig.

"What happened?" Josh asked. "Why'd you go to the hospital?"

"I don't know," Kyle said. "I just woke up there."

"That doesn't sound good."

"No." Kyle paused. "So, what do you remember from the other night?"

"You think your hospital thing was from the Rio?" Josh said.

"No. So, back to the Rio. What happened?"

"Memory fuzzy?" Josh grinned. "Those margaritas giving you trouble?"

"Yeah, I guess."

"Nothing much happened. We hung out and got drinks and some food. I brought you home. That was about it."

"I guess that's pretty much what I remember," Kyle said. But something important had happened, too. He also saw the Moira-look-alike. Did Josh remember her? "Was there a woman?"

Josh snickered. "Man, there's always a woman."

"I mean in particular."

"Yeah, you got worked up about some girl when we were leaving. But you only caught a glimpse of her. I didn't really see her."

"That was last night, right?"

"Yeah," Josh said.

"What did I do today?"

"You're asking me?" Josh shrugged. "I don't know. All I know is you didn't play basketball."

Kyle struggled to remember. He did errands. He went to lunch at that pancake place by himself and waited forever before eating alone. He did more errands. He woke up in hospital. "I guess I did errands." He only remembered one timeline. That meant he didn't overwrite anything.

Josh finished off his beer and stood up. "Good luck figuring all this stuff out."

It looked as if Kyle would need luck, and a lot more, to figure out what was going on. "Thanks."

Josh left.

Kyle sat and sipped his beer, considering things. The hospital visit probably meant someone else rewrote the timeline, and he didn't remember the original one. That was weird to think about.

The alternative was his previous Traveling had scrambled his brain somehow, and he didn't want to consider that.

If there was a renegade Traveler out there somewhere, it had to be the mysterious Moira-look-alike. What leads did he have about her? He may have seen her at that bar the other night. But who knew when or if she'd ever go back there?

From an overwritten timeline he did remember, Kyle knew Oliver's friend DeShaw had seen her in Oliver's neighborhood. Did she live in the neighborhood? If so, if Kyle set up some kind of surveillance, sooner or later, she'd show up, and he could find out about her. If not, setting up surveillance there wouldn't help.

He needed to think outside the box. Unfortunately, ordering yourself to think outside the box didn't make you think outside the box.

After sitting around his hotel room for a couple of hours, stewing, he decided to go out for some fresh air and walk around. Outside, it was a surprisingly nice warm spring day. The sun shone, and the breeze blew as he walked south toward Oliver's house.

At one corner, while waiting to cross the street, Kyle noticed a 'Lost Dog' flier on a telephone pole for Bitsy the apricot Labradoodle, complete with a color photo of Bitsy. Under the picture was a phone number and the word Reward.

"Duh!" He smacked himself on the forehead. Within moments he had his mobile out, calling Moira, asking her to email him a photo of herself.

Kyle plastered the university campus, Oliver's neighborhood, and downtown near the Rio with his Lost Girl fliers. Before he even returned to his hotel room, his mobile phone rang.

"Who the hell are you?" a woman demanded. "And why are you putting pictures of my roommate all over town?"

"My name is Kyle," he said carefully. "What's your name?"

"I'm not telling you anything," she said. "How do I know you're not some kind of perv?"

"If your roommate is the woman I'm looking for, I think we might be related."

"How could you be related to me?"

"No. I might be related to your roommate."

The woman on the phone didn't answer.

"Hello? Are you there?"

Chapter Forty-Five
Kairi: Boulder, Colorado, 2019

Some loud banging woke Kairi. Judging by the Big Ben and the Eiffel Tower posters, she was home in her dorm room, and she was dizzy. Dakota's stuff was there, too, but she wasn't. Who was banging on her door? Where was Dakota? Was she all right? And when was it?

"Chica! Answer the door already! Did it work? Chica?" That had to be Diego.

"Calm down, already," Ethan said. "Maybe she's not back from the past yet."

"It's mid-afternoon," Diego said. "She should be back."

They sounded like they knew all about time travel. That couldn't be right. She groaned as she clambered out of the nice soft, warm bed. Ugh. She ached all over. She shambled over to the door and pulled it open.

Diego jerked back. "Eek. You look awful."

Ethan shook his head at him. "Nice, D. Why don't you just kick a girl when she's down?"

Kairi's mind was reeling. It was Diego and Ethan, and they knew her. They also seemed to know about time travel. "What's the date?"

"March thirtieth, 2019," Ethan said.

That was her present, wasn't it? "Do you know if Dakota is okay?"

"Yes." Ethan dipped his chin. "We waited until she left to knock. You said she wasn't allowed to know about the time travel."

Thank God Dakota was okay. That was a relief. She relaxed a bit.

But they called that unearthly din knocking?

"It's Saturday," Diego added. "And you're beat-up like you said you'd be. Some people," his voice rose, and he grinned at Ethan, "said they weren't sure they believed you."

"And by some people, you mean you, right?" Ethan raised an eyebrow.

"To be clear," she said, pointing at them, "you guys know I can time travel?"

"Sí," Diego said. "Of course. You saved mi amor." He gestured towards Ethan.

"You remember that?"

Ethan glanced down the hall and then turned back to her. "Maybe we should come in and talk?"

She shrugged and stepped away from the doorway. "Whatever."

She got back in bed, pulled the pillow behind her back and leaned against the wall.

The guys came in, Ethan closing the door behind him. They both sat down opposite her on Dakota's made bed.

It hit her: Dakota's bed was made, and she was up and out on a Saturday morning. She was living with responsible-Dakota. That meant Dakota was doing well. That was good.

The guys stared at her.

Finally, she said, "What? What do you want to talk about?"

"You just look so horrible," Diego said. "Just like you did way back in November 2009 after the fight and last March when we found you in the hospital."

Ethan frowned and poked him.

"Sorry about the horrible comment," Diego said and looked down at the floor.

"So, now that we've established I look horrible--thanks, by the way--what are you doing here?"

"You said we had to leave you alone over spring break because you had important business to attend to, but when you got back on Saturday, we'd start our new mission," Ethan said. "Don't you remember?"

She felt dizzy. She shook her head. That didn't help at all. The room spun.

She clutched the bed as the room revolved around her.

"Remind me. What's the new mission?"

"You helped me, and you said you helped Dakota," Ethan said. "We thought it was time you helped yourself. We discussed it."

"Really?" She hadn't been expecting that. "We didn't want to do something heroic like stop nine-eleven?"

"We did discuss that," Diego said. "But Ethan thought it would probably be very difficult, and we should work up to it."

"We should work up to it?" she asked. "Are you saying we're some kind of team?"

Ethan shrugged. "We just offered to help you."

"Yeah, we owe you, chica, remember?" Diego said.

Their former conversation was starting to become less hazy. The three of them did discuss this stuff. "And when you say I should help myself, you mean what?" The whole Josh thing seemed hopeless at this point. She remembered more of their previous discussion. "I should try to find out what happened to my parents? Find out why I was found in the middle of the street?"

"Sí."

"Yeah."

She probably could use some help. And she didn't want to ask Dakota; that hadn't worked out well last time. "So, you guys have really known about my time traveling for all these years?"

"Only since last year when you popped into the hospital right in front of me," Diego said.

"And nothing bad happened to you?" Kairi asked.

"It's not as if we've been spreading it around," Ethan said.

She shrugged. "Okay. I accept your offer."

"Excelente!"

"Great!"

They both beamed at her.

She couldn't help smiling back.

"Let's go get some breakfast and strategize," Ethan said.

"I could eat," she said. "Just let me grab a quick shower."

Kairi couldn't believe it when they pulled up at the pancake house. "Here?" She looked at them.

"What do you mean?" Diego asked.

"I figured you'd know some special gourmet place with exquisite decor," she said.

"Because we're gay?" Ethan shook his head. "Sometimes gay guys just want some pancakes."

"Yeah, we come here all the time," Diego added.

She ordered some Belgian waffles topped with blueberries. "I never said I didn't enjoy the pancake house. And blueberries are a super-food, aren't they?"

Diego ordered an omelet and Ethan ordered a dish called fruity-tuity something.

"Ah ha!" she said. "That sounds like a gay dish if I ever heard one."

"What? I enjoy pancakes." But he smiled.

When the waitress tried to take the menus, Kairi held on to hers. "I might order some dessert," she said.

Both of the guys laughed.

"You might need some dessert for your waffle?" Ethan said.

Diego grinned. "I like this chica."

"I agree," Ethan said, grinning as well. He leaned over the table. "So tell us what happened this week. You've been pretty closed-mouth about it. All you said was this was when it all began."

She glanced around the room and it appeared no one else was in earshot. "Okay. It first started..." When had it started? It was just at the beginning of spring break, this week. That was it? It felt as if she'd lived a lifetime this week. "It actually started last weekend, at the beginning of spring break."

"Like six days ago, spring break?" Diego asked.

"Yeah."

"I don't understand that," Ethan said. "You told us a year ago you could time travel."

She wasn't sure she understood either. "Up until about a week ago, I lived my life like a regular person except future-Kairis came to visit me periodically. One future-Kairi told me I would learn how to time travel this week."

"That's consistent with what you told us," Ethan said.

"What happened this week?" Diego asked.

"I was on a road trip down to Texas with my boyfriend, er, fiancé. He asked me to marry him." She sighed. Josh. That ship

275

had sailed. She needed to forget Josh.

Diego's forehead wrinkled. "You didn't have any fiancé last week. Or boyfriend." He wiggled his eyebrows. "When did you meet him? Is he hottie-hot-hot?"

Ethan gave him a long look and then turned back to her. "How hot is this guy? He'd have to be pretty damn hot if you got engaged right after you met him."

"Never mind. Everything's changed," she said. "When this whole thing started the hottie-hot?, er, Josh, was my fiancé. We were driving down to Padre Island, but we got caught in a tornado down in Oklahoma."

"I think I heard about that tornado on the news!" Diego said.

"Me, too," Ethan said.

"Yeah, so I time traveled to avoid the tornado," Kairi said. "That was the first time."

Or was it? What had that cop said about when she was a baby? "Wait a minute." She'd been found in the middle of the street as a baby? Maybe that had been the first time she'd time traveled. Maybe that's why no one came to claim her. Maybe she had actual relatives somewhen in time. She should try to find them. Ooh, what if they could time travel too?

"Earth to Kairi," Ethan said.

"Um, so yeah, where was I?" she said.

"You time traveled to avoid a tornado," Diego said. "But I don't understand how could that guy be your fiancé so suddenly. Where is he now? Are you still together?"

"No." She shook her head. "We're not together anymore. Like I said, everything's changed. I changed my timeline." She pointed at them. "Like I changed the timeline for you guys."

They looked at each other and Diego grabbed Ethan's hand.

"I seem to remember all the timelines but no one else does. Anyway, I went back in my own past a few times to try to change it back to when Josh and I were engaged, but it didn't work. People, including Dakota, kept getting hurt. I had to give up on Josh." Her eyes felt heavy.

"Like that old movie Butterfly Effect," Diego said.

"Yeah, sort of like that," Kairi said.

They were all silent for a few moments, pondering loves

276

that got away. At least she was. She wasn't sure what they were pondering.

"So, anyway, this past week I ran into Diego several times, actually, although he doesn't remember them all. And he asked me to save Ethan. That part you know."

They squeezed each others' hands, nodding.

"I still don't get how the actual time travel works," Ethan said. "Explain that."

"I don't get it either. I've been trying to understand it," she said. "There was a neurophysiology professor at the university that was helping me. She had a lucid dream-something-device. It looked like a big metal helmet."

"Whoa. Hold the phone," Ethan said. "Neurophysiology? A professor? What does the time travel have to do with that?"

"I didn't mention that earlier? How the professor helped me learn to control it?"

The two of them looked blank.

Ethan shook his head slightly. "To be honest, you didn't tell us much of anything. You said we had to wait until now. Why did you think we were so anxious to see you today?"

"I'm not sure you really understood anything about time traveling before, chica," Diego said.

"You know I time travel when I dream," Kairi said.

There was a deafening crash next to them.

The waitress stood there staring at her. Their meals were all over the floor, right along with the broken plates. The waitress glanced at Diego and Ethan still holding hands and sitting very near each other in the booth.

"It's a play," Kairi said. "We're working on a play."

"Yes, we're thespians," Diego simpered in a super-gay way.

Ethan tried not to laugh.

"Oh," the waitress said. "I'm so sorry about your food. I'll put the order back in right away and, of course, it's on the house." She rushed off to say something to one of the busboys.

"Anyhow," Diego whispered, "what's next?"

"I was just reminded of something a cop told me when I traveled back to 2014," Kairi said.

The busboy came over and started sweeping up the mess. He kept throwing furtive glances at them, though, which really made Kairi wonder what the waitress had said to him.

The three of them looked at each other, unwilling to continue the conversation with an observer.

Finally, the busboy finished up and left.

"Uh, so where were we?" she asked.

"You just said a cop told you something in 2014, don't you remember?" Ethan asked.

"Yes, I remember that," she said. "It was only a few minutes ago."

"But you didn't remember that we were supposed to meet you at your room today?" Ethan asked.

A light bulb started going off. "It's almost like every time I get back from time traveling, I get all dizzy and disoriented and it screws my memory up."

Ethan and Diego glanced at each other, and then Ethan said, "That would explain today in your dorm room."

"My dorm room?" She paused.

They glanced at each other again.

She smiled. "I'm kidding. I remember you guys coming to my room. It was an hour ago."

"So you were saying you were in trouble with the cops in 2014?" Diego asked.

"Yeah, sort of," she said. Kairi and past-Kairi had gotten into a fight and she'd called the cops. She wasn't about to get into that though, it would be too embarrassing.

Someone next to the table cleared her throat. "Here you go. We put a rush on it." It was the waitress. She put the plates on the table. "That must be some play you guys are putting on."

"You have no idea, honey," Diego said.

As they dug into the food, Kairi wondered if she could actually find anything out about her family. At least now she had a place to start.

After they'd polished off most of their pancakes, waffles, and omelet, Ethan said, "Okay, what about the cops in 2014?"

"In 2014 a cop told me he'd found me as a baby back in 1999 in the middle of the street."

"So, you're going to go back to 2014 to check it out?" Diego asked.

"No. I'm going back to 1999." Again.

Chapter Forty-Six
Kyle: Boulder, Colorado, 2019

Kyle waited nervously at Boulder Brews. Every time the front door opened he held his breath, waiting.

The woman who'd called him about the Lost Girl wouldn't tell him her name and wouldn't tell him her roommate's name. Basically, she wouldn't tell him anything about anything. Kyle could only get her to meet him at a coffee shop to discuss things. He'd loaded up his phone with pictures of relatives including several of Moira and of Australia. Hopefully, he could convince her to introduce him to her roommate or, at least, tell him her name.

Yet another attractive college-aged woman entered the coffee shop. Who knew coffee shops were such good spots to meet women? That reminded him of Liam. Was Liam up to his old tricks picking up women? Did Liam miss him?

Kyle perked up as the newcomer scanned the room as if she was looking for someone.

Slowly, she approached him. "Are you the guy from the phone?"

"Yes," he said. "I'm Kyle. I put up the fliers. I'm looking for my cousin." He wasn't sure the mystery woman was his cousin but he figured it sounded plausible.

The strange woman just stood there, frowning. Even grumpy, she was hot in a sorority girl type of way.

Kyle started to panic. She was his only lead to the mysterious rogue Traveler. He decided to try to do what Liam would do. "What's your name?" Liam would definitely buy her a drink. "Can I buy you a coffee?"

She shrugged. "Yeah, okay."

She ordered a latte and after he paid they went back to one of the tiny bistro tables. After she took a sip, she said, "I'm Dakota Moore."

"Nice to meet you, Dakota. See, that wasn't so hard, was it?" He grinned. "It's a real pleasure to meet a sheila like you. I'm Kyle Barada."

"You already said that." But she smiled back. "What's your accent? Are you from Down Under?"

"Yep, mate. And how about your roommate? Is she from Down Under?"

"Carrie? No. She's from right here, Boulder, born and raised."

Bloody hell. Could that be true? If she was American, she couldn't be a member of Kyle's family. "C-a-r-r-i-e?"

"No. It's K-a-i-r-i."

"And what's her last name?"

"Johnson."

"Thanks." That didn't make sense. It wasn't an aboriginal name. Was it possible this woman wasn't the rogue Traveler? "And where do you guys live?" Kyle felt unusual.

Dakota leaned back in her tiny bistro chair. "Wait a minute. You're acting like a cop or a stalker or something. Why do you want to know all this stuff?"

"Like I said, I'm looking for my cousin." It didn't sound like this Kairi was the woman though.

Dakota crossed her arms in front of her.

Kyle was losing her. "And I appreciate fine sheilas." He forced another grin. But he felt odd, as if he'd had this conversation before.

"I don't know," Dakota said. "I'm getting a weird vibe. I think one of us needs to leave now."

"Aw, sheila, don't be like that." Kyle paused. "But I'm getting a weird vibe, too. Déjà vu."

"Really?" Dakota said. "Me, too, actually. What the heck?" She took the lid off her coffee and licked the foam off the inside.

Hell, she was really attractive. Trying not to stare, Kyle looked away. "Somebody else told me they got déjà vu recently.

Who was it? Damn. I can't remember."

"Who cares? Since when is déjà vu important?"

But that didn't sit right with Kyle. Something was going on here. What if déjà vu was important? What could it mean?

"Kyle? Earth to Kyle?"

When Kyle met Dakota's eyes again, she seemed irritated.

"You're the one who called me here," Dakota said. "Now you're blowing me off?"

"You're right. I'm sorry. I really want to meet your roommate." He picked up his phone. "Can I show you some pictures of me and my family? You can look at them and tell me if your roommate Kairi looks like she might fit in."

"They aren't pornos or something are they?"

"No." Where was she getting that? Americans were strange. He flipped through some pictures. "So, here's the whole clan before I was born at my grandparents' anniversary party." Grandfather David looked happy there. Kyle didn't think about how Grandfather looked writhing on the sidewalk. "And here's my parents and me and my brother, back in happier times." When Mom and Dad were still alive.

When he got to Moira, he said, "Here's a recent one of my cousin Moira with her parents, Raymond and Jessie."

Dakota glanced over at him and licked her lips. What did that mean?

Women were so cryptic. He kept going, showing her the family compound in the country and all the rest.

Dakota finished off her coffee at about the same time he got through the pictures. She carefully placed her empty cup on the little table. "I'll admit your family does resemble Kairi, especially that Moira girl." But Dakota stopped talking as if she was afraid to reveal any intel on Kairi. Why was she so protective of her roommate? What were they to each other?

"So? Can I meet your roommate and show her the pictures?"

"I don't know," she said slowly.

"Can I ask why you're so protective?" he asked.

She pursed her lips, distracting him. "She's not just my roommate, she's my sister."

Kyle felt his eyes narrow. These two women looked nothing

alike. How could they be sisters? "Oh?"

"You say that like it's weird," she said. "Like we're not sisters. We're sisters!"

"I don't think I did," Kyle said. Why was she getting so worked up?

She stood up. "I don't have to take this!"

"I'm sorry!" he said. "If I implied something, I apologize."

"Screw you!" Dakota gathered up her things and flounced out.

Kyle watched her storm out the shop's front door. "What did I do?" Women were impossible to understand.

Back at his hotel room, Kyle tried to google both women but couldn't find anything despite knowing their first and last names. Damn.

Too late, he realized he should have followed Dakota back to her place. But wouldn't that make him a stalker?

No, he wasn't a stalker, he was a spy. That was it. He was on a mission to discover who Kairi was and how she fit into the family. He was really helping her, that's what he was doing.

A powerful feeling of déjà vu came over him. "Weird."

What he should do was Travel back a couple of hours and wait for Dakota to come out of Boulder Brews and then follow her home.

Another déjà vu niggled at the back of his mind. "Bloody weird."

He stood up to go lie on the bed.

But he wasn't supposed to Travel. He sat back down on the couch. He'd decided it was too dangerous. He'd sworn to himself he wouldn't do it any more.

Unless it was life or death.

This was life or death, or at least almost as important. He stood up.

No, it wasn't. He sat down, feeling like some kind of freak. Up, down. Up, down. What the hell was wrong with him?

He needed to talk to someone, that's what he needed. Liam. He needed to talk to Liam. Liam understood what was going on.

Kyle grabbed his mobile and pressed speed dial.

"You've reached the phone of studly Liam Bowes. Please

leave a message, unless you're a sexy Sheila. Then, leave two messages, and I'll get you as soon as possible."

"Dammit!" So much for his Traveling sponsor.

Somehow, Kyle was standing right over the bed. He had no recollection of walking over to it. He had to get out of his hotel room before he Traveled.

He grabbed his hoodie and bolted out the door. Josh. He could call that Josh guy. Then it hit him Josh was the guy who'd had déjà vu the other day. Did that mean something?

He dialed.

Josh picked up. "Hi, Kyle. What's up?"

"Can we get together to talk about the other day? You got déjà vu, didn't you?"

"Yeah. I guess." He paused. He didn't sound enthusiastic. "When were you thinking of?"

"Now."

"I'm at work, dude. Now isn't a great time."

"Come on. It's important."

Josh exhaled loudly. "Okay. Come on over to the Physics Building." He gave Kyle directions to his office.

Kyle caught the bus and got off at one of the campus stops. He sauntered under the underpass. He walked through campus, past the UMC, past a big parking lot, past the Music Building. As he walked, the déjà vu feeling was building up in his brain. "What's going on?"

As he walked past some dumpsters behind one of the dorms, the smell of greasy old pizza boxes and skunky stale beer about bowled him over as déjà vu blew up in his mind.

"What the bloody hell is going on?"

Chapter Forty-Seven
Kairi: Boulder, Colorado, 1999

Kairi was back in 1999, the night the cops found the baby version of her in the middle of the street.

It was dark and cold. There was a loud blaring noise. Two very bright lights focused on a little pink fuzzy bundle in the middle of the road.

Past-her popped in by the side of the road as a cop parked his patrol car in the middle of the street and got out.

She crouched behind a bush, taking in every detail.

Past-her made no attempt to hide. Kairi had half a mind to tell her to take cover, but on second thought didn't want to deal with the nausea that dealing with another version of herself seemed to provoke.

The cop picked up the bundle, baby-Kairi, wrapped in a blanket. "Well, aren't you a little cutie? What are you doing here? You shouldn't be here in the middle of the street. Where's your momma and daddy?"

Past-her did duck down a little when the cop turned around and headed back to his car with baby-her.

The officer got in the car and started talking on his radio.

Past-her stretched towards the car to hear what he was saying. She was not successful, as Kairi knew she wouldn't be.

When the cop drove away, past-her popped away.

Kairi was pretty sure she knew where the cop was going: the police station.

She'd brought a bunch of 1999 quarters with her to use as money, and, yes, the bank teller thought she was weird when she asked for them. But she didn't have any trouble catching the bus over to the police station.

When she walked in the front door, an officer with the giant mustache looked almost asleep at the front counter. "Yes, can I help you?"

She opened her mouth. She'd been planning on asking about the baby that was just brought in. But if she did that, they'd probably think it was her baby since they looked like each other. And she was pretty sure the police frowned on leaving poor defenseless babies in the middle of the street in any time. Crap. She closed her mouth.

She glanced back out the door. "I, uh, thought someone was following me, so I ducked in here to get rid of him. How's it going in here tonight? Any excitement?" Like any baby-hers being brought in?

"Someone following you?" The uniformed officer stood up, revealing his beer gut and also revealing the prominent gun in the holster on his belt. "That doesn't sound good." He strode around the counter to the front door, opened it, and looked out into the night. "I don't see anyone." Something about him and his sandy hair and his mustache was familiar. Where did she know him from?

"Oh, good." She nodded. "You must have scared them off. Thanks. I appreciate it." She shuffled her feet. "So, nothing going on here? Nothing at all?"

The officer came back inside and sat down at the counter again. She noticed his nametag said Taylor. "Can I call you a cab, Miss? You really shouldn't be out and about at this hour by yourself." Wow, he was good at ignoring random questions.

If she got a cab, where should it take her? Back to the middle of the street where baby-Kairi had been found? She guessed she could stay there and watch for something weird happening.

Then Kairi had a light bulb-over-the-head moment. If baby-her appeared in that location in this time, maybe that meant she'd been in that same location at another time when something bad happened. "Thanks for your help, Officer Taylor. Say, I was wondering if you could tell me if there have been any accidents at a certain intersection in town?"

He ran his thumb and forefinger down his mustache, considering. "That depends. Were there any fatalities?"

285

Fatalities? Oh, no. That would make sense. Her parents. It would explain why they didn't look for her. She swallowed. "Yes, I think so. A man and a woman."

"If there were fatalities, then, yes, we would have a record of it."

What would the records say about her? Was a baby involved? Did they think the baby died? "Is there any chance I could get that information?"

He rifled through some forms on the counter. "Yes, you just need to fill out this form with the address and dates of interest, and we'll mail you the information in about two weeks."

"Two weeks!"

He jerked back. "What? Not fast enough for you? We have to look up files in the file room, and depending on the dates, the files might not even be on-site. It's standard procedure."

"Please," she said. "It's an emergency. I'm here in town looking for missing relatives. I heard a rumor they were in an accident in the Martin Acres subdivision. It would be something in the last year." Or the next year--but she couldn't say that. "Probably. Can you look it up, please?"

He stared at her for a few moments. "Why did you lie about why you were here?"

"I'm scared no one will help me," she said.

"You think some relatives died?" He stroked his mustache again. "That is sad. Do you have missing relatives, then? Did you fill out a missing person's report?" Whoever this guy was, he seemed like a decent sort.

She had no idea if anyone filled out a missing person's report because she didn't know if she had any other relatives to do it. She certainly hadn't filled out a missing person's report. And she didn't know what names to put on the report for her mom and dad. How could she explain that? She couldn't get into it. "My, uh, Mom did. That's all handled. Can you just look up the traffic accident info for that area?"

"I'll give it a shot," he said, picking up the phone and pushing some buttons. "Mavis? Yeah, can you look up possible traffic accidents this year in Martin Acres? Yes. Two fatalities." He glanced at her.

She nodded.

"Yes. A man and a woman." In a lower voice, he asked her, "How old?"

"Uh..." How old would they be? What year was it again? Her brain felt a little Swiss-cheesy. She couldn't do the math. She guessed. "In their twenties."

"Yeah. In their twenties." Officer Taylor's mouth turned down. He looked sad. "ASAP. Call me back here at the front desk. Thanks." He put down the phone. "You're in luck. Mavis is a whiz with the records. If anyone can find it, she can."

"Great," she said. Go, Mavis. She leaned on the counter.

Officer Taylor settled back in his chair.

They had nothing to say to each other. She looked around the room: a front door, white walls, a couple uncomfortable-looking benches, the big counter with some desks and chairs behind it. Boring.

"Maybe you should take a seat," he said.

"Thanks." She went and plopped on a bench. The hands on the clock across the room moved in slow-mo. She put her hands in her pockets, finding a bunch of quarters. She pulled them out to double-check the dates.

The phone rang. Officer Taylor got it on the first ring. "Yes, this is Officer Taylor. Oh, hi, Pam. Sure, I've got a couple of minutes."

Kairi froze. Pam? Could that be Pam Taylor? Her hole-y brain seemed to recall her foster mom, Pam, saying she'd been married to a guy named John Taylor.

"Social Services?" he said. "A baby?"

Shit! They were talking about baby-Kairi! This cop was her foster dad!

"I'm not sure. That sounds like a lot of responsibility." He glanced her way, still wearing his sad face. "I don't think...." He paused.

Now she remembered where she knew him from. He was the guy from Pam's wedding photo. And the guy who wouldn't let her in his house after the tornado. He seemed to be arguing with Pam, albeit very politely.

He didn't want her. He'd seemed pretty nice up until now. But he was the reason her life was so screwed up. He was the reason Dakota's life was so screwed up. The quarters were digging into her palms because her fists were clenched so tight.

"A marriage is a partnership, Pam. We have to decide these things together." The volume of his voice started to rise. "It sounds like you've already made up your mind. Why did you even bother calling me then?" He slammed the handset down in the cradle. After glaring at it for a few moments, he blew out a breath and leaned back in his chair.

"Everything all right, there?" She was dying to know what he'd say about why he didn't want baby-her.

"Fine."

He'd say nothing, apparently. Check. Maybe he should pay for what he'd done to her and Pam and Dakota or for what he would do. If she touched him while she was time traveling, would he feel nauseated? There was one way to find out. She shoved her quarters back in her pocket and lurched up.

At the same time, the phone on the counter rang again. "Yes, this is Taylor. Shoot, Mavis." He glanced at her again.

She sat back down.

Officer Taylor put down the phone. "I'm sorry, Miss. There haven't been any fatalities in that whole area for the last ten years at least."

Damn. Her mind was reeling. How could that be? She was ninety-nine percent sure the accident must have happened in that location. What did that mean?

"If you come back here tomorrow during regular business hours, they might be able to tell you more, but I doubt it."

Was it possible the accident hadn't happened yet? "Okay. Thanks." She was confused about Officer John Taylor. He seemed like a jerk when it came to fostering little kids, but he was helpful here and now when he didn't need to be.

"So, if there's nothing else?" he said.

Kairi could translate a request to leave when she heard one. "No. Thanks." She went out the front door.

Kairi went forward a year and repeated the whole thing, albeit by the book. She filled out the sanctioned paperwork and popped two more weeks into the future to get the official report.

When she pulled it out of the post office box, her hands were shaking so much she could barely tear the envelope open.

TEMPORAL DREAMS

She devoured the report, which unemotionally outlined the deaths of Jack and Laurie Djaru, both twenty-two years of age and Australian citizens, in a one-car accident in February 1999. She felt her eyes fill until she couldn't focus on the page.

She finally knew what had happened to her parents.

In February 1999, Kairi popped into the intersection of Martin Drive and Ash Avenue, unfortunately, directly in the path of an oncoming car. It was pitch black, and the headlights blinded her. She stumbled and fell to her knees on the asphalt.

The car honked and swerved. It jumped the curb and, going too fast, plowed into a telephone pole. The front of the little car crumpled up like aluminum foil with a horrible screeching noise.

"Oh, no!" Were they hurt? She ran to the car with speed she didn't know she had. She ran as if lives depended on it.

At the car, the metal pinged and groaned. The engine steamed. When she looked in the front seat, at first, all she saw was blood, lots and lots of blood. In the backseat was an empty baby's car seat. And then, in the front, she realized the bloody disaster was a man and a woman, a brown-skinned couple who looked like her, holding hands. Were they her parents?

They didn't move.

Chapter Forty-Eight
Kyle: Boulder, Colorado, 2019

Outside one of the dorms on the CU campus, Kyle couldn't figure out why he had such a strong feeling of déjà vu. When he started walking away from the dorm, it decreased. As a test, he walked towards the back door of the dorm. It increased. Weird. He checked the map on his phone and determined it was Baker Hall.

There was something important about Baker Hall? What could it be?

Josh texted him. I thought you were stopping by?

Kyle texted him back. Almost there.

As he rushed to the Physics Building, he kept glancing back at Baker and shaking his head.

When he finally got to Josh's office, Josh seemed grumpy. "So, what was the emergency?" It was a tiny room with two desks, three rickety chairs, and two bookcases that barely fit in the small space. The desks were covered, and the bookcases were crammed with papers and books.

Kyle sat down in one of the chairs. "Something weird is going on. I keep getting this déjà vu feeling."

"Why is that weird?"

"You said you got déjà vu the other day, too, right? It seems as if it's getting more and more common." Could it be linked to Traveling, somehow? But would that mean Traveling was more and more common? That didn't make sense.

"Okay, assuming I believe you, I guess that's weird." Josh's gaze slid to the computer on his desk.

"Josh?" Was Josh even listening to him? Kyle needed to get a handle on this déjà vu stuff so he could get a better handle on

Traveling.

Josh looked back at Kyle. "But even if it is true, what of it? I'm busy. I'm in the middle of an experiment for one of my classes."

Bam. Finally, Kyle's disquiet solidified into an idea. He needed to do an experiment. What if déjà vu was a sign that the timeline had been rewritten? That would be easy to test. "Since you like experiments, what would you say to a time travel experiment?" And then maybe if he found when the timeline was being rewritten, he could figure out who was rewriting it.

Josh snorted. "I'd say that sounds cool but highly improbable."

Kyle grinned. "Then hold on to your bloody hat, mate."

Lacking a better venue in the Physics Building, Kyle and Josh were going to do their experiment in the lounge at the top of Gamow Tower. It was empty at the moment, and there were a bunch of seventies-era orange couches. The whole place looked like it hadn't been touched since the seventies, but with the breathtaking three-hundred-sixty degree view of campus, who cared?

Kyle couldn't help being drawn to the window overlooking the sports stadium. "Do you ever come up here to watch the games? What do you guys call it? American football?"

"Usually, I'm working or studying." Josh turned out the lights and led Kyle to one of the couches.

Kyle lay down and closed his eyes.

"You claim what you're wearing travels with you, right?" Josh asked.

Kyle opened his eyes.

Josh made a weird face. "If so, apparently, you travel with a little buffer of air or whatever around you."

"Yeah," Kyle said. "And I'm pretty sure my body disappears. So, get ready."

"How does it work?" Josh asked. "The time travel." His expression got even odder if that was possible.

"What's wrong?" Kyle asked.

"I'm getting a really strong feeling of déjà vu."

"I think we're onto something," Kyle said. "Quit talking, and let's get this experiment going." He closed his eyes again and focused on his breathing. In. Out. In. Out. Once he was in a relaxed state, he thought: I am The Dreaming. I feel all of time. I access all time.

In his mind's eye, he saw himself in the tiny elevator with Josh in Gamow Tower, saw them walk to the elevator, saw them talking in Josh's office, saw himself walk into Josh's office, saw himself getting a text message from Josh, saw himself loitering by Baker Hall, saw himself walking across campus.

He materialized in the underpass under Broadway, whipped out his phone and texted Josh. Running a bit late. On my way. And then he jogged over to the Physics Building.

When he arrived, panting, he stood in the doorway of Josh's office, hands on his knees. "Can you do me a favor?"

"There you are." Josh tore his attention away from his computer. "What's the favor?"

Kyle was regaining his breath. "Can you text me? I'm not sure my mobile is getting texts right."

"Yeah." Josh grabbed his mobile.

"Wait. I want you to send me a certain message."

"Whatever." Josh shrugged. "What's the message?"

"I thought you were stopping by?"

Josh sent the text.

Kyle let the other-Kyle text him back: Almost there. "Now," he said. "How do you feel?"

"Besides thinking this is a waste of my time?" Josh asked. "You're not almost here; you're here."

"Yes." Kyle nodded. "Anything else?"

"Well..." Josh's brow furrowed. "I'm getting a déjà vu feeling."

"Yes!" Kyle threw his fist up.

"I'm confused," Josh said.

"I'm not," Kyle said. "I'm a time traveler, mate! I'm time traveling right now!"

"Yeah, right." The corners of Josh's mouth turned down. "Mate."

"I'm about to show up, and I won't know anything about this conversation we're having right now." Kyle turned to the hall. "See you in a few!" He jogged back to the elevator, rode upstairs, ran down the short hall to the physics lounge and then lay on the couch.

When he opened his eyes, Josh was staring down at him. "What the fuck? You, you..." He pointed at Kyle. "You disappeared for a few minutes, then reappeared out of nowhere."

Kyle sat up. "I told you I was a time traveler. I just time traveled, mate." He took a moment to savor the experience. He just Traveled, and there were no catastrophes. He could save his parents.

Josh sat down next to him on the couch. "Yeah, but..." He examined Kyle. "I guess I didn't believe you. So, how does it work? The time travel." He made a weird face.

"Let me guess," Kyle interrupted him. "Déjà vu."

"Yeah. How did you know?"

"That's what we were just testing. Déjà vu. Remember?" Kyle himself tried to remember the new timeline. After some initial confusion when Kyle arrived in Josh's office, it had all proceeded the same as before. Including Josh asking him how time travel worked when he lay down on the couch. "Hmm. Actually, mate, I think your déjà vu, here, now, is just regular déjà vu. You asked me how it worked," he looked at his watch, "ten minutes ago."

Josh shook his head. "Ugh. I'm getting déjà vu of déjà vu. I'm so confused."

Come to think of it, Josh did say he had déjà vu about ten minutes ago. What did that mean? Kyle didn't recall any overwritten timelines where Josh specifically asked him how Traveling worked. Could that mean Josh knew the mystery Traveler and had asked her? "Join the club," Kyle said. "Are you sure you don't know any other time travelers?"

Oh, wait, that Dakota girl gave him the name. "Kairi Johnson?"

Josh just looked at him.

Could that Dakota be the Traveler? "Dakota Moore?"

"Who the hell is that?"

Guess not.

Kyle's brain was racing. He knew he was onto something

with the déjà vu. Déjà vu did seem to be connected to Traveling. He was definitely on the track of the mystery Traveler. What with Josh and Baker Hall, the whole thing seemed located in the center of the university. What did that mean? Could the mystery Traveler, the one causing all this déjà vu, be here?

He walked all the way around Baker Hall, and the déjà vu feeling was centered at the northwest corner. He decided he would plant himself there and watch who came and went. Luckily, the campus was still dead because of spring break. The parking lot there was pretty much empty.

He went back to his hotel to get his rental car.

Kyle had almost fallen asleep when two men emerged from the back door. As they walked by his car, he got a very strong feeling of déjà vu. That was weird, and it had to be a clue.

He burst out of the car.

The two men flinched and stepped away from him. One looked Spanish or Mexican. They were both very handsome--not that Kyle noticed such things. One of them looked very familiar.

"What the hell do you want, hombre?" the Spanish one asked.

The other one said, "I have to warn you, we know karate."

What was that about? "I'm sorry," Kyle said. "I just thought I knew you. Do I?"

"What do you mean, do you know us? Either you know us, or you don't. Are you loco? We don't know you."

What had he stepped into? Or were all Americans so belligerent? "Sorry. You look familiar." Kyle forced a smile. "My name's Kyle. I think we've met, haven't we?" He knew him from hospital. "It's Diego, right? We met at hospital." Come to think of it, hadn't meeting Diego given him a case of déjà vu before?

The baby-blue-eyed one whispered something that sounded like, "Psst, psst, does look like Kairi."

"Kairi?" Kyle said. "Do you know her? I'm her cousin. I've been looking for her." What now? It was spring break. Maybe she was on a trip? "Is she back from her trip?"

"Her trip?" the Spanish one's eyebrows raised way up. "You know about her trips?"

"I guess he is her cousin," the other one said.

"But I thought she said she didn't know her family. He's acting suspiciously. We shouldn't tell him anything."

If Kyle had had a spidey sense, it would have been tingling. They seemed to be implying Kairi could take some kind of special trips.

Was it possible Kairi was the rogue Traveler?

That would mean she was his cousin.

But how did she learn to Travel?

And what had she been doing to the timeline?

Chapter Forty-Nine
Kairi: Boulder, Colorado, 1999

Kairi's brain didn't seem to work. She was staring at a bloody couple in a crumpled car. They didn't move. Why didn't they move? Who were they? She couldn't think. She couldn't turn away. She should do something. What should she do?

She didn't know how much time passed before she felt a hand on her arm. "Young lady? Are you okay?" a woman asked.

Kairi turned to face an elderly woman in a flannel nightgown, plush robe and slippers.

"My husband is calling the police." She glanced in the car and shivered. "Oh, dear." She reached into the car. "I used to be a nurse." She touched the necks of the man and the woman in turn. Why did she do that?

The former nurse withdrew from the car. "I'm sorry, honey. They're gone." She patted her shoulder. "Did you know them?"

Oh, Jesus. Kairi sank to the sidewalk. Were they relatives? They were, weren't they? They were her parents. She killed her parents. She lay on the ground, eyes overflowing.

When the ambulance roared up, sirens wailing, she realized she was freezing. That probably had something to do with the fact that the ground was freezing. She sat up.

The elderly Good Samaritan directed the EMTs to her. Why?

The EMTs rushed over. "Lay down, Miss," one said. "Can you tell us your name?"

"Where does it hurt?" said the other.

Her heart hurt. It was broken into a million minuscule pieces. She just looked at them.

The woman said, "I'm not sure if she was in the accident or

not, but I think she's in shock."

One of the EMTs was running his hands along Kairi's limbs. "I don't think she has any broken bones."

The other said, "I don't see any blood." He shined a light in her eyes. "Pupils are equal and reactive."

She squinted and turned away. Why wouldn't they just leave her alone?

The first EMT said, "I'm going to help you up, Miss. Just take it easy." He made Kairi stand up.

The other guy inspected the interior of the car. He blanched and started talking on his radio.

The first guy walked her toward the back of the ambulance.

Kairi felt like some kind of robot, an empty shell with nothing underneath her hard lifeless skin.

The EMT made her sit and then lie on the gurney in the back of the ambulance.

Kairi came to in a small uncomfortable bed in an ugly hospital room. She was sick and tired of waking up in strange places. And sick of hospitals.

And sick of strange times. What the hell was the date, anyway? If there was any kind of a God, it was before she murdered her parents so that she could undo it.

She was wearing one of those horrible hospital gowns. Those things made a person sick in and of themselves. Where were her clothes?

"Nurse! Nurse!" she said.

A woman about her age rushed in. "What's wrong?"

"I need my clothes. And what's the date?"

The nurse opened a drawer. "Relax. They're right here. What's your name?"

She got out of bed and lunged for her clothes. "What is the date? I'm not kidding."

"It's February twenty-fourth."

Kairi was already shimmying into her jeans. "What year?"

"What do you mean, what year? Did you hurt your head?"

"What year!" She let the gown fall to the floor as she slipped her shirt over her head.

"1999."

Dammit! She was too late.

She needed to go back in time and try to save them.

But she was exhausted, and she felt like shit.

She decided to go home and regroup and rest up.

She needed a better plan of attack.

Kairi traveled back to the evening on Saturday, March thirtieth, 2019. Her dorm room was empty. And, yes, she did double-check, and it was filled with her belongings. It was definitely her room. And Dakota's.

On her desk, she found a note.

We got tired of waiting around for you. Call us when you get back. Love Diego and Ethan.

Even though she'd been sleeping a lot lately, she still felt exhausted. She didn't know if she had the energy for a dissection of where she'd gone wrong, et cetera, et cetera.

She also felt hungry. She couldn't even remember the last time she ate. Her plan of attack was apparently going to start with ordering a pizza.

Even though her dinner arrived in thirty minutes or less, she managed to doze off before they called from the parking lot. At least she didn't time travel anywhere in the meantime. She checked. She trudged down the hall with her keys and wallet to the back door.

When she swung the door open, the delivery guy yelled, "Kairi? Kairi Johnson?" He wasn't wearing a uniform, but he was carrying a large pizza, so whatever. She guessed anything went on spring break.

"Yeah." She opened her wallet. "What do I owe you?"

"Nothing," he said.

She narrowed her eyes at him. "Say what? That's not what you said when I ordered it."

"Hi, Kairi," the man said. "My name is Kyle. I'm your cousin."

What were the odds that the pizza delivery guy just happened to be her long-lost cousin? Zero. She was too tired for this crap. "What are you talking about?"

"At least I think I'm your cousin."

"I don't have any cousins." The March wind blowing through the open door was cold. "Just give me the damn pizza and go away."

"You don't care that I'm your cousin? But I've been searching for you." He stepped toward her. "And I must tell you something: you've got to stop Traveling. You're screwing up the timelines."

He knew she could time travel? "Timelines? What the hell are you talking about?"

"Can I please come in?" He seemed kind of pitiful. "Please." He tried to smile. "If it means anything, I can time travel too. It's dangerous. I, ah, accidentally killed my parents."

"So did I!" Kairi gestured him inside.

Back in her room, she loaded up a paper plate with a ginormous piece of pizza and took a swig of soda. "Explain." She took a big bite of hot, cheesy goodness.

"I thought you'd be at least a little happy to meet me," he said. "Dakota said you didn't know your family. I can tell you all about them."

"You know Dakota?" she asked, chewing.

"What?"

Possibly he didn't speak pizza. She put down her cup and plate. "I'm sorry. This is all just a bit hard to understand. My cousin just happens to be the pizza delivery guy and just happens to know my roommate? Do you want something from me?"

"What? Oh, I'm not a pizza delivery guy. I bought the pizza from him when he drove up. I needed to talk to you." He paused. "Is there any chance I could have a piece, too? It smells really good."

She should have figured out he wasn't the pizza guy. He had a weird accent that the guy on the phone hadn't had. He looked so hungry and, yeah, pathetic, she couldn't help feeling a little sorry for him. "Sure, dude. You paid for it."

He grabbed a piece, and the room was silent for a solid minute as they both enjoyed chewy, cheesy goodness.

Kairi didn't know about her mystery cousin, but she was starting to feel better with food in her stomach and caffeine buzzing in her veins. She took a breath before inhaling the next piece. "Are you really my cousin?"

He was still eating, so he nodded.

"What's that accent? Where are you from?"

He swallowed. "Australia. I'm from Australia. So are you. We, you, have a big family. There's a bunch of aunts and uncles and cousins."

She found that hard to believe. If she had any kind of family, much less a big family, why didn't they come looking for her?

"And that's not all. We're aborigines."

"Abor-whats-its?"

"Native people of Australia. We're special. We have a unique and powerful connection to the land and time itself via The Dreaming."

"I didn't understand any of that, but I'd like to." She took a bite of pizza.

"I just wish I knew who your parents were," he said. "Are you sure you don't know?"

"Laurie and Jack Djaru."

"Djaru! I should call my uncle. He might know them, or at least know about them." He pulled a phone out of his pocket and looked at it. "But what time is it in Australia now?"

She shrugged and kept chewing.

"Dakota said you didn't know anything about them."

"Yeah, about that." She pointed at him. "How do you know Dakota?"

"I said I've been searching for you." He took another piece of pizza after glancing her way for approval. "Dakota hasn't been cooperating. She's very protective of you."

Go, Dakota. Kairi knew Dakota had her back in any timeline. She sobered. Unfortunately, the current timeline was screwed. "I just found out about my folks. I killed them. If you're really my cousin, you have to help me undo it."

He frowned. "Traveling is so bloody dangerous. I don't understand why. Actually..." He moved away from her on the bed. "Touching is fatal, you know. You didn't touch your parents, did you?"

"Touch them? No, I didn't touch them. What's wrong with you? And why did you just move away from me?"

He looked like his puppy had just been run over in the street. "My parents died because they touched a Traveler."

Kairi shook her head. "That doesn't make sense. I touch

people all the time. I've even touched myself when I was time traveling." That didn't sound right. "Not like that."

"Not like what?"

"Never mind." He was oblivious to the sexual innuendo. She finally relaxed a bit for the first time in she-didn't-know-how-long. This guy might actually be her cousin.

Could it be she'd found her family at long last?

And he was a time travel expert. He'd be able to help her save her folks. Thank goodness, all her problems and all this confusion were finally over.

Then, Dakota burst into the room, wild hair framing her face. She reminded Kairi of the overwritten druggie-Dakota. "Oh, no!" she said. "It's the stalker!"

Chapter Fifty
Kyle: Boulder, Colorado, 2019

Oh, no. Not that Dakota chick again. Why didn't she like him? Kyle held up his hands in surrender. "Relax, sheila."

She glowered at him. Why did he say that? Damn that Liam.

"My name's not Sheila!" Dakota said. "See what I mean? He's a freak."

Kairi stopped stuffing food down her mouth for a moment. "What's going on? How do you two know each other?"

Dakota pointed at him. "This joker has been putting posters around town saying you're lost?" she made the air quotes "--and trying to get people to call him about you."

"I said I was looking for you, Kairi," he said. "I had to do something. I didn't have much to go on."

"Wait a minute." Kairi turned to Dakota. "You knew about this guy? You knew I might have a relative in town, and you didn't mention it? You know how important family is to me."

"I thought I was your family." Dakota backpedaled. "And I'm still checking him out. I was going to tell you as soon as I knew it was safe."

Kairi raised her bushy eyebrows--they were just like Kyle's. "Really? And what does checking him out entail?" She looked Dakota up and down. "Going out with your friends?"

"I was just trying to protect you," Dakota said. "You've been acting so weird lately."

Kairi bolted up. "Weird! I'll have you know I saved you from being a drug addict, from being paralyzed and from ODing!"

Just how many times did this girl rewrite the timeline? No wonder everything was so screwed up.

"See," Dakota said. "You're proving my point. You're not

making any sense." She turned to the door. "I wash my hands of the whole thing. You two deserve each other." She flounced back into the hall and off for parts unknown.

Kairi looked at him. "Sorry about that. I'm sure she meant well."

"What did you mean you saved her from ODing and that other stuff?" he asked.

She just stared at him for a second. "I guess I can talk with you about this." A smile broke out on her face. "Awesome! You can tell me what I did wrong. I had a heck of a time fixing things."

Did that mean she successfully fixed things? That would be amazing. Maybe she could tell him what he'd been doing wrong. Maybe he could learn something from her, find out how to save his parents. "Tell me about it."

Kairi told him a long, complicated story that started with a guy named Josh and a tornado and ended with popping into the middle of a street and forcing her parents into a telephone pole at high speed. At the end of her tale of woe, she grabbed his hand. "You have to help me save my parents! You just have to!"

Kyle automatically jerked backward away from her, pulling his hand away, afraid two Travelers touching would be dangerous.

At his reaction, Kairi said, "What? What's wrong?"

But he didn't feel sick at all. Why not? "I was taught it's too dangerous for Travelers to touch."

"I feel fine," she said. "Oh, you're thinking of when we're time traveling, and we touch another one of ourselves who's time traveling. Yeah, that did make me a little sick to my stomach."

A little sick to her stomach? That was all? Wasn't that how people in his family died? He didn't know what to say to that.

"So what should we do? To save my parents?"

He considered the situation carefully. He needed to see her in action. He needed to learn from her. "In your latest trip, you caused your parents' car accident?"

She nodded vigorously.

"Well, let's go back and try to stop that." Based on his past experiences, Kyle wasn't super optimistic, but they had to start somewhere.

Back in February 1999, in the middle of the night, a cold wind blew down the residential street. Kyle was chilly and very tired, and grumpy. He'd just spent the last twenty-four hours traveling from Australia, and it had cost him almost two grand, but he couldn't figure out any way around it. In 1999 he'd been living in Australia, so he could only Travel to Australia.

He was waiting for his cousin Kairi to pop into the middle of the street, and he was going to swoop in and move her out of the way of oncoming traffic. So far, there'd been no traffic. The intersection was dead.

Hopefully, when they touched, neither one of them would die or be in need of hospital.

He checked his watch again. According to Kairi, she should be here any second.

And there she was. One second the intersection was empty, and the next, a woman stood there, looking disoriented.

He ran out into the middle of the street, seized her, and pulled her over to the sidewalk and back behind some bushes. Touching her didn't seem to make him sick.

She was not happy, squirming and writhing in his grasp. "Let go of me. Who are you? I'm here for a reason. This is important!"

"Shut up, Kairi," he whispered. "I'm your cousin Kyle."

"Cousin? What?"

"Shut up! You told me you were about to cause your parents' death. I'm here to stop you." He pointed at the car now approaching the intersection.

She froze, staring at the car.

The car tootled along the road and suddenly veered into a telephone pole.

"Oh, my God!" Kairi jerked toward the car. "Let go!"

Kyle didn't let go of her. "You don't want to see that again. And you can't do anything for them."

"Let go of me! You don't know that. I might be able to help."

"You can't! Just calm down and let me think." He did not let go of her arm.

Kairi didn't calm down, but at least she didn't bolt into the street, and she did shut up. As she stared at the car, her eyes overflowed. "I don't understand," she whispered. "Why did they crash?"

"Do you remember any timelines when you knew your parents?"

She slowly shook her head. "No."

"Well, the good news is you didn't cause the crash," Kyle said softly.

She just looked at him, tears rolling down her face.

Kyle pulled her into his arms. "I'm sorry about your folks, Kairi."

She sobbed into his chest.

"We will fix this, just not here and now," he said. He patted her back.

They had to be able to fix this because if they couldn't save Kairi's parents, they probably wouldn't be able to save his parents. And that was unacceptable.

Back in their present, in Colorado, Kyle and Kairi woke up in his hotel room.

She sat up and leaned against the headboard. "That was brutal."

Kyle stayed horizontal. "How do you feel? Dizzy?" He felt normal.

She shook her head. "Fine." She glanced at him. "Why?"

He scooted up and leaned against the headboard too. "When we rewrite the timeline, we get dizzy. We didn't affect the timeline just now, so no dizziness."

"Oh." Her eyes got shiny. "My parents are still dead. I don't understand what happened. Why did they crash?"

"I don't know." Clearly, they needed a better plan. "We did learn something important."

"What?"

"We can interact with each other while Traveling with no ill effects." Why was that?

"Why is that important?"

"Just trust me: it is." It meant neither one of them would die.

Kyle and Kairi hashed things through for hours and finally devised a new plan. Kyle was going to Travel back to earlier in that fateful day and stop Kairi's parents from getting in their car that night.

He was going to save her parents, and then she was going

to save his parents.

"Like Strangers on a Train," Kairi said. "Only instead of killing people, we'll be saving people."

What did trains have to do with anything? "Whatever you say."

Back in 1999, again, Kyle approached Jack and Laurie Djaru, putting baby Kairi into her car seat. "Jack? Laurie?" He was amazed at how familiar they looked. Laurie resembled his mom when she was young, and Jack resembled his Uncle Ray.

The couple turned to face him. Laurie stepped between Kyle and the baby.

Jack took a step toward him. "What?" He took another step. Kyle didn't know what it was about him, but he was menacing. "You're in our clan, aren't you?"

"Who are you? Are you Traveling?" Laurie asked. She looked to Jack and then glanced at Kairi. "Oh, no. Is something about to happen?"

"Yes," Kyle said. "You can't get in that car. You'll make Kairi an orphan."

"Oh no!" Laurie gasped, and she turned to her baby.

Jack narrowed his eyes. "What are you doing? We're not important. We left that life behind on purpose. Why are you saving us?"

"Kairi's important, and she needs you."

Laurie took Kairi out of the car seat, clutched her to her chest, and rocked back and forth, whispering something.

"What about those paradox things?" Jack asked.

Laurie interrupted him. "Forget paradoxes. We can't leave our Kairi." Still cradling the baby, she approached Jack and Kyle. "We'll do whatever you say."

Almost too late, Kyle realized something was wrong with their car. "And check out your car."

Jack looked at his wife and his child and finally nodded. "Okay."

Back in his present, in Colorado, Kyle woke up in his hotel room. He inspected himself. Was he dizzy? Only slightly. He guessed that made sense. He didn't change his own timeline.

TEMPORAL DREAMS

He grabbed his phone to call Kairi.
Her number wasn't there.

Chapter Fifty-One
Kairi: Boulder, Colorado, 2019

Kairi was hanging out at Boulder Brews, having a mocha, which she really needed, when a crazy man came right up to her and started babbling.

"Kairi! There you are," he said, sitting down at her table. "Thank God I found you." He had a neat Australian accent like her folks did.

She held out her hand to block him. "Whoa, dude. Do I know you?" It was turning into a weird day. About an hour ago, she'd been minding her own business unpacking from her Cancun trip, and she'd been overcome with dizziness. She fell right on the floor of her bedroom. Her sorority sisters rushed in from all over the house and tried to help her.

The housemother even said they should call an ambulance.

But Dakota convinced them to wait and see. The last time an ambulance had come to the house, it hadn't ended well for the sorority.

When Kairi could finally get up, she was torn between going to the hospital and going out for a monster fix of chocolate and caffeine. The mocha won.

The guy rubbed his hand over his face. "You don't know me? At all? Think carefully."

She examined him. With his skin tone and flat nose, he did remind her of her dad. The stranger looked like he could be a relative, but it was just the four of them in her bio family. "I don't know you. Who are you? Why do you know my name? How did you know I was here?" She still felt a little jittery and grabbed onto the table as she lifted her mocha and took a sip.

He held up his finger. "Wait. You feel sick, don't you? Dizzy."

Geez. How bad did she look? "How do you know that?" She narrowed her eyes. "For that matter, how did you know I'd be here?"

"Your, uh, brother, Lowan." He paused and shook his head slightly. "He told me you'd be here."

She was going to kill that kid. How did he even know? Oh, yeah, she'd called home looking for Mom when she felt sick and got him instead. "Who. The. Hell. Are. You?"

"Oh, sorry." He frowned. "My name is Kyle. I'm your cousin. I should have mentioned that."

At his words, she felt a tickle of weirdness. Great. Just what she needed on top of everything else.

From the top of Kyle's shaved head to his Indigenous All-Stars (whatever that was) t-shirt, hoodie, jeans, and weird tennis shoes, if she'd had a cousin, he would look like this guy. But that was impossible, wasn't it? Mom and Dad said all their relatives were dead.

He was staring into her eyes, but it wasn't creepy for some reason. He seemed desperate. "I just saved your parents, and your, ah, brother, I guess. I need you to save mine. You promised."

She was too tired for this crap. "What are you talking about?" The weird feeling intensified.

He pointed at her. "And now you're feeling déjà vu."

Now that he mentioned it, she realized he was right. "How could you possibly know that?"

"I'm your cousin. Our family is special." He grabbed her hands. "You have to listen to me. I'm a time traveler. I saved your parents. You owe me. You're a time traveler, too. You have to save my parents."

She didn't pull away. His handholding and desperation didn't seem creepy. But her lack of alarm was itself alarming, considering.

She extricated her hands. "I don't know if you're really my cousin. I don't see why my parents would lie about that." Was it possible they didn't know about this guy? "Just a minute. I'm going to try my mom again."

She pulled her cell out of her purse and speed-dialed Mom. It went straight to voicemail. What had she said she was going to do today? Kairi couldn't remember.

Back to the Kyle guy. "Even if you are my cousin," she said. "I'm not buying that we're a family of time travelers. That doesn't make any sense. How gullible do you think I am?"

He stared at her for a moment more and then leaned back in his chair, his eyes seeming to fill. "Bloody hell," he whispered. He leaned over, cradling his head in his hands.

Was he crying? She hated to admit it, but she felt sorry for the poor guy.

"Are you okay, dude? Uh, Kyle, was it?" She reached over and patted his back. "I'm not against helping you. I'm just not who you think I am."

He sat up. "But you are." Now, he had a kind of wild look in his eyes. "I'm sure you are. How can I convince you?"

"Gee, I don't know. Proof?" Like that would ever happen. "Listen, do you have some friends or family I could call for you? I'm a bit concerned. You seem a little crazy or something."

"That's it!" He grinned and took his cell out of his pocket.

That Kyle guy begged her to stay until his friend showed up. He seemed so pitiful, she couldn't say no.

When his friend did show up, she was very glad she'd stayed. He was gorgeous, from his dark-brown wavy hair to his gray-blue eyes, to his firm-looking pecs, to his jeans hugging what appeared to be an awesome ass.

"Kairi, this is my friend Josh," Kyle said. "Josh, this is my cousin Kairi."

She got a strong feeling of déjà vu.

Josh held out his hand for a shake.

When he looked into her eyes and smiled, something happened: she felt instantly and completely happy. She'd never experienced anything like that before. She couldn't help beaming back at him.

When their hands touched, she tingled everywhere--and she did mean everywhere.

For his part, he raised his eyebrows and opened his eyes wider. "Have we met before, Kairi?"

It seemed as if she'd known him forever. And it seemed as if she'd known him all over. She flushed. "I'm not sure. I don't remember meeting you before. But, somehow, it feels like we have."

Kyle stood up. "I was right." He pointed from one to the other. "You do know each other."

Josh cradled her right hand in both of his. "Well, we know each other now. And I will ensure we continue doing so for a long, long time."

A thrill raced up her spine. Why did touching him, knowing him, feel so right?

"I'm not sure what to say," Kyle said. "I'm glad you guys hit it off. I'm sorry to interrupt whatever this is, but I have an emergency. Lives are at stake. My parents' lives. Can we please sit down and talk? It's life and death."

Seemingly reluctantly, Josh let go of her hand and sat in one of the tiny bistro chairs.

Still buzzing all over, she followed suit. She didn't even remember standing up. "Go ahead. I'm listening." Her eyes were drawn to Josh, and she couldn't seem to pull them away.

"Josh knows I can time travel," Kyle said. "Tell her, Josh."

He smiled, and Kairi melted again.

"Yesterday Kyle and I did what he called a time travel experiment," Josh said. "He lay on the couch in the physics lounge and disappeared into thin air. Then he predicted that I was going to get déjà vu."

She quit staring at Josh's mouth and straightened in her chair. "I have déjà vu now." When she wasn't peering directly at Josh, she felt a bit more normal. She didn't know what was going on with her, but it was significant.

Josh smiled at her again. "Me, too!"

She started to tingle again. Look away, Kair. She looked at Kyle.

"Oh, good grief." Kyle sighed. When he saw her looking at him, he appeared to relax. "Déjà vu is a symptom of time travel."

"What does it mean with Kairi and me in this case?" Josh asked.

She didn't look at him, but she could feel the edges of her lips tugging upwards like they wanted to smile.

"In this case, the two of you knew each other in another timeline," Kyle said. "You had a strong bond."

What she felt about Josh was strong and bond-like and definitely unusual. She wanted there to be some kind of logical explanation. She risked a glance his way.

His lips stuck out ever so slightly and curved up. Wow, they looked kissable.

And what would they feel like kissing her? Her lips? Her neck below her ear? The little hollow at the base of her neck? Her breasts? She started to heat up again. This had to stop.

Look away, Kairi! But she felt her lips curve up in harmony. She forced herself to turn back to Kyle. "Okay. So. There is clearly something going on here. I'm not sure what it is." She wanted to glance back at Josh but didn't let herself.

She tried to shake it off, shaking her head, but that made her dizzy again.

Josh scooted his chair closer to hers and their knees touched under the table.

A wave of fire traveled north from her knee. What was she saying? She scooted her chair away from Josh's. "Um. Where was I?" She focused her eyes on Kyle.

"You were about to agree to help me save my parents," Kyle said.

"You were about to agree to go out with me," Josh said.

At the same time, her cell rang. It was Mom.

"We need to talk, Kairi," she said.

Chapter Fifty-Two
Kyle: Boulder, Colorado, 2019

In the coffeehouse, Kyle was freaking out. He'd finally tracked down Kairi, and she had no memory of their Strangers on a Train agreement. He was very disappointed. He'd finally let himself get his hopes up again, let himself think he might be able to save his mom and dad.

And he was mad at himself. He should have seen this coming. Only The Traveler remembered the overwritten timeline.

She was on her mobile right now, not saying much, her expression getting darker and darker as she listened.

Josh leaned towards him. "Thanks for introducing me to Kairi. I've never felt like this before. Do you think we did know each other in another timeline?"

Kyle shrugged. He didn't care about Josh and Kairi's love life. He had more important things on his mind.

"Do you think we could have been together, you know, a couple?"

"I don't know, mate," Kyle said. "She'd said something earlier, but I don't remember."

"Yeah," Josh said. "It feels like we've known each other longer." His gaze was drawn back to Kairi. He drank her in greedily. Kyle thought it was a little unsettling.

"Maybe you should get going, Josh?" Kyle said.

Kairi hung up her mobile, scowling.

"What's wrong?" Kyle asked. "Who was that on the phone?"

"My mom." She seemed to avoid looking at Josh. "My parents have been lying to me my whole life. I can't believe it. We're Australian. Aborigines. We have all kinds of relatives living back in Australia." She shoved her phone into her purse. "And, there's more. Mom said our clan has powers. She wouldn't get into it on the phone. She said she and Dad had to tell Lowan and me in person." She shook her head.

Kyle figured I told you, so it was probably annoying.

"So?" Josh asked. "Will you go out with me?"

Kairi still didn't look at him. "Yeah. But I can't focus on that now. Kyle told me all this for a reason. Right, Kyle?"

Hurray. They might finally get back on track. "Yes."

Before he could get anything further out, Kairi said, "In fact, maybe you should leave, Josh. You're kind of distracting." She glanced at him and flushed, and quickly looked away.

Josh looked crestfallen. "Can I at least get your phone number?" He pulled his phone out.

"Yeah." Without glancing at him, Kairi pulled her phone back out and handed it in his general direction. "I'll input my number in yours. You input your number in mine." The two of them punched numbers for a few moments and then handed their phones back.

"So, then, I guess I'll go?" Josh reached for her hand.

At his touch, she recoiled as if he was on fire. But then she swiveled and looked into his eyes and smiled tentatively. "Sorry. It's not you. You're great. I'm in an odd place right now. I look forward to your call."

Josh stood up. "Okay. I'll call then."

"Okay," she said. "Sounds good."

"Let me know if you need anything, Kyle," Josh said.

"Okay," Kyle said. "Thanks. Bye."

He didn't seem to want to, but Josh turned and left.

Once he was gone, Kairi visibly relaxed. "Sorry if I was weird there."

"Ah, okay," Kyle said. "What was going on with you two?"

She shrugged her shoulders up and down. "I don't know. Love at first sight? Whatever it was, it was bizarre. Anyway."

"Anyway?"

"Are we going to time travel or what? How do we do it?" She paused for a moment. "I can't believe I'm about to say this, but do you have a time machine?"

Kyle smiled. "No." He tapped his forehead. "This is our time machine."

In Kyle's hotel room, Kairi lay on the bed. "I don't think my parents would be too happy about this if they knew about it," she said.

"Do you think they're against Traveling?" he asked. "Aren't you supposed to meet to talk with them about it?"

"I meant I didn't think they'd be too happy about me going to the hotel room of a strange man I just met and lying on his bed."

"But we're cousins," he said.

"So you say."

"But?"

"Relax," she said. "I believe you. I believe all this crazy stuff. I believe you're my cousin. I believe we can time travel. I can't explain why. But it feels right." She crossed her arms over her chest and crossed her legs. "Let's get this show on the road." She closed her eyes. "You said this was just a test to see if I could do it, right?"

"Yeah." Kyle wasn't entirely sure he could teach Kairi to Travel on the spur of the moment. He rubbed his hands together. They were cool for some reason. He must be nervous. "My Uncle Ray helped me with my first trip. I guess I'll say to you what he said to me." Kyle cast his mind back. "You can access The Dreaming," he said. "You have the power. Feel all of time flowing through you. It's you. You're it. You are The Dreaming."

Everything seemed to stand still in the hotel room.

After a few moments, Kyle got short of breath and had to gasp air in. "Kairi?"

She opened her eyes. "Yeah? When are we going to get started?" At his expression, she added, "Or did we just start? Was that supposed to do something?"

"Yeah," he said. "Do you feel any differently?"

She shook her head. "Not really."

"Dammit." Kyle realized he'd had years and years of training, learning to calm himself and reach another state of consciousness. He glanced at Kairi, who wiggled her eyebrows at him. "How did you do it before?"

"Do what? Time travel? I don't remember."

"Dammit." He wracked his brain. "It's a different state of mind, sort of like meditation. Do you know anything about that?"

She sat up. "Is transcendental meditation the same thing?"

315

If she knew about transcendental meditation, maybe this would work. "Yes! I think so. Do you know how to do that?"

"No."

Bloody hell. Kyle blew out a breath. "Then why did you bring it up?"

"I've heard of it," she said. "I think my sorority sister, Dakota, does that kind of thing as well as lucid dreaming and out-of-body experiences and other woo-woo stuff."

"Really? A sorority girl does that stuff?"

Kairi grinned at him. "I hate to break it to you, dude. We are in Boulder."

He knew where they were. How stupid did she think he was? "So?"

"I'm just saying there's all kinds of weird hippie stuff around here," she said.

"Lucid dreaming sounds perfect," he said. "Is there any way your sorority sister could help you do that?"

She shrugged. "I'll give her a call and see."

Kyle was very annoyed. He couldn't believe he agreed to sneak into a sorority house dressed as a girl. At the moment, he was crouched in the bushes outside, waiting for Kairi to bring him a wig.

"Psst! Kyle, where'd you go?" Finally. It was her.

"I'm here. Did you get it?"

She crept into view. "Yes. Here you go." She handed him a sorry-looking bright pink wig.

She had to be joking. "You expect me to wear this?"

"Yeah. I brought some makeup, too." She rifled her pockets and came out with small plastic cases.

"Why do we have to do this?" This had to be some kind of trick.

"I told you. Men aren't allowed upstairs in our rooms. Dakota's meeting us in our room with something she called a lucid something-or-other." She reached out toward his face with a small stick. "Close your eyes."

He did so and felt her brushing something on his eyelids.

"Open your eyes." She smiled at him. "Cute." She reached out with another stick.

Kyle closed his eyes again.

"No. You keep your eyes open for this one." The stick got closer and closer to his eyeballs.

"Don't poke me in the eye."

"Relax. I've been doing this for years." She brushed stuff on his eyelashes.

"And finally." She opened a cylinder and twisted it, and a column of red stuff came out.

"Oh, I know that one," Kyle reached for it. "It's like lip balm."

"Right." Kairi had an odd expression on her face, and he put on the lip stuff.

He handed it back. He needed to keep focused. This was for his mom and dad.

"And the wig?"

"You do it." At this point, he was resigned to the whole thing. Whatever it took to get his parents back.

She placed the wig on his head and adjusted it a bit. "Now pull up your hood."

He did.

"You look cute. I'm gonna say you're my cousin."

"I am your cousin."

"Well, there you go." She grabbed his arm and pulled him up. "Maybe you shouldn't talk. Your voice is too low."

As they walked toward the front door of the sorority house, Kyle wondered if he'd see any sorority girls hanging around in their underwear. Maybe being forced to wear makeup wouldn't be so bad.

No one stopped them as they tramped up to the third floor. They went inside one of the small bedrooms, and Kairi closed the door behind them.

She sat down on the bed. "Make yourself at home. Now we just have to wait for?"

The door swung open, and another girl started to come in.

Kairi jumped up. "Sorry, Sophia." She raced to the door. "We're busy."

"What are you doing?" Sophia asked. Kyle wished Kairi would get out of the way. What was Sophia wearing? He couldn't get a good look.

"Dakota, there you are," Kairi called down the hall. "I'll talk to you later, Sophia."

Dakota? Was that the same girl who was her roommate in the other timeline? Uh oh. Kyle braced himself.

"But…" Sophia said.

Dakota slipped through the open door, carrying a full plastic grocery sack. "A girl cousin?" She glanced back at Kairi. "I thought you said your cousin was a guy."

Kairi slammed the door behind her and locked it. "He is a guy."

"Oh, he's you-know," Dakota said. "I get it."

Apparently, Kyle disliked Dakota in every timeline. He pulled off the wig. "I'm not you-know!"

Dakota smothered a laugh. "Whatever, dude." She pulled a strange-looking helmet out of the bag.

"What the hell is that?" he asked.

"This is a lucid dreaming something-something," Dakota said. "I, ah, borrowed it from Mary's lab. Wait, I recorded what she said about it." She pulled her phone out and pushed a button.

A tinny voice wafted out of the phone. "This is my lucid dream induction device. It's based on mnemonic initiation. It detects when you've entered REM sleep and triggers an auditory tone, flashing lights and a small vibration. Whichever triggers you detect are incorporated into your dream and thus remind you to dream lucidly."

"I'm getting déjà vu," both Kairi and Dakota said at the same time.

"Good!" That meant they'd done this before in an overwritten timeline. They were definitely on to something.

The woman's voice continued. "Reality testing is used to determine if you're dreaming or not. You can try to stick your finger through the palm of your hand, or hold your nose closed and see if you can breathe without using your mouth, or pinch yourself."

Dakota leaned over and pinched Kairi.

"Ouch," Kairi said.

"Déjà vu," they both said.

"You can also flip a light switch," Mary said. "They usually don't work in dreams. Or look inside a book. They're usually blank in dreams."

Dakota did something with the phone. "I think that's it."

If Kyle understood this device, it was perfect for their needs. He wished he'd had something similar when he'd been a kid trying to learn how to Dream. "I think this'll work." He reached for the helmet. "Kairi lay down on the bed."

She did so, and he handed her the helmet. She had to sit up again to put it on.

Kyle leaned down and looked at the wires. The device needed a power source. "Do you have an electrical outlet?"

"Of course, dude," Dakota said, shaking her head. She plugged it in.

"Now what?" Kairi asked.

"Now we have to be quiet and let you go to sleep," Kyle said. "When you hear a tone, or see flashing behind your eyelids, you'll know you're asleep. Then, I want you to remember, to think about..." What? "A little while ago when you put the makeup on me."

Kairi snickered. "Sounds fun."

"The concept behind all this is you can access that time from this time," Kyle said. "Time isn't what you think it is. It's not an arrow. It's all everywhere."

"Cool," Dakota said. "What will we see?"

"This is just a test to see if she can do it. If it works, we'll see Kairi disappear," Kyle said. "Don't be alarmed, Dakota."

"What do I do?" Kairi asked.

"Just try to dream," Kyle said. "This first time, you probably won't go far." He just hoped she went. "Is everyone ready?"

Dakota nodded. "Yep."

"Yes," Kairi said.

Kyle and Dakota sat there silently for quite a while. Kyle himself may have dozed off when Dakota shrieked. When he looked back at the bed, Kairi flickered and reappeared.

As soon as she solidified, she bolted upright and tears cascaded down her cheeks. "Oh, my God. Oh, my God. Oh, my God." She kept repeating it over and over.

Chapter Fifty-Three
Kairi: Boulder, Colorado, 2019

It all came back to Kairi and she couldn't stop saying, "Oh, my God." It was all so much, all the old timelines breaking over her like waves on a beach.

The first one, where she was so lonely and sad and defensive and mad, beaten down by her encounter with Chad, but recovering--with Josh's help. All those good times with Josh, from clinking champagne glasses to licking maple syrup off each other, to boring but wonderful stuff like just studying together at the library.

The second one, when she went back and saved the younger, still-optimistic still-innocent Kairi from Chad. She'd been so feisty and loved Dakota so much. Then, sweet, generous Dakota ended up living on the street, begging (or worse) for food and drugs. And, then, worst of all, Dakota dead of an overdose at the age of seventeen. Ultimately, saving Dakota again after paralyzing her.

The final timeline when Kyle gave her her parents and her brother was the most amazing, but to her, until now, it had seemed like the only one.

She felt like an insignificant speck of sand, roiling in the salty ocean, trying to stay on top, near the sky, near the air. She grabbed onto whatever was nearby.

Kyle. "Hold on, Kairi." He held her in his arms. "I know it's a lot. Hang on. It'll calm down." He held her up.

Finally, she felt like a person again. She focused on his face.

"Are you okay?" he asked.

"Yeah, are you okay?" Dakota asked.

She nodded. "I think so."

This man, her cousin, gave her back her parents. This man gave her her brother. She gripped him tight, feeling the tears overflowing again. "Thank you. Thank you. Thank you for my mom. Thank you for my dad. Thank you for my brother. Thank you for my life. I can never repay you." She was too overcome to continue.

He patted her back awkwardly. "There, there."

Eventually, she was all cried out. She let go of her cousin. Her cousin! She leaned back. "Sorry about all that."

He didn't seem to know what to say.

"Are you sure you're okay?" Dakota asked.

"I'm sure." She turned back to Kyle. "I'm sorry it took me so long to thank you for what you did for me."

"That's okay. I get it. You didn't understand what happened."

She straightened her spine. "Now what can I do for you? I'm at your disposal. I'll do anything. Anything. I'm serious."

He looked at his shoes. "I do want to try to help my folks."

She nodded. "We're going to save your parents. Absolutely. What's the plan?"

After a lot of hashing and rehashing, Kyle convinced her to join him back in 2004 in Sydney on the day his parents died in this most recent timeline. He'd summarized what happened with the car accident and being stuck in the middle of it.

He'd maintained the best way to change the timeline was to stop others from changing the timeline. And he'd said she evidently had an unusual immunity to ill effect from touching Travelers. She wasn't sure what the origins or consequences of that were, but she was glad about it. She thought it meant she was in less danger when she Traveled--and that sounded like a good thing.

So long story short, they were going to stop everyone from going to the scene of the accident. Kyle had said she was the secret weapon, because no one knew her.

She was determined to help Kyle as much as he'd helped her. They would save his family.

Even though it was the plan, Kairi couldn't believe she was back in 2004. At the airport. Going to Australia. Her blood was racing. Her heart was jackhammering. Would anyone here now figure out she didn't belong?

Kyle was as good as his word and the ticket was there waiting for her at the United counter. She flashed her fake ID at the employee, and smiled. A little later she repeated it at the security checkpoint and that was it. All that worrying for nothing. Thank goodness one of her sorority sisters had an ID-making setup in her room. The under-twenty-one sisters usually kept her pretty busy, but she'd managed to fit Kairi in. She sauntered right down to the gate. No problem.

Kyle met Kairi at the Sydney airport. But she was so tired and out-of-it she almost didn't recognize him. She never had been able to sleep on planes.

"Kairi?" he said. "Are you all right? You don't look so good."

"Yeah." She nodded. "Any chance I can get a nap before we go off and save the world?"

"Sure." He took her arm in his, and they stumbled off.

"Kairi!" someone, a man, whisper-shouted at her. "Wake up."

She was lying in a strange bed, with a strange man lying next to her. As she took in his face, she realized it was her cousin Kyle. And she was on a time travel mission. Holy shit.

"What? Why did you wake me up?" She still felt like crap from the long trip here to Australia. Australia! "And what are you doing here in bed with me?"

"I'm here to wake you up in case you start Traveling in your sleep. You're new at it, I thought there was a chance you might not be in total control of your powers." That actually made sense, at least as much as any of this did.

She heard a noise from the other room that sounded like a doorknob turning. "Is someone else here?" she whispered. "Where are we?"

"We're at our corporate apartment. It's a safe-house," he said. "We have to hide." He grabbed her wrist and pulled.

"Hide? Why?"

"Just come on!" He dragged her out of the bed and into the closet. He pulled the doors closed after them.

She could still see into the bedroom through the slats in the closet doors. "I don't understand. Why are we hiding?"

"This isn't exactly a sanctioned mission," he whispered.

"So the person who's here now is on a sanctioned mission?"

But then a middle-aged man ambled into the bedroom.

Kyle whispered, "Ray. Bloody hell."

"What? Who's Ray?"

"Shh."

The man glanced at the closet.

They both froze.

The man walked to the dresser and opened the top drawer, taking out underwear, socks, and a new shirt wrapped in cellophane. Then he turned and walked into the bathroom, partially closing the door behind him. They heard the shower turn on.

"We need to get out of here," Kyle said.

"Why?" Kairi asked. "I don't understand what's going on. If he's here in your apartment, isn't this Ray guy one of your relatives, one of our relatives?"

"Come on!" He slowly opened the closet doors and they crept through the bedroom. Once they got out into the family room, they ran.

Kyle quietly opened up the front door and they slipped out. He closed the door behind them.

They stood for a moment in the hall. For her part, Kairi tried to calm her heart. Nothing like adrenaline to wake a person up, apparently. "What's going on, Kyle?" she asked.

"You don't understand." He pointed at the closed door. "That's Ray from my time, from our time, from 2019--at least he looks the same age. He shouldn't be here." He shook his head. "I never did understand what happened with my folks back here. Especially my Traveling dad. He knew better than to get mixed up with his past self and his past wife."

"So what do we do?"

"I hate to say it, but this is more complicated than I thought. We need more information," Kyle said. "And I can only think of one place to get it."

Kairi and Kyle loitered around the corner from some

office building. He'd said they had to wait for someone named Charlotte to get into work.

She was practically dozing off when she heard a woman loudly say, "Young man! I say, young man!" Kairi peeked around the corner.

Next to her, Kyle was riveted by the scene.

No wonder. She quickly realized the woman, presumably Charlotte, was yelling at some other version of Kyle. And from the looks of him, it was Kyle from her time. "This reminds me of Back to the Future when Marty travels back and sees himself?"

"Shh! I'm trying to hear what they're saying."

She leaned against the wall. "Don't you know what they're saying?" she muttered.

After a few minutes, he leaned back and said, "Okay, they're gone. Come on. We need to go. We have to get inside before the other Kyle comes back."

This whole thing was surreal. She followed Kyle into the building, and they went up some stairs. "We have to try to avoid Ray," he said over his shoulder.

"Don't we know Ray is in the shower?" she asked.

"That's the Ray from our time, not this time," he said, as they entered a public foyer area.

"Oh, right." Would she ever get all the time traveling stuff straight?

The woman jumped up from her chair. "I thought you said I wasn't in the loop?"

Kyle glided over to her desk.

At the same time, she looked him up and down. "Oh, no. You're dressed differently. You're a different version of that young man." She sank down in her chair. "What's going on? It can't be good with so many Travelers here."

"Charlotte I do need your help," Kyle said. "First of all, who else is here in the office?"

"No one," she said. "I'm the only one here." She glanced at Kairi, seemingly noticing her for the first time. "Wait. Who's this now? Another Traveler? She looks like a Traveler." She glanced back at Kyle.

"Who else has Traveled here?" Kyle asked.

"No one," she said. "Just you, Mr. Barada."

"Not Ray?" he asked.

"Ray Barada? No," she said, eyebrows rising. "He's not allowed to Travel."

That comment seemed to strongly affect Kyle.

In the meantime, the poor woman was getting more and more freaked out. Someone needed to reassure her--they needed her help--and it didn't look like it was going to be Kyle. Kairi took a step forward. "Hi, Charlotte is it?" She smiled at her.

She nodded.

"Thank you for helping us. My name is Kairi. This is Kyle. It's an honor to meet you."

"Thank you," she said quietly.

"We're not here to cause any trouble," she said. "Just the opposite, in fact."

"What's my mom's mission today?" Kyle asked abruptly.

"Your mom, Rebecca Barada?" Charlotte asked. "She doesn't have a mission scheduled."

"But then why..." Kyle trailed off. He pulled up a chair and sat down.

Kairi yawned. Now that the excitement was ebbing again, her jet lag was catching up to her.

"Can I get you some tea, honey?" Charlotte asked.

"That would be nice," Kairi said. "Coffee would be nicer." She smiled.

"I can do that." She smiled back and stood up and walked over to a kitchenette.

Charlotte brought the three of them cups of coffee. It cleared Kairi's mind.

For his part, Kyle seemed to be in a daze. She guessed she could understand that, all the players were his relatives, people he loved.

She didn't have that problem. They were all strangers to her. They needed to get this show on the road. She didn't come thousands of miles and many years to sit around. "Kyle?"

He looked up at her. "Huh?"

"What's happening?" she asked. "Do we need a new plan?"

He just looked at her.

"Maybe, if your mom isn't Traveling Charlotte could divert her from the accident. And your dad of this time, too?" She peeked at Charlotte.

She nodded. "I could call a mandatory meeting at the Training compound in the country."

"Okay," Kairi said. "Good. That just leaves Traveling Kyle and his Traveling dad, what's his name?"

"Riley," Kyle mumbled.

"Riley," Kairi said. She felt her mouth tug down in a frown. "And what about the shower guy, Ray? Do we need to worry about him?"

"Oh, yeah," Kyle said. "We need to worry about him. He's not supposed to be here."

"What shower guy?" Charlotte asked. "Who's the shower guy?"

Kyle turned to her and said in a strange voice, "Ray."

"Ray?" Charlotte asked. "You mean he's Traveling? He's forbidden from Traveling."

"You said something about that before," Kyle said. "I don't understand what you're talking about."

Charlotte opened her mouth and then closed her mouth. Finally, she said, "I shouldn't say. I don't know the details but Ray's ancestors did a bunch of stuff they weren't supposed to do while Traveling."

That sounded intriguing. "Wow," Kairi said. "Like what?"

"They acquired riches." That didn't sound so bad. "People were murdered." Okay, bad. What the hell was she getting into here? Charlotte continued. "So, as part of their punishment, he and his descendants aren't allowed to Travel--unless they're the only clan members left."

"Well, that doesn't sound good," Kairi said.

Kyle didn't say anything. He just glowered.

"And, ah, Kyle really shouldn't interact with his other self," Charlotte said.

"Okay," Kairi said. "I'll take the other Kyle and Riley." She turned to Kyle. "Can you deal with this Ray guy?" She wasn't chicken. She could deal with a potential murderer--she just didn't want to. That was her story and she was sticking to it.

"Oh, yeah," he said. "I can deal with him."

It looked like they had a new plan. Hopefully this one would work.

Chapter Fifty-Four
Kyle: Sydney, Australia, 2004

Back in 2004 in the offices of Time Advantages, Inc., Kyle's mind was racing as Kairi and Charlotte talked.

Kyle couldn't believe Ray was here in 2004 on the day his parents died. It was doubtful he had a valid reason for being here. A lot of Ray's behavior that Kyle had thought merely odd was now cast in a very suspicious light.

And if what Charlotte had said about Ray being forbidden to Travel was true, how could he be the official Traveler in Kyle's current timeline? Had Ray somehow squashed his Traveling prohibition?

Hadn't Mom mentioned Ray when she'd spilled all that info about the reporter Lachlan Harris? At the time, Kyle hadn't thought it was suspicious that Mom revealed so much information so easily. But he should have, she was a trained Agent. That information set a series of disastrous events into motion. Kyle'd sought out Lachlan, which eventually led him to the car accident in 2004, which led to his parents' deaths. Could Ray have engineered that? How? Was he that manipulative?

Kyle's mind was reeling. He started to feel dizzy, and leaned over resting his head on his hands.

"Kyle?" Charlotte rubbed his back. "What's wrong, honey?"

Kyle sat up. "I think someone's been working against me." He had a horrible thought: could Charlotte be in on it? He stared into her eyes.

"Oh, no." She put her hand in front of her mouth. "What do you mean?" She looked genuinely surprised and horrified.

"I think someone's been trying to kill my parents," Kyle said. "And maybe me."

Kairi asked, "Who?"

"Ray Barada," Kyle said.

"Oh, no!" Charlotte said.

"I don't get it," Kairi said. "Why would this Ray guy try to hurt you and your family?"

Kyle said, "There can be only one Traveler at a time."

"Why is that?" Kairi asked.

He resisted the impulse to give her a dirty look. She hadn't had any training, after all. "It wasn't initially clear to me because it's never supposed to happen. But I think I figured it out. Each Traveler is responsible for a timeline, a version of reality, so if there's more than one, the realities have to fight for dominance."

"I didn't know that," Charlotte said.

"Me neither," Kairi said.

"I'm not sure anyone really knew," Kyle said. "My dad Riley's line is now the official Travelers, so, they are the only ones supposed to Travel."

"What does all this have to do with Ray?" Kairi asked.

"He wants to Travel," Kyle said. "If Riley's entire line is dead he apparently has free rein." He felt his face stretch into a grimace.

"It's hard to believe Ray would kill so many relatives just to Travel," Kairi said.

"The traditions and regulations of Traveling are very strict," Charlotte said. "They've been developed over the generations and they can't be broken."

"What happens if they're broken?" Kairi asked.

"Execution," Kyle said.

Kairi gulped and then said, "What?"

"Ray's line used to be the official Travelers," Charlotte said. "But his grandfather completed a number of unsanctioned missions with the express purpose of personal gain, to accumulate money and property." Charlotte continued. "When he was confronted with evidence of his crimes, he tried to run and the clan was forced to execute him."

Kyle bet tried to run covered a myriad of sins.

"Did Ray know his grandfather?" Kairi asked.

"Yes." Charlotte nodded. "In fact, the whole clan had to witness the execution."

"Ray must have been a little kid though," Kairi said. "Surely, they didn't make him watch it?"

Charlotte's eyes took on a haunted look. "That's before my time, but I'm afraid they did. It was a difficult time."

"That's not right," Kairi said. "A kid shouldn't have to see that."

"No," Kyle said. "Executions are barbaric. But it doesn't excuse him trying to kill other people. He has to be stopped and punished." Kyle clenched his fists.

"It might explain it though," Kairi said. "Are you sure we, er, you, should go up against him? Maybe it's too dangerous."

Kyle had never felt like this. He wanted to hurt Ray. He wanted Ray to feel as bad as Kyle had when his parents died. "I said I can deal with him and I can." He stood up. "Charlotte, get the key to the weapons locker. We're gearing up."

After a moment of hesitation, Charlotte got a key out of her top drawer. Kyle and Kairi followed her to the stairs.

"Do you even know how to use a weapon?" Kairi asked him.

He resisted an urge to snap at her. She hardly knew anything about Traveling and knew nothing about the years of training he had to go through, including weapons training. "I know."

The three of them tramped down the stairs and then down the basement hall to get weapons. Kyle realized he might not make it through this mission. Well, as far as he was concerned, it was Ray or him. One of them wasn't going to make it back to 2019.

Charlotte was unlocking the large weapons locker. "What do you want?"

Kairi held up her hands. "Nothing for me, thanks."

"You're taking a pistol at least," Kyle said.

"But I don't know how to shoot it," she said.

Charlotte was turning from Kyle to Kairi and back again as if she was watching a tennis match.

"You're just going to persuade Traveling-me and my Traveling-dad to turn around and go home," Kyle said. "A pistol is a good persuader. They're pussycats. All you need to do is point a gun at them and they'll cave." Since they're unarmed. Arm them and you've got another story. "You don't have to take any ammo if you don't want."

"I guess that would be okay," Kairi said.

He hoped he wasn't putting her in too much danger. "Just don't get within arm's reach of them," Kyle added. He didn't think her touch would be fatal or vice versa, but better safe than sorry.

"Uh, okay," Kairi said as Charlotte got out a pistol and a harness. Kairi took off her coat and handed it to Charlotte. Charlotte handed her the harness.

Kyle stared at the gun rack. They had a lovely assortment of guns from throughout the ages. The SIG 550 would be nice. He picked it up.

"That's going to draw an awful lot of attention," Charlotte said.

Kairi was putting her jacket back on over the gun.

Reluctantly, Kyle decided Charlotte was right. He put the SIG back in the rack and picked up a Heckler and Koch MP5K.

"Now, try drawing it," Charlotte said to Kairi.

Kairi successfully drew her pistol.

"Good," Charlotte said.

Kyle tried sighting the H and K down the hall. Not bad.

"You guys seem to have a lot of different guns here," Kairi said, slipping the gun back in the harness. "Are they from different times?"

"Yes," Charlotte said.

"Any from the future?" Kairi asked. "I mean the future compared to now, 2004."

"Yes," Charlotte said. "The H and K is also pretty noticeable, Kyle."

"How does it work?" Kairi asked. "How do you bring weapons here from the future?"

"The same way you don't Travel naked," Kyle said, putting the H and K back.

"Oh." Kairi frowned. "I hadn't thought about that too much before."

He picked up a Glock 19.

"Good choice, Sir." A Glock 17 was what she'd given Kairi. "The Australian Federal Police use the Glock 19, or at least they will."

Kairi gave her an odd look. "Are you a Traveler, Charlotte?"

"Me?" she said. "No."

He felt his mouth turn down in a scowl. "Quit Moneypennying me, Charlotte."

Kairi snickered.

"What?" Charlotte asked. "Oh, the James Bond character?" She tried to suppress a smile.

Kyle grabbed a box of ammo, opened it and loaded his weapon right then and there. He put the rest of the box in his jacket pocket, took off his jacket, laid it carefully on the shelf, put on a gun harness and holstered his weapon.

"That's a lot of ammo, Kyle," Kairi said.

Charlotte wisely didn't say anything.

Kyle put his jacket back on, ammo jingling in the pocket. "We need to be prepared. People have died."

Kairi's eyes seemed to grow moist, but she just nodded.

At least one more person was going to die if Kyle had anything to say about it.

Charlotte and he had given Kairi their best suggestions on how to intercept the other Traveling-Kyle and Traveling-Riley. So Kairi was on her way to find Traveling-Kyle.

In the meantime, Kyle made his way back to the safe house. Hopefully, Ray would still be there.

When Kyle approached the apartment building, he saw Ray walking down the sidewalk in the other direction. The sidewalk was crowded, but Kyle was sure it was him. He quickly fell in behind him but Ray stepped to the street and hailed a cab. "Damn."

Kyle hailed his own cab. Thankfully, one stopped quickly. Kyle jumped in and said, "Follow that cab," pointing ahead of them in weekday traffic.

The cabbie turned around. "Seriously, mate?"

"Yes! Go!"

The cabbie shrugged and pulled out.

Kyle followed Ray to the corner of Eddy Avenue and Elizabeth Street, the site of the accident. "Bloody hell," he whispered. But it was hours before the accident was supposed to occur. What was Ray up to?

"They're stopping," the cabbie said. "What do you want to do?"

"I'm getting out," Kyle said and handed him some time-appropriate bills. It was good having Charlotte's support. He got out of the cab and skulked down the sidewalk, keeping Ray in view.

Ray ducked into a storefront. Kyle froze. Should he follow him in? He decided to wait outside for him to come out. Forty minutes later, he was a nervous wreck. He kept sliding his hand inside his jacket to touch the grip of the Glock. Where the hell was Ray? Why was he here?

And then he felt something hard jab into his back. He turned and saw Ray's unsmiling face. "Ray? What are you doing?" he managed to stammer out.

"You are a persistent little shit, I'll give you that," Ray said, digging the barrel of something into Kyle's back. Kyle couldn't get a good look at it, but this--gun in the back--was a classic training scenario.

Trying to get out of it, Kyle twisted around, but when he looked into Ray's eyes, he remembered Ray and his wife Jessie raising him and Oliver like their own sons in this timeline. He remembered family dinners with Ray, Jessie, their daughter Moira, and Oliver and Kyle sitting around the kitchen table. They'd talked about what happened in school or at the company. They'd been there for each other. How could Ray be evil?

When he finally focused on the-Ray-here-and-now he barely had time to think, That gun looks weird, before he heard a sizzle, smelled ozone, and his whole body roiled with pain. Everything went black.

Chapter Fifty-Five
Kairi: Sydney, Australia, 2004

Kairi was in the past, in a strange country, thousands of miles from home. When she imagined traveling the world, it was not like this. Suffice it to say, she was nervous. All that talk of the big baddie Ray had scared her, and the guns scared her--not that she was going to let on in front of Kyle. He'd surprised her. He'd seemed kind of wimpy when they'd met in Colorado. He'd let her dress him as a girl, after all. But he did seem to know what he was doing with those guns. Personally, she was imagining her gun-harness-combo was a cute new type of accessory.

She took a deep breath and tried to calm down. One nice thing about Australia: everybody had those neat accents. She strode out of the Time Advantages, Inc. office building to confront Traveling-Kyle. Kyle had told her that after Traveling-Kyle talked to his mom in the coffee shop, he'd staked out the office building for hours. All she had to do was find him outside here.

The sidewalk was crowded, but he was pretty easy to spot. There weren't that many brown-skinned folks walking by and there were even fewer folks just loitering. She marched right up to him.

"Kyle Barada, go home," she said, forcefully, she hoped.

After looking flustered for a few moments, he asked, "You sound American. How do you know me?"

"I'm a Traveler. My name is Kairi. And you're about to fuck things up royally. Go home, back to your own time."

"You know about Traveling? Since when do we have American Travelers?"

Kairi briefly toyed with the idea of getting her gun out. "Yeah. Focus, Kyle. You're about to kill your parents, your mom and dad. Dead." That was harsh, but she really needed him to skedaddle.

He paled. "Why should I believe you?"

What had the other Kyle told her to say? Oh yeah. "You saw Liam's junk, more than once, I might add. And it was circus-freak huge." She was suddenly curious to meet this Liam guy.

"How do you know that?" Kyle said. "I would never tell anyone that."

"You did tell me that," she said. "In the future. While you were grieving about killing your own parents."

His eyes darted from her to the front door of the building to the surrounding crowd, as if he was looking for something or someone. "But..."

"Give it up, dude," she said. "Go home."

He shook his head slightly. "All right," he finally said in a resigned tone.

"In fact, I'll take you inside and Charlotte will help you get on your way."

"Really?"

"Yep."

He nodded. Score! She steered him right inside those front doors. One down, one to go.

Kairi and Kyle didn't have quite as much intel on where to find Traveling-Riley. The only place they knew he'd be for sure was the corner of Elizabeth Street and Eddy Avenue, so that's where she went.

It was several hours before the accident, so for all she knew, she'd be stuck waiting for a while. She paced all the sidewalks around the intersection until she saw a familiar-looking man walking with a purpose towards a building.

She crept closer, trying to decipher if he was Riley. He did look a lot like Kyle--or at least the way she imagined Kyle would look if he were forty. Actually, come to think of it, Riley looked a lot like her dad. She really needed to nail down the family tree at some point. Exactly how were they all related?

Riley, probably, went right up to a battered metal exterior door and knocked on it.

It swung open and revealed Ray. He smiled at Riley, but

she didn't think it looked convincing. For his part, Riley looked surprised to see Ray.

Wait a minute. If Ray was here, where was Kyle? Could Kyle have missed Ray at the safe house?

The two forty-something Baradas stood talking in the doorway for a few minutes. Strike that. They stood arguing.

Kairi brushed her phone in her pocket with her fingertips. She wished she could call Kyle on his cell, but of course, their phones didn't work here, or, now. Whatever. Damn. If she knew the phone number at the safe house, she could call Kyle on a landline.

Ray seemed to want Riley to come inside the building. Riley didn't seem to want to. He shook his head vigorously. They both raised their voices, but she still couldn't quite make out what they were saying.

She crept a little closer. The beauty of this situation was neither one of them knew her, so even if they saw her, they wouldn't know she was Traveling. She crept a little closer yet.

"The ancestors were very clear, Ray!" Riley said. "You aren't supposed to Travel! How do you even know how to Travel?"

"I'm trying to help you, Riley," Ray said. "Why won't you let me help you?"

"You aren't allowed to help me!" Riley said. "As the designated Traveler I order you to go back to your present and cease Traveling at once."

"But Rebecca's in danger, Riley," Ray said. "Don't you want to help her? I have evidence that Rebecca is about to die in a traffic accident."

"Don't make me convene a clan family council, Ray," Riley said with steel in his voice.

Ray just looked at him with disdain.

Kairi shivered. Something about his expression was unsettling. That Ray was a scary guy.

Ray put his hand in his jacket pocket. Did he have a gun? Would he shoot Riley?

Riley tensed.

She reached her hand under her jacket and clutched the gun in the harness. The two men still hadn't noticed her. Would she have the courage to pull the gun if she had to? What if it made things worse?

But all Ray did was take out some papers and shove them at Riley. "Here. You can read all about it if you don't believe me. Rebecca dies here, at this intersection, in approximately two hours. Come back when you're ready to let me help you, unless you don't care about your wife." He went back inside and slammed the door.

Riley stared at the papers, clearly battling if he should read them or not.

Kairi knew she needed to convince Riley to go back to his own time. And there was no time like the present. She took a step forward and then another and another. "Uh, Mr. Barada, sir?"

He jerked back. "Who are you?"

"My name is Kairi." She took another step. "You don't know me, but I'm a Traveler like you."

He jerked back again. "If that's true, you need to stay back."

"I don't think we're in danger because I'm not your descendant."

He looked skeptical.

"But we're getting off-track," she said. "I'm here to get you to go home, back to your own time. Things don't go well here today. Several people die. You die."

"Why should I believe you?" he asked, regarding the papers in his hand and then the door.

She wondered if Ray could see them. She wondered if he really was the bad guy. So far, she hadn't seen him do anything bad. "Kyle thinks Ray's arranging things so he can be The Traveler."

"Kyle's here?" Riley looked around. "He's Traveling? Is he all right?" He frowned.

"Kyle is here, working on something else. He's fine." She really hoped he was fine. Where was he, anyway? "But maybe we should move off the street to talk about things?"

"If Kyle's Traveling, does that mean I'm dead?" Riley asked.

She nodded. "I'm afraid so. Kyle and I are here to try to stop that."

"As you pointed out, I don't know you. So I say again, why should I believe you?"

"That's a good question." Why should he? She had a brainstorm. "What about Charlotte? You know her, right? She'll back me up. You need to go straight home to your time and not interfere with whatever Ray's got cooked up here."

"I do know Charlotte." His eyes went somewhere far away.

"Come on," Kairi said. "Let's go back to the Time Advantages offices. Charlotte will straighten this out."

Back at the Time Advantages office, Charlotte seemed surprised to see Riley. Finally, she said, "It's nice to see you, Riley." Maybe she was surprised at how old he appeared.

"Wow, Charlotte, I can't believe how hot you are." Riley's eyes drank her in. "I mean, I just saw you at home, but you look..." Was there something going on between these two?

"Anyway," Kairi said, "Charlotte, tell him to go home. He didn't believe me."

"Actually," Riley said, "Ray gave me these records." He held out the papers that he'd read in the taxi. "This afternoon the accident is going to be a temporal crux. I should stay."

"Ray? Can I see those?" Charlotte grabbed them and paged through them. After only a few moments she looked up. "These are forgeries."

"How can you tell?" Riley asked.

"I'm in charge of records," she said. "I always put a secret code in. These don't have my code."

"You do?" he asked. "I didn't know that."

Go, Charlotte. Good for her.

"What's the code?" Riley asked.

"I'm not telling you," she said. "It's an extra layer of security. In fact, I shouldn't even have told you there was a code." She glanced away. "Shoot."

"It's okay, Charlotte," Kairi said. "We won't tell anyone. So, Riley, what do you say? Are you going to be cooperative and go home?"

"Are you sure it's what I should do, Charlotte?" He gazed at her.

Charlotte nodded.

"Okay," he said. "Can I use The Dreaming Room to go home?"

"Of course." She grabbed his arm and led him away.

Kairi sat down in an office chair. Two down, none to go. She rocked this secret-Time-Agent thing.

Charlotte soon came back.

"That went surprisingly smoothly." Kairi took off her jacket in preparation for giving back her new accessory.

"I'm not surprised," Charlotte said, sitting down at her desk. "Travelers are well-trained. Except for Ray, evidently." She was now holding the papers Ray had given Riley.

"So, what do the forged papers mean?" Kairi was still trying to put all this together. "Ray's trying to trick Riley and the others to all go to this car accident? What does that accomplish?"

The phone on Charlotte's desk rang. She held up her finger as if to say, hold that thought. "Time Advantages, Inc. This is Charlotte. How may I help you?" She listened for a few moments.

Then, she said, "No, Rebecca. You are required to attend the meeting. It's mandatory." She paused. "There is no emergency here in town. Forget what Ray told you. Yes, we're on it. Go to the meeting."

She hung up and turned to Kairi. "There's the other shoe. Ray told Rebecca that Riley was in danger at that intersection. She was all ready to drop everything and go there."

Charlotte pursed her lips and then tapped them with her finger. "I hate to say it, but getting Travelers to interact with themselves is a pretty elegant way to kill them." She pulled out some paper from the drawer in her desk. "So, at least in one timeline, Ray convinced Rebecca and two versions of Riley to be at the same time and place and got them to interact and therefore kill each other. I need to make a record of all this."

When Kyle said Kairi interacting with herself was special, he wasn't kidding. Why didn't she die? Why was she special? She'd have to investigate when all this was all over.

"Before you get all wrapped up in your report, can I give you this gun back?" Kairi asked. "It makes me uncomfortable. I was worried I'd have to pull it on Ray, but nothing really happened."

"Ray?" she asked. "You saw Ray?"

"Yeah. I saw the guy Kyle and I saw earlier in the shower. That's Ray, right? And he looked the same age."

338

Charlotte brow furrowed. "But what about Kyle? Did you see him, too?"

"No. I don't know where he was."

"Did you call the safe-house?"

Kairi shook her head. "I don't know the number."

Charlotte immediately picked up the phone and dialed. After a few minutes, she hung up. "No answer. I don't have a good feeling about this. Where's Kyle?"

"I have no idea."

Chapter Fifty-Six
Kyle: Sydney, Australia, 2004

Kyle came to in a strange room filled with abandoned office furniture. He was tied to an old chair. He had no idea where his gun was. Or Ray.

He tried to break free, but while the ropes appeared old, they held strong. "Bloody hell!" He jerked impotently back and forth in the chair, causing it to wobble. Could he break the chair?

There had to be an easier way. He tried to calm down so he could think more clearly. He focused on his breathing, making it more smooth and even as he'd been taught in Training.

That was it. He should just Travel away. It was doubtful the whole chair would Travel with him.

He closed his eyes. He breathed deeply and evenly. "I am The Dreaming." All this, the words, the relaxed state, were symbols, triggers that put Kyle in touch with Everything.

In his mind's eye, he saw Ray tying an unconscious Kyle in the chair, he saw Ray holding up unconscious Kyle in the elevator. Ray's face was beet red and he was covered in sweat. That looked like as good a time as any.

Kyle emerged in the elevator.

Ray flinched and dropped his hold on the other Kyle. "Shit!"

The other Kyle fell to the floor of the elevator with a slumping thud.

"Surprise!" Before Ray could pull the gun he was clearly reaching for, Kyle punched him in the chin with a sharp right hook.

"Oof." Ray staggered and fell against the wall of the elevator. His eyes stopped focusing on Kyle, and he shook his head slightly as if trying to shake the punch off.

Should he punch him again or try to get the gun? And where

was the other-Kyle's gun? During Kyle's moment of indecision, the elevator pinged.

The door slowly opened.

Ray drew his gun and pointed it at Kyle.

But Ray's gun didn't look like any gun Kyle had ever seen. "What the hell is that thing?" Kyle said. The grip looked normal and the barrel was cylindrical but the rest of it looked like science fiction, all flares and dials and wild colors.

Ray leaned heavily against the elevator wall. His right arm shook as he pointed the whatever-it-was-gun at Kyle. "Heh, heh. Yeah, I bet you've never seen anything like it. It's an electromagnetic gun, from the future."

The future? Ray had a gun from the future? How?

"When I'm in charge of the company, I'm going to change everything. Forget all the rules and regulations. Forget all the piddly corporate crap, and especially forget the executions. You have no idea what Travelers can really do, or what this thing can do." Ray stood up and used his left hand to adjust something on the gun. "It has different settings." Kyle was guessing the setting he'd already experienced wasn't the strongest one.

The elevator doors slowly started to close.

"Bloody hell." Kyle darted out of the elevator, leaving Ray and the other Kyle inside.

"You better rescue your younger self, Kyle," Ray called out through the closing doors. "Who knows what I might do to him? He is such a pain in the ass, after all."

Kyle was still right outside the elevator. As the doors started to open again, all he could see was the barrel of that weird gun. "Shit!" He ducked just in time to avoid a beam of electromagnetic energy. "Shit! Shit! Shit!" He ran down the hall and hid behind an old metal desk. This was not going well. He really wished he could call for reinforcements but his mobile wouldn't work.

Where was Kairi? For that matter, what time was it? Had the big car accident happened yet? Were his parents alive or dead? All Kyle really had to do was keep Ray from setting things in motion, right? Or was it too late already?

Kyle peeked out from behind the desk. Ray had stepped out of the elevator and was pointing his weird gun in Kyle's general direction. At least that meant the other Kyle was safe in the elevator for the moment. Kyle ducked down behind the desk.

A loud thrumming noise echoed down the hall from the direction of the elevator. Was it moving? Did that mean someone on another floor had pushed the button?

"I know you're here somewhere, Kyle," Ray said. "Come on out. I won't kill you."

The loud thrum stopped.

Kyle smelled ozone and then the metal chair in front of the desk jumped and sizzled, as if it had been hit by lightning. Ray would kill him in a heartbeat.

The elevator must have started back to this floor because the loud thrumming sound resumed. Was someone else going to get caught in the crossfire? Kyle couldn't let some innocent bystander get hurt. Maybe he could use the desk drawer as a kind of shield. It was made of metal. Maybe it would reflect the beam. He eased the drawer out quietly. It was filled with old office supplies.

The elevator got closer and closer. Maybe it would pass right by their floor.

But he needed something non-conductive to hold the drawer with so he didn't get electrocuted. Rubber bands? There were a ton of them here. Kyle started laying them out over the edges of the drawer.

"I wouldn't want the other-Kyle to get away," Ray said and pushed the elevator call button before it passed them.

The elevator pinged, and the doors started to open.

It was now or never. Kyle pulled the sleeves of his hoodie down below his fingers, and grabbed the drawer where the rubber bands were. He jumped up, holding the drawer in front of him. "I'm here! Don't hurt the other-me!"

"You fool," Ray said, right before he pulled the trigger.

Kyle smelled ozone again and felt a tingle through his fingers and the drawer jerked backwards, pushing Kyle back.

At the same time, Ray screamed, but it was quickly silenced.

"Shit," a woman said. "Ray?" It sounded like Kairi.

Kyle peeked out from behind the drawer. "Kairi?"

"Oh, my God!" she said. "Kyle?"

Kyle came out from behind the desk. Ray lay on the ground

in the hall, smoke rising from his chest.

"He's dead!" she said. "And I thought you were... You're just lying here in the elevator."

He walked towards her.

"Why are there two of you?" she asked. "What happened?"

"More importantly," Kyle said. "What time is it? Has the accident happened yet?"

"No." She checked her watch. "We've still got an hour at least."

"Did you do what you were supposed to do?" he asked. "Are my parents safe?"

"Yes." She nodded. "I think so. Your parents of this time are safe in the country. Charlotte escorted both the Traveling Kyle and the Traveling Riley back into The Dreaming Room and watched them leave." She glanced around the hall. "What happened here?" Her eyebrows rose and she pointed at Ray's gun lying on the floor next to his hand. "What's that?"

"It appears Ray had an actual ray gun, from the future." Kyle leaned down to pick it up. It was hot. He gingerly put it in his jacket pocket.

"Ray had a ray gun?" She giggled. "That's kinda funny."

Kyle giggled, too. His adrenaline was still racing. It was just hitting him that this might all be over. He might have saved his parents. Take a breath, mate. He tried to slow his breathing.

"We have to clean all this up," he said, pointing at Ray and the still unconscious other-Kyle in the elevator. As he looked down at the man who'd raised him, now with a smoking hole in his chest, he was still having trouble facing the fact he'd tried to kill him. He shook his head. He'd grown up in this timeline thinking of Ray as a father figure. He was so confused.

"Damn," he said. "We need Charlotte."

"Uh, she's down in the car," Kairi said.

Kyle woke in The Dreaming Room. As soon as he made the slightest move, he was overcome with vertigo, memories shifting and rearranging, coalescing. The timeline where Ray raised him faded. The timeline where his folks were divorced and he was estranged from Mom and Oliver faded.

Replacing them were many, many memories of Kyle and

his brother and his Mom and Dad, happy and healthy. He remembered the four of them sitting around the kitchen table, eating, talking and laughing over the years. He remembered his dad teaching both he and Oliver cricket and the three of them bowling and batting and laughing on the pitch Dad built in the backyard.

He remembered Mom and the rest of the family teasing him as he went on his first dates, awkward and uncomfortable in his fancy clothes. He remembered his folks being so proud of him as he graduated high school, and even more proud when he graduated university. They were proudest of all when he started working at the company.

When the room finally stopped spinning, Kyle's cheeks were wet with tears.

"Phew." Shaky, he got up out of the chair and wobbled his way to the door of The Dreaming Room.

As soon as he opened the door, a roar of sound assaulted him. He ducked before he realized it was people cheering and clapping for him.

"Kyle!"

"Yeah!"

"Awesome, mate!"

He saw his Dad and Mom and Oliver and Liam and Charlotte and the rest of his friends and family smiling and laughing.

"You afraid of some clapping there, mate?" Liam took a step forward, holding out his hand.

Kyle straightened and stepped into the arms of his loved ones. After a lot of hugging and backslapping, and yes, a few tears, Dad got out some bubbly and started pouring.

"To Kyle!" Dad said once everyone had a glass.

"To Kyle," everyone said, raising their glasses.

They all sipped.

"Don't get me wrong," Kyle said. "I appreciate being appreciated, but what's going on? What's all this for?" Usually only the Traveler knew when a timeline had been changed.

They laughed.

Mom came up and put her arm around his shoulder. "We know you foiled Ray and saved us all." She glanced over at

Charlotte. "You saved our lives, you saved the company."

"Yeah." Dad came up and put his arm around Kyle. "For all we know you saved the future."

"When Ray disappeared," Mom said, "Charlotte figured it out. She has some special records system she won't explain to us."

"We can never thank you enough, son," Dad said, voice getting thick.

Kyle had a hard time talking around the lump in his throat, too. "Thanks, Charlotte."

She smiled and dipped her chin.

His pocket started ringing. He reached inside, around a ray gun, and pulled out his mobile.

"Hi, Kairi," he said. "It worked!"

Chapter Fifty-Seven
Kairi: Boulder, Colorado, 2019

Kairi was on the phone with her new cousin. "It worked," Kyle said. "Thank you!"

"Thank you!" She looked across her folks' living room at her mom and dad and her brother Lowan on the couch. Even though she had a lifetime of memories with them now, she still couldn't believe how lucky she was. Family was precious. She'd never forget that.

Dakota bounded into the room. "Don't you have a hot date, Kair? Why are you on the phone? Oh, no. That's not him calling to cancel is it?"

Why would Dakota say that? "Gotta go, Kyle," she said. "Keep in touch."

"Oh, I will," he said. "We make a good team. Until our next mission, then. Bye."

"Wait." She looked at her cell. "Our next what?" But he'd hung up already.

"Can we finish our discussion now?" Mom asked.

"Of course," she said. Mom and Dad had been leading up to telling Lowan and her that they had the potential to be time travelers, but they hadn't managed to spit it out yet.

"Are you guys gonna sit?" Lowan asked Kairi and Dakota.

"Yes," Kairi said sitting in the love seat. "Please continue."

"Yep." Dakota plopped down next to her.

"So, we think it's time that you two," Dad paused, "and apparently Dakota, learn about your heritage. We come from the native peoples of Australia."

"Where all those convicts went?" Lowan asked.

"Hush, Lowan," Mom said.

"Yes," Dad said. "But as I was saying, we were there before the English. We were the native Australians. We're Australian Aborigines."

"We have a bunch of relatives in Australia," Mom said. "In fact, my sister Rebecca Barada lives in Sydney with her family."

"A bunch of relatives?" Lowan asked. "That's not what you said before. Why did you lie?"

Mom frowned at him.

Rebecca Barada? Wasn't that Kyle's mom? They really were cousins. Kairi chuckled.

"And our clans are special," Mom said.

"I was getting to that," Dad spared her an irritated look. "We have access to all of time through The Dreaming." He looked around the room expectantly. What was he, pausing for dramatic effect? Get on with it already. She had a date.

"Sometimes it's referred to as Dreamtime," Mom said, also looking around expectantly. Were they waiting for a big reaction? They weren't going to get it from Kairi. She already knew all this. "Every one of us exists eternally in The Dreaming."

"Huh?" Lowan said.

Dakota looked confused which was a pretty common look for her, come to think of it, in every timeline.

"They're trying to say we can time travel," Kairi said.

"What!" Lowan jumped up off the couch.

Dakota said, "We can?"

Kairi turned to her. "I'm sorry, D. Not you."

"How do you know that, Kairi?" Mom said.

"Yes, young lady," Dad said. "What are you talking about?"

Lowan jumped up and down. "Someone explain what's going on!"

Kairi sighed. She had a lot to tell them. "Dude, you can time travel when you dream. I've done it a bunch of times."

Mom and Dad gasped. There was the big reaction.

"But it's pretty complicated," Kairi said. "And dangerous. And there's a lot of rules." She felt her nose scrunch up.

"No way!" Lowan said.

"I think you owe us an explanation," Dad said.

She swallowed. Did she really want to get into all of it? They might get a little upset, hearing about the timelines where they

347

were dead. On the other hand, they were family, and family was supposed to be there for each other. Kairi knew that. Now.

She cleared her throat. "Actually, in my first few timelines you guys were dead..."

Dad expelled a big burst of air.

"What?" Lowan yelled.

Mom's eyes were moist with tears.

"Me, too?" Dakota asked quietly.

Kairi reached out and squeezed her arm. "Don't worry, Dakota. You were only dead once."

"I think you better explain yourself, young lady," Dad said.

She almost smiled. She still got a kick out of being called young lady, even though she was twenty-one and had moved out of the house. It was a quintessential Dad term. She had a dad! And a mom! And a brother!

"Yeah! What the hell, Kairi?" Lowan said.

"Okay, Lowan, technically, you weren't dead. You never existed."

His face paled and he fell back down on the couch.

A tear escaped Mom's eye and rolled down her cheek.

Kairi felt bad. "I didn't mean to upset you all. I'm sorry."

"Just tell the story," Dad said.

"I was found by the police alone in the middle of the street," she said. "I eventually found out I time traveled to avoid a fatal car accident in which both Mom and Dad died." Now all four of them looked totally miserable.

"So I grew up an orphan, in foster care. No one ever adopted me."

Dakota squeezed her hand. Kairi had talked her folks into adopting her in the current timeline.

"I'm so sorry you had to go through all that, honey." Mom stood and came over to hug Kairi. "The whole reason we moved away from home was to separate you kids from the whole Traveling thing. We were trying to keep you safe." She sat down next to Kairi on the love seat, putting her arm around her.

"Back up a minute," Dad said, face grim. "How did you say we died?"

"Car accident." Kairi stared at him, hoping he wouldn't ask for more details.

"What happened?" he asked.

"Well, Kyle thinks your car was sabotaged," she said slowly.

"Sabotage!" Dad's eyes flashed.

"Oh, no!" Mom said.

"Are we in danger?" Dad asked.

"No. I went to Australia and helped Kyle foil the bad guy, Ray Barada."

"Australia! Cool!" Lowan said.

"How can you be sure we're safe?" Mom asked. "Is Ray in jail?"

"Uh, well, actually, Ray sort-of died," Kairi said. "He's dead."

"Whoa!" Lowan said. "My sister's a bad-ass! Who knew?"

"You killed someone, Kairi?" Dakota asked.

"Kyle did it," she said. "But it was self-defense. Ray attacked him with a ray-gun and Kyle reflected the ray back at him."

"A ray-gun! Cool!" Lowan said. "I want a ray-gun. I want to time travel."

"None of this is cool, young man," Dad said.

"I can't believe you had to go through all that, Kairi," Mom said. "I'm so sorry."

She shrugged. People had to play the cards they were dealt.

"Growing up alone must have been scary," Dakota said.

"Actually, D, I had you in every timeline." She turned to her, feeling her eyes grow heavy with moisture. "You've always been my family, and you always will be."

Dakota's eyes filled, too. She nodded.

"You said you eventually found out about Traveling," Dad said. "How did that happen?"

"I, uh, time traveled to avoid a tornado."

"What!" Mom jerked back on the love seat. "All this and a tornado, too?"

Kairi nodded.

"You weren't hurt, were you?" she asked.

"No," Kairi said. "But my fiancé Josh was..."

"What?" Mom said. "You had a fiancé? What happened to him? How badly was he hurt?"

"Josh?" Dakota asked. "Isn't the guy you're going out with tonight named Josh?"

"Yeah," Kairi said. Why did Dakota have to put it together?

"You're not old enough to be engaged," Mom said. "You have to finish your degree."

"You're engaged and you didn't tell us about it?" Dad said.

"No," Kairi said. "I'm not engaged. This is our first date in this timeline."

"Can we go back to the ray-guns and time traveling?" Lowan said.

There was a knock at the front door. They all turned to look at it.

Shoot. Talk about bad timing.

"Aren't you going to get that?" Dakota asked, halfway to the door already. "It's got to be him, the hottie-hot-hot."

That reminded her, Kairi needed to re-do a favor for Diego. But, she could do it tomorrow and it'd be like it had always been, right? That was a definite plus of time travel.

Dakota swung the door open. "Josh! Welcome to our home. It's wonderful to meet you."

"Yes, come in. Come in," everyone said.

Josh seemed a little nonplussed. "Uh, hi. Thanks. Is Kairi here?" He looked past Dakota, saw Kairi and waved. "Hi."

She rushed up to the door.

"Where are your manners? Aren't you going to invite your young man in?" Mom asked.

"Yes, I'm sure we'd all like to meet him and get to know him," Dad said.

Dakota moved out of the doorway, and Josh stepped in.

His earnest gray-blue eyes and uncertain smile reminded Kairi of that first timeline when he'd asked her to marry him. Her mind reviewed all the wonderful times they'd had from drinking champagne to celebrate their engagement to just hanging out. He seemed to be the same great guy.

But she was not the same woman. That other Kairi had been so lonely and naïve, and frankly, a little desperate. She wasn't that girl any more. She didn't need Josh any more. Would Josh even like the new Kairi? Did she want him to?

Kairi's family stared at him like he was Jesus or maybe the devil.

"Is this a bad time?" he asked. "We can reschedule if you

want."

He was a good man. She would be lucky to spend her life with him. "Now is a perfect time," she said. "We are not rescheduling."

"Wait a minute," Dad said. "Do you have a job, young man?"

"You don't have to answer him, Josh," Kairi said.

"No. It's okay. I'm a senior here at the university."

"What happens when you graduate?" Mom asked. "Do you have a job lined up? Are you moving away?"

"Let's go," Kairi said. She was embarrassed they were giving him the third degree.

"I've been accepted to the graduate school here," he said. "I've got a teaching assistantship all lined up."

"What does that pay?" Dad asked.

"Oh, good grief," Kairi muttered. "We're going." She practically dragged Josh out the front door. "Bye, everyone." She waved behind her.

"Bye Kair," Dakota said. "I'm gonna want details."

"We'll resume our conversation later," Mom said.

Kairi closed the door behind them.

"Your family is kind of intense." Josh smiled.

"Yeah. Sorry. They're pretty over-protective." She loved his smile. She smiled back at him.

"So, where to?" he asked. "I was thinking dinner. How do you feel about sushi?"

She faced him. "I'm not sure if this is the right thing to do, but I'm going to tell you the truth."

"Uh, okay." He gulped. "You don't like sushi?"

"No, I like sushi." She shook her head. "But that's not the point. What I'm trying to say is I'm strongly drawn to you. I feel like we have a connection." She knew better than to say, I think you're my soulmate. She also knew better than to say, We were engaged in another timeline.

He smiled, and the edges of his eyes crinkled. He took her hand, and she felt a tingle travel up her arm. "I'm strongly drawn to you, too, Kairi." He lifted her hand to his mouth and kissed it gently. Now she was tingling all over. "I've never felt anything like it."

She pulled her hand down and lifted her lips towards his.

They kissed. It felt like heaven. Flowers flowered. Rainbows rainbowed. Fireworks fired. She pressed her body against his, and they fit together perfectly. She felt warm all over.

When they came up for air, he said, voice husky, "Your place?"

"Sorry. Boys aren't allowed upstairs in the sorority." And she didn't think she could dress Josh up to make a very convincing woman.

He pointed at her parents' house. The two of them still stood on the front stoop.

She shook her head. "No. They have a full house. What's wrong with your place?"

"Roommate. Let's try that again." He kissed her again.

She was all too happy to try it again. "Mmmm." Practice makes perfect, after all. She had a feeling they were going to need lots and lots of practice in the coming months and years. She couldn't seem to stop smiling.

"On the other hand," he said, "nothing wrong with my place, nothing at all." He grabbed her hand as they started strolling down the front walk.

"You know, it's kind of weird," he said. "I have a really strong feeling of déjà vu right now. Does that ever happen to you?"

She laughed. "You have no idea." She stopped and turned, smiling at him. The sunset bathed both of them in a golden glow. "But you will. I've got a story for you." She resumed strolling. "But, later. It'll keep."

They were going to have a whole new glorious adventure together.

He kissed her hand again. "I can't wait."

Neither could she.

Science Fact: The Physics of Time

Time is a complex concept. People typically think of time in terms of units such as seconds, minutes, hours, etc. On Earth, humans historically defined units of time such as day, month and year in terms of astronomy. A day is the amount of time it takes for one rotation of Earth on its axis. A month is the amount of time it takes for the moon to complete one orbit of the Earth. A year is the amount of time it takes for Earth to complete one orbit of the sun. Smaller units of time such as the hour, minute, and second are then just subdivisions of these. But units of time are completely arbitrary. Humans could have defined time units in other ways. Time units are not time.

How does time behave? According to physics, microscopic processes are hypothesized to be time-symmetric, meaning it's equally likely they will proceed forward or backward in time. A fancier name for this is time-reversal invariance. Obviously, this is not what we experience in real life. If you shatter a cup, there's no scenario in which it flies back together again. The reason for this is the second law of thermodynamics which states entropy, or disorder, always increases. Thus, macroscopic processes exhibit an arrow of time. Time seems to proceed in only one direction, i.e., into the future. We could call this the asymmetry of time.

But what is time? Physics says time is mathematically the same as space. Physicists combine the three spatial dimensions with the temporal dimension to create four-dimensional spacetime. Special relativity is the theory that relates space and time and has been proven by experiments. According to special relativity people observe time dilating, or stretching out, if they are moving relative to each other or if they are different distances from gravitational masses. For example, clocks on Earth actually run slightly slower than clocks on GPS satellites. This is called time dilation and is due to the very nature of spacetime.

Some mysteries of time remain to be fully explained. Why does the asymmetry of time exist? What does it mean for time to be like space? What is the spacetime continuum?

For more information and details about these and other topics, check out the Physics Is Fun website: www.physicsisfun.net

Thank you for reading *Temporal Dreams*. I hope you enjoyed it!

- For more info about me or my work, please go to my author website, http://www.lesleylsmith.com/. Sometimes, I post links for free fiction downloads!
- Please check out the Physics Is Fun website www.physicsisfun.net for lots of information about fun physics topics.
- Reviews help other readers find books. I appreciate any and all reviews.
- A sneak peek of my new novel, *The Quantum* Cop, follows.

--Lesley L. Smith

The Quantum Cop
Chapter One

If I'd known my morning was going to split into two possibilities, I would have bought two cinnamon rolls—one for me and one for the other me.

"What time did you get into town last night?" my cousin Ryan Martin asked me.

"About one a.m. Thanks for leaving the door unlocked, and thanks for letting me stay with you guys." We stood on the corner across from campus, waiting for the light to change. We were on our way to work and had just stopped at Boulder Brews for coffee and cinnamon rolls. Ryan was the chief of the university police, and I was a new physics professor.

"I'll be out of your hair as soon as I can." Shifting my bookbag on my shoulder, I took a big bite of my roll. It was still warm with gooey cream-cheese icing. Mmm. My other hand was starting to cramp as it held the almost too-hot paper cup of coffee.

"No hurry, Madison," he said. "But if you're still staying with us when the baby's born, you'll have to help out."

"My pleasure." I squinted up at him. The sun was as blinding as a laser. Colorado definitely seemed sunnier than Missouri. I wished I'd worn sunglasses. I wished I owned sunglasses. "I volunteer to help no matter where I'm living." Who wouldn't want to help with an adorable little baby?

"Thanks." He smiled at me from his six-foot-plus height. "So, are you excited about your new job?"

As I stood there, it was taking all my self-control not to break into a happy dance right there on the sidewalk. "Does a supernova spew heavy elements?"

He raised his eyebrows at me.

I grinned. "That's a yes. I'm excited. I've been working towards this for the last decade. It's a dream come true."

"What did Ted say about it?" Ryan asked, staring at me. "Did you guys break up?"

My boyfriend Ted was still back in St. Louis. Debating what to say, I took a sip of coffee. "We didn't break up, but it wasn't pretty."

"Tell me what happened," he said. "You owe me. I confided in you when I was getting ready to propose to Sydney. And look how good that turned out. Five years of bliss."

"True." I pointed at him with my coffee cup. "And now a little one on the way. How many more days until she's due?"

"Nice try, but you don't get to change the subject that easily. What happened with Ted?"

"At first, he seemed supportive," I said. "He said congratulations and everything."

"And then?" He prompted.

"He asked me if I took the job—as if there was some question about it." My voice started rising. "Obviously, I took it. Anybody would take it, which is what I told him. Then he got all whiny, asking what it meant for him and me. He actually brought up that we had talked about talking about getting married." Some coffee slopped out of my cup as I gestured with it.

"Talked about talking?" He laughed. "So, he didn't ask you to marry him or even talk about getting married? I never liked the guy."

"I know." The crowd waiting to cross the street was getting quite large. There must have been twenty or thirty people on the sidewalk. "Geez, this is a long light."

"Don't change the subject," he said.

"I knew Ted was just upset because he loves me, and he thought I was leaving him, but I started getting a little torqued. So..."

"So, let me guess, you blew up at him?" Ryan asked.

"Yeah, there was some yelling then." I grinned. "But later we made up, and let me tell you, the make-up sex was great."

He frowned. "Too much information."

I laughed. "You're such a guy, Ryan."

I took another sip of coffee and thought about Ted. It was wonderful being with a guy like Ted, who actually understood what I did for a living. Mentioning elementary particles like quarks and neutrinos to most folks made their eyes glaze over.

I was still thinking about him when the walk sign finally lit up, and I absentmindedly stepped off the curb into the crosswalk.

Something slammed into me. My coffee and cinnamon roll flew out of my hands in slow-mo, and my book bag thumped against my back before taking its own trajectory. My left leg and hip crumpled as I hit the pavement with a splat. As my fingertips dug into the gravel and asphalt, I struggled to lift my head up off the ground. What was going on, and why didn't it hurt?

"Oh, my God. Madison," Ryan screamed as he dropped his coffee and kneeled over me. "Madison, say something. Are you all right?"

I knew I should answer him, but I felt like I was separated from him, separated from everything, by layers of cotton batting.

Curiously, I had also hesitated before stepping into the crosswalk, and a car had whizzed by against the light. I felt odd, disconnected.

Ryan screamed and lurched forward into the street. He knelt over a woman lying in a heap in the crosswalk. "Madison, say something. Are you all right?" Who was he talking to? It couldn't be me. I was right here on the sidewalk.

"Did you see that?" a bystander said. "She just flew into the air."

Students in a variety of leggings, jeans, and t-shirts crowded around to get a look at the woman who had apparently been hit by a car.

I craned my neck to get a look. She was in her late twenties, of average height and weight, had long blonde hair, and was wearing a killer suit. Actually, her suit looked just like mine. Come to think of it, the rest of her looked just like me, too. I stared. Was she blurry?

One thing was clear: Ryan looked really worried.

As I lay in the street, to my left, a car's tires squealed as it backed up and swerved around me and the other people in the crosswalk.

My fingers on the asphalt looked blurry and insubstantial.

A couple of the bystanders yelled. "Hey, watch it."

"Hey, you can't leave."

"Come back here."

Ryan stuck his face right in my face. "Madison, please answer me. Blink or something."

This fuzzy, floaty feeling couldn't be good. I concentrated on lowering my eyelids.

He nodded. "Good. Can you talk?"

The entire world had shrunk to Ryan's freckly face, and his eyes bored into mine through his wire-rimmed glasses.

I should be able to talk. I used to be able to talk, didn't I? This whole scene was just wrong. It was all wrong. I should still be on the corner.

I looked at the corner, and there I was, still standing on the sidewalk. That was much better.

On the corner, the guy standing next to me said, pointing, "Is that your twin?"

I didn't have a twin. Was that me in the crosswalk? I looked down at my panty-hose-clad legs and the sidewalk under my shoes. I was still standing on the corner. I could feel my bookbag weighing down my right shoulder and my big toe chafing against my fancy shoe. I looked kind of blurry.

The woman in the street looked kind of blurry, too.

"I'm calling 911," one of the bystanders yelled.

I was getting a nagging sense of déjà vu. Had I been blurry before? Had I been in two places at once before?

Standing on the corner felt better, more right. I focused on that. The morning rush hour traffic on highway 36, a half-block away, sounded like ocean waves breaking on a beach. My heavy bag, filled with books and papers, kept banging against my hip as I shifted my weight slightly. Both my hands were full, one with a very hot paper cup of coffee and one with a cooling pastry. It was really too much to carry at once. Geez, that cup was hot. My toe hurt as it pressed up against the inside of my fancy shoe.

How could I be standing on the sidewalk and lying in the street at the same time? How could I be in two places at once?

359

My odd feeling of déjà vu solidified into memory…

I tripped headlong into frigid water. I gasped and couldn't breathe. An icy liquid vice crushed my chest. I didn't even have enough air to scream for help.

And at the exact same time, I felt warm sun and a light breeze on my face as I crouched on the deck of a boat. I'd been in two places at once back then, too.

Now, apparently, I was standing on the corner, and I was lying in the street at the exact same time.

In the street, I thought, a car must have hit me. Excruciating pain started to seep into my awareness.

I struggled to calm down. Focus, Madison. You can get out of this if you focus like you did when you fell off the boat. Back then, I focused on the situation I wanted, and the other one disappeared, leaving only memories.

I knew which circumstance I preferred now—the one where I still had the cinnamon roll and wasn't crumpled in the crosswalk. I picked that possibility.

Purposefully, on the sidewalk, I opened my mouth wide and took a bite of roll. I tasted sugary sweetness on my tongue. Bite. Chew. Cinnamon was real.

The woman lying on the ground surrounded by crouching people was dimming. I did my best to ignore her. She was not real. Not real. Not. Real. I was real, not her.

On the corner, I jostled my coffee, and a few scalding drops fell on my foot. Ouch.

The other woman faded away.

I did it.

The people trying to help injured other-Madison stood up in confusion.

"Where'd she go?"

From the distance, a siren approached.

"Madison, is that you?" Ryan asked. "What just happened?" He stepped back onto the curb, his face ashen. "I could have sworn I saw you get hit by a car. But here you are." He shook his head. "Madison, answer me." Ryan's face beaded with sweat beneath his sandy brown hair, and steam grazed the bottom of his glasses where they touched his face. "What the hell's going on? Are you okay?"

Not sure I could talk, I nodded. That was a close one. Too close.

We were jostled as more people came up from behind and joined the crowd.

"C'mon, let's go," someone in the crowd said.

"You've got the walk signal."

"Go for Christ's sake."

Students flowed around us into the crosswalk.

Glancing up at the decreasing red numbers in the walk signal, my hands started shaking violently. Coffee slopped out of the cup, splashing onto the sidewalk. I dropped my partially eaten cinnamon roll. I looked down at the splattered curb, reluctant to step into the crosswalk. I couldn't move.

The ambulance pulled up, and the EMTs jumped out.

"Who got hit?"

Everyone who hadn't crossed the street yet pointed at me. "Her."

"That lady, there."

I tried to take a sip of coffee to calm down, but my shaking hands just spilled more on the curb.

The EMTs came up to me.

"Miss, are you all right?" the balding one asked. "You shouldn't have moved."

"We need to assess your injuries," the other said.

I shook my head. "Near miss." I attempted a smile. "Wasn't hurt." Thank God.

"Glad to hear it," one of the EMTs said.

"No," Ryan said, shaking his head. "I saw her lying in the street."

"You don't look so good," an EMT said. "You better let us check you out."

"I'm fine. Need to get to class. Right, Ryan?" I looked at him for support.

"Madison, you should let them check you out," he said uncooperatively.

They led me over to the back of the ambulance.

"I wasn't hit by the car," I said repeatedly. I was starting to get a huge headache, though. "I have to get to class. I'm a professor. It's my first day. I can't be late on my first day." I needed to put this bizarre incident behind me ASAP.

I jerked away from the ambulance and started speed-walking to campus. When I reached the safety of the other curb, I sighed in relief.

Were that tall, good-looking kid and the chubby Asian kid next to him staring at me? I was careful not to make eye contact as I walked past them.

"Madison, come back here," Ryan yelled after me. "I need to know what the hell just happened."

But I couldn't explain it to him. I didn't understand it myself. Yet.

www.ingramcontent.com/pod-product-compliance
Lightning Source LLC
Chambersburg PA
CBHW070635180626
46817CB00006B/2128